TEQUILA STRAIGHT UP

REMEMBERING THE

RULES

BY TERRY POCA

TEQUILA SUNRISE
BREAKING THE RULES

TEQUILA STRAIGHT UP
REMEMBERING THE RULES

Coming soon:

TEQUILA SHOTS
MAKING THE RULES
A NOVELLA

TEQUILA MARGARITA
FORGETTING THE RULES

TEQUILA STRAIGHT UP
REMEMBERING THE
RULES

Terry Poca

Beach Book
Publishing, LLC

This is a work of fiction. Names, characters, places, and incidents either are products of the author's imagination or are used fictitiously and are not to be construed as real. Any resemblance to actual events, locales, organizations, or persons, living or dead, is entirely coincidental.

Beach Book Publishing, LLC
PMB 136
1750 Powder Springs Road, Suite190
Marietta, Georgia 30064-4861

Copyright © 2014 by Terry Poca
ISBN 978-1499745283

Cover art by Noelle Pierce, Selestiele Designs

www.terrypoca.com

DEDICATION

To my family:
Mama, Jeanie, Ann, Brandi,
Briana, Allen, and Preston.
And my hero, Bill.
Thank you for believing in me.

Hugs. Love. Mwah!

Acknowledgments

I must thank my family, friends, encouraging beta readers, and writer friends.

I want to give an enormous thank you to my supportive family. Mama, Jeanie and Ann: a special thanks to y'all for encouraging me since the release of my first book *Tequila Sunrise ~ Breaking the Rules*. Hugs and kisses to my husband Bill who has encouraged me from the beginning and a big thank you to Brandi, Briana and Allen, and Preston. I love you all.

I owe many thanks to my beta readers: Ann Sparks, Atalie Andressen, Noelle Pierce, April Cochran, and Carolyn Dunn, and all the others who read and critiqued *Tequila Straight Up*. My love and hugs to you all!

Noelle of Selestiele Designs: You did it again. You are AWESOME. Love and hugs.

CHAPTER ONE

The broiling August heat pushed the Atlanta temperature into the high nineties, and although the AC blasted inside the car, Celeste felt the warmth of the afternoon sun against her cheeks. She'd used her all-natural, powdered makeup, dusted her cheeks with a touch of blush, and applied a shimmer of lip gloss hoping for a fresh-faced appearance. She prayed the SPF really worked—she could hardly be a femme fatale with a face full of freckles. Not that being a seductress mattered to her anymore, especially since she'd given up men.

"You need to drive like you're on your way to a Neiman sale." Trudi turned to Celeste.

"I resent the implication I'm a shopaholic," Celeste said. Okay. She liked to shop, but Trudi didn't need to rub it in

"You'd be there as soon as the doors open." With a personality as fiery as her hair, Trudi had the tendency to call things as she saw them. Sugar coating wasn't her strong trait. And they both knew Celeste wouldn't miss a sale. "But at the rate we're going, we'll never make Becca's party on time."

"I can't be late to my own wedding shower." Becca, sitting in the back seat, grabbed the headrest to pull herself forward, accidentally yanking Celeste's newly straightened hair.

"Ouch." Celeste pulled her captured strands free of Becca's desperate fingers. "Lighten up. I promise I'll get you there."

She inched her Acura forward a few feet before the light turned red again. She frowned at the line of cars stretched in front of her on Peachtree Street. Nothing like the rush-hour crawl of traffic in Midtown Atlanta.

Celeste risked a glimpse at Trudi in the passenger seat. She couldn't help but grin at the image of the pit-bull attorney holding a gift bag embossed with two glittery wedding bells.

"Be careful holding that too close," Celeste said. "You don't want to cause your own matrimonial clock to tick." She glanced in the rearview mirror at Becca and Patrice. "Right, girls?"

Trudi lifted a skeptical brow. "No need for concern…that won't happen."

"There's someone for everyone," Patrice replied, dreamy, dark eyes the focal point of her pixie face, a new short hairdo poking out from her head in raven spikes. Ever the optimist, especially when discussing love, Patrice never thought of anything without a rosy glow. "You haven't met him yet. That's all."

"Not everyone can be as lucky as Becca and Marcus," Celeste said.

Becca, her brown eyes sparkling with happiness, hooked a loose strand of blonde hair behind her ear and grinned at Celeste's reflection in the rearview mirror. Since meeting her fiancé, Becca's life had been an ecstatic whirlwind.

"I am lucky, aren't I?" She grinned.

"If Celeste doesn't focus and find a side street to get us to the freeway in a hurry, you won't be lucky enough to arrive at your wedding shower before all of the guests." Trudi ended the conversation like a judge slamming down a gavel. She shoved the gift bag into the backseat. "Here, take this. It's from Patrice and me."

"Why are you giving this to me now?" Becca asked. "Shouldn't you give it to me at the shower?"

"This isn't exactly a Stock the Bar gift, nor is it appropriate for a coed get together." Trudi's smile was sly. The afternoon sunlight streaming through the window haloed off her red hair and cast a flaming glow, and her green eyes slanted at a feline angle. Sometimes she looked wicked. "Go ahead and open it."

"Yes, do." Patrice clapped her hands.

Celeste moved the Acura forward another car length before the light turned red again, and she slammed to a stop. Damn light. They would be late for Becca's wedding shower. Celeste heard the crinkling sound of tissue, and she turned around in time to see Becca dig through wads of sparkly tissue and pull out the largest, longest dildo Celeste had ever seen. She stifled a startled gasp.

"What am I supposed to do with this?" Becca asked, her face flushing a quaint shade of crimson as she stared at the work of sensual art, realistic down to every curve.

If she hadn't been behind the wheel, Celeste would have doubled over with laughter at the expression on the bride-to-be's face. She couldn't blame Becca for her reaction. The thing was hideous. And purple. Bright glow-in-the-dark purple.

"Have fun with it, honey," Trudi said. "I'm sure you and Marcus can think up a few uses for it on your honeymoon."

"Seriously, Trudi, what is *that* for?" Celeste asked, wiping a tear from the corner of her eye.

"It's for Becca to tap into her hidden erotic resources," Patrice said, recording the impromptu gift in her bridesmaid's notebook. She was the self-appointed historian for Becca's wedding, documenting every aspect of the fun-filled road to matrimony, and she took her role seriously.

"Check it out. There're multispeeds," Trudi said. She grabbed the dildo and flipped on the switch. The *dong du jour* pulsated and writhed as it rotated in a circular motion.

"Put it away." Celeste jerked Trudi's hand, pulling the toy from the view of the foot-traffic on the sidewalk. "People can see that thing."

"Titillating, isn't it?" Trudi asked. "The prospects are endless."

"Won't that hurt?" Becca asked. She grabbed the gift of love and turned it off. "It doesn't look natural." She dropped it back in the bag and made a yuck-face. "What's it made of anyway?" She stared at her hand.

"Gel that warms up to body temperature when in use. Feels real and slick, doesn't it?" Patrice asked and grinned, her words belying the innocence on her face. "And no, it won't hurt." She laughed. "Trust me."

The light turned green and Celeste made a left finally moving toward the freeway.

"Explain again, who's hosting this Stock the Bar?" Celeste asked, changing the subject while she merged onto I-75 north and headed toward the suburbs.

"George," Becca said with an uncharacteristic snap in her voice. Apparently, Celeste had managed to tap the last reserve of patience from her typically mellow friend. "You already know that."

"Marcus's brother, right?" Preoccupied with work, Celeste hadn't paid much attention to all of the wedding plans, although she had managed to make the first dress fitting appointment on time. If she wanted a snowball's chance in hell of being the as-of-yet unnamed maid of honor, she really needed to get with the program and concentrate on Becca's wedding.

"Yes," Patrice replied. "And don't get any ideas. He's married."

"Even if he was single, I wasn't going to 'get any ideas,'" Celeste said, watching in the rearview mirror for a split second before zipping her attention back to the slow moving traffic. She understood that tonight was Becca's time, and she had no intention of discussing her recent decision to swear off men for a while. "I'm not the least bit interested."

"Yeah, right," Trudi said. "And I wear panties every day." From the corner of her eye, Celeste saw Trudi grin.

Celeste ignored the comment and didn't bother to respond to Trudi's insinuation that she couldn't resist a man. She would call a girlfriend meeting in the next few days and give them the lowdown. Struggling with her career ladder, Celeste had tired of the dating game. Her thirtieth birthday loomed in six months, and she was ready for the next step—news anchor. She'd paid her dues for the past three years reporting overnight murders and car crashes on the scene at six in the morning. The time had come for her to advance, and focusing on the opposite sex would distract her.

"Do you want me to give you a run down on the wedding party again?" Patrice asked.

"Yes, please." Celeste intended to listen carefully as she drove and would commit everything to memory. "Shoot."

"There's the best man and three groomsmen—"

"Three? I only remember two brothers." Celeste guided the car into the right lane so she could swing onto I-285 west toward Vinings. "And the best man is a cousin?"

"And the third is another friend. And Marcus's brother and his wife are hosting the Stock the Bar party."

"His wife's a real sweetie," Becca said. "Y'all will love her."

"Yeah. Right." Trudi didn't try to mask the sarcasm in her voice. "You know how I'm always looking for new women friends."

Celeste laughed, thinking about Trudi's intolerance for the female species. "Okay, so there are the two brothers, a friend and a cousin. Anything else I need to know about?"

"It doesn't matter, you won't remember anyway," Patrice said.

"But you do need to know that Max is the best man," Becca added. "He's from south Georgia and works on the family farm."

"Oh. The infamous Max." Trudi sighed. Celeste could hear the lust ring through the purr in her voice. Trudi was always on the prowl for a new victim.

"What do you know about Max?" Celeste asked, her curiosity piqued.

"Only that Becca claims he's almost as hot as Marcus. I can't wait to meet him in the flesh."

"Hands off." Becca's voice held an abnormally waspish tone. "I've already explained to you guys. He's in an emotionally fragile stage in his life."

"Emotionally fragile?" What had she missed? Celeste didn't recall hearing anything about someone being in a precarious state of mind. "Remind me. Who's Max and why is he unstable?"

"I didn't say he was unstable," Becca said. Celeste could imagine, from the impatient tone in Becca's voice, the pout on her face. "His wife ran off with the youth minister. Left him alone with two children."

"She left without her kids?" Celeste asked. What kind of mother would desert her children? She couldn't imagine. And the poor guy—desertion was a nasty betrayal.

"I know, right?" Patrice said. "She was their mother, and she left them. And her husband."

"Needless to say, Max was devastated," Becca said, concern etched in her voice. "When she first disappeared, no one knew where Sissy was for a month. She's been in California for over two years, and they're divorced now."

"Sissy. What kind of name is Sissy?" Celeste asked. The name didn't fit someone so narcissistic, so audacious, that she would desert her family.

"Apparently, she wanted out," Trudi said. "But, in my humble opinion, he shouldn't be so wounded. If someone didn't want me anymore, I'd say to hell with them."

Celeste glanced over at Trudi.

"You have an interesting view on relationships."

"Let's not talk about Max," Becca said. "I feel bad for him. He's really a sweet guy. He didn't deserve being treated in such a disrespectful way."

"You're right," Patrice agreed. "Let's talk about Celeste's hair. It looks spectacular by the way."

"Thanks, I'm tired of it being a curly mess."

"It's going to kink back up when you're out in the humidity," Trudi said.

"Trudi." Becca and Patrice reacted in unison.

"I'm stating the facts, girls." She pointed ahead. "Turn left here, and the house should be the fourth on the right."

Celeste guided her car parallel to the curb and killed the engine. All four doors opened, and they piled out. She had braced herself for the shock of moving from the chilled, air-conditioned interior into the clammy August heat, but as soon as she exited into the late afternoon sunshine, the humidity tugged at her hair. Before the night was over, her hair straightening effort would be a damn waste of twenty-five bucks. Celeste exhaled a defeated sigh.

After locking her car, Celeste fell into place behind Trudi, and they followed Becca up the sidewalk, with Patrice fussing over her as if she were royalty. There was no doubt in Celeste's mind that Patrice intended to be named maid of honor.

When Trudi stopped dead in her tracks, Celeste managed to make a quick sidestep and avoided a collision without breaking her ankle—a small miracle considering the four-inch, spiked heels on her sandals.

"Holy celestials," Trudi gasped, her words whispered on a breathy sigh. "Greek deity incarnate." Trudi jogged forward and grabbed Becca's shoulder, holding her back. "Who…is that hunk standing next to Marcus? Is he—"

"Hey, don't bruise the bride, if you don't mind." Becca shifted her shoulder away from Trudi's death grip, and lowered her voice. "That's him."

Celeste shifted her attention from her friends to the mammoth Victorian house, searching for Marcus on the crowded, wrap-around porch. Marcus stood, in all his gorgeous glory, next to the only man on Earth who could possibly give him a run for his money.

Celeste stared at the stranger. His profile was classic. The slope of his forehead, the bridge of his nose, the curve of his lips, and the solid line of his jaw and chin were all perfect. His black hair, clipped short on the sides and back, was longer and wavy on top. If he weren't so handsome, he'd have qualified as pretty. The sleeves of his chambray button-down were folded below his elbows and his jeans were neatly pressed. What had she heard about men who ironed their jeans? Anal retentive? Gay?

She dared another appraising look. He was beautiful. Luscious, drop-dead gorgeous. Her knees turned to jelly, and her left ankle turned inward causing her to teeter, for a brief moment, on her heels. Too bad she'd sworn off men.

"Him who?" Patrice asked, shifting her attention from Becca to the house.

"Max." Becca lifted her hand and waved at Marcus, who motioned for her to join him on the porch. She nodded and held up her finger indicating for him to give her a minute.

"So that's the infamous, heart-broken Max Riley." The green in Trudi's eyes glowed. She thrust out her chest and straightened into her best man-eater pose. "Ggggrrrrr."

Becca tried to scowl at Trudi, but a naive sweetness lined her brow instead. Celeste held back a laugh. Becca was about as vicious as a teddy bear, even in her bridezilla state.

"I told you to leave him alone." Becca glared at Trudi. She shifted her warning to Patrice and finally Celeste. "And I mean all of you."

"Hey, don't look at me," Celeste said, holding up the gift bags in a shrug of defeat. "If he can't push my career up the ladder, I'm not interested. And I'm pretty sure small-town boy can't help me in the metro Atlanta broadcast market. So I'm not the one you need to worry about." Celeste pointed at Trudi. "She is."

CHAPTER TWO

⧽⧼

"Good, they're here," Marcus announced, waving his hand toward the front gate.

Max watched his cousin's face break out in an idiotic grin. He was always amazed how love turned the manliest of men into a pile of mush. Max turned around in time to see Becca and three other women in a heated conversation. Becca waved at Marcus and turned to talk to her friends, before the foursome made their way up the sidewalk.

A tall redhead in a skin-tight purple dress took the lead. She was a hot number—and every stride she took confirmed she knew it. She was too hot for her own or anyone else's good, if you asked Max. Her walk could be described as a sass-shay—emphasis on the ass. She definitely shayed it.

Next to her a tall, slinky woman, model-thin, strode with an elegant grace on impossibly high heels. Max wondered why women did that to themselves—spikes couldn't possibly be comfortable. She wore a sundress that flowed around her thighs, showing a good four inches of leg above her knees, and he couldn't help but notice her long brown hair bouncing with each step she took. She was the TV reporter he'd seen on the local morning news reporting a pileup on the freeway.

A petite brunette glued to Becca's side matched her every step and didn't seem to have attention for anyone other than the bride and a notebook she held in her hand. Max smiled to himself. Women and weddings. Happy and excited one minute, upset and crying the next. But he had firsthand knowledge that women could be unpredictable. His smile faded.

He'd learned the hard way when his ex decided to get involved with charity work at the church. Sissy had thrown herself into volunteering. Every Thursday night she'd help the youth minister with the Sunday School lessons for the preteens, and she would stay after potluck dinners on Wednesdays, supposedly to help clean up, all the while ignoring Max and the kids. He should have known things were amiss. The Jezebel. She ran off with the damn youth minister and didn't have the good grace to leave a note. She'd left Max under the scrutiny of the law for over four weeks, before she surfaced—alive and well—in California with Pastor Dick. A total scandal. And an embarrassment.

Becca pushed past the redhead and led the way up the stairs and onto the porch while Marcus moved through the crowd of guests to greet her. Marcus scooped his future wife into his arms and bent his head to give her a welcoming kiss. She tilted her face to meet his lips, appearing as gloriously ecstatic as Marcus. Max smiled at the two of them, glad he was capable of experiencing happiness again. Grounding himself had taken him awhile.

Max'd been a conflicted wreck when Sissy first left, his entire world tilted on its axis, his life like a sailboat adrift without any wind. After the initial shock wore off, he'd become bitter, wallowing in self-pity, until he realized his children needed him. And they needed him happy. Especially Neecie. She'd been only two years old when her mother deserted them.

Max brought his memories to a halt when Marcus, Becca, and her three friends maneuvered their way toward him. He shifted away from the porch post and straightened to his full height.

"Hi, Max," Becca said. He leaned down to hug her, and she in turn wrapped her arms around his neck. "It's good to see you again."

"You, too." He eased away from her embrace and grinned. "I'm glad I was able to make the trip for the party. I was afraid I wouldn't be able to get away, but Dad promised he could manage the farm without me."

"You needed to get away," Marcus said and clapped him on the shoulder, pulling him forward. "Let me introduce you to the bridesmaids."

The redhead stepped in front of Becca, shoved her handful of gift bags to the leggy one standing behind her. She pushed her hand at him, and he instinctively clasped hers in greeting.

"Hi, I'm Trudi Steward." Her lips curled into a provocative, come-on smile. "A pleasure to meet you."

Her hand gripped his in a confident shake, and he could swear he heard her purr—or had she growled? His mouth morphed into what he was sure resembled a grimace of fear, but he tried his damnedest to pull his lips into a smile.

"Welcome to Atlanta," she said. "I promise to make sure you have a *real good time.*"

She gave him a wait-until-later look and dropped her lid in a lascivious wink. Max gulped, and the hairs on his arms bristled when his self-preservation instincts soared to alert. Becca reached over and grabbed Trudi's arm, and Max silently thanked her, wondering if Trudi might be listed as a modern definition for predator in the dictionary.

Becca tugged Trudi's hand. "Let go," she said. "Don't scare him off. We need him as our best man."

"Give the guy a chance to get acclimated to the city." Marcus laughed. "He's a country boy, not accustomed to all you aggressive urbanites."

"I'm not an urbanite." The short brunette giggled as she closed her notebook and stepped closer, holding out her hand in greeting. "I'm Methodist," she clarified.

Max didn't respond, gauging whether she was serious—she was—and weighing the odds whether the petite one was as pushy as Trudi. He resisted the urge to wipe his hands on his jeans before he made physical contact with her, and after a slight hesitation, he reached out and shook her outstretched hand. Her grip was soft, and none of Trudi's assertiveness zinged through. He breathed a sigh of relief.

"I'm Patrice," she added. "Nice to meet you. I'm documenting absolutely everything about the wedding, so I'll need to interview you, since you're the best man." She dropped her hand and opened her notebook, pulling out a pen from the side of her purse. "What's your birthdate—"

"Not now, Patrice," Trudi said. "Let Max unwind, enjoy himself. This is a party. You'll have time to fill out your little journal later." Trudi stepped toward him again, bringing the hair on the back of his neck to attention, when Becca sidestepped in front of her and ushered her third friend forward.

"Last, but not least, this is Celeste."

He gazed down at her and favored her with a genuine grin, and she in turn flashed her megawatt smile. He recognized it as the same one she used on camera.

"Hello," she said, stiffly. Short and sweet. She shifted the collection of gift bags to her left hand, freeing her right for the obligatory shake.

She reminded him of a World War II pinup girl. Her shoulder-length, brown hair hung in soft waves, framing her perfectly oval face, her skin flawless except for a dusting of freckles across her nose. Her glossed lips appeared ready for a kiss. His perusal lingered a moment too long on her mouth, and when she licked her lips, he glanced up to her most arresting feature—her eyes: a bright sky-blue, fringed with thick dark lashes. She blinked and brought him back to reality, and he remembered his manners.

"Hello, pleased to meet you." He took her hand, but when he gripped her palm, her fingers remained rigid, the bogus, movie-star smile plastered on her face. The best he could tell, she was wound up tighter than a politician the week before election. What in the world would cause such an attractive, talented woman to be so tense? She let go of his hand, and his palms were sweating. Flustered, he couldn't remember the last time a woman had gotten under his skin. The idea left him unnerved.

"Likewise, I'm sure," Celeste said. She hadn't been prepared when she peered into his face and the full force of his masculinity hit her. Perfection. And a downright sin God had created such a specimen, cranked him full of testosterone, and unleashed him on unsuspecting females. More particularly, her. Apparently the holy divinity had an evil sense of humor. And Celeste had always imagined God as a woman. Not anymore. He must be a man with a crappy sense of humor. Too bad she didn't date divorced men with children, and more importantly, that she'd sworn off men. She sighed. Her timing and luck always sucked.

She inhaled a lungful of humid air, and another chunk of hair coiled back into place. From beneath lowered lashes, she gave him one last glimpse before she turned to Becca.

"Where should I put your gifts?" she asked.

"I don't know," Becca answered. "Let's ask George." Becca reached for Trudi's hand. "Come on, let's find a safe corner for you."

"I'll be back to entertain you," Trudi said, a split second before she had no other choice but to turn and follow Becca.

Celeste held back a laugh. Trudi the man-eater at her finest.

A mixture of panic and apprehension flickered across Max's features, but he quickly recovered, and Celeste allowed her gaze to linger on his hot, dark eyes. Eyes far too alluring. Eyes that hinted at an invitation to trouble.

He grinned, and a bolt of lust shot straight to the crevice between her thighs. And if she didn't know better, she'd swear the heat melted her new silk thong.

"Later," she said, glad the smile he cast her way appeared sincere and free of fear. Mischievous maybe, but at least, free of fear.

She walked away and forced herself not to look back. The man was an enigma. Was he wounded and vulnerable? Or hot and dangerous?

CHAPTER THREE

Would the night never end? Celeste stood with her back against the wall, trying not to stare at the receding hairline of her captor.

"Right." Celeste nodded her agreement, not paying a bit of attention to what the balding young man before her yammered on about. Who was this guy? She wished someone would cram a fork in her cranium and put her out of her misery.

She took a sip of wine and scrutinized the room, searching for the nearest exit. She should know them all, since she'd spent the entire night exiting a room every time Max entered. Her heart hitched up into her throat when he and Marcus came through the door laughing. She tried to crouch, but the little sawed-off bastard who had her cornered wasn't tall enough for Patrice to hide behind, much less Celeste in four inch heels. From her chest upward she loomed exposed, and she was trapped.

"So, when can we expect to see you sitting behind the desk reporting the *real* news?" he asked, blinking like a frog eating its dinner. "Instead of the shit news from the side of the road?"

The ballsy asshole. Her eyebrows rose in affront. She gritted her teeth and flashed her newscaster's smile.

"What makes you think I want a news anchor position?" she asked politely, instead of saying, *why don't you crawl back under a rock where you belong* like she wanted to. A surge of resentment pursed her lips. Did she have a neon sign above her head proclaiming "Stalled Career?" Was it blatantly obvious to all the viewers that her coveted position loomed beyond her reach and that the network had filled the latest anchor slot with yet another newcomer?

"I would think a striking woman such as you would want an anchor position. You deserve to be in front of the camera the entire broadcast, not just a few minutes." He grinned and licked his shiny mouth, oily from the wings he'd sucked down earlier. Flattery could get most people anywhere, unless they were bald, five-four, and on the make. With greasy lips.

"Well, you're wrong," she said, defending herself while looking down at him. "Some of us enjoy the excitement of reporting the news as it happens. To be in the moment, enjoy the exhilaration of being on the scene." She stepped around him, making a deliberate attempt to avoid brushing against him, hoping her departure would be understood as a polite, but obvious turn-down. She tried to smile. "If you'll excuse me."

"News? In the rain before the sun comes up?" He laughed, a riled glint in his eye. Possibly her exit hadn't been polite enough. "I'm not buying that. You want to know what I think?"

She stopped and turned around. "Not really."

"I think you want news anchor, and you want the position badly." The insolence of his scrutiny tensed her stomach muscles as if she'd been sucker punched. "You're beautiful enough, smart enough, but something's missing."

She didn't bother to answer him—he'd hit his mark, and his words stung with their intended malice. Her belly clenched in self-doubt, but Celeste smiled at him, determined not to show him how close he'd come to the truth.

She turned and dodged her way across the room. How could a frog of a man be so perceptive? Must be his eyes, bulging and all-seeing, taking everything in from both sides of his head. But he qualified as a dumbass because he didn't understand that being intuitive didn't make him a prince.

Celeste glanced over her shoulder as she left the family room. No sign of Max or the girls. She scanned everyone's faces again when she darted through the kitchen. She headed out the back door, across the porch, and into the dark solitude of the backyard. Finding a nice quiet spot to soothe her wounded pride suited her at the moment.

When her sight adjusted to the thick velvety dusk, she spied a pair of Adirondack loungers on the far side of a small, but nicely landscaped garden. She made a beeline, taking note of the orderly plantings of begonias still in bloom in the late summer heat.

After settling onto the chair, Celeste threw her purse onto the ground and kicked off her sandals. She stretched her legs and wiggled her toes, luxuriating in the relief from the high heels.

Celeste took another sip of chardonnay and placed the wine glass on the arm of the chair. She scrutinized the backyard, taking in her surroundings. They'd done a decent job with the landscaping. Even her mother, the June Cleaver of the modern world, would be impressed. She closed her eyes, shutting out the dim light of the evening, and breathed in the fresh clean smell of cut grass. A symphony of crickets chirped their evening serenade and katydids screeched in the distance. She needed to go home more often and spend an occasional night at her folks' house. She'd forgotten the sounds and smells of life outside the city.

At thirty, she'd chased her dreams for years, knowing what she wanted—the celebrity of being hometown Atlanta's number one news anchor. Who knew? Maybe she could move on to bigger and better positions, such as *Good Morning America,* and follow in Diane Sawyer's footsteps. Or Oprah's. Maybe she was destined to rule the afternoon prime spot of TV talk host.

Her only problem was her tendency to stumble over words when she read the tele-prompters. She did a slam-up job during the on-the-scene newscasts, but put her behind the desk and have her read the prompter, and she sometimes tripped over the words. Making hash out of the news seemed to be a self-induced sabotage.

But she would overcome all obstacles. She was getting better, and being news anchor was what she'd always wanted. The same career her mother had given up so she could be a stay-at-home mom. Celeste couldn't believe her mother had resigned from her spot as daytime anchor when her oldest brother was born. Why would a woman choose motherhood over a promising career? She'd never understood why and probably never would.

But if she didn't get her act together, she might find herself destined to remain a newscaster and never attain her dream. Celeste jerked her purse open and dug through the clutter until she reached the bottom, stretching her fingers out and searching for a Hershey Kiss, one of her few indulgences. She always carried a few in her purse for times when she needed comfort. The smooth chocolate melting on her tongue reminded her of when she was a little girl—after she'd scraped her knee or felt sad. Her mother would kiss the top of her head and present her with a foil-wrapped candy. She would hold Celeste close and hum a tune, usually "A Spoonful of Sugar" from Mary Poppins, while the sweet cocoa melted and her hurt went away.

She located a particularly evasive Kiss in the bottom of her purse and unwrapped the candy with relish, her salivary glands almost screaming in anticipation. She leaned back against the wooden slats of the chair, propped her feet up, closed her eyes, and slipped the chocolate into her mouth, waiting for its magic to work.

Max was across the room when Celeste escaped through the back door. He followed as quickly as he could, but by the time he dodged his way through the crowd, she'd disappeared. He walked outside and stood at the top of the stairs, listening to the din from within. Most everyone had piled inside while a handful of guests still gathered on the front porch, near the bar. Once he adapted to the darkness, he started down the steps. When he stepped onto the flagstone walkway, he spotted movement in the corner of the yard. He squinted in order to see.

He'd spent the majority of his evening trying to get the image of her eyes and lips out of his mind, and the remainder of the night wanting to talk to her. Which wasn't a good idea. He had no business trying to engage her in conversation. He didn't trust women any further than he could throw them, and he didn't need one muddling up his life. Then the image of her licking her full, pouty lips would jump back into his head, and he'd think about taking the time to get to know her a little better, and his resolve would drop. But every time he'd spot her, she'd disappear soon after. He'd missed out on the opportunity to speak with her at least six times. Not that he was counting.

He watched her from across the lawn while she appeared to frantically search through her bag. Hopefully not for her car keys. He didn't want her to leave. Or did he? She must have found what she was looking for because she put her purse down and relaxed. He couldn't pinpoint the reason, but she intrigued him. And how could walking over and saying hello hurt? Or asking her about her day? About her life, her favorite color, her favorite movie?

Who was he fooling? He didn't have any business pursuing her. A big-time news reporter in the city had nothing in common with a horticulturist from south Georgia. Max should go back in the house, search for Marcus, and ask for the keys to the loft, so he could leave before he found himself in over his head. But instead, he started walking toward her, and he didn't have a clue what he would say to her when he got there.

"Where have you been all night?" Max asked when he walked up the pathway. Well, that should fall into the category of the all-time lamest line.

Startled, Celeste sat up, gulped a lungful of air, and began thumping her chest.

"Oh my God." She coughed and thumped more. "I think I swallowed it whole."

"Are you okay?" He sprinted the last few steps to reach her. "Swallowed what? Here drink this." He grabbed the glass sitting on the arm of the chair and handed it to her.

She took a gulp, tears rimming her lower lids. He resisted the urge to reach over and wipe them away.

"Oh, thank God." She hiccoughed. "It went on down." Relief washed over her face and erased the concerned wrinkles from her forehead. She slumped back against the chair. "Woo." She dabbed at her lids with the pads of her fingers. "That was close."

"What were you eating?"

"A chocolate."

"Chocolate?" There was no way she was eating candy. He'd be willing to bet good money, sugar never passed between her lips.

"Yes. A Hershey Kiss to be exact." She challenged him with her tone.

"As in a cone-shaped milk chocolate?" He sounded skeptical, but he couldn't help himself.

"You don't believe me?" She must have heard the doubt in his voice too.

"It's that," he paused. "Well…you're awfully thin."

"I beg your pardon?"

"What I mean is…" He stalled, not sure where to go. Why had he mentioned her weight? Didn't he know better? But he hadn't talked to a woman alone for over two years and hadn't used a pick-up line in over ten. He'd spent way too much time working and way too little time honing his social skills. "You need to come down south and let my grandma fatten you up." He inwardly cringed. No doubt that comment would impress her. Not. He was doing a bang-up job, about as well as a man with a shovel digging a hole. And from the evil glint in her eyes, a very big hole. He should have stayed in the house.

"Fatten me up?" She raised her manicured brows and stared down her freckled nose, the edge of her lip lifting in an Elvis snarl. The crater he'd dug got deeper. "Your grandmother?"

"Yeah, Big Mama."

"You call your grandmother Big Mama?" Celeste said. "That's absolutely horrible. Doesn't she take offense to such a derogatory reference to her weight?"

Max laughed. "Big Mama is four feet eleven and weighs all of ninety pounds."

"I guess I don't understand." He appreciated the gentle curve of her shoulder and arm as she reached for her purse and pulled it into her lap.

"Her name is not about her size, it's about her. She's a force in and of herself. She rules the roost, and nobody crosses Big Mama. She always gets what she wants. I'm surprised they didn't nickname her Camille after the storm, but she's been Big Mama since 1955 when she and Papa Joe saw *Cat On A Hot Tin Roof* in New York. She told Papa Joe the night of the show that she would always be his Big Mama and nine months later my daddy was born. She's been in control of the family ever since." He sized Celeste up again. Beautiful, but he normally preferred women with curves, some padding on their hips. "Big Mama could cook you up a meal and put some meat on your bones."

"I can't afford to have *meat on my bones*. I work in front of the camera. It adds fifteen pounds." She huffed, and her puckered brow translated into *are you for real?*

"I heard it was ten." He wanted to keep her talking. He enjoyed watching her lips open and close as she spoke. If possible, her mouth appeared more kissable than it had earlier.

"On me, it's fifteen." She scowled her exasperation at him. "I'm sure your grandmother—"

"Big Mama," he corrected.

"Yes, well…I'm sure B…Big Mama," she stuttered, "is an excellent cook. But in the interest of my career, I believe I'll pass on the fattening-up opportunity." She pushed her feet back into her sandals and started to stand. "If you'll excuse me."

"Let me start over." He held out his hand and stopped her from rising.

"There's no need." Celeste sat forward, ramrod straight, and pulled her features into an uptight expression, casting glances that rivaled the negative temperature of a polar ice cap. Talk about striking out. Other than scare her, he couldn't imagine what he'd done to deserve such a cold shoulder. Except the weight comment. Damn. He'd really lost his touch.

Celeste hated she had to act like such a bitch, although his comment about her weight had taken her aback, the main reason she found herself on high alert was the fact he was so damn sexy. She feared she would heat to a full boil if she didn't get away from Max the Magnificent. The cozy corner of the garden was intimate, he was extremely close, and he was beyond gorgeous. The mere act of looking at him was driving her crazy. If looks could make you come, she was on her way to a big O, and she prayed he wouldn't move any closer because she'd have no other choice but to jump him.

Then she remembered Becca's orders. But had she actually promised Becca she'd keep her hands off of him? On the verge of asking to see his tan lines, she remembered the show stopper. He had kids. She'd never dated a man with offspring, and she didn't intend to start now.

"Really," she reiterated, "I see no need to start over."

"Ah, come on," he said, and flashed his killer smile as he settled next to her on the footrest, trapping her on the Adirondack chair. "Don't tell me you aren't going to give me the chance to try my best line."

"And what would that be?" she asked. He mulled over his response, and she wondered why she led him on, torturing herself in the process. She needed to engage him in conversation like she needed a hole in a condom. Not in this millennium.

"You look so good I could put you on a plate and sop you up with a biscuit." He wiggled his brows and seemed pleased with himself, while he flashed an enticing grin and lured her to places she should never go. Make that *would never* go.

"Sop? A biscuit?" She ignored his mouth and instead focused all of her attention on his eyes. "You're kidding, right?"

His gaze slid from her face all the way down her legs and back up again, settling on her mouth and causing her breath to snag in her throat. He must have worked a charm on her because she couldn't quit watching him. His dark eyes, alluring and dangerous, were framed with lashes too thick and long for a man. Another cruel joke of nature. Focusing on his eyes seemed risky, so she forced her sight past his shoulder. "That line works for you?" she asked.

"Of course not. It's funny as hell. Who honestly uses a line like that?" He laughed, his belly chuckle warm and infectious. As her laughter joined his, some of the night's tension disappeared, and she relaxed a little.

"I don't know...*The Dukes of Hazzard*?" she said, enjoying the sound of his voice and conveniently forgetting Becca's mandate.

"Exactly. That would be a Bo line if I've heard one." He hummed a tune and quoted a line about good ol' boys meaning no harm and modern day robin hoods then ended with a loud, "Yee-haw."

"And that would be?"

"The theme song to the *Dukes*," he said. Disbelief clouded his face, as if she should know.

"Oh please, you cannot know the theme song to that hokey show." He really was a country boy. With kids.

"And why not? I'll bet you know the theme song to a few of your favorite shows."

"Favorite show?" She laughed. "It takes a real man to admit *The Dukes of Hazzard* is a favorite."

"My daddy and Papa Joe didn't miss one episode, and neither did I. Started watching the show when I was four," he said, a tinge of defensiveness in his voice.

"I didn't mean to imply…" She paused, not sure what else she should say. She couldn't very well tell him she thought, although he was breathtakingly gorgeous and naively charming in a precarious way, he was a bumpkin from the country. And she'd been warned to stay away. So she began again. "What I really mean is that I didn't intend any offense."

"None taken." He brightened, once again all handsome charm.

"I'm sorry, I'm not normally this bitchy," she said, regretful she'd acted so uptight. "I've had a rough day, make that week…actually year, and Becca told us…"

He waited a moment for her to go on, but she stalled, knowing she shouldn't tell him about the caveat.

"What?" he prompted.

"Becca requested we stay away from you," she confessed in a rush, and consequently experienced an intense case of guilt. She'd called out her best friend, knowing good and well Becca wouldn't want him to know she'd warned the girls to stay away from him.

Then Celeste made another mistake and caught his gaze again.

"We? Who's we?" His eyes, sweet and dark, triggered a hot wave of desire straight to the pit of her stomach, which spread a warm ache to the flesh against her twisted thong. He was too close.

"Trudi, Patrice and me." Was she under a spell? Celeste clamped her loose lips, determined not to say anymore.

"Why would she do that?" He sounded disappointed.

"She explained that you've been through a bad time…about your wife."

"She told you about Sissy?" Shock radiated across his face, a trace of hurt exposing itself in the pained cloudiness of his eyes, the strained lines around his mouth. "Why would she mention Sissy?"

"Becca didn't mean any harm," Celeste said. "She was concerned for you." Celeste tried to laugh, to lighten the mood, but the sound came out strangled and forced. She took the last sip of her wine. "I assume she didn't want us to go on the attack when you might not be ready," she stalled again. "You know."

"I'm not sure I do."

"Well, believe me or not, but Trudi can come on quite forceful sometimes."

Max laughed. "I not only believe you, I experienced her myself."

"Oh no," she exclaimed. "She got to you?"

"She cornered me briefly, but Becca swooped in and steered her away. The last time I saw her, she was enjoying the attentions of the bartender."

"Poor Steve," Celeste said.

"Who's Steve?"

"A special friend of Trudi's. She has a thing for waiters and bartenders."

"Ah, I see." He didn't appear as if he did.

"She's a damn fine defense attorney. If you ever need one, hire her," she said. "But she works hard and when she plays, she plays harder. She prefers to keep things simple. Fun. Uncomplicated." Celeste twirled the stem of the empty glass between her palms. "Can't blame her. I understand. Relationships get in the way of our true goals, if we allow them to. That's why I've sworn off dating for a while. I need to concentrate on my career, go after what I truly want."

"What would that be?" he asked, and he appeared genuinely interested. Did she dare confess her ultimate aspiration?

"One of these days I plan on being the number one news anchor in Atlanta." She sounded much more confident than she felt. There. She'd voiced her dream out loud for the universe to hear. And to Max Riley, a complete stranger.

"And I know you will," he said with conviction.

"Thank you." His simple words had triggered a disconcerting moment of introspection. Why had she confessed to him? She'd never been compelled to express her goal to any of her men friends. And his expression of complete faith in her without any hesitation whatsoever gave her a satisfying sense of competence. "Thank you very much."

"For what?" He smiled and tilted his head, watching her through marginally lowered lashes.

"For saying that. Confirming your belief in me." She glanced away, embarrassed by her sudden openness. "That was kind of you."

"Why wouldn't I want the best for you? For you to attain your dreams?" he responded, reflective. "All of us should be able to reach our goals. God gave us talents, and He wants us to succeed. He wants you to believe in yourself and go after what you want and to fulfill yourself."

"You sound like an evangelist." She took another hard, assessing once-over of him. "Have I seen you on television before?"

"Hardly." He laughed his wonderful belly laugh again. "I'm a far cry from being a preacher man." He looked at her empty glass. "Can I get you another wine? I'll go grab a beer and get you a refill, if I could entice you to stay out here with me for a while longer?"

She pondered his proposition, before deciding against spending any more time with him. "I can't. I promised Becca."

"But you aren't dating men anymore, and I'm not looking for anyone to date. What can the two of us talking possibly hurt? You aren't really breaking a promise, especially if I ask you to have a drink with me."

Celeste recognized the sincerity of his invitation, and she had the distinct impression that her hanging out for a while was important to him. She yearned to stay, but knew she should leave. In the end, her compulsive side won.

"Sure, but instead of a glass of wine, can you make that a shot of tequila, please?"

CHAPTER FOUR

ॐॐ

While Max waited for the bartender to shake the tequila over ice, he decided it was time for him to get with the program. Even though he hadn't engaged in an intimate conversation with a single female in years—make that a sophisticated and career-oriented woman, ever—he was still first and foremost a Riley. He could hear Big Mama browbeat integrity into his head, reminding him of his family values, reinforcing his confidence, encouraging him to always be a simple man, a good man, and to always be upfront. No puttin' on airs, as she would say. And consequently, he'd grown into a self-reliant, self-sufficient, positive, strong adult. He was proud of who he'd become and couldn't think of a good reason not to allow his confidence to shine through. He'd go back to the garden and allow Celeste to see the real him.

Max walked across the lawn balancing two old-fashioned goblets. The time had come for him to break out of his rut and have some fun. Emotionally, he'd moved on a long time ago. He deserved to finally relax and enjoy himself; everyone knew Sissy had. When she'd first left, he'd beat himself up trying to understand where he'd gone wrong, ultimately deciding the problem had been Sissy, not him. The hardest thing for him to acknowledge was the probability she'd never loved him at all. That, and the fact she left the kids, which hurt the most, even more than the embarrassment. She'd married him to escape her dysfunctional family life, and after a few years, a secure family wasn't enough, and she craved more. Who would have ever thought Pastor Dick would be the ticket? Must have been the thrill of seducing a married man. The forbidden. The taboo.

Max approached the flagstone walkway and forced himself back to the present. He was in town for the weekend, and on Sunday he'd head back down south, back to the routine of his life, back to the children. All he wanted to do was enjoy the company of a beautiful, intriguing woman for a change. He deserved the simple pleasure of a nice conversation. No strings attached. Maybe when he returned home, he'd try dating again. Possibly he was ready after all.

"Here you go," he announced when he returned to the intimate corner where Celeste sat in the dark. She jumped at the sound of his voice.

"You need to stop sneaking up on me like that," she said, clutching her hand to her chest. "Be still my pounding heart."

"I have that effect on women." Max laughed. "Sorry, I didn't mean to startle you. Didn't you see me coming?"

"I had my eyes closed," she said, sitting forward. "What have we here? Those aren't shots." She motioned toward the glasses.

"I hope you don't mind," he said, settling down on the footrest. "But I took the liberty of ordering your tequila the way I prefer mine." Her dark hair seemed curlier than it had earlier, and soft wispy ringlets framed her ivory face. He couldn't make out the dusting of freckles, but he knew they were there. She was an incredibly attractive woman.

"And how is that?" she asked, all beautiful-eyed and pouty-lipped. She had the most kissable mouth he'd ever seen. Possibly he'd misjudged which of the three bridesmaids was the most dangerous because he was certain the redhead didn't hold a flame to Celeste.

He tried to focus. What had she asked?

"How do you prefer your drink?" she asked again. She tilted her head to the side and gave him a peculiar look.

"Chilled and straight-up," he managed to say as he handed her the glass. "Good tequila does not require lime and salt. Excellent tequila is like a fine brandy that is to be sipped and enjoyed, not gulped and swallowed."

"You're a tequila connoisseur?" she asked, incredulous, doubt showing on her face. She lifted the drink in the air so the light of the moon reflected off the clear liquor.

"Exactly."

"So the bar is stocked with a liquor you deem the finest quality."

"They have a bottle of silver tequila, triple filtered for an incredibly smooth taste and that makes it one of the finer sipping liquors," he said. "But there are other quality brands. I'll have to introduce you to them all, and we can discuss which one you think is the best. Whether you prefer the silver over the gold, the aged to the others."

"An intriguing challenge. A *ta-kill-ya* taste test." Her full wattage smile almost blinded him. As if he wasn't already a little punch-drunk. "I like the idea, but I can only drink one tonight since I'll be driving later, and I don't think you'll be in town long enough for us to taste them all."

"There's always the wedding," he said. "Isn't the reception a given time and place for people to indulge? Go a little crazy?"

"I suppose."

He interpreted her words to have the same meaning as Big Mama's "we'll see," which always meant "no." But he didn't intend for her reluctance to spoil his fun.

"How about a toast to our first drink together? Tequila straight-up." He lifted his glass to hers, and she raised hers to meet his. He clinked the crystal. "Here's to women's kisses, and to tequila, crystal clear; not as sweet as a woman's kiss, but a damn sight more sincere."

"Oh my," she said, putting on an affront as if she'd been insulted, but a smile tweaked the corners of her mouth. "You trust tequila more than women? So you must like having your feet pulled out from under you. How about this toast? One tequila, two tequila, three tequila, floor?"

"Point taken." He laughed again, enjoying himself. "Now swirl it in the glass and allow it to release its full aroma, and smell it." She followed his lead, sniffing gingerly, and waited for her next instructions. "Sip it slow, let it roll over your tongue and hold it in your mouth for twenty seconds allowing it to warm up so you can enjoy the rich flavor before you swallow."

She followed his directions, took a dainty drink.

"Hmmm. Excellent. I've always picked up the shot glass, licked the salt, swallowed, and bit a lime." The moonlight reflected in the blueness of her eyes. "You've taught me something new."

"Good to hear," he said, lower than he'd meant to, his voice hoarse with the sudden desire to kiss her. Max shifted his gaze to her mouth. She ran her tongue across her upper lip and pressed her lips together, and all he could think about was what her incredible mouth might taste like. Celeste leaned forward and one of her curls bounced loose from her shoulder and brushed against his arm, wafting a scent of vanilla and almonds, making him dizzy.

She took another sip of her drink, and Max watched her every move, from the gentle curve of her neck across her shoulder and down her arm as she put her glass on the side table. Then she reached over and took his glass away too. His attention moved back to her face, and she leaned toward him. She wound her arm around his neck, and the softness of her skin, her aroma and warmth, the pure sensuality of her closeness, intensified his perceptions, honing all his senses to an extraordinary pitch. He lifted his face, and when he did, she pressed her mouth against his.

And she had him.

As much as she'd tried to not to make eye contact, Celeste knew the minute he'd lowered his voice, his whisper gruff, that she would kiss him. The tequila pulsed through her blood, and she prayed that two sips wasn't enough to cause her loose lips to sputter something entirely impetuous, such as *Do me now, I'm yours.*

His mouth was warm and soft, and she could taste the piquant liquor on his lips as she breathed in the scent of him. He smelled fresh and crisp, with a hint of spice, a manly aroma reminding her of the outdoors and sunshine. Her heart raced. Her senses in chaos, she melted her mouth against his and moaned, the ache of wanting him vibrating through every nerve in her body. And then he took over.

Max reached up and lifted her off the chair, settling her into his lap, his mouth tasting her as if he was a condemned man and she was his last meal. Her lips parted and he teased her with his tongue, delicate at first, until he deepened their kiss, his arms wrapping around her, pulling her closer, pressing her breasts against the hardness of his chest. No longer a brushing kiss, sweet and innocent, but full-fledged hot and all tongue. Her nipples ached and hardened against the flimsy silk of her sundress, and she felt herself get wetter with each throb of her sprinting heart.

When he finally pulled away, they were both breathing hard.

"Yowza," she said against his ear, as he leaned his forehead to hers and took a restraining breath.

"Incredible," he murmured, teasing his mouth over hers, while flicking her lower lip with his tongue and nipping a playful bite. "Where have you been all my life?"

"Looking for you," she said, half in jest. She peered heavenward to determine if the fireworks were real or only in her head, but all she could see was a pitch dark sky, not one star in sight.

"And now you've found me," he said against her cheek, his breath tickling a salacious dance across her neck. She ducked her head to escape the sensation, inadvertently squirming her rear into his lap, and found herself enjoying the delicious pressure of him against her. "So what's next?" he asked.

His Adam's apple moved as he talked, and she found herself tempted to lick her way up his throat and reclaim his mouth, showing him a thing or two.

"Let me kiss you this time," she said, her voice throaty with lust. And she did.

Celeste planted butterfly kisses along his neck, along his jaw, the scratchiness of his whiskers against her lips exciting her more, as she continued to trail light kisses across his cheek, finally claiming his mouth as hers. A quivering heat flared in her stomach, igniting her blood, warming her skin. She felt flushed and hot, her curls sticking to the nape of her neck, while her tongue did a gluttonous dance with his. She'd never reacted this insatiable over a kiss before, and she feared that she'd never taste enough of him.

He groaned, deep in his throat, and the sound reverberated through her, stimulating her already overloaded senses. His arms tightened around her waist again, and she knew he wanted her as much as she wanted him, the promise of incredible sex evident in every thrust of his fabulous and capable tongue. She imagined the many ways he could use his talented appendage and started plotting when she could see him again. Where they could consummate what they'd begun in a garden owned by strangers. Then she heard Becca calling her name from a distance, and she wrenched her mouth away. Back to reality.

"Oh my God, oh my God." She dragged herself away from his grasp and sat back on the chair. "I can't believe I did that."

A short silence ensued, while Max studied the ground, and she felt a heated blush spread across her cheeks. Disappointment flooded through her. Not only had she broken her "no men" rule, but to make matters worse, she'd kissed the very man Becca had asked her to stay away from.

"I'm really sorry." She broke the silence. "I shouldn't have kissed you. This is my fault. I don't know what I was thinking. And after I'd been warned to leave you alone." She felt guilty, excited and hot and magnificent and titillated, but guilty nonetheless. She had no business sidetracking herself or him. She had her career. He had his kids.

She heard Becca call her name again, closer this time.

"I better go," she said, grabbing her purse and rising. Max stood along with her and reached for her arm, turning her around to face him. He gently placed his fingers under her chin and lifted it so she had no other choice but to look at him.

"Thank you," he said, simple and short. He reached down and grasped her fingers with his hand, rubbing his thumb across the back of her hand.

"For what?"

"Spending time with me. Talking." He smiled. "And the kiss."

"I really shouldn't have," she said, wanting to pull her hand away, but enjoying the warmth of his hand too much.

"Yes, you should've." He leaned down closer until he was inches away. "Tonight was one of those times that rarely happens to someone, a moment they never forget. And I'm glad I experienced it with you."

"Me too," she said, begrudgingly. She had the distinct impression he was the type of man who would reach beyond his own needs, always put others first, and that his generosity was more important than his receiving. "I need to go."

"Can I see you again before I go home?"

"No, I don't think so. I'm working all weekend." She lied, knowing she needed to stay away from him. Max Riley was a good man, and there wasn't a doubt in her mind that he could be a threat to her recent promise to stay away from men. And she certainly didn't need to create waves with Becca. But most frightening of all, she had a fear she could like him, and the last thing she needed was someone worming their way into her heart.

Max kept an attentive eye on Celeste while she walked through the garden and onto the porch, where she greeted Becca, and the two of them disappeared into the house. When the door closed and he could no longer see her, he realized he'd forgotten to breathe. He took a ragged breath and sat back down, picked up his glass and took a healthy slug. He swallowed too fast and the fiery liquor burned his throat and stung his sinuses. He chuckled at the irony. Sometimes, no matter how expert a person might be, the margin for error always existed.

He wished they'd had more time to talk before Becca had found Celeste and lured her away. He'd wanted to get to know her better, figure out what made her tick. In the little time they had together, he'd picked up on the fact she was sharp and witty. Funny. Serious about her career.

He could spend more time with her at the wedding in October. Two months wasn't that long of a time to wait. Or was it? He realized another day was too long. And then he understood.

Until Celeste had stepped away and left him alone, he hadn't known how lonely he'd been. Lonelier than he'd realized. If only he could figure out a way to see her before the wedding.

CHAPTER FIVE

❧✧

"I've never heard of such a thing," Celeste said. She and the girls sat crammed in the corner of their favorite bar on Wednesday evening, waiting on appetizers and drinks. "A pre-wedding family reunion? So the entire family can meet you?"

A disaster waiting to happen, if anyone asked her: nervous bride, apprehensive in-laws, grandparents, kids. The very thought made her skin itch. She resisted the urge to scratch. No need to draw attention to her unease.

"Actually it's one of their family traditions," Becca said. "They have a reunion every Labor Day weekend. They want me to come down and join them along with my folks and Grammy." Becca sounded nervous, but Celeste thought the latest crisis, although a horrible proposal, hardly seemed catastrophic enough to call an emergency girlfriend meeting. Until Becca added the clincher. "And they invited y'all to join us too."

"What?" Celeste jerked to attention, wishing her drink had already arrived. The reunion could be more of a predicament than she'd originally thought, and there was no way she would go. Becca would need to handle this one without her.

Celeste had already tried, unsuccessfully for the past five days, to forget Max Riley and their spectacular kiss, dreading every minute until the time she'd have to face him again. At the wedding. She'd figured two months would give her time to prepare for the inevitable meeting. Now this? "But that's weekend after next, not even ten days."

"It sounds like a bridal roast to me. Who knows what you might be subjected to? They'll probably put you on display and publicly decide whether you're good enough for one of their own. I wouldn't trust the in-laws," Trudi said, matter-of-fact. She glanced across the room. "Where's our server?"

"Yeah, it does sound scary," Patrice put in her two cents. "I wouldn't want to be you."

"No kidding," Celeste agreed, not wanting to be Becca or herself either. There was no way in hell she'd get within kissing distance of Max Riley. None. Whatsoever.

"I know. I totally agree, and even though they want my family there, you can't believe how relieved I was when they invited the bridesmaids too. I really think it would be a good idea if y'all come with me," Becca said. She gave each of them a pointed stare, her eyes large and brown. And begging. "I need y'all there."

"Marcus will be with you, and I have no desire to visit rural Georgia." Celeste felt a bolt of fear rush down her spine, causing her toes to tingle. The idea of seeing Max again was more than her starving libido could stand. This was not a good idea. At all.

"Where is it?" Patrice asked, jotting down notes in her cloth bound journal.

"Where's what?" Becca asked.

"Rural?"

"Rural, what? What are you talking about?" Celeste snapped, her nerves riding on the edge of a razor blade. Sometimes Patrice could be so dense.

"Rural, Georgia? Is it near another big city like Atlanta? Or Statesboro? I went to a party in Statesboro one time—"

"You're kidding, right?" Trudi asked, barely able to disguise the disparagement in her voice. "How do you keep your job?"

"Cut me some slack. I didn't do well in topography—"

"You mean geography," Trudi corrected, her eyes telegraphing her annoyance.

Patrice glared, her lower lip sticking out in her infamous pout. "I'm a receptionist. My skill set doesn't require I have knowledge on the location of every city in the state."

"I don't think you have knowledge of any city in the state," Trudi said.

"Girls. Girls. Settle down." Celeste said. Becca's pre-wedding jitters had rubbed off on all of them. After Becca had planned her first wedding only to wind up jilted after the rehearsal dinner, her being on edge was to be expected. But Celeste knew Becca had found her true soul mate in Marcus and the wedding would happen without any disasters. If the four of them didn't claw each other's eyes out first.

"I do too know cities," Patrice said.

"You do not."

"That's enough," Celeste said. She didn't want to listen to the two of them bicker. Once they got started, they would nip at each other for the remainder of the evening, and she'd already had a horrible day. She'd planned on going straight home and crashing for the night before Becca had called her summit. If she'd known the topic of the emergency, she'd have blown Becca off. Or not.

The four of them had known each other since sixth grade where they'd all been in the same homeroom, and they were more like sisters than best friends. They stood by each other through all the good times and the bad times. But there was no way in hell she could attend Marcus's family reunion.

"I'm not going," Celeste said, her voice firm. She cast a quick sideways glance at Patrice, then shifted to Becca and raised her eyebrows for emphasis. "Regardless of what city it is near or how much you need me."

"Of course, you're going," Trudi said with a sly look. "For two reasons." She squeezed her eyes in that I dare you way of hers and waited for Celeste to bite. Trudi could be tricky, that's why she was such a successful attorney.

"No. I can't go." Celeste ignored Trudi's bait. "I'm sure they'll need me at the station for weekend highlights."

"You never do the weekend news," Patrice pointed out, her pen poised above the page. "So what day is it?"

"What do you mean, what day is it?" Trudi asked between clenched teeth. "It's Wednesday."

"No, silly, not today. What day is the family reunion? I need to make a note in the journal and to put it on my social calendar."

"It's Labor Day weekend," Becca snapped, her bridezilla side beginning to show. "I already told you that."

Celeste couldn't help but smile. She always enjoyed it whenever Becca, usually a sweetheart, showed her bitchy side. It made her seem human, like the rest of them.

"Okay, got it." Patrice scribbled the date in the journal and closed it with a snap. She reached for her purse and pulled out a small Day Timer. "Now for my social calendar—"

"Social calendar? Cut me a break. As if you have one?" Trudi said.

"Bad day?" Patrice asked, batting her eyelashes. She must have felt the need to be a punching bag because she was purposefully provoking Trudi.

"Here's our waitress," Celeste pointed out the obvious, hoping to change the subject, as their server returned with a tray filled with drinks and chips. "I'm starved, aren't you?" She took the basket of chips and shoved it toward Trudi. "Here. Eat. I think your blood sugar might be low."

"Smartass," Trudi said. She smiled. "So what about the two reasons?"

"I beg your pardon?" Celeste played dumb. She knew good and well what Trudi meant.

"Two reasons?" Patrice perked up, grabbing for the journal. "Is this something I should record?"

"Oh, yes, indeed. Record this." Trudi fished again. "The two reasons Celeste will join us on the trip down south."

"Okay, shoot." Patrice sat perched with pen above paper, waiting.

"First," Trudi began. "We all love Becca, and we're the Three Musketeers, and we stand behind our d'Artagnan, as well as each other, giving support when and where needed."

Celeste felt her cheeks grow hot. Trudi was correct, and she knew, as did Celeste, that they all would support Becca if she needed them to.

"I thought you were d'Artagnan?" Patrice, a confused glaze clouding her features, tilted her head at Trudi.

"I did consider myself the wanderer of the group, but since Becca is marrying first, she gets the title and the three of us are the Musketeers," Trudi said. "You know that."

"I forgot."

"Surprising." Trudi turned back to Celeste. "And number two," she stalled for dramatic effect. Celeste had seen her use the same tactic in the courtroom during a trial.

"And?" Becca leaned forward, waiting, a tortilla chip poised in midair.

"Max Riley," Trudi said and focused her laser scrutiny on Celeste. "You wouldn't miss the chance to see him again, or allow me the chance to jump his bones if you aren't there to run interference."

"What?" Celeste was appalled. Was she that obvious? She didn't think anyone knew about her clandestine tryst with Max. "I don't know what you're talking about."

"Yes, you do."

"No, I don't."

"Well, I certainly don't, so will someone kindly explain what we're discussing here?" Becca did not seem pleased.

"This is better than I thought," Patrice gloated as she wrote furiously in the notebook. Becca's hand shot out and snatched the book away.

"Stop it. You can't write that down in my memory journal." Becca attempted a death glare. Normally a teddy bear, she now seemed more like a bridezilla on steroids. "What's this about you and Max?" She turned her wrath on Celeste.

"Nothing." Celeste gulped, her face growing hotter. She picked up the paper coaster and fanned her cheeks.

"What is this about?" Becca asked again and glared at Celeste before she zipped her attention to Trudi. "And jumping bones? I thought I warned all of you to stay away from him. Marcus is really worried about Max, and he purposefully requested that I ensure none of you, and I will quote, 'ate him up and spit him out.'"

"I didn't, I swear," Patrice lifted her hands toward the ceiling in surrender. "I didn't say good-bye or try to interview him for the book. I did exactly as you asked."

Like a good I-want-to-be-the-maid-of-honor, Celeste thought.

"You're off the hook." Becca pushed the book back to Patrice. "But do not write any of this down," she said through clenched teeth. Becca was seriously not happy. She leveled her regard on Celeste and Trudi. "You two, however, are not out of trouble. Trudi, what is this all about?"

"Ask Celeste." Trudi ricocheted the question and turned to look at Celeste, who squirmed under her glare. "Go for it, girlfriend. Tell us what you were up to in the garden."

Everyone stared, waiting, and Celeste fidgeted some more. She picked up her drink and took a swallow.

"In the garden?" Becca parroted, frowning at Celeste. "What is she talking about?"

"I have no idea." Denial was her best option at this point.

"Yes, you do." Trudi plied onward. "Tell us what happened in the garden."

"You were spying on me?" Celeste couldn't believe it. Trudi must have seen her and Max. And snooped.

Trudi laughed. "Actually no, I didn't. I suspected, but you confirmed my suspicions. You and Max were swapping...uh, stories, I take it?"

"Absolutely not," Celeste said, appalled. How could she have fallen into Trudi's trap? She should have known better. Now Becca knew Celeste had defied her request, and any chance Celeste had for maid of honor crashed and burned like a race car spinning out of control. She crossed her arms and pressed her shoulders against the back of the booth. She hadn't wanted to be MOH anyway. "We talked for twenty minutes. Tops. No big deal. He followed me out to the garden, he seemed lonely, and asked if I'd have a drink with him." She put on her best I'm-sorry-poor-pitiful-me face. "I promise nothing happened. No harm done. I swear." No harm to him, but possibly to her. She hadn't stopped thinking about him since.

"That might not be true," Trudi said.

"What do you mean?" A wrinkle of concern creased an unbecoming line between Becca's brows.

"Think back to Saturday night when we met for dinner. Did no one but me notice how disappointed Max acted when he found out Celeste wasn't joining us?" Trudi lifted one brow, reminding Celeste of the Wicked Queen in Snow White. "He seemed in good spirits when he first arrived, but then he sat silent and withdrawn during the entire meal. I think he has a thing for our Celeste." Trudi smiled, but Celeste would swear there was a sting of spitefulness ringing through her words. Or her suspicions were her own paranoia.

"You know," Patrice added, "you're right, now that you mention it. I did notice he seemed reserved. I thought it was a reflection of his delicate emotional state."

"He's not interested in me," Celeste said, knowing good and well their kiss had been magical. Their superb kiss. Why couldn't she forget it?

"And you're interested in him…you're blushing, and you never turn red," Trudi said.

"I can't believe this." Becca leaned back, her shoulders slumped. "Now I have to tell Marcus."

"Tell him what?" Celeste asked. "That his grown cousin talked with me, had an innocent drink." Not so much an innocent kiss, but she kept that to herself. "Really, Becca. I think you're overreacting."

"I am not." Becca's voice quivered and for a second Celeste feared that Becca would cry. "It's that—"

"Hey, what's going on with you?" Trudi asked, reaching over and patting Becca's arm.

"Yeah, girlfriend, it's not like you to get so upset over something so trivial." Patrice put her arm around Becca and pulled her into a hug.

"The wedding," Becca said. She leaned her head on Patrice's shoulder. "The date is getting closer, and I don't want anything to go wrong, to give Marcus any cause to…you know, break off our engagement."

"Oh, pleeeaasseeeee," Trudi said. She took a healthy draw off her drink. "The man is enamored. Forever. Like he would ever leave you." Trudi pursed her lips and tossed her head, her hair flickering like flames under the light of the tiffany swag hanging above the table.

"Of course he wouldn't," Patrice said, total disbelief on her face. "Is that what you're worrying about? That he'll cancel your wedding after the rehearsal dinner, and pull a Harold Houdini? That will never happen."

"Patrice is right, honey," Celeste said, concerned for her friend, but at the same time experiencing guilt that she'd played a part in causing Becca's insecurities to resurface. Although Harold canceling the wedding had been the best for both of them, Becca had been humiliated and hurt by the way he'd handled it. Telling her immediately after her parents spent a chunk on the rehearsal dinner, as well as the wedding, was inconsiderate timing to say the least. "Marcus is not Harold. Thank God. Harold was a wimp-ass, and you're lucky to be rid of him. Marcus loves you. Adores you. And there's no need to worry."

"She has a severe case of premarriage jitters, that's all," Patrice said. "Sweetie, it'll be fine. You've found your Prince Charming. No doubt about it."

Becca lifted her head and reached for her purse. "I still need to let Marcus know that Celeste talked with Max."

"You don't need to tell Marcus anything. Come on, I mean, really. I only talked to him." Celeste wished they could stop discussing Max; she was having a hard enough time forgetting him without him being the topic of discussion. "Really. Nothing happened. There's nothing to tell."

"Yes, I do need to let Marcus know," Becca said. "I'll have a clear conscious if I confess, so he'll know that I didn't keep anything from him. I'll ask him if he thinks it's really a good idea for y'all to attend the reunion, and," she pointed a finger at Celeste, "you do not move. I will be back to discuss this further." She slid out of the booth, pulling her phone from her voluminous designer bag as she walked away.

A silence settled over the three of them, each one eyeing the other until Celeste broke the quiet with a sizzling hiss tossed at Trudi. "I can't believe you did that."

"What?" Trudi asked, playing innocent, as best she could.

"You called me out. To Becca," Celeste said.

Trudi burst out laughing. "Come on, Celeste, it was funny. You should have seen your face."

"There is nothing remotely funny about this," Celeste said. "You think this will give you a better chance for maid of honor." She leaned out of the booth and scanned the surrounding area for Becca, hoping like hell she would come back and tell them the bridesmaids were no longer expected at the family reunion. She crossed her fingers under the table and prayed.

"I have a slam dunk on the maid of honor role," Patrice said, her tone gloating and assured.

"Have you now?" Trudi turned her full attention to Patrice. "What makes you so sure?"

"She's right, she has it," Celeste said. "And I think it should be Patrice. You certainly don't deserve it."

"Like you do." Trudi glared.

"Well, you don't." Celeste stared back.

"Focus," Patrice said, sounding disturbingly like Trudi. "What's actually the most important thing we should be discussing right now, ladies? Think." She turned from Celeste to Trudi. "I'm surprised, Trudi, that I'm the one who has to ask this next question." She swiveled back to Celeste. "So what happened in the garden? Did you…you know, get to third base? Is he hung?"

Celeste felt her mouth drop. It never ceased to amaze her that someone so sweet, so pixyish and innocent, could be such a sexual voyeur.

"I will not entertain you with an answer to that question."

"She made it to at least one of the bases," Trudi said. "Look at her light up like Christmas at the Griswolds."

Celeste felt her cheeks burn like a 103 degree fever.

"I knew it," Trudi said with a little too much glee. "I could tell something was up when he came to the bar and requested two tequilas straight-up, chilled, and discreetly walked toward the back of the house and disappeared into the dark. I knew it." She laughed. "I love you, Celeste, you never let me down."

"I wish I could say the same about you. You certainly let me down."

"How so?"

"Calling me out…Becca might not want me in her wedding. At all."

"She'll want you. But you won't be her cherished first attendant." Trudi snapped to attention. "Quiet, here she comes."

Celeste turned in time to watch Becca make her way around the tables, lifting her rear so she could squeeze between the packed chairs. She appeared to have calmed down and a smile turned up the corners of her mouth. She looked gorgeous, all blonde and happy, walking back to their booth. Love must do a body, and attitude, good.

"So?" Trudi asked as Becca slid back into the booth. "Do we need to draw and quarter her? Or will she be allowed to live?" Trudi glanced at Celeste and smiled, and Celeste wondered if she might not be serious.

"She lives. Everything's fine. In fact, Marcus said Max had a fantastic time and is in better spirits after his visit to Atlanta," Becca said reaching for her drink. "And," Becca turned to Celeste, "it seems that the request for the bridesmaids to accompany me came from Big Mama, so although I'm disappointed in you, Celeste, you must accompany me, and Marcus agrees. Because if Big Mama wants it—"

"I know, I know," Celeste said. "Big Mama gets it."

"Who the hell is Big Mama?" Trudi asked, her eyes darting from Becca to Celeste and back again.

"Do I need to write this down?" Patrice reached for the journal.

"So, it's decided," Becca said. "We're all going to the reunion."

"Oh, hell." Celeste groaned.

The country and farmers and kids, oh my. And insatiable, hot kisses. Oh no.

CHAPTER SIX

❧❧

Labor Day weekend arrived with warp speed, much too fast for Celeste. Why was it when you looked forward to an event time dragged, but dread something, and time fast-forwards, like a roller coaster spiraling downhill? Another freak of nature. Like men with thick, dark lashes that were far too long. And scorching kisses that could rock a girl's world.

"Focus," Trudi said with a snap. "Where do I turn next? We're so far south, God knows where we're heading, and the GPS is confused."

"It isn't confused," Patrice said from the backseat. "Since Becca gave us directions to drive through town and take the scenic route instead of using the bypass and going straight to the farm, the GPS thinks you're a dumbass for going the wrong way." She poked her head between the bucket seats and snapped her fingers at Celeste. "Are you going to read the directions or do you want me to?"

Celeste forced her thoughts back to reality. Attending the family reunion weekend was a bad idea; she knew she shouldn't have agreed to come. She took note of the wadded-up paper clutched in a death grip between her strained, white fingers. She glanced out the window as she smoothed out the directions. Wildflowers bloomed among the spindly pines and hardwoods, intermingled with a large oak here and there, and straight ahead stretched a length of two-lane blacktop without a sign of life in sight.

"Where are we?" Celeste asked.

"That is exactly what I'm asking you." Trudi gritted her teeth and shoved her D&G shades further up her nose. She gripped the wheel with both hands and huffed. Perturbed didn't come close to describing her. "Looks like the pit of hell. Miles and miles of hot asphalt. Am I hallucinating or is there steam coming up off the road?"

"You're not seeing things," Patrice said. "It's steam coming out of your ears because you've been dreading the weekend the entire way."

"I haven't been—"

"Yes, you have," Patrice said. "You kept saying you couldn't believe you were giving up Labor Day weekend to spend it in the country with a bunch of hillbillies."

"Actually as I recall it, we all lamented the fact we had to do this, and," Celeste interjected, remembering correctly that she'd been the one to call Max Riley a farm boy, "once we were outside the Perimeter and cruising down I-75, you were the one doing all of the talking. I don't recall Trudi having the opportunity to say much of anything." How could she forget? Patrice's ability to talk nonstop without taking a breath for miles on end had hypnotized Celeste into a stupor. "Trudi was only driving."

"Thank you, Celeste, I appreciate you standing up for me," Trudi said. "But focus. Where the hell are we?"

Patrice grabbed the directions. "According to this, we should be coming up on the city of Tyler." She shook the paper between the seats and pointed excitedly. "Look ahead. I see houses."

Celeste stared through the passenger window as they entered the quaint town and time seemed to crawl to a gracious meander. When they entered the reduce speed ahead zone, Trudi slowed to a whopping twenty-five miles per hour and crossed into the city limits of Tyler, Georgia, population 19,578.

Tyler was a small college town nestled in the southwest corner of the state, surrounded by farms and hunting plantations. Agriculture reigned supreme. Streets lined with one hundred year old southern live oaks led their way into the antebellum downtown square. Signs boasted of over sixty historic and beautifully renovated architectural structures and a collection of refurbished mid- to late nineteenth century small town buildings, as well as one of the most extensive assortments of domestic Italianate architecture.

They drove past one of the stately homes, recently renovated into a bed and breakfast.

"Somerset Hall. How beautiful." Patrice sighed.

"I wish we were staying here in town instead of with Marcus's relatives." Trudi groaned a deep-throated, mournful noise. "I really dread this whole weekend on the farm. I know it's totally unfounded, but I'm thinking outhouses, no running water."

"It can't be that bad," Celeste said, hoping she was right. "This is 2014. We're visiting the family farm, not a renovation project." She sent up a silent prayer, please let there be indoor plumbing. She studied the homes as they cruised past one after the other, all examples of beautiful architecture reminiscent of an era long gone.

Children played on the sidewalks and pedestrians took their time at the crosswalks. A sense of tranquility washed over Celeste, and she imagined that the residents of Tyler found their refuge from the outside world in the small, serene town wrapped in nostalgia. A place where rush hour wouldn't be the height of news, and they probably never had to report fatal pileups. Or a policeman being shot. Or a college coed, missing for days, found after being lured to her death by people she'd known. God, her job was depressing.

"I'm glad Becca suggested that we drive through Tyler. This is lovely," Celeste said, forcing her thoughts back to the beautiful town and its innocence. As the light turned green, Trudi drove onward, cruising through town.

"Picturesque, I'll agree," Trudi said. "But by far too calm for my taste. My law practice would fizzle-out in a place like this. Dry up like old leaves and blow away in the wind."

Her comment gave Celeste pause. She doubted they had a local television station, and if they did, the coveted positions of anchor were few and far between. A small town like Tyler would be career suicide for a reporter. Not that such a thought would ever cross her mind, but since it had, she needed to file it under yet another reason to stop obsessing over Max Riley and his lusciously heated kiss. Remember, she forced herself to think: farm boy with kids, rural town so small you could drive through the entire place in less than ten minutes, and he lived too far away for a booty fling. As they picked up speed on the south side of town, they passed the rolling hills of a cemetery dotted throughout with green tents.

"Wow, look." Patrice pointed, counting the tents. "It looks like three funerals are scheduled. A lot of people just died."

"Probably out of sheer boredom," Trudi said and stomped on the accelerator, propelling her Lexus over the speed limit, shooting them down the road, passing fields with row after row of crops stretching as far as the eye could see.

"I wonder what's planted out there?" Celeste asked, becoming dizzy watching the rows flicker like a strobe as they passed.

"Probably cotton or soybeans. Aren't they the agriculture staple of Georgia?" Trudi asked, disinterested, staring at the never-ending road ahead.

"You know better than that. Our main crop is peanuts," Patrice said.

"I don't think either of you know what you're talking about." Celeste stared out the window, wondering if they would ever reach their destination; the fields seemed to stretch on for miles.

Trying to overcome the vertigo triggered by the flickering strobe-like view of the field rows as they sped past, she looked upward at the clouds, puffy white against a pastel blue, outlined in a darker shade of azure, like a painting the artist forgot to blend. Similar to her career. Not merging, unfinished, and like the clouds, with no foreseeable balance in the near future. She leaned her head back and focused on the dark music playing on the CD: some soundtrack from a popular vampire movie.

After a painful period of no one talking, and another unfathomable amount of acreage disappearing behind them, the fields ended and were replaced by pines and hardwoods until the foliage thinned and an open area, dotted with live oaks dripping with Spanish moss, led the way to a drive marked with an entrance to Magnolia Oaks.

"Slow down, slow down," Patrice said, leaning forward between the bucket seats. "This is it." She pointed at the sign and read out loud, as if no one else could read. "Magnolia Oaks. We're here. Becca's directions say the house sits a quarter mile off the road."

"I'll call Becca and let her know." Celeste pulled out her cell and hit speed dial. "We made it, girlfriend. Be waiting on us." Celeste shoved the cell phone into her purse as her heart pounded against her chest and every survival instinct she had kicked to alert. She would hang close to the girls and ignore Max and his classic good looks. And she wouldn't allow herself to look into his dangerous, but dazzling, dark eyes. A muffled moan hummed at the back of her throat.

"Did you say something?" Trudi asked, as she braked and pulled the Lexus onto the drive.

"No, no," Celeste said, studying her fingernails. "I jammed my nail, that's all."

Trudi gave her a skeptical look, before following the winding avenue canopied by towering oaks and interspersed with an occasional magnolia.

"Oh, hell," Trudi muttered, and asked in her best southern drawl. "Where are we going now? Twelve Oaks?"

"Wouldn't it be Tara, Scarlett?" Celeste countered.

"No, Twelve Oaks had the trees, and in comparison, Tara was a dump."

"Blasphemy," Celeste drawled, laughing, attempting to ignore the nervous ping of her heart and her sweaty palms as they drove farther down the drive, getting closer to Max Riley. "No self-respecting southern woman would ever utter such sacrilege."

"I'm not southern. I'm from Atlanta."

"Hush your mouth," Patrice said, getting into the groove. "What would your momma say?"

"She'd agree," Trudi deadpanned, humorously. But she was serious. Trudi's mother was a hard-ass attorney, like her daughter.

Celeste heard Trudi and Patrice gasp, and then the scene before her registered. A wrought iron gate stood open, lined on either side with orange and red canna lilies, black-eyed Susans and some type of purple flower Celeste couldn't name. But it wasn't the gate or the flowers that took their breath away. Trudi slowed the car to a crawl as they took in Magnolia Oaks.

Gleaming white in the afternoon sun, Magnolia Oaks boasted eight stately, three-story columns stretching across the front, and a porch with a balustrade running the entire length. Wraparound balconies adorned the second and third floors, and flanked on each side of the main house were one-story wings. A porte cochere graced the side entrance where Becca and Marcus stood waiting for them. Becca grinned like a Cheshire cat and motioned them forward.

"OMG," Patrice said in a hushed tone.

A male peacock strutted past, its iridescent blue and green feathers trailing along, his plumage tucked neatly behind.

"You are kidding me?" Trudi's mouth gaped open in an unladylike manner. She pushed her shades on top of her head for a clearer look. "Is this for real?" She turned and stared at Celeste.

Celeste eyeballed the sprawling mansion in front of them and couldn't think of a single thing to say, so she nodded and waved at Becca as they drove under the portico. When she reached for the door handle, Trudi grabbed her other arm and pulled her around.

"You know what this means?" Trudi asked, her eyes bugged-out in disbelief.

Celeste mutely shook her head in the negative.

"OMG," Patrice repeated from the back seat.

Celeste turned in time to see Max Riley and an elderly couple walk out and join Becca and Marcus, everyone smiling in welcome.

"He's dirty, filthy rich," Trudi said. Her lips turned up in a slow curl and she winked at Celeste before she let go of her arm and put the car in park. "Bling, bling, baby."

CHAPTER SEVEN

᠅

Max watched Celeste close her eyes against the hot blast of air that greeted her when she pushed open the car door and got out, soft waves of her hair fluttering in the steamy September breeze. Patrice eased out of the backseat, and Trudi walked around the front of the car and joined them on the passenger side, while they all surveyed their surroundings as if they'd landed in Oz. The place could be intimidating, he knew.

Becca threw her arms around her friends and pulled them into a group hug. "I'm so glad y'all are here…it seemed to take y'all forever."

"We thought the same thing," Trudi said, disentangling herself from the embrace.

"Welcome to Magnolia Oaks. I'm Big Mama, and this is my husband, Papa Joe."

His grandmother pushed forward, extending her hand in greeting. Papa Joe shuffled behind her and joined in welcoming their guests. They all shook hands, but Max hung behind, not sure he was ready to face Celeste. He needed to get a grip on his thoughts and how he felt about seeing her again. Although he did admit to himself that he'd anticipated this day as much as he'd dreaded it, the desire to kiss Celeste again a steady internal battle.

"Y'all come on in," Papa Joe said. "I'll send someone around to unload your bags and park the car. Come on in the house and let's show you around before we all melt out here in this scorching Georgia heat." He took hold of Trudi's elbow and guided her, until Big Mama caught sight of his wayward appendage and jerked his arm away.

"Old coot," she muttered and pushed Papa Joe toward the loggia running along the façade, which connected the side wing to the main house. "Now lead the way to the front entrance."

"Max," Trudi said. She strolled toward him and held out her hand. He took it, and she gave him a hearty shake. "Good to see you again."

"You, too. Welcome," he said, his voice sounding odd. Something about Trudi put his teeth on edge; probably the fact that she looked like she ate men for breakfast, and not necessarily in a fun way.

"Hi Max," Patrice said, tucking her journal under her arm as she pushed her hand at him. "Nice place you have here." She blinked. "Big."

"Ostentatious comes to mind," he said and grinned, his gaze moving past her to Celeste who hung behind the others. She'd hiked her shades on the top of her head, pushing her curls away from her face, her lips shiny with a tint of gloss, the bridge of her nose still dusted with a few freckles. She wore a shift dress that brushed her legs a few inches above her knees. Simple but stunning, just as he remembered.

Becca scooped her arm through Celeste's and scooted her past him.

"Say hi to Max, Celeste," Becca said, casting a sideways look in his direction.

"Hi," Celeste said, offering a brief peek his way while she allowed Becca to drag her past, much too quickly for him to do more than say "Hi" back and catch the merest glimpse of her gorgeous baby blues.

Max turned to Marcus, who shrugged his shoulders, and fell into step alongside his cousin as they followed a few feet behind the others.

"What was that all about?" Max asked.

"Becca's a nervous wreck. She's a little high-strung about the reunion and meeting all of the family," Marcus said. "And even though she's glad the girls are here, she's concerned about you."

"Me?"

"Might be my fault."

"You want to explain?"

"Big Mama had talked to Mom, told her about how, after Sissy ran off, you changed. You weren't the same. Depressed, withdrawn. I'd picked up on it myself last year in Jacksonville when we met for the Georgia-Florida game."

"I'll admit, it's been rough. But how would you have taken it if the woman you loved, thought loved you, the mother of your children, the person you thought you'd spend the rest of your life with, ran off and deserted you? And your kids. That hurt the most, the fact she didn't give a backwards glance, just took off and left Charlie and Neecie." Max paused, an attempt to clear the confusion that still muddled his thoughts. "You'd hurt too."

"Exactly. And I understand," Marcus said. "So, I'll admit, I'd discussed my concern for you with Becca, and since she has the tendency to be a motherly type, she worried that her girlfriends might be too aggressive, and they wouldn't be a good—hmmm, how should I say it?—experience for you?"

"Tell her I can handle myself," Max said, silently swearing to himself that his emotions, as well as his libido, would remain under control. "No need to be worried about me."

But when he observed Celeste from behind, contemplating the soft curve of her rear and the flounce of her dress while it danced along the back of her thighs, he wasn't so sure that was true.

Expecting Big Mama to be older than God, Celeste was surprised by the perky woman guiding them across the verandah to the front door. By calculating everyone's ages, Celeste figured Big Mama had to be pushing eighty, although she didn't look a day over sixty-five. True to Max's description, she was tiny, barely five feet tall, and couldn't weigh a hundred pounds dripping wet, but her size and her personality had nothing in common. She was a force to be reckoned with; her firm, spry step and authoritative voice screamed tenacity.

"Aren't they cute?" Becca whispered in her ear, still holding onto Celeste's elbow with a firm grip, marching her along behind Trudi and Patrice like a sheriff guiding a prisoner to jail.

"I don't know if cute is the adjective I would use," Celeste whispered back as she took another good look at the couple holding open the front door and ushering the girls inside.

Big Mama's snow-white hair, pulled back into a neat chignon, was a sharp contrast against her tanned, elegantly lined complexion. An obvious lover of the outdoors, she'd taken care of her skin, and she glowed, all natural, not a trace of makeup. Her dark eyes were lined with thick lashes, and Celeste realized where Max got his dark looks.

Celeste took a quick glance at Papa Joe, standing inside the door grinning, as she passed him. He had a head full of thick, gray hair, still streaked by a few strands of stubborn black, looking oddly reminiscent of a movie star she couldn't quite place, until he smiled and curled his lip. Remington Steele. Her mother had loved Pierce Brosnan as the quirky private investigator. Still had a crush on the actor himself, actually, and Celeste could imagine him looking like Papa Joe in another twenty-five years.

Cute? No. Powerful and intimidating? Definitely.

Celeste stepped into the cool foyer and gasped. If she found the exterior amazing, the interior took her breath away.

"We're running late, so snap to," Big Mama said. "You girls need to get upstairs to your rooms, unpack and get back down to the pool. Has Becca gone over the weekend agenda?"

Agenda? Celeste, along with a confused-looking Trudi and Patrice, stared at Becca. Celeste tried to pull her arm away, but when Marcus and Max entered the foyer behind them, Becca held onto her for dear life.

"Not yet, Big Mama," Becca said. "I can show them to their rooms and explain everything to them. They'll be pleased to hear of all the lovely activities you have planned for us this weekend."

"Activities?" Trudi repeated, a cautious tone ringing through. Celeste imagined that her defense tactics were going into high alert.

Celeste observed the magnificent entrance hall and the sweeping staircase, the back wall of windows opening onto a terrace and a lawn with a sunken garden, rooms to either side of the foyer leading in opposite directions, and all the ceilings looming at least twelve feet overhead. Palatial.

"If it pleases you," Becca said to Big Mama as she guided Celeste to the staircase, "I'll go ahead and take them upstairs. First three rooms in the east wing. Correct?"

"Yes, and it does please me," Big Mama said. "I don't do those stairs any more than I have to these days." Big Mama turned to Marcus and Max. "Come on, boys, escort me back out to the pool. I need a drink, and we can entertain Becca's folks and her Grammy until she comes back down." With a "Yes, ma'am" and a grin, the two men took their grandmother by the arm, their size dwarfing her in comparison, and guided her through the foyer. She called over her shoulder, "Papa, make sure to get the bags up to the girls' rooms and get your backside out to the pool, snappy."

When Big Mama, Marcus and Max disappeared through the archway to the right and Papa Joe down the hall to the left, muttering something about a bossy old woman, Becca finally let go of Celeste's arm.

"Come on," Becca said starting up the steps. "I'll show you to your rooms."

"If it pleases you?" Trudi asked, disgusted. "Where the hell did that come from?"

"You'll understand after you're around Big Mama for a little while."

"East wing?" Celeste asked, absently rubbing the finger imprints from her arm as she followed Becca up the curving stairs, the step treads stained a deep mahogany, the staircase itself and the banister a pristine white. Were they in the White House?

"I know, I know, crazy, isn't it?" Becca sounded as in-awe as Celeste felt.

"Crazy. OMG," Patrice noted. "Crazy, crazy."

"Where the hell are we?" Trudi asked. "Did I fall asleep in a hot tub and wake up in a classic historical novel? Possibly this is Gone With the Wind? The Foxes of Harrow?"

"Foxes of Harrow?" Celeste echoed along with Patrice and Becca.

"Yes, did y'all not read it?"

"Never heard of it," Becca said, taking a right when she reached the top of the stairs. "This way," she instructed and took a left down a hallway that Celeste assumed must be the East wing.

"I thought we were all voracious readers and that's why we bonded," Trudi said, sounding disillusioned and stopping when Becca opened a door on the right.

"We all did read," Celeste said. "We didn't all read historical novels like you. I was into Victoria Holt, remember?"

"And I read Trixie Belden and Nancy Drew," Patrice added. "I don't know anything about Foxes of Yarrow."

"It's Harrow."

"Harrow, yarrow. It all sounds the same to me."

"Well," Trudi said, "think Southern, with a capital S, and plantation, with a nice thick drawl, and think lots of pretentious money. That should wrap it up for you."

"Oh no, the Rileys aren't pretentious at all." Becca pointed to the first bedroom. "This one's yours, Patrice. Trudi gets the next one and then Celeste. I'm on the other side of Celeste, sharing a room with Grammy. Mom and Dad are the next room down."

"Sharing a room with Grammy?" Trudi asked. "You're kidding, right?"

"No, afraid not," Becca said, a sad pout tugging at her mouth. "Big Mama doesn't believe in unmarried couples sleeping together before the wedding."

"I assume you haven't explained to the family how the two of you met?" Trudi asked, alluding to the afternoon when the girls had challenged Becca to indulge in a one-night stand; the day she'd first met Marcus. A sly grin sliced across Trudi's too perfect features, and Celeste witnessed horror filter across Becca's face.

"No, and don't you dare mention it."

"Don't let me have anything to drink. You know how loose-lipped I can get," Trudi said, baiting Becca and enjoying herself a little too much. "Possibly Celeste seducing Max isn't the only thing you need to worry about."

"Stop it, Trudi," Celeste said, following Becca down the hall. "You don't need to worry about me seducing Max," she whispered. "I plan to stay as far away from him as possible."

"Good," Becca said, a frown worrying her brow. She gave Trudi a dirty look, but quickly smiled when two gangly teenaged boys entered the hall carrying all of their bags.

"Hi guys," she greeted.

"Hey, where do these go?" the older looking one asked. Both boys had the same sailor-tanned good looks of the Rileys: dark hair and eyes, chiseled features, model-worthy good looks.

"Y'all want to tell Peter and Chip what bag belongs to whom?" Becca instructed. "Boys, these are my best friends. Trudi, Patrice and Celeste. My bridesmaids." She turned to the girls. "And these two handsome guys are Marcus's cousins. His Aunt Pansy's youngest kids. They're sixteen and fifteen. Cute, huh?"

"Nice to meet y'all," the cousins mumbled, embarrassed and uneasy in their teenaged skin, as they deposited the bags in the first three rooms as instructed and quickly exited the way they'd come.

"Come in here and explain this whole agenda thing," Celeste said entering her assigned room. Stopping short, she took in her surroundings and gave a low whistle. "I need to sit down." Her knees gave out from under her, and she collapsed on the four-poster, canopied bed. "Isn't this a little overwhelming for you?" she asked Becca, the sweep of her arm indicating the plush decor. "Because it is for me. I thought these people were farmers."

"They are farmers," Becca said. She straightened her shoulders and lifted her chin, everything about her stance and voice defensive.

"Well what the hell do they farm?" Trudi wanted to know, joining them with Patrice on her heels.. "The goose who lays golden eggs?"

"OMG," Patrice muttered again.

"Will you stop that," Celeste, Trudi and Becca said in unison.

"Sorry," Patrice said. She walked across the Oriental rug and opened the French doors exposing the wrap-around balcony outside. "This is like a movie."

"They don't think a thing about the house being...sort of," Becca waved her hands in the air, searching for a word, "flamboyant."

"Well, there's a word for you," Trudi said, settling on the bed next to Celeste. "How about grandiloquent?"

"Don't be nasty," Celeste said. She turned her attention back to Becca. "So what do they farm?"

"Peanuts and other things. I think there're some pecan groves, something about stock, old money, I don't know." Becca sat down on the bed with a whoosh and began to pick at her nails, while Patrice closed the balcony doors and moved toward the bed. "It caught me by surprise too. Marcus didn't exactly warn me. His mother's a Riley, but once she met Marcus's dad up at UGA, she assumed her role as an accountant's wife and put her Riley life behind her. Marcus and his brothers spent summers down here, working and hanging out with Max and their cousins, but he never thought life down here was out of the ordinary because to them it isn't. They have money, but truly, they're down-to-earth. I swear."

Celeste grabbed Becca's hands. "Quit picking at your nails; the last thing you need to do is mess up your manicure."

"So tell me about this agenda BM mentioned," Trudi said, folding her arms behind her head and leaning back against the pillows.

"BM?" Becca asked.

"Yes, BM, Big Mama."

"What's up with BM?" Celeste said, dreading Trudi's response even as she asked the question.

"You know, she seems like such a real pain-in-the-ass, I thought BM was a perfect nickname for her."

"Trudi." Patrice yelped and collapsed on the bed in a fit of giggles. "You are soooooo bad."

"Do not, I mean, do not call her that, that..." Becca said, "w...word."

Celeste slapped Trudi's leg. "She won't. Will you? You promise to play nice, don't you?" Celeste glared a warning at her friend.

"Okay," Trudi conceded. "I promise, no BMs." She sat up and took Becca's fingers into her hand, stopping her nervous picking. "I promise to be good. So what's on the agenda?"

Becca took a deep breath and Celeste, leaning toward her best friend, waited for her to speak. Becca let out a rush of air and started talking so fast, Celeste could barely keep up.

"Well earlier today, they had a pool party for the kids, but anyone under the age of eighteen has already been ushered in for game and movie night, there's twelve great-grandchildren, so this afternoon we're having a cocktail hour by the pool for the adults. And tomorrow is the big barbeque here at Magnolia Oaks, somewhere out there on the grounds near the lake," Becca made a swoop with her hand indicating outside, "that's when y'all will get to meet all the kids."

"Oh, goody," Trudi said. She didn't mask her cynicism. "That's exactly what I was hoping for on Labor Day weekend, a picnic with little no-neck monsters."

Celeste gulped. Kids? Good grief, kids were not her thing. Kids and animals gave her the hives, and she hadn't thought to bring her antihistamine.

"Don't be ugly, Trudi." Becca plowed on. "And Monday, we are supposed to do a trail ride, but the biggest plan of all is tonight."

"Tonight?" Celeste asked along with Trudi and Patrice.

"What's tonight," Trudi asked, suspicion ringing through. "You're scaring me."

"Well, every year the first night of the reunion, the entire family goes into town." She stopped, giving new meaning to baited breath.

"And," Celeste prodded.

"They, I mean, we, are hosting a cocktail reception and dance for everyone at the club."

"The club?" Celeste asked, fearing the definition. Cocktail reception and dance? This couldn't be good, so much for a small family gathering on the farm.

"Yes, the Tyler Country Club to be exact."

"Country club?" Patrice parroted. "As in exclusive membership?"

"Precisely," Becca said. "Get ready to be on your best behavior, girls. We're about to meet everybody who's anybody in the entire county."

CHAPTER EIGHT

୬ଡ଼ଵ

Celeste took a swig of wine and tried to calm her pounding heart. Country clubs made her as nervous as a cat in a rocking chair factory. She backed herself into a corner near a bushy palm and tried to stand as still as possible. Hopefully no one would notice her.

She looked for Trudi who was accustomed to the exclusive club scene. Trudi's parents, both hot-shot attorneys for a prestigious firm in downtown, had belonged to the Capital Atlanta Club for years. Celeste, Becca and Patrice always received one invitation for a Saturday swim party and the once a year birthday bash for Trudi at the club, but Celeste had always felt out of place, and she'd never gotten over the way the snotty rich kids knew they belonged and she didn't. Another strike against the rich, country clubbing Max Riley, which made three strikes, and he was now officially out.

The reception hall was packed. She couldn't believe there were this many elite people in such a rural area, but what did she know about the country? She spotted Trudi standing at the far side of the room talking to a red-faced man in khaki pants and a navy blue blazer. Typical club attire, she presumed, since every other man in the place was dressed similarly. Trudi practiced her magic as she took a dainty sip of her wine and flirted, the man grinning like a fool the whole while. Smitten, the poor guy was a lost cause. Celeste smiled; the girl could work it.

Celeste spied Patrice standing outside a wall of French doors, which opened onto a covered verandah where a scattering of table rounds swathed in linen and adorned with flickering candles beckoned guests to sit and relax. Nice ambiance, but the place outfitted to the nines still paled in comparison to Magnolia Oaks. Patrice, too, seemed to be in her comfort zone, but that was Patrice. Always naïve and oblivious, she never knew whether she belonged or not, so she always fit in.

Becca and Marcus stood with other family members in a reception line greeting their guests. Becca, all blonde and lush, glowed with sheer contentment. She'd certainly come into herself after leaving her oppressive advertising job and becoming the Lei D model. Her boss had been a chauvinist of the first degree. Celeste felt her heart skip a beat, delighted for her best friend and the love Becca'd found. She deserved happiness after the horrible way Harold had treated her two years before, breaking off their engagement the night before their wedding. Jerk. Men were such assholes. The thought reconfirmed Celeste's decision to stay clear of the opposite sex.

"Who put you in the corner?" a male voice asked, low and deep and uncomfortably close to her ear. Celeste jumped, sloshing her wine, and looked up to see a huge hulk of a guy who reminded her of a young Jethro Bodine. "Whoa there," he said, taking her wine glass and dabbing at it with his kerchief.

"You startled me," Celeste said, her cheeks burning. He handed her back the wine, and she took it, her hand still trembling.

"I'm sorry," he said. "I saw you standing over here all by your lonesome and couldn't help but come over and introduce myself." He held out his hand. "I'm John Hardy."

"Nice to meet you." Celeste shifted her wine to her left hand and extended her right. The unexpected gusto of his handshake took her by surprise and her wine spilled again. They both watched a splash hit the plush carpet underfoot. "Oh no, look what I've done," she said.

"Don't worry about it," John said, taking her by the elbow and steering her away from the shelter of the corner. He gestured to a passing server. "Marie, there's a little spill over here you might need someone to attend to," he said.

"Yes, sir, Mayor Hardy, I'll take care of it right away." She scurried away, leaving John to guide Celeste into the crowd.

"Mayor?" She gave him a perusing once over. "You have too honest of an appearance to be a politician." He laughed, a loud raucous laugh causing heads to turn their way, and she felt her earlier blush deepen, praying Max was nowhere close by. Why had she said that? It was a gaffe line in competition with all-time stupid things to say, like I carried a watermelon. "I meant too young," she said.

"I believe," he winked at her and led her toward the bar, "you meant exactly what you said, and that's perfectly fine with me, but to keep the record straight, I am an honest and trustworthy mayor, Miss—" he allowed the salutation to hang, waiting, his southern twang carrying "miss" out like a river.

"Celeste," she said. "Celeste Taylor. I'm one of the—"

"Bridesmaids for Marcus's wedding," he finished for her. "We heard y'all were coming to town, and there were quite a few of us looking forward to tonight for that very reason." They'd reached the bar, and he smiled down at her. "How about a glass of champagne?" He didn't wait for her to answer, but took the chardonnay out of her hand and turned it over to the bartender. "Champagne for the lady and me, please."

John handed her a flute filled with sparkling bubbly, took his own, and turned to guide her toward the verandah, his hand splayed across her lower back.

"Thank you," she said, allowing the mayor to escort her, while purposefully not glancing around for fear she'd see Max and her knees would give way. After eluding Max at the pool party all afternoon, she'd avoided making eye contact with him since they'd arrived at the country club, but she remained painfully aware that he was near.

John leaned down and whispered in her ear, "I believe that is another friend of yours talking to my partner over there. Let's join them."

"Your partner?"

"Yes, in our law firm." He grinned a nice pleasant smile showing white even teeth, but something about it made Celeste think of the big, bad wolf from Little Red Riding Hood. What big teeth he had.

"I thought you were the mayor?" She knew she shouldn't have believed him. After all, he was a man.

He laughed that loud guffaw of his, and Celeste cringed, refusing to look around to see who all stared their way this time.

"I'm a full time attorney by profession, but I'm an elected official as well. Mayor of Tyler is not a full time job, by any stretch of the imagination." He motioned her forward. "Here we are."

After introducing Celeste to his partner and he met Trudi, the four of them walked out to the verandah and joined Patrice and her new friend, then spent the next two hours listening to hometown stories, most of them suspiciously embellished, downing a few glasses of champagne, and dancing every line dance known to man: the Electric Slide, the Cha Cha Slide, the Boot Scootin' Boogie, and a few others she didn't know the names of. She didn't care too much for line dancing, but she'd rather be up and moving instead of listening to more of their stories and worrying about Mayor Hardy getting handsy. She'd managed to avoid any dance falling in the "slow" category, but the feat hadn't been attained without a huge amount of effort on her part. John Hardy hadn't become mayor without dogged determination, she was certain. And she wouldn't be surprised if his middle name was Persistence.

She'd tried all night not to look at Max, or watch as every single woman in the place came on to him, and she'd pulled a crick in her neck trying not to glance his way. To no avail. Out of the corner of her eye she'd seen it all. And by the stories John Hardy told, it was evident Max Riley had always been the envy of every man in the county. He was treated like the crown prince. She should have known.

After warding off an unsolicited pat on her leg, with a much too close whisper suggesting they find somewhere more intimate, Celeste excused herself and made a mad dash for the ladies room where she spent time fluffing her too curly hair and applying fresh gloss. On the way back to the verandah, she decided to take a breather and slipped out the side door and down the stairs into the garden, seeking some peace in the secluded darkness.

When he first saw John Hardy with Celeste, Max felt his temper rise but managed to tap it down. The first time. But the damn douche-bag stuck to her like glue for the remainder of the night. Not that Max dared get too close to her himself, but he didn't want John Hardy near her either. Then John had looked at him over his shoulder and winked, causing Max's blood pressure to skyrocket: his ears burned, his breathing became shallow, and his eyes narrowed to mere slits. The friggin' douche was egging him on. On purpose.

Nothing had changed since high school; the two of them always competing. John took it hard when Max made quarterback their junior year, and the competition continued when Max brought his new fiancée home to meet everyone, and John had made a play for Sissy. Hindsight, Max wished John had won that one. Would have served him right. John deserved Sissy and her two-timing, deserting ways. John Hardy was as shady as most of his business deals and the cases he won, and he couldn't be trusted any farther than Max could throw him. As bulky as John was, Max figured that couldn't be more than a foot at the most. Shady bastard. He'd been a dork growing up and now he was nothing more than an untrustworthy weasel.

"What you scowling about, boy?" Big Mama appeared at his side, sneaky as always.

Startled, Max turned his back to the verandah and shifted his attention to his grandmother.

"'Cause that brunette's over there with the mayor?" She said, observant as ever. She'd caught him temper-hot and red-faced.

"No, not at all. It's nothing to me who she's talking to."

"Don't lie to me," she said. "I know you and you know it. I helped raise you, the good Lord knows your mama couldn't have done it by herself, and I know when you're happy, when you're sad, and I know when you meet a woman you've got a hankering for, and," she turned and, to his horror, pointed at Celeste, "there's something intriguing you about that one there." She dropped her hand and stared up at him. "I've seen you watching every move she's made all night…you weren't obvious about it, I'll give you that, but I knew."

He grabbed her elbow and headed for the buffet. "Let's go check out the desserts," he said, desperate to divert her to another subject. "They have that strawberry pie that's your favorite."

She jerked her arm away from his grasp. "I can't eat strawberries anymore on account of the possibility I could flare up a case of diverticulitis. You ought to know that and not tempt me that way." Big Mama glared at him and mimicked an ingénue pout. "Hurts my feelings, you do me such a way."

Max grinned and sighed in relief. His tactic had worked; he'd successfully diverted her thoughts. Max sent up a silent thank you that she was such a drama queen when it suited her to be.

"Let's dance," he said as the DJ spun the beginnings of "Come Fly With Me." Big Mama loved Frank Sinatra.

"Let's go, handsome." She smiled and lifted her brow. "You remember all those dance moves Papa Joe and I taught you?"

Max took her hand and the two of them swung onto the dance floor amid a round of applause from the crowd. He waltzed her around, dipping and spinning, with graceful moves allowing for her age as well as her feistiness. As the song came to a close she looked up at him.

"Nice move, slick," she said. "You think you made me forget what we were talking about, enticing me with pie and dancing, but the fact is, I wanted to dance, and that woman sitting out there with John Hardy...the one you want for yourself...well, she just made her escape, all by her lonesome, out the back door." She paused, gesturing toward the garden. "But since you're not interested, I'm sure you don't care." She gave him a big wink and turned, leaving him alone on the edge of the dance floor, trying like hell not to look the way she'd pointed.

Celeste shot a nervous glance over her shoulder as she inched into the inky darkness. Even with the sky full of flickering starlight, she didn't realize nighttime could be so pitch black. She gauged her way by the tiny solar lamps, which cast a mellow warm glow along the crushed stone path, and the beckoning sound of a tinkling water fountain in the distance. The air had cooled down, and she finally relaxed, her heart easing to a steady beat when she heard a crunch on the gravel behind her. Her skin prickled, and she stopped in mid-stride. She eased her sandaled feet onto the dew-wet grass, hiding behind a tall, bushy hedge.

"We need to stop meeting like this." A strong, warm hand reached out and took her forearm.

She stifled a scream, and her heart catapulted into her throat, and as the voice registered she breathed a sigh of conflicted relief. Her stalker was Max.

"Oh my gosh, you scared the crap out of me," she said. "I thought you were Jethro following me."

"Jethro?" Max asked, easing closer to her, so close she could smell the crisp male scent of him, mixed tonight with a woodsy cologne. She sucked in a deep breath and savored the memory of the first night he'd been this close. "We have a Jethro in Tyler? I wasn't aware."

"No, I'm sorry, I shouldn't have said that, it's what I thought when I first saw him, that he looks like Jethro Bodine, but he doesn't act like him, he's much too sharp, almost shifty." Celeste cringed. She rambled like a blubbering idiot.

"Are you talking about Hardy?" Max asked and grinned his knee-melting smile. "Never thought about it, but I guess you're right. He does look like a Beverly Hillbilly." He slipped his arm through hers. "What are you doing out here, alone in the dark?" Realization dawning on his face. "Oh, I'm sorry. You were meeting him here, weren't you, and I've interrupted your rendezvous?" He dropped her arm and stepped away, the disappointment on his face evident.

"No, no, no," she said, horrified he would think she was in the habit of meeting men at parties and immediately roaming into dark gardens with them. "Absolutely not. I was escaping from him actually. That's why it startled me when I thought you were him. You know, like a Gotcha! kind of response?"

"Yes, I do know. But you probably don't want to stay out here too much longer or you might get carted off by skeeters."

"Skeeters?"

"You know, mosquitoes, those pesky little critters that would turn someone as sweet as you into a nighttime supper." His voice was warm.

"Sweet as me?" she asked, hiking her twang to a Southern Belle lilt. "You trying to charm little ol' me?" She tilted her head and splayed her hand across her chest. She knew how to play the perfect ingénue.

"Could I be lucky enough to have the chance to charm you?" While his voice was neutral, his stance wasn't. She didn't respond. "Because I would love to sweep you off your feet, right into my arms." He stepped closer and her breath hitched in her throat. "And kiss you again."

After a nerve-racking pause, she felt her cheeks burn under his intense gaze. Maybe she didn't know how to engage in such a coquettish seduction after all, because she couldn't think of a clever retort, except for take me I'm yours, but that didn't seem appropriate at the moment.

Max leaned down, closing the short distance between them, and Celeste instinctively pressed her hand against his chest. A razor-sharp jolt of desire blazed through her, her entire body tingling like an erogenous zone. She smoldered all over, and the thought of spontaneous combustion came to mind.

"Whoa, Romeo," she said, trying to sound normal and unaffected. The man was dangerous, and she needed to keep her distance. "Becca was worried about you? I believe she should be more concerned about me."

He tilted back his head and laughed that wonderful laugh of his, the one that comforted her and made her connect to him, as if she'd known him in a past life.

"How about allowing me to escort you back to the party?"

Max slid his hand into hers and started along the path. His hand radiated a sexy warmth, making her imagination run wild with thoughts full of naughty promises, and unable to resist, she followed.

CHAPTER NINE

࿐

Celeste's senses soared to high alert. She was aware of the crickets singing, the smell of the late-blooming roses perfuming the air, the drone of conversation from the party in the distance, and Max Riley's sexy ass so close, she would swear she sensed his pulse throb through her entire body with each beat of her heart. She sucked in a deep breath and prayed her knees wouldn't go wobbly.

"Tell me," Max asked, looking down at her, "how have things been going for you since we last spoke? Have you reported any exciting news stories lately?"

He wanted to talk about her job and news stories? Celeste couldn't believe she'd heard him correctly. Since she'd encountered him in the garden, she'd resisted the urge to grab him, to kiss him again. His nearness flared a tremulous heat in the deep pit of her stomach, and a zig-zag of lust pulsed between her thighs. And he wanted to discuss the news? Maybe giving up on dating hadn't been such a good call after all. Because it seemed, after only three months, she'd lost her finesse with men as well as her perception for whether a guy was interested. She would have sworn on a stack of designer dresses that Max was attracted to her too. It seemed she was wrong. She pulled her hand free and took her next stride a few inches from him, missing his closeness as soon as she stepped away.

"Let me think." She paused, trying to recall an attention-grabbing story. "A family locked themselves out of their house and thought it would be a good idea for their eleven-year-old son to shimmy down the chimney so he could unlock the door."

"That's worthy of sending a reporter to the scene?" Max asked.

"It is when it takes the fire department and a rescue crew three hours to free him after he gets stuck halfway down." She heard Max laugh, but she refused to look at him, determined not to drown in the dark pools of dreaminess that were his eyes, so she kept walking.

"You're kidding, right? People aren't really that dumb, are they?"

"Unfortunately, they are. More than stupid, actually. People are careless. They leave their children and pets in cars when the temperature is in the nineties, and you know in a closed up vehicle, it soars higher. They drive too fast. They're downright mean and evil. Shooting each other, stealing, murdering."

"It must get depressing, reporting those types of stories all the time."

"You have no idea how hard it is," she said. She didn't dare confess how much energy she spent trying to remain unaffected. Sometimes she felt drained from the effort. However, the reports were what they were. The news. And her job was to report them, so she struggled daily to not allow the stories to distress her.

"How did you wind up as a reporter anyway?"

"My dad worked for the station as a cameraman, still does actually. My mom was hired as the primetime newscaster, and that's how they met. They fell in love and she quit her career to be a stay-at-home mom, a housewife," Celeste said. "Can you imagine that? Giving up her career for children? Sometimes, I don't understand my Mom."

"I do. Her family came first. She wanted to be the best mother she could be, so she made a choice. It makes perfect sense to me. I think your mother sounds like a great person."

"She is. Don't get me wrong...Mom is fantastic. I simply don't understand her giving up her career, that's all." Celeste stopped and turned to glance up at Max. They obviously had nothing in common if he didn't understand her point. As far as she was concerned, her mom trading her spot as the daytime anchor for a full-time housewife was huge. The family could have come later.

They'd made their way back through the garden and were at the bottom of the steps, the din from the party louder, idle chatter, laughter, and the clink of glasses filling the air.

"I think family is one of the most important things in life. The number one priority. Or it should be," Max said. Celeste thought she heard remorse ring through, a quiver in the low rumble of his voice, a shadow of hurt in his eyes, and she remembered his wife and what she'd done to him.

"I agree. Family is important, and I love my parents and older brothers, even though they tormented me relentlessly when I was younger," she said. She knew the significance of family, and she might not be overly close to her brothers, but she knew they would have her back if she ever needed them. And she'd have theirs.

"Enough about families," Max said. "Did your dad help you get your job?" He'd redirected the conversation, and Celeste silently thanked him.

"Not directly, but I'm sure it helped that he'd worked there for years when I applied for an internship. Afterwards, I was hired full time, and as most beginners at the station, I started out answering phones, printing out script pages, scanning the news wires and unclogging paper jams in copy machines. Although it sounds trivial, it's all important."

"I'm sure any and everything you contributed would be important. You were learning the behind-the-scenes. Good stuff."

"Exactly. One unanswered phone call or a misplaced script page could wreck a newscast. I paid my dues, learned the ropes, and clawed my way to news reporter."

"Do you love it?"

"Love it?"

"You must, it's your dream, what you want. You must love being there, in the moment, reporting news as it happens. That's exciting."

"Yes, it is thrilling, but more importantly it's necessary for me to reach my goal." She thought of the whole process as a necessary means to the ultimate end: sitting behind the desk as news anchor, where her mother should have been. She started up the steps and heard Max follow. When she reached the verandah, she stopped, and he stepped into place beside her, taking her hand again and leading her toward the open French doors.

"Would you like a drink?" he asked, guiding her toward the bar at the end of the room.

"No, thanks, I'll take a soda, a Diet Coke, please." She felt lightheaded, a little dizzy from the earlier glasses of champagne.

And the nearness of Max, all raw sensuality and male yumminess, only added to her woozy-headedness.

"I can't talk you into your next sample of tequila straight-up?" he asked, smiling down at her as they neared the bar. "I did promise to expose you to different varieties and blends so you could decide on your favorite."

"No, I'm good for now, maybe later," Celeste said, the idea of drinking tequila bringing back memories of a few too-late nights, the wild-child liquor firing her inner spirit to the point of dancing on a table or two. She glanced around the room from one person to the next, and if she wasn't mistaken, everyone in attendance had zeroed in on them like a missile locked on a target. Celeste gulped. Dancing on the table in Tyler, Georgia, didn't seem like a good idea. "Definitely soda, please."

"Soda, it is." Max let go of her hand and stepped away to get their drinks, leaving Celeste alone. She fidgeted, trying to resist the urge to assess the crowd and confirm her suspicion that everyone still stared at her, but her eyes had a will of their own. She looked across the room into the drop-dead stare of Serena, Max's mother, who stood like a shadow next to his father, Brick.

Celeste had met Serena earlier by the pool. The cool, sophisticated champagne blonde with piercing blue eyes and perfect features had been glued to her husband's side, as she was now. They were like Siamese twins. The two obviously doted on one another, and the fact that Serena now glared at Celeste from thirty feet away, instead of gazing dreamily at her husband, gave Celeste the impression she'd committed a major faux pas. Even from the distance, Celeste could see Serena's arched brows lift, crinkling her otherwise pristine forehead, and Celeste knew the hateful glare couldn't be good.

"Here you go." Max's voice made her jump again. The man wreaked havoc on her nerves. Maybe she should have gone for the tequila after all.

"You've got to stop doing that," she said. He stood beside her, too close and sexy, holding a soda and a beer. He lifted his chin and nodded his head toward a table in the far corner of the room.

"Let's go sit over there, it's less crowded, and it appears that most everyone has wandered out onto the terrace."

Were they at the same party? The room was still packed, and as best she could tell, Brick, who only watched Serena, was the one person not staring their way. She turned to Max who seemed as oblivious as his father. For all of his good looks and manliness, there was still something refreshing, almost guileless, about him.

"Are you sure we should—"

"Yes, I'm sure," he said. "Come on."

He balanced the two drinks in his one palm, took her by the hand with the other, and led her to the table he'd pointed out. Thoughts of nobody puts Celeste in the corner flashed through her head, but she followed him anyway.

Max set the drinks on the table with an exaggerated flourish and pulled out the chair for her to sit. Celeste laughed, a bubbly, happy giggle that made her feel thirteen again. He settled in the seat beside her and stretched his long legs out in front of him. He picked up his beer and lounged back, taking a swig. She reached for her glass and studied him as she sat back, struck again by his sheer beauty; she took a sip to wet her suddenly dry throat. The man was simply gorgeous.

"Tell me more about you," he said. "I want to hear about what you were like as a little girl. I bet you were cute. Funny."

"Me?" Celeste scrunched her nose, and he laughed. He touched the tip of his finger to her nose.

"Yes, you." He sat forward and leaned his elbow on his knee, narrowing the distance between them.

"I don't know if I would describe me that way, but all we've been doing is talking about me," she said. "Why don't you tell me more about your life at Magnolia Oaks?" She locked eyes with Serena, whose earlier stare had graduated to a penetrating glare. "Or tell me about your parents and why your mother is sending me death threats?"

Max swiveled his head, lifted his hand and waved. Serena jerked her shoulders back and jutted her chin. She whispered in Brick's ear, and he looked their way before he took Serena by the arm and led her away, his arm wrapped protectively around her shoulders.

"Don't pay her any attention. Serena can get worked up sometimes," he said.

"Serena? You call your mother by her first name?" she asked, incredulous. The only person Celeste knew who would come close to calling their parents by their given name would be Trudi, and even she called her parents Mom and Dad.

Max shrugged his shoulders. "She wanted me to. I'm sure you've noticed, my parents are rather," he cast a glance over his shoulder toward the French doors through which his parents had exited a moment before, "hmmm, how should I say it? They're...devoted to one another."

"Yes, I did notice," Celeste said, trying to keep her face neutral and not show her shock. Or to say aloud that "fanatical" was more like it.

"Serena isn't exactly the nurturing type. She couldn't be bothered with a baby. So Big Mama's the one who took care of me most of the time and raised me. But, in the long run, I think I lucked out. Big Mama and Papa Joe did all right by me, and in turn, I think I'm a good father."

"That's right," Celeste said. "You have children." The dreaded topic: little people with short legs and no necks, grimy faces and snotty noses. Men with children—a big taboo on her list of rules.

"Yes, two. A boy and a girl." Max beamed, proudly. "Charlie is six and Neecie just turned four. They're hell on wheels, but I love 'em." He took a swig of his beer. "You'll meet them tomorrow at the picnic."

She tried to smile, but her cheek muscles jerked and froze, and to her horror, her upper lip twitched.

"Meet them, yes, I suppose I will." Oh goody.

"Well, considering they're the flower girl and ring bearer for Marcus and Becca's wedding, it's inevitable."

"Oh. Becca didn't mention that." A brief thought of an emergency girlfriend meeting to discuss the fact Max's children were part of the wedding party flashed through her mind, but she immediately nixed the idea, knowing the topic of the meeting would be a confession of her interest in Max. And she wasn't, in any way whatsoever, interested in him.

At all. And if she kept telling herself that, hopefully it would come true.

"Really? I'm surprised she hasn't."

"She's been so preoccupied with the wedding plans and being the Lei D girl, she probably didn't think about it." A realization dawned on her. "Do you think your mother is angry with me for talking with you? Are you still married?"

"I. Am. Not. Married," Max said. His jaw clenched and the vein in his temple throbbed with each word. "I'm sure Becca mentioned that my ex-wife deserted me and the kids. She's been gone for two years, and my attorney tracked her down and served papers on her over a year ago. The first year, every time he'd find her, she'd move."

"On purpose? Like she was deliberately avoiding being served?"

"Who knows?" His brows rose a fraction and he shrugged his shoulders. "Or cares. I haven't spoken with her since she left. Not one word."

"Do you miss her?"

"Absolutely not. But Charlie did at first. He was four when she left and he has some memories, but Neecie was a toddler and doesn't remember her at all. That's what makes me the angriest, her walking away from her children."

"I'm sure her leaving hurt you too." She didn't know what else to say.

"In the beginning, but after a while I realized we'd been living a lie for a long time, and I should have seen it coming. But that's twenty-twenty, as they say." He smiled and she wanted to wrap her arms around him and kiss all his hurt away, but instead she reached over and cupped his cheek with her hand.

"She's a fool," Celeste said.

"No doubt about that," Max agreed. "I can't understand how she could leave her own children. She was never who I thought she was."

The DJ returned from his break and started off with a slow rumba-sounding jazz tune by Michael Bublé, and a few dancers ventured onto the floor. Max took Celeste's hand and stood, tugging her up with him.

"Dance with me," he said.

She leaned into his arms, and he pulled her toward the dance floor.

"I don't know," she said, struggling with whether to say no or to follow her instinct and enjoy it. "Aren't you worried what everyone will say?"

"Absolutely not. Do I impress you as a man who is concerned with what others think and say?" With a lift of his arms, he twirled her into an embrace, and she melted against him as if she'd found home. The faintest smile turned up the corners of his perfect mouth. "Because if you think that's who I am, I need to introduce you to the real me."

He swung her onto the dance floor, and she managed to keep up with his lead, the song a melodic blend of horns and cha-cha rhythms, and she swayed along with him as they claimed the dance as their own.

She loved his strong hand against her back supporting her, the warmth of his palm as he held her hand and led her, the brush of his muscled thigh rubbing against hers. A palpable heat ignited in her belly and curled a burn of passion between her legs and from the glint in his dark eyes and the hardness pressed against her leg, he felt it too. He grinned, and she was lost. He had her.

Max held her tighter, and Celeste dared to peek at the crowd. From the wide-eyed expression of the guests, everyone was well aware of the attraction between them. She might as well have done the tequila shot and danced on the table. To hell with decorum.

"I think we're quite the scandal," she whispered, her voice sounding breathy even to her own ears.

"And you think I care," he asked, dipping his head and blowing a tickling breath across her neck. Celeste relished the heat of the wild, reckless excitement Max generated as he swung her around the dance floor, oblivious and uncaring of the stares cast their way. "What do you say—why don't we get out of here? Away from so many inquisitive people," he said, raising and lowering his brows in a quick, provocative move, his smile promising outright sensuous delights.

Her heart palpitated while horns blared the resounding finale, and the song ended. Damn, Max Riley. He was making the fact she'd sworn off men a hard commitment to keep.

Before she could respond, he walked off the dance floor straight for the exit door, holding her hand and pulling her behind him.

Chapter Ten

❧

As soon as they pushed through the door, Max took the lead and led her down the hall their footsteps muffled on the carpet. He made a beeline for a side entrance he remembered well from his youth and guided them wordlessly down the hallway, strategically passing potted palms along the way, until they reached the door. He pushed it open and pulled her outside.

"Wait," Celeste said and tugged at his hand. "Where are we going?"

"Some place quiet," he said, fueled by her nearness and the sudden desire to be alone with her.

"But I left my purse on the table."

"Is there anything of value in it?" he asked, scanning the side of the club, looking for one of the parking attendants.

"My gloss and ID."

"The servers will turn it into security…we can pick it up tomorrow," he said, anxious to escape and be alone with her. He caught the eye of the head valet, who'd worked at the country club since the beginning of time, and motioned with a quick wave of his hand.

"Are you sure?" Celeste asked. "I wouldn't want to be any trouble."

"Trust me, you're no trouble at all," Max said, and impatient, he started across the parking lot, guiding her along. The air was warm, the sky filled with stars, and he zeroed in on his Porsche, beating the valet by a few steps. "I'll take those," he said and held out his hand. The valet grinned and tossed the keys into his open palm.

"Just like old times, Riley," he said and darted back through the maze of parked cars.

"What did he mean by that?" Celeste asked. Max opened the passenger door and held out his hand to help her in.

"Nothing, he's worked here a long time, and he thinks he's a comedian," Max said, feeling oddly skittish for a man who'd once been known for his game. He shut the door and hurried around to the driver's side and slid behind the wheel, starting the car with a flick of his wrist.

"Is this wise?" Celeste asked, her voice sounded a little giddy. "I'm not typically impulsive."

"I haven't done anything spontaneous in years." Max stole a glance at her as he backed out of the parking space, and she almost blinded him with the full wattage of her smile. "It's been a long time since I took myself by surprise, and I think the time has come for me to break a pattern in my well-organized routine." He gunned the motor, propelling them forward through the exit and into the dark night. "You don't mind that I chose you to break it with, do you?"

"Well, yes and no," she said, the hesitancy in her voice belied the grin on her face. "Becca will strangle me, Trudi and Patrice will razz me unmercifully, your mother will probably lace my drink with arsenic, and who knows what Big Mama will do to me?" She reached over and grabbed his forearm. "What is her favorite means of torture?"

Max laughed. "If you were six and in deep shit, you'd most probably have to decide between a spanking with her little red belt or a switch. After agonizing over which might cause the least pain and you choose the belt, chances are you'd be sent outside to pick out your own switch."

"But I thought I picked the belt?"

"That's part of the torture. You decided on the belt, but she changed it on you, and there's nothing worse than picking out the whippy, little stick that you know will make you dance. Unless you picked the switch and she pulls out the belt instead. You can never win with Big Mama, she'll outsmart you every time. But believe it or not, Big Mama is probably enjoying every minute of this."

"How's that?"

"Well for one, you're torturing Serena." Like Celeste was torturing him: sitting so close, within touching distance, the smell of vanilla filling his nostrils. He gripped the wheel tighter.

"There's a two?" she asked. She shifted in the seat, turning his way, and from the corner of his eye, he saw her curls bounce against her shoulders. Her honey-toned skin glowed soft as silk in the pale light from his dash, and his fingers itched to find out for themselves how smooth and warm she was.

"And Big Mama likes you," he said.

"She likes me?" Celeste sounded incredulous.

"Yes."

"Why?" She leaned across the console, and her arm brushed his. Her skin was warm pressed against his, and a rush shot through him from the simple pleasure of her closeness.

"Because I like you," he said, and the admission scared the hell out of him.

"Oh," she said. "Is that why you chose me to be, uh…spontaneous with?"

"It's not enough to do something because you want to," Max said, hoping, even though he didn't fully comprehend it himself, she'd understand that his wanting to be alone with her was more than impulsive. "You have to trust your instincts, and if you wait to do something until you're sure it's right, you'll never do anything."

"Interesting philosophy. Have you always lived by that belief?"

"No," he said, realization dawning on him. "I think I just figured it out myself."

He turned onto the dirt road that led onto the backlands of Magnolia Oaks and opened the sunroof as he slowed the car to a crawl.

"Where are we?" Celeste asked, sitting up straighter, moving away from him. She shot an apprehensive glance out the window.

He missed her warmth as soon as she moved.

"I thought we'd go out to the lake, and we don't have to pass by the big house if we come in the back way."

"The lake? Where we're having the picnic tomorrow?"

"Yes, but we're going out to my cabin. It's on the south end of the lake, closer to the fields, and the picnic'll be at the pavilion on the north side, closest to the house."

"It's sort of scary out here," she said, peering ahead.

Max followed her line of vision and tried to imagine what a stranger might see: the headlights illuminating the dirt road twining ahead until it disappeared into the darkness, thick foliage and trees lining their way on either side.

"No, it isn't scary." He put his foot on the brake and stopped the car, killing the engine and the lights, the darkness engulfing them, the warm glow of the moon and stars their only light. He released his seatbelt so he could turn freely in order to see her better. "Take in your surroundings. It's peaceful. Beautiful. You're in God's country." He wanted to reach for her, brush her hair off her shoulder, plant a kiss in the curve of her neck, to taste her pulse against his lips, but he resisted. She needed to be comfortable, and he wanted her to respect the nature surrounding them. "Close your eyes and listen to the night sounds. Do you feel the balminess of the air?"

Celeste leaned her head back and followed his instructions. The crickets and katydids sang their lullaby.

"Do you smell it? Hear it?" he asked.

"Hmmm, yes. Smells like wet dirt and fresh cut grass, reminds me of watermelon on a summer's day," she said, reaching over and taking his hand, entwining her fingers with his. He caught his breath, and she opened her eyes. "And if you kissed me right now, this would be perfect."

Max reached for her seatbelt and unlatched it, freeing her to move closer, and she took advantage of her freedom and maneuvered next to him. With her so near, he was conscious of everything about her. The soft swell of her breast, the rise and fall of her chest with each breath she took, every delicious curve from her hips down to her thighs, the way her hair curled in ringlets.

And the aroma of vanilla floating around her, reminding him of Christmas cookies and all things safe and secure in life. Her warmth radiated through him, and he allowed himself to relax and enjoy the moment.

He framed her face with the palms of his hands, luxuriating in the cool smoothness of her cheeks, and he lowered his face until his mouth met hers.

Celeste twined her arms around his neck as his lips melted against hers, and she lost her breath in the heat of the moment, asphyxiation coming to mind, but she didn't care. What a lovely way to go. He tasted of beer and sweet promises, and when his hand brushed her breast as he engulfed her in an embrace, her nipples peaked hard and tight against the French lace of her bra. He teased her lips with his tongue, and she opened to him, allowing him to claim her, the kiss no longer a lovely light kiss, but a hungry, demanding one. When her tongue touched his, she felt his breath hitch in his throat, and he kissed her harder, deeper, an unquenchable need evident with each thrust of his tongue, and her body throbbed in blissful response. He wanted her as much as she wanted him.

Struggling with the console and the tight confines of the front seat, she leaned into him, wanting his hand on her breast, the scent of him combined with the earthy smells from outside driving her crazy, sending tingles of desire throughout her body and moisture between her thighs. She pushed against him, and he sucked in a breath; her skin prickled against the chilled heat in the humid night air. No doubt about it, the man was making her hot. She was on fire, and he was her flame.

"You're driving me insane," he said against her lips, his mouth barely moving, but she tasted every vibration of his voice all the way down to her toes. He slid his hands under her hair and cuddled her neck. "Hmmm, moist."

"You have no idea," Celeste said, thinking how wet she was in other places. "How about your cabin? Maybe we should continue this at your place." Acting like a teenager in a full make-out session in the front seat of a car was not her thing.

Max drifted away from her neck and gazed at her, his face still inches from her.

"Forgive me, but you're so delicious, I got carried away." Max smiled. "Where are my manners?" He pulled away and started the car, revving the engine and turning on the lights, then shifted the gear into drive. He kept one hand on the wheel and guided the car down the road while he rested his other arm across her shoulder, his fingers tickling her neck and playing with her hair.

They rode in silence for the few minutes it took to wind their way through the woodlands until the foliage and trees thinned, and the scene opened up on the lake, the moonlight shimmering its silver reflection on the ripples of water.

"Oh," Celeste said. "How beautiful." She turned to Max, delighted. "It's so idyllic."

"I love it here," Max said as he pulled up next to a small cabin about twenty feet from the water's edge. He turned off the car and got out, and with a quickness, he was opening the passenger door for her. He held out his hand, and she took it cautiously, wondering why she was here, where they were going with this innocent seduction?

"Come on, let me show you around," Max said.

Celeste exited with his help and took in the scene before her. A front porch wrapped around the side of the cabin onto a deck that ran along the back of the cabin facing the water, and a dock that led straight into the lake. A small pontoon rocked in the rise and fall of the water, bumping against the dock with a muffled thump. They walked along a path of crunchy pea gravel, her heels sinking and throwing her off balance.

"Be careful." Max reached out and steadied her, and she grasped his arm, his muscles rock hard underneath her hand. He guided her up the stairs to the front porch where a wood swing graced one end and an old cane rocker sat at the other. He opened the door and reached inside, turning on a smattering of overhead, recessed lights. He stepped aside so she could enter. The room was spacious, but cozy, with a fireplace in the middle of the far wall, and a bank of windows facing the lake on either side. A small kitchen and dining area were part of the main room and two doors led to either side of the cabin.

"That's my bedroom," Max said, pointing to the right. "And my office is over there." "What do you think?" He swept his arm, indicating the common area.

She stepped further into the room. A brown leather couch faced the fireplace and two overstuffed chairs in a muted plaid were placed strategically to each side, with rust-colored, velour throws tossed carelessly across the backs of each. A coffee table piled high with magazines and books claimed the middle of the floor, and a flat screen TV was mounted to the stacked rock above the mantle.

"I think it feels like home," she said.

"Good answer." He grinned. "I designed it myself." He walked over to an entertainment unit and flicked on the stereo, a light jazz tune coming to life from speakers installed overhead.

"Nice job." Celeste kicked off her heels and padded barefoot across the planked hardwood floor to enjoy the view of the lake. The moon, half full, shone its silvery light in a stream across the water, the reflection dancing on the ripples, her earlier response to the scene now more poignant since she was inside the comfortable warmth of the cabin. "You have a beautiful place. Do you stay here all the time?" She watched his reflection in the glass as he walked up behind her, and she felt him close the distance between them.

"Not all the time. I built the cabin two years ago, after Sissy left. I sold our house in town and the kids and I moved back to Magnolia Oaks," he said. "Needless to say, Big Mama was tickled to death to have the kids at the big house, but I needed my own space, and she knew it. She suggested I build a place out here so I could have a retreat, a place of my own."

"Big Mama's a wise old soul, isn't she?" Celeste turned.

Max smiled and stared toward the middle of the lake.

"Yes, she is. She knows how much I love the water, and the lake has always been a catharsis for me. The cabin has been a refuge and provided a special healing for me." He glanced her way, a sheepish expression settling across his handsome features. "I've never brought anyone out here before."

"I'm honored," she said, apprehensive, unsure what his confession meant.

"No. I mean, no one," he said. As his perfect mouth moved, forming the words, his lips puckered in an enticing, need-to-be kissed way.

"No one?" she reiterated, hoping he'd repeat the words and she could watch his mouth move again.

He shook his head in the negative. "You're the first person ever to visit."

"Not even Big Mama?" she asked.

"No." There was that tempting pucker again. If only he would reach out and touch her, she'd jump his bones on the spot.

"The kids?" she asked trying to refocus her thoughts.

"No," said his damn seductive kisser again. Her mouth watered as desire multiplied at an alarming rate and took over every one of her brain cells.

"Well, I probably don't need to ask about your mom," she said, forcing her thoughts to focus on anything other than his sexy mouth, but her imagination had grown legs and was currently sprinting a marathon. She'd be a molten mess if he said "no" one more time.

"Absolutely not. Too rustic for her taste." Max grinned.

"In that case, I'm flattered." Honored to be alone with him at his cabin; the one person to ever share his special retreat.

"Can I convince you to enjoy the next taste test of your tequila education?" he asked and beamed his playful smile, the one that seemed to secretly promise fun things to come.

"Sure, why not?" Celeste studied her surroundings. "I don't see any enticing tables or an audience in the room."

"Excuse me?" Max wrinkled his brow.

Celeste laughed. No need to bring up table-dancing. "Never mind. Why don't you make those drinks, and I'll wait for you outside. I believe your catharsis of a lake is calling me. I feel a healing coming on." In more ways than one, but he didn't need to know all her thoughts.

"Sounds like a plan," he said and ushered her through the sliding glass door. "I'll be right out."

"I'll be waiting at the end of the dock," Celeste said, and a shiver of anticipation slithered up her spine.

CHAPTER ELEVEN

৯৩৪৫

Celeste leaned backwards, bracing herself with her arms, holding her face skyward and enjoying the ticklish coolness of the lake as she splashed her feet in the water. She didn't realize there were still so many stars; she figured they'd all faded amidst the brightness of city lights, but she was wrong. They were all still alive, twinkling bright against the pitch-dark, country sky.

She took a deep breath of pine-scented air. The aroma washed over her like an adrenaline rush, recalling the hungry need of Max's last kiss, and she couldn't wait to taste him again. Possibly nature was the original aphrodisiac.

The sliding glass door opened and closed, and Celeste felt Max's footsteps vibrate along the wooden slats, but she didn't turn around, choosing instead to anticipate his nearness with each advancing step. Her skin prickled with expectation, and when he arrived and squatted next to her, she wasn't disappointed. He handed her a drink, his fingers brushing hers, and a jolt of fervor surged through her.

"Here you go. This is an Añejo. Typically, they're aged in wood barrels for at least a year and acquire a deep, smoky resonance that's instantly recognizable if you're a whiskey drinker. However, this particular tequila has been aged for over three years and has an almost peaty, caramelized flavor reminiscent of fine brandies," he said and settled on the dock beside her. He'd changed out of his khakis and dress shirt into a pair of cargo shorts and a T-shirt. He was barefoot, and he shrugged his shoulders. "I had to get more comfortable. I hope you don't mind."

"No, not at all." Her voice sounded velvety, thick with desire. She hoped he hadn't noticed, but the man was hot as hell, sexuality personified.

"So should we toast?" he asked, holding up his glass.

"Of course," she said, raising hers to his. "It would be a sin to drink without one."

"Here's to you, my sweet Celeste, may you enjoy your new tequila test." He smiled. "How's that?"

"Silly," she said, returning his contagious grin.

"Now you," he said. "What's your toast?"

"A toast to you, Max Riley extraordinaire, may you always have a head full of hair." She clinked her glass to the edge of his and erupted in a fit of giggles, and he joined in her laughter.

"That works for me," he said, and took a slow sip, watching her while she drank. "What do you think?"

"Hmmm." She tilted her head and let the liquor flow over her tongue as he'd taught her a few weeks before. She swallowed. "A little heavier than the blanco. I think the silver is smoother, but I'll wait to make my final decision until I've tasted more." She took another sip.

"Would you like to take the pontoon out on the water?" he asked, standing and pulling her up with him. "There's nothing more peaceful than a moonlight ride across the lake."

"Is it safe?" she asked. She'd never been on a lake at night before.

Max laughed. "Of course. It's a private lake, and we'll be the only ones out."

He helped her step off the dock and onto the boat, guiding her to the seat behind the captain's wheel. He opened a compartment and pulled out two life vests.

"You can put one on if you'll feel safer, but if you choose not to, you know there's one beside you in case you need it." After untying the boat from the dock, he engaged the engine, and the motor puttered and roared to a full throttle, and he inched the boat onto the lake.

Celeste eased back and enjoyed the drone of the motor, sipping her drink and relishing the tranquility, the peace surrounding her. Who knew? She took it for granted, living in Atlanta, that congested living quarters, traffic, and thick air were the way of the world.

Max, his muscles rippling under his T-shirt, held onto the wheel, turning it slightly, guiding them toward the center of the water. And when he reached for his drink, his biceps flexing with the movement, she thought she'd come out of her skin. His muscles looked rock hard. She took a gulp of her drink.

"How's this?" he asked over the roar of the motor, turning to her. She hadn't realized how large the lake actually was until the last glimmer of light from the cabin disappeared from view.

Celeste lifted her drink in acquiesce instead of trying to answer over the din, not sure she could muster more than a croak. The man had her in a tizzy.

He killed the engine and then headed for the front of the pontoon.

"This is my favorite spot," he said. "It's the center of the lake, and you can't see land." He opened the bench seat and pulled out a blanket, fluffing it upward and allowing it to flutter into place on the deck. He turned and smiled at her. Her breath caught in her throat, and her pulse raced as he strolled toward her, sure-footed as the pontoon bobbed in the water. He grabbed his drink and held out his hand to her. She took it and, hoping her knees hadn't turned to jelly, allowed him to pull her upward and guide her toward the blanket.

Max enjoyed how small her hand seemed, engulfed in his, and he tightened his grip. He knew he didn't have any business getting involved with someone from Atlanta, especially someone with an up-and-coming career. But she was different from other women he'd met, and it had been so long since he'd wanted to spend time with someone. Sharing his special place on the lake couldn't hurt anything. Or anyone. All he wanted was a little time alone with her.

"Do you come out here often?" she asked, and her voice floated like a reverent whisper across the cool night air.

"Almost every night after the kids go to bed," he said. "I come out and count the stars. Unwind." He winked at her. "Commune with nature."

"So how does one 'commune' with nature?" she asked and flashed her camera-ready grin. A man could get lost in a smile that happy. He attempted to clear his thoughts and forced himself to concentrate on the topic.

"Like this." He settled down onto the comforter, lying back and stretching out, positioning his hands behind his head. He looked up at her, still standing and watching him as she sipped the last dregs of her drink. He sat back up and took her empty glass away. He reached for her hand. "Come on. Join me, and I'll show you."

She eased down next to him, careful to arrange her dress around her legs, and mirroring his pose, she placed her hands behind her head.

"Like this?"

"Yes. Exactly like that," he said. He propped himself on his elbow, not allowing his body to brush against hers, knowing if he did, he wouldn't be able to resist touching her. And he wanted to. "Close your eyes."

She rolled her head to the side in order to see him, a confused wrinkle creasing her forehead. "I thought I was supposed to look at the stars?"

"But first you need to concentrate and listen to the night."

"The night?"

"Yes, for all the sounds of the night, and you need to take deep breaths in order to take in all the aromas around you. Once you experience the energy of nature coursing through your blood, you open your eyes and float to the heavens and become one with the stars."

"Are you for real?" She seemed skeptical, and Max laughed.

"No, but humor me," he said, cringing inwardly. He'd been too lyrical.

She finally closed her lids and breathed, following his instructions.

Her breasts rose and fell with each breath, and she appeared to relax, her face looking luminous in the pale moonlight. She undoubtedly was the most beautiful woman he'd ever met. Her mouth, perfect and full, begged him to kiss her, but he wanted her at ease and to enjoy the peace of the night like he did. He needed to share his solitude with her, and the admission exposed his vulnerability, because he hadn't wanted to share himself with anyone in a long time.

Max leaned closer, still careful not to touch her. "Do you feel it?" he asked in a whisper.

She nodded, and he jerked when her hand brushed against him, the softness of her skin running shivers up his spine.

"Should I open my eyes now?" she asked.

"Not yet," he said, his instructions as much for himself as they were for her, acutely aware of her hand on his arm. He didn't want to rush anything. "Be patient, a minute more."

Celeste surrendered a sigh when his breath tickled across her shoulder. Patience be damned. The man must be a bloody saint. She opened her eyes and found him watching her, and when he leaned nearer, she prayed he would kiss her again.

"Look at the stars," he said, his voice low and thick. "Do you feel it?"

"I think so," she said. Like hot lust and the need to jump him, but she stared upward instead, conscious of how near he was. She was tempted to close the miniscule distance between them and lick her way up his throat and claim his mouth. Kiss him until they floated to the moon.

"What do you feel?" he asked. His lips were next to hers, and she could almost taste him.

She wanted to say free, but she couldn't make her vocal chords form the words. Instead she simply nodded. Engrossed in the dark pools of his eyes, she pressed against him when he touched his mouth to hers.

His lips were warm, and she could taste the tequila on his tongue. She hummed while she reveled in the fervor of his kiss, his mouth delicate at first, but more demanding when she kissed him back. His hands skimmed across her breasts, her nipples peaking at his feathery touch, and an intoxicating pleasure fluttered in her belly. His hands caressed her body, moving downward along the curve of her waist, across her hip and down her thigh to the hem of her dress. He nibbled at her lips before his mouth drifted lower, trailing butterfly kisses along her throat. She sucked in a breath when his fingers brushed the skin above her knees and began an unhurried trail up the inside of her thigh.

On instinct, her legs tensed, and he pulled away.

"I'm sorry," he said. "I shouldn't—"

"Yes, you should," she said. Her heart raced, a frantic beat, leaving her breathy. She laced her arms around his neck and pulled him closer. She kissed him, an impassioned, ruthless kiss, taking it to the next level, the musky tang of sexual promise in the air.

She maneuvered closer, arching into him, hotter for him than she'd ever been for anyone. Missing his touch, she groped for his hand and guided him back to where he belonged. As he found the route he'd deserted earlier, she couldn't concentrate on his mouth anymore. His fingers slid between her legs, and her mind catapulted into space, like a rocket on its way to the moon. Maybe this was what he'd meant about becoming one with the stars.

Communing with nature was downright fabulous, but when his hand roamed back down her legs, Celeste moaned in frustration. Did he not realize he was going the wrong way? U-turn, please. She dared a peek at him, and he smiled as he took the hem of her dress and inched it up her thighs, the tantalizing silk trailing against her skin, the idea his hand moved along with it satisfying. When he reached her hips, she adjusted herself so he could pull it up and over her head. He discarded her frock with a flick of his wrist, leaving her exposed to the night air. Clad only in a matching lace thong and see-through bra, for some surprising reason, she felt at ease. Natural. Normally, getting naked in front of someone new always made her nervous. But not under the stars with Max Riley.

"God, you're perfection," he said, kneeling above her.

Her skin glowed smooth in the moonlight, and she sent up a silent prayer, thankful for loofahs. Almost nude, her nipples were tightened into peaks and pressed against the confines of the lace bra imprisoning them, and when he reached out and traced his finger around the edge of first one and then the other, every hair follicle on her body peaked into goose bumps. He ran his hand across the plane of her belly, luckily flush after a week of limited carbs, and flattened his palm and traced his way across her hips and followed the direction of her thong, a nice sharp vee pointing straight to where heaven awaited. If only he was getting naked with her.

"Hey," she said, bracing herself on her elbows. "This is not fair. I'm almost undressed and you still have all your clothes on."

"Trust me," he said. "We don't need me to take my clothes off yet. Why don't you let me pleasure you?" he asked. "Relax and enjoy being in tune with nature." He wiggled his brows, and she laughed.

"How's a girl to turn down such an incredible offer?"

"You shouldn't," he said and lifted her leg, dipping his head to meet her ankle, and his mouth started its ascent.

Celeste leaned back and enjoyed the velvety softness of his lips and tongue on her leg, his fingers leading the way. Who knew that nibbling and sucking one's ankle and leg could ignite such a hot heat? She moaned and arched her pelvis, about the same time that he reached her knees, and when he swirled the tips of fingers against the backside of her leg and his tongue flicked a happy dance, she thought she'd go insane with the need to have him reach his final destination.

He licked his way up both her legs, and his hands still moved ahead of his mouth, roaming along the soft skin of her inner thighs, brushing lightly against her thong. He stopped and teased his fingers across the lace, lifting the edge of the elastic and taunting her. She pushed her hips forward, wanting him, and she growled in frustration when his hands pulled away, leaving her wanting more. He shifted his hands upward across her abdomen, higher and higher as the anticipation of his touch transferred to her breasts.

Celeste bit her lip as he massaged her nipples, his fingers dusting across the outside of her bra while his mouth lingered along her inner thighs, his tongue flicking and darting a path. He slipped his one hand under her back and, with the finesse of a maestro, unhooked her bra and pulled it away, casting it aside. His hands slid away from her breasts and past her stomach, continuing downward and before she realized it her thong took a ride down her legs and past her ankles. Max dipped his head between her thighs and as a finger slid inside her and curled into the perfect spot, his mouth found the most wonderful place to suckle. Damn, the man was good. Talented to the extreme, she thought before she went mindless and decided she should enjoy the ride.

Celeste moaned under his touch and pressed her hips against his lips, giving in to the heat of the moment.

"More, more," she said. She pulled him toward her, her pelvis pushing forward, and obviously the perfect gentleman, he obliged.

He pushed in another finger and curved them both, searching for her special spot, and she stilled for a moment, knowing he'd find it, and when he did, she groaned.

Bingo.

"There, there," she said.

He did something utterly amazing with his tongue while his fingers danced inside her, and she writhed against him, making mewing sounds. A brief flash of guilt flashed through what little brain matter still functioned, but at the most wonderful moment of her life, she could have cared less. Guilt be damned. She was on her way to the moon. A free ride, compliments of the most talented Max Riley.

The heat of his mouth against her, his fingers finding nerves she didn't know existed, the tension winding and tightening inside her like a coil ready to spring and spiral upward, she moved against him, anticipating every possible pleasure he could give her. And pleasure didn't come close to describing her out-of-the-world experience as his tongue fluttered and flicked against her, driving her to the edge, her body clenching with expectation, her orgasm building and building and building. Celeste knew he was about to rock her world.

Her climax reached its countdown, and she was on a trip of no return.

Ten. She pulsed against his hand.

Nine. She quaked.

Eight. Her toes curled.

Seven. Her toes straightened.

Six. Her stomach contracted.

Five. Her groin pulsed.

Four. Her body quivered.

Three. Every nerve in her body shattered.

Two. She cried out in the darkness.

One…Lift off.

And she saw stars.

CHAPTER TWELVE

Too satisfied to feel self-conscious, Celeste stretched, wiggling her toes and luxuriating in the afterglow of a perfect orgasm while she drifted back down to Earth, wondering if the landing would be as fabulous as her entire experience. With her senses on high alert, every nerve in her body tingled as Max kissed her inner thighs, murmuring something she couldn't hear because her heartbeat still thudded inside her head.

"What?" she managed to ask, reluctant to give up the ecstatic exhilaration that coursed through her. She had never been so in touch with herself and wanted to delight in every nanosecond while reality drifted back to normal.

"I hope you enjoyed that," he said, his voice low and soft and no longer muffled. She forced herself to lift her lids and face him. He watched her over the plane of her belly and smiled, proud but bashful at the same time.

"Love would be more like it," she said. As soon as the sentence escaped her lips, she regretted her choice of words, hoping the use of the L word wouldn't drop like a bomb.

"Good to hear," he said, unaffected, and she breathed a sigh of relief. She had to give kudos to a man who didn't shy away at the mention of a word interlaced with commitment.

She enjoyed every intoxicating kiss as he tracked his way up the length of her torso until he reached her neck where he nuzzled a final peck, before he stretched out beside her. He propped himself on his elbow and gazed down at her.

"I needed that," she said.

"I'm glad I could oblige."

She turned her head so she could see him better. "Seriously, that was incredible. Do you think it was," she lifted her arm, her muscles still weak from their earlier nerve overdrive, and limply indicated the sky and lake, "the scenery."

"I'd like to think I had a little something to do with it." Max laughed and then sobered. "But making love under the stars is incredible." He played with a wayward curl and twined it around his index finger.

"I totally agree," Celeste said. "To hell with sex in the city." And she almost meant it. But Atlanta was home, and she couldn't very well travel four hours south every time she needed an earth-shattering big O. A shiver of regret coursed through her as she thought about what a wonderful time she'd experienced, and she sighed.

"What's wrong? Are you cold?" Max asked, concern puckered his brow. He reached for the edge of the blanket.

"No," she said, sitting up and pushing his hand away, pulling her knees up in order to hide her nakedness. She wrapped her arms around her legs and rested her chin on her bent knees. "I'm—" She stopped herself. She didn't know how to explain her feelings and didn't really think she needed to, even if she had an inkling of what to say. Possibly her mind-blowing orgasm had destroyed a few of her integral brain cells. The ones she couldn't afford to think without.

"How about a swim?" he asked sitting up beside her.

"Out there?" She pointed toward the dark, rippling water, the moonlight skipping across its surface as far as she could see. "By myself?"

"No, goose," Max said, and in one magnificent move, and an incredible display of rippling muscles, reached behind and pulled his T-shirt over his head. "With me."

"I don't know about that." Celeste looked back at the water, beautiful in the moonlight, but dangerous in its mysterious depths. "How deep is it?"

"Probably about fifteen or twenty feet through here," he said.

"That's pretty deep." Swimming wasn't her strong suit, and she wasn't sure indulging in the sport in a secluded lake at midnight was such a good idea.

"Have you ever swum with the devil in the pale moonlight?" he asked, his voice teasing, playful.

"Skinny dipping?" she ventured. Swimming naked with the most gorgeous man in the world? The suggestion began to sound impossible to resist.

"Exactly," he said. He stood. Unbuckled his belt, unzipped his shorts, and allowed them to slide down his legs and pool at his feet. He stepped out of them and kicked them aside. "Since I had the pleasure of undressing you earlier, would you like to return the favor?" he asked and indicated the waistband of his boxers.

She moved from sitting to a kneeling position, shaking her head in the negative, meaning the entire time to shake it in the positive, but her arms wouldn't move. His erection surged against the cotton. He was enormous. And the ache to know what he'd feel like inside her left her speechless.

"Suit yourself," he said, turning his back and dropping his boxers to the ground. The most perfect ass she'd ever seen sauntered to the back of the pontoon. He called as he dived into the lake, "Last one in—"

The splash drowned out his last words, and Celeste stood and walked to the edge, straining to see where he'd surface in the dark, murky water.

She heard a bubbling splatter and saw him surface and tread water twenty feet from the stern.

"Come on in," he said. "The water's perfect."

"I'll bet it's cold." Not that she couldn't use a cooling off.

"When you first jump in. You'll warm up once you start swimming."

"Are there any creatures in there?" she asked, peeking over the ledge, trying to see into the depths.

Max laughed. "What do you mean? Like Loch Ness?"

"Don't say that." She stepped away, thoroughly spooked. She believed in the Scottish legend. Who knew? Maybe someday she'd be assigned to report the sighting that finally proved Nessie existed.

"The only monster in this lake you need to worry about is me, and I promise I'm on my best behavior." He started to swim toward the pontoon, his arms slicing through the water like an Olympic swimmer.

"I'm not afraid of you," she said, laughing. Monster? Not. Teddy bear was more like it. Maybe Becca was right and Celeste should leave the man alone. He seemed too good to be true. But a weekend fling couldn't hurt anything. Or anyone. Could it?

After all, he'd shown her a joyous, climatic good time communing with nature. She should reciprocate. And she'd enjoy every minute of it.

Celeste stepped forward again, gathering the nerve to take the plunge. She knew he told the truth and she had nothing to fear, but she still felt apprehensive. The idea of diving into the darkness, the water swallowing her, made her linger a few seconds longer. There had to be fish swimming around in the depths somewhere. But more curious about him than she was afraid of what lurked below the water's surface, she lifted her arms and followed him into the lake.

Celeste disappeared in a spray of water, and Max doggy-paddled, waiting, until she emerged in front of him two feet away.

"You lied," she said, laughing, kicking her feet and bobbing in the water while she reached up and pushed her hair away from her face. "It's bloody cold. I think every inch of my body is tightened up into a giant goose bump."

"I might have failed to mention that the interpretation of water temperature might be subjective." He felt a tinge of guilt. After tapping down his natural instinct to ravage Celeste earlier and nearly blind and deaf with lust, he thought he'd lose his mind. He'd needed a dip in the lake to take his passion down a notch. And now as she floated in front of him, her firm breasts hovering along the water's edge, her nipples taut, he wondered if he'd made a bad decision. His libido ramped up and bounced along with her as she bobbed close, but still too far away. Skinny dipping to chill down his passion? What was he thinking?

"I'll race you," he said and pushed away, swimming toward the middle of the lake.

He heard her kicking, following behind.

"Where to?" she asked.

Away. Anywhere. As long as he wasn't so close to her. He didn't need to be tempted, everything about her body lean and compact. Everything about her perfect. She intrigued him, and he liked her. Max knew he needed to focus, and swimming through the icy cold would help. He hoped.

He allowed his mind to shift gears as he slowed down his strokes and eased into a comfortable pace. After Sissy left, Max'd stayed to himself for over a year, until his friends finally dragged him out and insisted he have a good time. And he had. Once or twice. But his attraction to Celeste was different, and he knew he wanted his first time with her to be special, to be more than a casual fling. But was getting involved with a career-oriented city woman practical?

"Hey," Celeste said from a distance. "You win."

Max stopped swimming in mid-stroke and turned. Celeste floated in the water, halfway between him and the pontoon.

"I need to turn back," she said.

"I'm sorry, hold up," he said and started his way back toward Celeste and the boat. He covered the distance between them and slowed to arrive at the ladder at the same time as Celeste.

"What a workout," she said in a huffed breath, pulling herself up the steps and back onto the pontoon. "Where were you planning to race to?" Her teeth chattered, and she shivered in the night air.

"I didn't think that far ahead," he said. "You make me a little crazy." He followed her up, stepped past the blanket, grabbed two towels, and tossed her one.

"I thought you were training for a triathlon," she said and cast him a puzzled look.

She wrapped the towel around her, covering her nakedness from his view, and he thanked the Lord, hopeful he could regain some of his good sense.

"Once we dry off, we can dress and I'll take you back to the big house."

"We're not going back to your cabin?" she asked. She sat down on the bench seat, and her eyes widened in surprise. "I thought maybe we'd¬—"

"No. I think I should probably get you back, it's already past one."

"The bewitching hour. The time when no good things come to pass?" she said, and he knew she meant it as a question by the way she lifted her eyebrows and smiled.

"Something like that," he said and, fighting the urge to sit down next to her, settled into the captain's seat instead.

"The clock struck twelve, and I'm no longer the princess, but a simple cinder-wench."

"Pardon?" he said, not sure he understood what she meant.

"Never mind." She started the search for her clothes. "I can't find my thong," she said. She straightened, holding her bra and dress. "Do you know where it went?"

He walked over to help her search. "We were right here." He motioned to the spot on the blanket. "And I was about here." He backed up a pace. "Then I slid it down your legs and tossed it over there." They both followed his line of motion straight to the opening on the side of the pontoon where they'd entered earlier. "Oops."

Celeste rushed over and gazed into the water. "Do you think my thong," she poked out her lower lip and finished, "fell overboard?"

Max pulled back the blanket and searched around one last time, but didn't find the missing underwear. He pushed his hand through his hair and turned to face her. "Appears as if that might be what happened."

"Oh." She sounded disappointed. "I liked those."

"You did pack more than one pair, didn't you?" he asked trying to lighten the mood.

"Yes," she said with her lip jutted out in an identifiable pout.

"I'll buy you another, I promise. Don't be sad." He assumed tossing her favorite thong overboard wasn't scoring him any points.

"No worries," she said. "But I do wear a size four, in case you're in Victoria's Secret any time soon." She smiled her beautiful grin, and Max forgot about everything except how good he felt when she looked at him that way. "Now turn around so I can dress."

"I think it's only fair, if you keep your back turned while I dress," he said.

"Deal," she said and waited while he picked up his clothes. "You go first."

He faced the bow and had the distinct impression she watched every move he made while he stepped into his boxers and then his shorts. After he zipped his pants, he gave it a beat before he asked, "Ready?"

"Almost," she said, and he heard a faint ruffle of clothing as she dressed.

"Let me know when," he said, thinking she'd had plenty of time to get into her slip of a dress and bra.

"Okay. Now."

He turned around, and she sat there, grinning like a kid locked in a candy shop.

"Nice show," she said.

"I'm glad you enjoyed it."

"Come tell me about," she spread her arm and indicated with a sweeping gesture, "all of this. And you."

He walked over, and now fully clothed, felt in control enough to sit next to her, but he still left a safe distance between them.

"What do you want to know?"

"The history of your farm, what you grow here," she said and smiled. "When you were born? Your sun sign?"

Max laughed, settling against the backrest, glad to think of something—anything—other than Celeste and her sweet scent and the softness of her skin. Or the dusting of freckles across the bridge of her nose. He glanced at her and wished she'd quit smiling at him; it threw him for a loop. What was his astrological sign? He studied his feet and thought for a moment, and then he remembered and dared another glimpse her way. "I'm an Aries, a fire sign. March 30."

"That's good."

"It is?"

"I'm Libra," she said. "An air sign."

"Air makes a fire burn higher," he said, but thought hotter. Sissy had been a water sign. Not a good thing for a burning flame. "What else do you want to know?"

"Tell me about Magnolia Oaks. Has your family owned it long?"

"Since the 1800s."

"A long time." Her voice held a reverent tone.

"Very. The railroad came through southwest Georgia in 1861 and after the War Between the States—"

"You mean the Civil War?"

"No," he said. "I mean the War Between the States. Aren't you Southern?" he asked.

"Well, yes. I'm from metro Atlanta."

"Then you know all true Southerners never refer to it as the Civil War?"

"I do now. I stand corrected."

"I'm glad I helped you see the error of your way," Max teased. "After the war a lot of northerners started coming down—"

"Don't you mean Yankees?" she asked and smiled.

"Exactly. A lot of wealthy northerners came down to vacation during the winter months, in fact this entire area of southwest Georgia became known as the Winter Resort of the South. At first they came down for the therapeutic pine-scented area, supposedly it helped pulmonary problems, but I don't buy that. I think it was more for the hunting and fishing, the social aspect. The winters were mild, and there was horseracing and fabulous golf courses."

"Around here?" She sounded doubtful.

"Yes, around here. Tyler's small, but there are larger towns nearby, well known for their history. And back before the turn of the twentieth century the tourists discovered it was cheaper to buy the land and refurbish or build than it was to come down and stay in the resort hotels in the bigger towns."

"Where?"

"Where what?"

"Are there bigger towns?"

"Ah, come on. We're not in Timbuktu," he said. She must think he was a total back woodsman. "We're civilized here."

"I'm kidding. So your family stems from rich Y...," she stumbled over the word, "Yankees?"

"No, my ancestors were the original owners. Our family was awarded the acreage during the 1820 land lottery and then continued to acquire more land in two-hundred fifty acre lots. They farmed cotton and crop vegetables, and struggled during the war and afterward. But they stuck it out when others had no other choice but to sell out. Papa Joe's grandfather was determined to persevere and continued to plant crop vegetables and peanuts. And in 1922 when his daddy's banker urged him to invest a portion of his seed loan money each year into Coca Cola stock, he did it." Max smiled. "Brilliant. And the rest is history."

"So your family is rich as Croesus because of peanuts and Coca Cola?" She smiled her mind-numbing grin.

"Croesus?"

"The king of Lydia," she said. "Never mind. Rich as the Vanderbilts?"

"Not quite the Vanderbilts, but still...isn't it great?" Max asked. "Come on, peanuts and Coke? You can't get more southern than that, now can you?"

"You still plant peanuts?"

"I don't. My daddy does, carrying on the tradition with the peanuts and pecan trees, but a few years ago, I talked Papa Joe into giving me a thousand acres to start growing organic produce." Proud of his success with his portion of the business, Max smiled. "I've been quite successful. I provide organic vegetables to a few major grocery chains and restaurants."

"Organic?"

"You got it. Growing vegetables free of any toxic chemicals that offer healthier choices while saving the environment, and I use practices that produce healthier soils while keeping the air, the ground and water systems free of toxic pollutants."

"I like that about you. I like it a lot."

"Thanks," he said, taking a deep breath, his chest swelling with pride. It meant a lot to him that she respected his passion. "I'm a member of the Organic Growers Association, as well as the Georgia Produce and Southwestern Produce associations. I was on the board of the Organic Growers until two years ago when I had to step down." He stopped, remembering why. "For personal reasons, but you already know about it." He didn't want to ruin his special moment with Celeste by mentioning Sissy's name out loud. "I have a horticulture degree from UGA. They want me to teach over at Tyler Community, but I don't have the time."

"Impressive," she said, nodding her head.

"If Big Mama didn't have every minute of this weekend crammed with picnics and parties, I would take you out and show you my operation."

"That would have been nice."

"Maybe you could come back down some other weekend, and I'll give you the grand tour, all 8,500 acres. Peanut fields, pecan groves, my organic operation?"

"Maybe," she said, but by the way she stretched out the may in maybe, he was confident she meant no.

"You sure I can't convince you?"

"Hmmm, we'll see."

Max knew what that mean, and what was he thinking anyway? He needed to stop thinking with his little head and allow his big head to make the decisions. He had no business inviting her down to Magnolia Oaks as his personal guest. Exposing her to the kids as anything more than one of the bridesmaids was ludicrous.

He stood and headed toward the bow. "It's probably time to get you back to the big house," he said. He would control his impulsiveness for the remainder of the weekend. One way or another.

CHAPTER THIRTEEN

❧❦

Celeste awoke with a start and stared straight into Trudi's face inches from her own.

"Get up," Trudi said, her voice a strangled hiss. "Or you're going to be in deep shit."

"What?" Celeste pushed herself up, leaned against the headboard, and tried to clear her thoughts.

"I know what time you came in," Trudi said in a whisper, the scowl on her face accusing and suspicious. "And so does Becca."

"What are you talking about?" Celeste decided playing dumb would be her best bet.

"You came sneaking in at two a.m. I heard you tiptoeing down the hall, there's a board between my room and yours that squeaks. Your door opened, I heard whispers, and then the door closed and the floorboard squeaked again." Trudi continued in a huffy whisper, her words hurled in accusation. "I peeked out my door in time to watch Max turn the corner." Trudi put her hands on her hips and glared down at Celeste. "That particular piece of information Becca doesn't know." Then she added with emphasis in her normal voice, "Lucky you."

Celeste threw her legs over the side of the bed. She should have known if anyone caught her it would be Trudi. Trudi didn't miss a thing. Never had. Probably never would.

"I've been here since midnight," she said.

"Yeah, right. And I'm a virgin." Trudi reached out and pulled Celeste by the arm, tugging her to a standing position. "Come on, Sleeping Beauty. The whole damn family is downstairs enjoying a buffet breakfast that would put the Capital Atlanta Club to shame." She pushed Celeste toward the bathroom. "And everyone is asking where you are."

"Me?"

"Yes, you." Trudi shooed her on. "Now go. Pull it together, before you have some explaining to do. Such as why your hair looks the way it does?"

Celeste reached up and grabbed a handful of curls. The swim in the lake had destroyed her straightening job. "Oh, crap."

She rushed into the bathroom and rummaged through her bag, tossing her makeup on the counter. Celeste groaned. She'd forgotten her flatiron, and there'd be no other choice but to wear her hair au natural for the remainder of the trip.

"What's wrong?" Trudi asked, leaning against the door frame, her arms folded across her chest while she studied Celeste. "Forget something? Please tell me it's not your birth control?"

"No," Celeste said. "My flatiron." And as far as she was concerned, much more disastrous. She watched her reflection in the mirror and pulled out a spiral of hair until it straightened. With a scrunched face she let go and allowed the unruly curl to spring back into a perfect ringlet. "What am I going to do?" She moaned.

"You're going to scrunch it. Now get a move on, I'm giving you fifteen minutes to pull it together before I drag you down to the dining room. We don't need to cause any drama for Becca. This is her weekend."

"You're waiting on me?" Celeste asked. A surge of gratitude calmed her jumbled thoughts, and some of the tension building in her spine subsided. She didn't want to make her tardy entrance alone.

"I'll be right here." Trudi stepped back into the bedroom. "I'd never send you into that lion's den alone. Those Riley females could probably eat you for breakfast and start on me for lunch. Now hurry up."

Celeste amazed herself when she managed to jump in the shower, scrunch her hair, apply a smidgen of makeup and pull on a pair of capris and a halter top in record time. Lucky for her, Trudi waited almost thirty minutes before she dragged Celeste through the house. She marched her down the winding staircase and straight into the dining room where most adult members of the Riley family, including Max, and their guests sat talking over the remnants of a phenomenal breakfast. Celeste's stomach growled when the scent of bacon greeted her. Although she made it a rule to never eat bacon, rules were made to be broken. Her stomach rumbled again.

"Here's our late-sleeping bridesmaid," Big Mama said. Everyone turned their attention toward the doorway, and Celeste felt a heat burn its way up to her now curly hairline.

"It's the fresh air," Trudi said. "Too pure, not enough smog, caused her to sleep right through the alarm clock." Trudi moved away and left Celeste to brave the stares alone.

"Good morning," she said to no one in particular and took a tentative step, purposefully avoiding Max who sat at the far end of the table. She hadn't had time to reflect over last night in her wild haste to get ready, but she'd certainly had all the time in the world while she'd lain in bed unable to sleep during the early morning hours. Trying to figure out why Max brought her back to the house instead of his cabin had plagued her until she'd finally fallen into a fitful sleep sometime after five. No wonder she'd overslept. Any other man in the world would have taken her to the cabin and been all over her. Why hadn't he?

"There something different about your hair?" Big Mama asked, giving Celeste a once over.

"Yes—"

"Come on," Big Mama said. She pushed her chair back, stood, and motioned Celeste forward. "Come on. We need to fix you a plate and get some nourishment in you. You don't look like you eat more'n a bird. Need to get some meat on those bones."

"Yes, ma'am." Celeste ventured past the longest dining table she'd ever seen. She didn't take the time to count, but she guessed there had to be at least thirty chairs, and the mahogany sideboard, laden with every breakfast food imaginable, stretched a good eight feet. Big Mama grabbed her elbow as she passed, ushered her to the stack of plates and pushed one in her hand.

"Here," she said and scooped up a pile of bacon with the tongs and plopped them on the plate.

"I don't—"

"Yes, you do. Don't is not in our vocabulary here at Magnolia Oaks. Don't never could. Now take some of the grits." A scoopful of white glop dripping in melted butter joined the crisp bacon, and Celeste felt her arteries harden. Her traitorous stomach growled again. "And here's some of my cheesy eggs. Don't I make the best cheesy eggs in the world?" she called over her shoulder.

A chorus of "yes, ma'ams" answered from behind, and Big Mama continued to usher Celeste down the buffet, scooping and piling food on the plate until Celeste's wrist ached from the weight, and she imagined she'd need a wheelbarrow to get it to the table.

"That should be enough," Big Mama said. She placed a fluffy white biscuit on the mountain of food. "For your first helping."

"First?" Celeste said in awe. She didn't eat that much food in a week, let alone in one meal.

"Yep, the first go round," she said. She faced the room full of Rileys. "Don't we always eat seconds?"

Another echo of "yes, ma'ams" answered her, and when Celeste turned around, she realized she had two choices of a place to sit.

At the head of the table near Becca and her parents, but Celeste immediately nixed that as her choice because Becca's mother made her nervous. A retired high school English teacher, she always corrected everyone's grammar, and she never forgot anyone's mistakes. Mrs. Sanders had the annoying habit of remembering the most embarrassing tidbits of someone's life at the most inopportune times. She was a walking, talking database of awkward moments. Not that she meant her recollections mean-spirited; she was a little dingy and didn't know when not to speak. Bless her heart. And, of course, that option included Becca with her accusing glare.

Her other choice, at the opposite end of the table, was where Max sat next to his parents.

Dilemma.

Big Mama decided for her when she took her plate and hiked it down to the empty seat next to Max and motioned with a wave for Celeste to follow.

"If you don't put a move on, this food's gonna get cold. Come on now." Big Mama glanced from Celeste to Serena and said something Celeste couldn't understand, but a few of the nearby Rileys chuckled as Celeste claimed her assigned seat.

"Good morning," Max said, smiling one of those grins reminiscent of the Cheshire cat. "I trust you slept well."

"Very, thank you," she said as she fluffed the linen napkin across her lap and stared at her plate oozing with butters and gravy and melted cheese. "I can't eat all of this," she said to Max from the side of her mouth. She caught Serena staring at her from across the table, and Celeste attempted a smile but couldn't manage to move the muscles in her cheeks.

"You'll have to," Max said.

"Or you'll be answering to Big Mama," Brick said. "She'll take offense if you don't eat. Mama loves to feed us."

"How do y'all stay so fit?"

"Hard work, and lots of it. Right, son?"

"Yes, sir," Max agreed. Celeste scrutinized her food, and Max reached over and brushed his fingers along the edge of her shoulder. "Your hair is—"

Celeste grabbed a ringlet and tugged. "Curly."

"I like," Max said. "I like it a lot."

Celeste picked up her fork and stabbed at the bacon, breaking it into pieces. "Oh my."

"Eat it with your fingers." Max reached over and picked up a piece, took a bite and held it toward her. "Bite," he said. She followed his instructions and the wonderful flavor of the bacon danced across her tongue. Her taste buds shuddered in delight as the hickory smoked, fatty goodness melted in her mouth.

"Uhmmm," she said.

"Good stuff, huh?" Max grinned.

Next she scooped up a wad of grits, but before she could raise it to her lips, Max stopped her. "Wait, those need salt."

"Mama doesn't add salt to anything," Brick said. He looked lovingly at his wife who still stared at Celeste, unblinking. Silent. The woman was eerie, but at least her stare held none of the malice Celeste had seen the night before. Maybe drinking wine brought out her hateful side.

Max sprinkled a dash of salt on her food and took her fork and re-scooped the grits. "Now try them."

They were delicious. Apparently, her mother didn't know how to cook grits because hers never tasted so good. But you couldn't expect a girl from Pittsburgh to know how to prepare a southern favorite. Max continued to watch her as she dipped her fork into first one item and then the next, taking tentative nibbles at first and digging in for second ones after the initial taste. The food was fabulous, but after small tastings of everything on her plate and enjoying a huge mouthful of biscuit, she couldn't eat another bite.

"I'm done," she said and pushed the plate away. "No more."

"Sshh." Max hushed her, looking down the table at Big Mama who regaled Becca and her parents with one of her stories. "Don't let Big Mama hear you, or she'll be down here spoon feeding you."

Brick laughed. "Don't think he's teasing. She'd do it, wouldn't she, Serena?" The still-staring Serena blinked and nodded. "She forced Serena to clean a plate or two until the two of them reached an understanding."

Celeste couldn't imagine what the understanding might have been unless it was Big Mama hoping the woman would eventually starve herself to death. Serena couldn't be any bigger than a size four. And Celeste could eyeball someone's size like a judge on America's Next Top Model.

"Hey, Dad, help me out," Max said, a scheming hush to his voice. "Run interference for me. Distract Big Mama and I'll get rid of the evidence." He nodded his head toward the head of the table, and Brick stood and walked toward his mother, calling on his way. "Mama, don't we need to get those butts on the smoker?"

"Son, those butts have been on that smoker since last night," Big Mama said, focusing her attention on her son while Max pushed his empty plate in front of Celeste. He took the opportunity to disappear through a side door with her full one.

Celeste breathed a sigh of relief, only to find Serena still watching her.

"You won't tell, will you?" Celeste held her breath, fearful the woman would rat her out and she'd be faced with another plate piled with food. The Riley to her right stood and left her alone at the end of the table with Max's mother.

Serena smiled, a ghost of a smile that didn't register as sincere. "I won't tell, but while I have you alone, I'd like to make sure you and I have an understanding."

"Pardon?" Celeste hoped she'd heard incorrectly; there was something ominous about the way Serena had pronounced understanding.

"You heard me," she said again, the fake smile now frozen in place. "You can't have him."

"Who?" She knew damn well who who was, but she played dumb all the same, stalling, hopeful Max or Brick would return in time to save her. And she'd been so happy about pulling one over on Big Mama and ditching the food. Serena was a definite buzz kill.

"Max." Serena reminded her of Trudi for a brief second. Matter-of-fact. No emotion. Straight forward. "He should be with the mother of his children."

Celeste nodded unable to break eye contact with Serena.

"He has children. Children who want their mother, and he doesn't need some upstart from Atlanta playing with his emotions." Serena broke their stare long enough to glance down the table in time to see Brick start back their way. She zeroed in on Celeste, talking rapidly. "I'm sure you're a nice girl, a sweet girl, but Sissy needs to come home and be a mother to her children. We do not want any more scandal in this family. And Max doesn't need you confusing him."

"I think it's up to your son whether he wants to reunite with his ex or not," Celeste said, not sure why in the world she sparred with the mother from hell. "And from what I understand, he's already divorced."

"The formal proceeding has been completed. True. But what a man thinks he wants and what he really needs are usually two different things. He's hurt, but he'll get over it as soon as Sissy comes home." Serena tapped her blood red fingernails on the tablecloth. "He still loves her. Mark my words."

"What are you two chatting about?" Brick asked as he leaned down and kissed Serena on the cheek. "I missed you while I was gone," he said and smiled, pulling back Serena's chair so she could stand.

"We were talking about how Miss Taylor can't wait to get back to Atlanta. She thinks the country air is giving her hives." Serena lifted one eyebrow in challenge, a silent dare for Celeste to deny the topic of their conversation. When Celeste remained quiet, Serena produced a satisfied smile. "You'd probably be best served to return to Atlanta as soon as possible. And try oatmeal soap for your skin. It works wonders on rashes." Serena took Brick's hand and allowed him to guide her away without a backwards glance.

Hives? Rashes? From fresh air? Hardly. More like from the Mrs. Danvers of a mother, Serena. Celeste pushed her chair back and stood up, searching for Trudi and Patrice. She needed to talk to her friends.

"You." Big Mama pointed at Celeste. "You, come help me in the kitchen. We need to get a few things ready for this afternoon's cook out."

"Me?" Celeste gulped. She didn't know how to cook.

"Yes, you," Big Mama said, making her way to the door. The remaining Rileys laughed and Becca blinked, looking confused, and her mother and Grammy both stood.

"We can help," Mrs. Sanders said.

"No, you can't. I want her." Big Mama stopped and pointed at Celeste.

"But I don't know how to boil water, I won't be of any help—"

"Sure you can."

"I'll help," Trudi said, rising.

"No, you stay where you are. You might break a nail." Big Mama glared at Trudi until she sat back down. "I want her." She hooked her finger in Celeste's direction and crooked it in a come-with-me motion.

"Seriously, Mrs.—"

"How many times do I have to tell you, girl? Call me Big Mama. Now come on in this kitchen and help me get the side dishes ready."

"You might be better off allowing Trudi to help."

"Her?" Big Mama jerked her thumb at Trudi. "I can guarantee you, I'd have to send that girl for some cooking lessons before she could be of any help," Big Mama said with a scoff, giving Trudi a scornful frown. "She's too prissy and full of herself. Now you, on the other hand, are teachable. Follow me."

Celeste held back a laugh. For the first time in her life, she saw Trudi speechless. Old people apparently said anything they pleased. She assumed, after the age of retirement, manners no longer held a place on one's priority list. Celeste cast a sympathetic glance at Trudi who smoldered with an unbecoming shade of red splashed across her cheeks. The color clashed with her hair. Celeste wondered how Patrice had managed to stay off the radar and noticed her sitting next to Trudi, unobtrusively scribbling in her notebook. Celeste shrugged her shoulders and lifted her hands at Becca, who indicated she should do as she was told and nodded toward Big Mama's retreating back.

Celeste mouthed back, "You owe me," and followed BM down the hall.

"You know," Big Mama said as Celeste tracked behind, "it was my idea to invite you girls along with Becca for our family reunion. I thought it would be nice to meet her bridesmaids since we already know the groomsmen. I got the idea when Max came back from that party in Atlanta all happy. Seemed like his old self again. Made me wonder which one of you girls had curled the feather in his cap. Once Max found out I'd invited y'all, he was all excited. And I knew I was right. 'Course, I'm always right." She stopped and turned around to make sure Celeste followed, and satisfied when she saw her, she turned back around and continued on her way. "I've been watching, and I can see it written all over his face. I would make a bet you're the one he's got a hankering for. And I certainly hope it's not the red head."

"Hankering?"

"He likes you."

"Me? Oh no, I don't think so." If he'd had a hankering for her he'd have taken her back to his cabin and made passionate, wild love to her, but he hadn't. He'd escorted her back to the big house as fast as the pontoon could putter across the lake. His well-bred offer for her to come back and visit another time had been only that: a courteous invitation. He hadn't meant it. And helping her out with the plate of food didn't count either. He was being polite, and the task gave him a reason to escape because he hadn't returned.

They passed a smaller dining room that opened onto the verandah and another small room to the left. Celeste peeked in.

"That's the butler's closet," Big Mama said without turning around, convincing Celeste the woman had eyes in the back of her head.

"And here's my pride and joy." Big Mama stepped aside so Celeste could follow her into the huge kitchen. "What do you think?"

"Wow." The kitchen was worthy of Better Homes, a perfect blend of country style and high tech. The yellowed, pine flooring shone in the morning light, the crisp white walls contrasted against the black marble countertops. The cabinets were white and a few of them sported glass fronts where brightly colored dinnerware sat on display. Across one wall was a state-of-the-art grill, two stoves and three ovens, all of which would have made Rachael Ray salivate. A weathered-oak work table graced the middle of the floor. Obviously a cook's heaven. "Nice."

"You like?"

"Yes, it's comfy." Although huge, the room conveyed a sense of coziness and contentment. Windows allowed sunlight to spill into the room from three sides and a small fireplace nested in the corner with two Queen Anne chairs facing it. She could imagine sitting in front of the fireplace on a cold winter's night reading a good book, while she sipped hot cocoa and warmed her toes.

"Good, I'm glad you like it." BM walked over and plopped down in one of the chairs. "Now come here so we can talk."

"I thought we were going to cook?" Celeste realized everything was already prepared. Both ovens were turned on, and she could see casseroles bubbling, and a row of pans covered with foil were lined along the table.

"Let you cook?" Big Mama snarled her upper lip. "Do you think I'm crazy? I might be old, but I still have my good sense." She tapped her forehead with a gnarled finger. "Come over here," she said with a softened tone. "I want to talk to you about my boy."

"Max?" Celeste didn't know why she asked, she knew good and well BM didn't want to talk about Brick. She sat down, ramrod straight, and waited.

"Oh, relax," Big Mama said. "I ain't gonna bite ya." She leaned back against the wingback. "I was afraid after that little bitch Sissy turned his world upside down, he wouldn't be able to love anymore. But there's something about you he's a-liking. He seems to be alive again." She turned her head and peeked at Celeste. "And that makes me happy. So I need to know what your intentions are with him. Because he's a good man and he doesn't need any more hurting."

Celeste gulped. Trudi had been right. The Riley women were eating her for breakfast. First Serena and now BM. Big Mama continued to peruse Celeste, waiting for her response.

"I need an answer here."

"Mrs.—" she stopped herself, "I mean Big Mama, I think you might have read him wrong this time. I don't think Max is interested in me at all."

"Of course he is."

"Well, not according to his mother. She seems to believe—"

"When did you talk to Serena?" Big Mama sat forward, and from the look on her face, Celeste would bet her blood pressure had sky-rocketed. "What did she say?"

"She seems to believe that Max still loves Sissy and that Sissy will be back."

"Huh." Big Mama scoffed. "That ain't happening, and that boy doesn't love her. Not sure he ever did. Biggest mistake anybody could have ever have made, bringing that gold digging piece of baggage home with him." She observed Celeste. "Is that what you're up to?"

"No, ma'am, not at all. I had no idea, and to be honest, I came down to be supportive of Becca. She's one of my best friends and I love her. I'm happy for her and she wanted us to come along because you were so gracious to invite us, and we all came and I want to have a good time and be supportive—"

"You already said that," Big Mama said.

Celeste stopped rambling and tried to regroup her thoughts. "Well, what I meant to say is that I'm confident Max isn't interested in me," she said. Or he would have slept with her last night, but she couldn't very well tell his grandmother that. "And I'm not interested in him either."

"Yeah, right." Big Mama clearly didn't believe her. "You're into him, and he's into you, and now I need to make sure you know how to cook, so come on and let's go over a few things before you go out and meet the children."

"The children?" Celeste swallowed a lump of fear that congealed in her throat. The last thing she wanted to do was meet the little no-necks. The whole trip wasn't turning out as she'd planned.

"Yes, Charlie and Neecie. Of course, you need to meet his children."

Little people with short legs and no necks, grimy faces and snotty noses. Oh, hell.

CHAPTER FOURTEEN

৵৽

Celeste closed the door to her assigned bedroom and turned around to face Trudi and Patrice.

"How can we have an emergency girlfriend meeting without Becca?" Patrice asked. "I don't think that's right. Having a meeting behind her back, and she's the bride. The reason we're here."

"Becca wouldn't approve of what I need to talk to you about," Celeste said. "I really need you two to help me figure out what's going on."

"What do you mean?" Trudi asked. "Isn't it evident? You have the hots for Max, Max has the hots for you. Becca's freaked out about it, but she'll get over it. End of story. Now can we go down to the lake? Papa Joe mixes one killer martini." Trudi headed for the door, but Celeste grabbed her arm and stopped her.

"No, wait. It's not that simple. I need your advice." Celeste knew she sounded pitiful, and acting pathetic was not the best way to garner Trudi's sympathy and counsel, but she'd never felt so helpless before. "Please sit down and listen."

Trudi and Patrice both sat on the edge of the bed and waited. Celeste gathered her thoughts and started to pace. She focused on her feet as she talked.

"You're correct, I do have an attraction to Max—"

"Uh. Duh," Patrice said. "Like we don't know that already." She opened her notebook and began to write.

Celeste reached over and grabbed the journal away from her. "Do not write that down."

"Hey, that's mine," Patrice said. "Give it back."

"Promise you won't write any of this down." Celeste glared at her.

"Okay," Patrice said without any sincerity as she clicked the pen closed and put it aside.

Celeste waited.

"What?" Patrice asked.

"Put it on the bedside table."

"Are you for real?"

Celeste nodded and waited while Patrice placed the pen out of reach, and only then did she hand back the notebook.

"That bridesmaid journal's going to be the new Sex and the City before the wedding happens." Trudi laughed. "I'll buy the first copy," she said to Patrice and turned back to Celeste. "Okay, we understand that you've had an epiphany and you realize you're attracted to Max. Is that what we need to discuss? Because I thought you had seduction under control. You know what to do."

"It sure appeared that way last night," Patrice said, and she turned to Trudi. "Didn't you think they looked romantic dancing together?"

"The next best thing to public sex with clothes on," Trudi said.

"We most certainly did not look as if we were doing," Celeste stopped herself, unable to say the word, "… that."

"Oh yes, you did." Patrice chortled her silly laugh, and Trudi joined in.

"You couldn't have slid a piece of paper between the two of you," Trudi said between laughs. "And you don't think anyone noticed?"

"It was hotter than hot," Patrice said. "More like an inferno."

"Enough," Celeste said. "Okay," she added in a sardonic tone. "I get it. We were on fire, blazing with undeniable passion. The two of us so into one another it was as if we were alone in a room full of people."

"Oh that's good, real good," Patrice said, excitedly, grabbing her pen. "Can I write that down?"

"No." Celeste said in time with Trudi.

"Are you going to give us the sordid details or do we have to guess?" Trudi leaned back on her elbows, crossed her leg and swung it back and forth.

"There aren't any—" Celeste stopped and felt her face grow hot, and she could tell from the fire in her cheeks, she was beet red.

"Yeah, right. We're not buying it." Trudi sat back up, uncrossed her leg, and leaned forward. "Is he as good as he looks like he would be?"

"Do tell." Patrice moved closer, sitting on the edge of the bed.

"He's better than good."

"Aha. I knew it. Go ahead and confess it all, no need to make me interrogate you," Trudi said, gloating.

"Suffice it to say the man is a phenomenal kisser."

"I could tell by the shape of his mouth," Patrice said, nodding eagerly. She licked her lips. "Soft and yummy—"

"Enough," Trudi said. "Let Celeste tell us her story. She called an emergency meeting and I want her to get to the point." Trudi jerked around. "Spill. What's the problem? He's a fantastic kisser. Go on."

"He's quite talented with his mouth and hands."

"I could tell that too," Patrice added quickly, darting a glance at Trudi as she moved a foot further down the bed, an arm's length away.

"So what's your problem?" Trudi asked. "He's talented. Great mouth. I don't get it."

"Well, I didn't either," Celeste said.

"What?" Trudi asked.

"Get IT." Celeste cringed when she emphasized it. Were they going to force her to explain her lack of getting laid in detail?

"Get what?" Trudi asked again.

"IT," Celeste clarified, her cheeks burning hot. She couldn't believe them; they were going to force her to say it aloud.

"Huh?" Patrice chimed in.

"I mean—we…he," Celeste said, but before she could explain, Trudi interrupted.

"You're telling me he…you, the two of you…didn't?" She finally understood.

"Right." Celeste breathed a sigh of relief.

"Oh." Trudi and Patrice chorused.

"And therein lies my problem," Celeste said. "What does it mean?"

"Is he gay?" Patrice asked.

"Oh, please, no, of course not. Anybody with any kind of gaydar knows that man is one hundred percent straight. There is nothing the slightest bit swishy about him." Trudi chewed on her bottom lip, thinking.

"His mother warned me to stay away from him. Said that I shouldn't confuse him or mess with his emotions. Mentioned something about his ex, said she needs to come home and be a wife and a mom to her kids."

"His mother said that to you?" Trudi asked. "When?"

"She cornered me at the table this morning, and she told Brick that I'd said I have the hives."

"Do you?" Patrice asked, lifting Celeste's wrist and inspecting her skin.

"No. Absolutely not." Celeste jerked her arm away from Patrice's grasp.

"Because you can get the hives from sexual frustration." Patrice nodded her head knowingly. "I know."

"TMI," Trudi said. "Focus. You're getting off track here." She stood and walked over to the French door and gazed out at the verandah. "Did he not make a pass?"

Celeste felt her face flush again. Trudi wasn't making this easy.

"Let's leave it at the fact I enjoyed myself, but no, we didn't sleep together. And I really shouldn't want to have sex with him. You know my rule. No divorced men and absolutely no men with kids. And he is geographically undesirable—and the GU factor is concerning. He has triple strikes against him. He's already struck out before the game can begin. Besides, I've sworn off men. It's all about my career now."

"But he's soooo hot," Patrice said.

"Exactly, and I couldn't resist, and I'd pretty much decided I'd go for it. A weekend fling. I mean, what could it hurt?" She stopped and glanced over at Trudi, and Celeste couldn't help but wonder what was going on in Trudi's sharp, fast mind. "Then Big Mama had a talk with me in the kitchen and tells me that Max has a 'hankering' and he doesn't deserve to be hurt again."

"Hankering?" Patrice asked, confused. "Is that like a handkerchief?"

"No," Trudi said, exasperated. "It means he has the hots for her."

"Why didn't she say that?" Patrice asked. "That's what's wrong with the world today. People won't come out and say what they mean. We're always trying to figure out—"

"Enough. Stop it," Trudi said and walked back across the room, chewing on her lip. "He's obviously attracted to you." She stopped in front of Celeste. "No doubt about it."

"Well, I do have a doubt, that's why I called this meeting."

"His mother's warned you to stay away," Trudi said.

"And so did Becca," Patrice said.

"Big Mama mentioned he doesn't deserve to be hurt. Becca warned you to stay away, and so did Serena, although for different reasons. No one wants you to hurt Max," Trudi said. "And I'd be willing to bet that Max feels the same way."

"You think that's it?" Celeste asked, trying to remember anything he might have said or done to give any indication that Trudi's conclusion was correct. She couldn't think of anything. Other than he was a really sweet guy, who'd been dumped by his witch of an ex, and he probably was leery of being hurt again. Which made sense. "He's worried he'd get hurt. That's it. Deep down I realized as much, but I didn't want to admit it. I know I can't get involved with someone with children and who lives so far away. I have my career to think of, and he's vulnerable, like Becca warned, and I can't hurt him."

"No doubt about it. So consider yourself lucky and heed the warnings from the women in his life. Stay away. No weekend fling. No getting involved with Max Riley."

"But Big Mama seemed to think that the two of us would be good together, and she mentioned me meeting the kids. Not that I was looking forward to meeting them."

"I can sympathize," Trudi said. "Kids can bring extra conflict into a relationship. But now that you've decided there won't be anything between the two of you, you don't have to worry. Meeting them should be insignificant."

"I like kids," Patrice said. She grabbed her pen off the table. "Can we go now?"

"Not yet," Celeste and Trudi said together.

"Although it's a shame to miss out on such an incredible specimen of manhood," Trudi said. "Consider yourself lucky. You won't be breaking your own rule. You do remember your own rules, don't you? You won't become involved with a divorced man with kids, however brief and insignificant it might be. Two kids, very young ones, I might point out." Trudi took Patrice by the arm. "Let's go down and find Papa Joe and indulge in one of his martinis before they unleash the little monsters on us." They walked to the door, and Trudi turned. "Coming?" she asked Celeste.

"I'll be down in a few. I need a minute."

"Are you sure?" Trudi asked. "Because we can stay."

"Yeah, if you need us, we're here for you," Patrice said.

"No, y'all go ahead and meet up with Becca. She probably needs some support about now. I'll be fine."

They didn't move.

"Really, I'm fine. I want to be alone for a minute. That's all."

Celeste sat on the edge of the bed and heard the door close, and then the floorboard in the hallway squeaked. She put her head in her hands and massaged her temples. Max's reluctance to get involved was totally logical. Made perfect sense. After all, her first rule was to never date divorced men with children, and her most recent rule of no dating at all was crucial to get her career where she wanted it.

Trudi was right. Celeste needed to remember her rules and avoid getting tangled up in any type of relationship with Max, no matter how tenuous. No more hot, fabulous kisses. No more wonderful, talented mouth and hands. No fling.

But how the hell would she make it through the next two days and manage to stay away from Max?

CHAPTER FIFTEEN

꙰

"You can do this," Celeste said to herself. She'd masterminded a plan while she'd changed from her capris into a sundress.

With the entire family in attendance, as well Becca's family and the girls, there was quite a crowd. Celeste had calculated the exact number, counting off first Big Mama and Papa Joe and making her way through the list of their children, grandchildren and spouses, and the great-grandchildren. No way could she remember everyone's name, but she did remember the number. Thirty-nine in all. That many people should offer enough distraction to remain engaged with others, while she managed to avoid Max and his kids during the afternoon picnic.

To start, she would mingle with Marcus's brothers, Andy and George, and their wives. After all, she'd met them at the Stock the Bar party, and they'd been more than welcoming since she and the bridesmaids had arrived. She would hang with Max's Aunt Pansy's older daughters, they were in their early thirties, both married with kids, and she could think of something to talk about, to bide the time, and stay clear of Max. If she could float around like a social butterfly during the picnic, when everyone went back up to the big house to watch the football game, she could feign a migraine and disappear for the evening. She'd worry about tomorrow later. After all, it would be another day.

Armed with her plan, she paused on the hill behind the big house and sucked in a fortifying breath before walking down the slant of manicured lawn leading to the pavilion. Taking her time and glad she'd had the foresight not to wear heels, she strolled in a pair of flat sandals she'd bought for a steal at a Neiman sale two weeks before. Think shoes, not Max. She could ignore him. She would.

A Moonwalk bounced with little munchkins flying into the air and falling back down again and again while their anxious mothers waited outside. Under the covered picnic area several helpers placed food on tables covered in red-checked cloths, while Big Mama ordered them about, pointing while directing their every move. A smaller gazebo closer to the lake housed a bar where Papa Joe entertained Trudi and Patrice. Trudi tilted back her head, the afternoon sun glinting off her hair, and laughed at something Papa Joe had said.

Becca and Marcus were talking with their parents and Grammy, while further away from the picnic area another handful of cousins and the older kids indulged in a family softball game. From the number of the crowd, it appeared she was the last to arrive. Again. She walked through the afternoon heat toward the activity around the lake. Celeste squinted up at the sky, clear and blue, a puff of clouds floating overhead. Nice day for a picnic.

Scoping for Max, she scrutinized the family gathering again. After all, she'd need to know where he was in order to avoid him.

Her breath hitched in her throat when she spied him, and her plan detonated. He stood behind a young boy, his arms wrapped around him as he helped the little guy swing a bat almost as long as he was tall. From the looks of him, she assumed he was Charlie, Max's six-year-old son. Cute kid. But of course, she knew he would be. Max laughed when the bat teetered and his son looked up at him with a lopsided grin. Then, to her dismay, Max turned, saw her and flashed his heart-warming smile. Her heart flip-flopped, and she gulped. Evading him would be harder than she thought.

Max smiled and waved when he saw Celeste standing on the periphery of the lawn, her wispy dress fluttering in the breeze. Anxious to talk with her again, he'd been waiting for her to show up for the last thirty minutes.

After breakfast, he'd searched for her downstairs and discovered that most everyone had retired to the main room. The front room, as Big Mama called it, was so large it housed two fireplaces and separate sitting areas with four huge sofas and a spattering of tables and over-sized chairs. His teenaged cousins had been deep in a game of chess, and a few others indulged in games of Parcheesi and Sorry while The Lion King played on the big screen and the little kids sat engrossed by the story. After realizing Celeste and the bridesmaids were nowhere to be found on the lower level of the house, he'd given up his search and spent the remainder of the morning with Charlie and Neecie, waiting for time to pass.

And now there she was, standing apprehensive and gorgeous in the afternoon sun, the sight of her causing his heart to thump wildly.

"Hey, Charlie, why don't you have Uncle Andy help you with that swing? He has a few tricks up his sleeve," Max said.

"Tricks?" Charlie perked up.

"Sure, he knows how to swing a bat better than Babe Ruth." Max turned to his older brother. "Can you show Charlie the ropes on how to position his bat and eye the ball."

"Sure," Andy said and knelt down next to Charlie. "Okay, slugger, here's the deal."

Max slapped his brother on the back and knuckled a playful punch into Charlie's shoulder. "I'll be back and I expect you to show me everything Andy's taught you."

Charlie nodded, his features fixed and serious, reflecting his determination. "Sure, Dad."

By the time Max turned around, Celeste was almost to the lake. He'd need to sprint to catch up with her, but he hesitated, remembering Serena pulling him aside earlier and giving him a lecture about family and, more importantly, their reputation.

Apparently, she felt the Rileys were held to a higher set of morals, and she insisted any liaison with Celeste would be more scandalous than Sissy running off with Pastor Dick. Max didn't share her point of view. Especially when she started rambling about the possibility of Sissy coming home and how he should be prepared to take her back.

Like hell he would. He'd divorced her, and it'd be a cold, cold day in the pit of a volcano before he ever considered taking her back.

He didn't understand Serena's logic. He could hardly compare a man moving on with his life to a woman deserting her children and husband. Somehow it didn't run a close parallel at all. Sometimes Serena really pissed him off, but he always listened respectfully and nodded. No sense in arguing with her. He'd found that out a long time ago.

Max glanced at his parents who'd joined Big Mama under the pavilion, his father's hand resting lovingly on his mother's back. What the hell? Celeste was at Magnolia Oaks, and he might as well enjoy her company for the weekend. Spending a little time with her wasn't as if he were asking her to meet his children, to stay forever, and live happily ever after. A little flirtation couldn't hurt.

After all, he deserved some happiness too, and without further reflection, he took off jogging across the grass.

"Hold up."

At the sound of Max's voice, Celeste stopped and waited, allowing the inevitable to happen. So much for her plan. She could hear his steps thud against the dense grass and felt him when he stopped behind her, his breathing deep and even. She turned around.

"Hey," she said and held her hand up to shade the sun, wishing she'd thought to bring her shades. Hiding would have been easier behind a pair of huge sunglasses. "Great weather."

Max glanced upward. "It is now, but rain is coming."

A white fluffy cloud drifted overhead, the sky blue, the sun shining, and she laughed. "Good thing you didn't become a meteorologist." She dared to look him in the eye. "Because I'm afraid you might not have done very well."

"No, seriously," he said, taking her elbow and walking, gently guiding her along with him. "Look." He pointed to the trees lining the field and leading into the woods surrounding the property. "See how the leaves on the hardwoods are turned upward. It'll rain before nightfall."

Celeste followed his pointing finger and sure enough the leaves were turned, their underbellies lighter, a shimmering mosaic of green and silver as they reflected the sunshine, glimmering and dancing in the light afternoon breeze.

"Amazing," Celeste said. "Is that what it means? Really?"

"Wait and see." Max nodded and smiled. His eyes crinkled and his mouth turned up at the corners in a confident, proud smile. He didn't seem egotistical, simply self-assured. "I'm a helluva forecaster. You should have your station give me a call and offer me a position."

"That would be something," Celeste said, thinking how seldom the weathermen seemed to hit the mark with their predictions. "A forecaster who actually gets the weather correct." She laughed and he joined in, chuckling along with her.

They'd stop walking, and she realized they were still a good thirty feet from the bar by the lake, and after an awkward silence Max spoke.

"I drove over to the club this morning and retrieved your purse."

"Thanks—"

"I have it and your shoes," he said.

"My shoes?"

"You left them at the cabin last night."

"Wow. Thanks. I'd forgotten about them."

"No problem. About last night, I'd—"

"Here y'all are." Big Mama's voice boomed from behind, startling Celeste, and her hand instinctively fluttered up to her chest where her pulse raced ninety to nothing. "Glad to see y'all found each other."

"We were on our way to get a drink," Max said, and Celeste wanted to ask we were? But instead she smiled and nodded her head in agreement, thankful Big Mama had interrupted when she did. Celeste really didn't want to know what Max had planned to say about the prior evening. Her cheeks flushed hot at the memory.

"Good," Big Mama said. "Me too." Big Mama squeezed between them and linked her forearms through each of theirs, dragging them toward the gazebo, amazingly strong for someone her size and age. "Papa Joe should have already poured my Dewars, and by now the ice should have melted a little. The way I like it." She gave them each an all-knowing appraisal. "I didn't mean to interrupt. Y'all go ahead…so what are we talking about?"

"We were talking about—"

"The weather," Celeste said, not sure where Max planned to go with his explanation.

"No need wasting any time on that discussion. It's going to storm," Big Mama said, as self-assured in her answer as Max had been with his. "But we'll have time to eat and enjoy ourselves and get everything cleaned up before it hits."

Celeste couldn't believe what she was hearing. Did these people own a crystal ball? The weather report hadn't mentioned anything about rain, and she didn't see a dark cloud in the sky.

When they arrived at the gazebo, Papa Joe handed Big Mama her drink. Her fingers, still elegant although slightly gnarled with age, wrapped around the highball, and she winked at Celeste. "Train 'em right, my dear."

"What will you have, young lady," Papa Joe asked.

"Nothing for me," Celeste said.

"What?" Trudi asked. "You're not drinking? You really should try one of Papa Joe's martinis. The man can rock a cocktail."

"He sure can," Patrice said. "Please, sir, can I have more." Patrice placed her empty glass on the bar, and Papa Joe went to work shaking her another one, while Max reached into the cooler and pulled out a beer.

"You sure you don't want anything?" he asked Celeste, and he held out an enticing frosty bottle with crushed ice slithering down its side.

"No, none for me," Celeste said, knowing a drink might lower her resolve and foil her plan. As if understanding her dilemma, Trudi took hold of her arm.

"Let's walk over and grab you a tea," she said. "Excuse us, we'll be back in a few." She guided Celeste away from the bar. When they walked out of earshot, she released her arm. "Well, that was close. What were you and Max talking about? You acted as if you needed to be rescued."

"I did. Thanks," Celeste said. "I planned to avoid him, but he caught me off guard. And then BM swooped in for a tackle."

Trudi laughed. "No worries, my friend. I'll take care of you."

Celeste breathed a sigh of relief. If anyone could run interference for her, it was Trudi.

When lunch was served, Trudi ditched her in order to grab another cocktail, but Celeste managed to slip away in the confusion of everyone going through the buffet line. She took her plate and wandered away from the pavilion, making her way toward a set of barns: one large, the other smaller and farther away.

Celeste found an old, weathered picnic table on the far side of the largest barn and settled on the bench ready to dive into her food. She was ravenous; she hadn't eaten anything since breakfast, and it was almost three o'clock. Wishing she had a cold, frosty beer to go along with her pulled pork and slaw, she took a sip of unsweet tea. She shouldn't have refused the offer of a drink earlier, but she wanted to keep her wits about her, fearful alcohol would lower her defenses, and she'd find herself enjoying Max's company too much.

She scooped an unladylike amount of pork onto her fork and took a mouthful, enjoying the sweet, succulent meat that melted in her mouth. No doubt, Big Mama knew how to smoke a butt. The woman was pure genius. If Paula Deen still ruled supreme, she'd need to relinquish her crown.

After engulfing everything on her plate, having no need to eat like a bird when there were no men around, she turned her back to the table and propped herself on her elbows. She scanned the horizon and was amazed to find that the once blue sky was a hazy gray, the sun now hidden by a low bank of darker clouds. She smiled. Well, she'd be damned. Maybe it would rain after all.

Hearing a shuffling sound, Celeste turned around. A little girl with long, blonde curls ran around the corner and skidded to a stop in front of her. Then Charlie ran around the barn, close on her heels.

"Neecie, stop. Big Mama's gonna be mad." He slid to a halt beside his sister, and they both stared at Celeste, their eyes large and unblinking.

"Who aw you?" Neecie asked. She eyed Celeste with a conflicting mixture of interest and surliness.

"She's one of the bridesmaids," Charlie said in a low whisper, sounding as if it were a disease. He tugged on her arm. "Come on, before Big Mama finds out we're down here, and we get in real trouble."

"Bwidesmaid?" Neecie perked up, her fascination peaking, while her unfriendliness slipped away. "For the wedding?"

"Yes, I'm Becca's friend." Celeste smiled. She supposed all little girls, no matter how young, were intrigued by brides and weddings. She always had been.

"My name's Neecie," the little girl said and stepped closer to Celeste. Her eyes were blue, lined with thick lashes, her cheeks, pudgy and round, were pink, and below her small, upturned nose, she had perfect, cupid-bow lips. She reminded Celeste of a china doll, a living perfect specimen of a faultless angel. Celeste wondered if she took after her mother, then frowned at the thought. Why did she care what the runaway ex looked like? She didn't. And the two little people standing in front of her were part of the reason Max was off limits. That and the fact she'd sworn off men. Neecie tilted her head to the side. "You're pwetty."

"Thank you," Celeste said. "So are you."

"No, I'm not," Neecie said and stepped in front of Celeste to lean against her knees. "What's your name?"

"Celeste," she said.

Neecie's plaid, cotton jumper was soiled with dirt, and a smear of something that could be chocolate stained the front of her bodice. Celeste winced and resisted the urge to hold the little person a good arm's length away. Her sundress was dry clean only.

"Lest?"

"That'll work," Celeste said.

"You wanna see my kitties?" Neecie asked.

"No, Neecie," Charlie said. "We need to get back. Everyone's going to the house to watch the game."

"I don't wanna see no stoopid game," Neecie said. "I wanna show Lest my kitties. You wanna see them?"

"Sure." Celeste agreed, somewhat reluctantly. Second to kids, animals weren't really her thing. Her father and older brothers always owned large, intimidating dogs for pets. German shepherds and rottweilers, the kind of dogs that would snarl and scare her, although her brothers insisted that the canines from hell were only smiling at her. Right. Those dogs didn't smile; they anticipated having her for dinner. And cats would have been out of the question. Her mother was allergic, and the dogs would have made mincemeat pie out of them. She did win a goldfish at the fair one time and named it Betty. But Betty only lived two weeks, and her father flushed her down the toilet. Celeste and animals weren't a good mix. She gritted her teeth and caved. "Sure, let's go see them."

"Good," Neecie said, grinning from ear to ear, her little four-year-old teeth, even and pearly-white, showing through a contagious smile. Neecie grabbed Celeste's hand and took off down the dirt trail heading for the smaller barn, pulling Celeste along with her. Charlie fell into stride behind them, a protective shadow, lingering a few steps in their wake.

"We really need to go back, Neecie," he said again.

"No," Neecie replied and continued on her quest.

"What's your kitty's name?" Celeste asked.

"Her name's Punkin."

"Punkin?"

"She means Pumpkin," Charlie said.

"Oh. Pumpkin. I see, well that's an interesting name."

"Teresting?" Neecie observed her from under her thick lashes, waiting for Celete's explanation.

"You know, fun, different. You don't think of a cat being named Pumpkin."

"Why not?"

"I don't know." Celeste laughed. Why couldn't you name an animal after a vegetable?

"Big Mama says we can name them anything we want," Neecie said with a stubborn jut of her chin. Her expression clearly conveyed that she thought Celeste was a dumb ass.

"Well, if Big Mama says it, it must be true." How could one argue with a law set down by a local deity?

On the back side of the barn, Neecie fell down on her knees, oblivious of the dusty dirt beneath her as she reached with grubby fingers into a wooden box turned on its side and scooped up a cat and pulled her into a bear hug. A litter of kittens scattered when she exposed them.

"Oh, your cat has babies," Celeste stated the obvious.

"Yep, six of 'em," Charlie said from behind. Celeste jumped. She'd forgotten he was there.

A fluffy orange and white ball of fur sprung forward and waltzed a happy sideways dance toward Celeste. She knelt down on her knees and held out her hand. With razor sharp claws, the kitten took hold of her dress and pulled itself into her lap.

"Ouch," she said. Mewing softly, the kitten butted its head against her hand.

"Rub her," Neecie said, dropping the mama cat on the ground. "She wants you to pet her."

Celeste reached out and scratched the kitten under the chin. The ball of fur enjoyed it far too much and began a rumbling serenade, pushing its head closer. When Celeste pulled her hand away, the kitten snuggled past her waist and began to inch its way up her chest, digging in, and after another half dozen heart-felt ouches from Celeste, the kitten managed to climb its way to her shoulder. Neecie doubled over in a contagious belly laugh.

"That kitty likes you, vewy much," Neecie managed to say through another eruption of giggles as the kitten nuzzled its face into the crook of Celeste's neck.

"That tickles," Celeste said, the kitten's soft fur grazed against the tender area of her collarbone, causing her skin to prickle.

"She's giving you kisses." Neecie sobered. "That means she loves you. You should be her mommy."

"Yeah," Charlie said, causing Celeste to jump again. "They'll be ready to give away in another week or two. You should take her, she likes you."

"Oh no, I couldn't," Celeste said, pulling the kitten from her shoulder and settling it into her lap.

"Why not? She loves you."

"How do you know it's a girl?"

"We can tell," Charlie said. He sounded grown up, so knowing for someone only six years old. "She's a girl. Besides, Big Mama said the orange and white ones are girls, and the black ones are boys, for sure. And Big Mama knows everything."

"Does she now?" Celeste asked, beginning to wonder if maybe they were correct about Big Mama and her all-knowing capabilities.

"We have puppies too," Charlie said, quietly. "You wanna see 'em?" He seemed apprehensive, as if he was afraid she'd say no.

"Sure, why not? I'd love to see your puppies." She took the kitten from her lap and settled it back in the box next to its litter mates. She held out her hand to Charlie, and he hesitated a moment before he finally took it. "Lead the way," she instructed, as she lifted herself to a standing position, brushing loose strands of hay from her backside with her free hand. So much for her sundress. It'd need more than dry cleaning after her farm adventure.

Neecie jumped up and ran across the barn toward the open doors at the opposite end. "The puppies are out here," she said over her shoulder, before she disappeared around the corner. Charlie picked up his pace, tugging on Celeste's hand, and she walked faster to meet his gait.

A step behind Charlie, she exited through the doors and stopped in mid-stride, pulling her hand away from his grasp, every muscle in her body tensing on high alert. Warning whistles zinged through her as her rear clinched in fear.

Not more than ten feet away, a kennel housed a litter of black and tan puppies. Puppies, her ass. There were seven big black and brown animals with domed foreheads, long muzzles, black noses, and brown, beady eyes, and they were large enough to knock her down and have her for lunch. Their large ears stood erect, their long necks arching forward, their bushy tails swinging back and forth. German shepherds.

And Neecie stood on her tiptoes reaching for the latch to unhook the gate.

CHAPTER SIXTEEN

❧

"No," Celeste tried to shout, but the command came out sounding like a garbled screech. Bordering on hysteria, she stood paralyzed, her feet glued to the ground as her knee caps jerked in fear.

"Neecie, don't you dare." Charlie yelled at his sister. He turned around, placing his hand on Celeste's arm and stared at her, tilting his head to the side. "You okay?"

Celeste wanted to scream hell no, but managed to shake her head in the negative and take a tentative step backwards, her mind racing to determine how many steps it would take her to reach the safe haven of the barn and slam the door shut, all the while trying to judge if she could make it before the dogs were set free.

Charlie gave her another unblinking glance, before he took off in a trot.

"Neecie, no. Big Mama doesn't want them running loose during the picnic."

Celeste's pulse hitched when the tip of Neecie's fingers pushed the latch free, and the gate swung ajar. One huge snout pushed the gate open and a small horse of a dog galloped toward her, and Celeste willed her feet to move, but all she managed to do was shake in fear, every childhood terror returning. She felt her eyes bulge wide, as her muscles tightened, and her upper lip broke out in a film of perspiration. A scream of pure horror gurgled in her chest, but the dog lunged at her before the sound escaped her lips. Stepping backwards, she tripped over her own feet as its paws landed on her thighs and knocked her over. She was being attacked by a half-grown German shepherd.

A rough, scratchy tongue licked a slick swath up the side of her face, and a soft, furry muzzle tickled her ear. In the background, she heard Neecie break-out in a fit of giggles and even Charlie laughed.

"I tink Sarge likes Lest," Neecie said, close by, and Celeste felt the little girl settle down by her side, next to the dog.

Celeste opened one eye.

Neecie wrapped her arms around Sarge's neck and nestled her face in his fur.

Celeste pushed herself up on her elbows and searched for Charlie. He herded the puppies back into the pen and re-latched the gate, preventing the other dogs from escaping again. She took the opportunity to scoot backwards, putting distance between herself and Sarge, keeping a watchful eye on him, although he appeared preoccupied with Neecie as the two of them engaged in a playful joust of pushing and nudging each other.

She hadn't realized she was holding her breath until her heart kicked in like a runaway train and her pulse pounded in her ears. Rolling to her hands and knees, she managed to stand up and backed away on shaky, wobbly legs. Sarge turned his attention from Neecie back to her and his ears perked to attention. Celeste met his gaze, but immediately diverted her eyes. Never look a dog in the eye. Where had she learned that? Probably from her father after the family dog, King, a large white German shepherd, had knocked her down and bit a hole in the neck of her sweater. Her father had called King off of her in the nick of time.

"Don't be scared," Neecie said. "Sarge won't hurt you." She grinned and Celeste could see an impish-twinkle beacon through her too-blue eyes.

"Yeah," Charlie said, as he returned from the now locked and secured kennel. "He's a good dog, but Big Mama hasn't finished training them, so they haven't learned all their manners yet." He studied the ground in front of him and scuffed the dirt with his sneakers, trying to hide a smile. "Sorry he knocked you down."

"He wanted to play with you," Neecie said. "He wikes games." She lunged at Sarge and grabbed him around the neck, pulling him onto the dusty ground and rolling around with him. "See. He's havin' fun," she said before breaking out into a belly laugh.

"Stop it." Charlie walked over and pulled Neecie away from Sarge, yanking her to a standing position and putting his hand on the dog's neck. Sarge, with his tongue hanging out of his mouth, all lopsided and happy looking, sat down and looked up at Charlie. "You're still scaring her." Charlie jabbed his thumb toward Celeste, who, like a total freak, stood as still as a statue. Her mouth gaped open, her tongue drying out, so she forced her lips to close, but she still couldn't speak.

"If I bring Sarge over and introduce him to you, will you shake his hand?" Charlie asked. "He knows how to shake."

Celeste moved her head from side to side and took a step backwards.

"Ah, come on," Neecie said. "He wikes you. He gave you a vewy big kiss."

"Was that what that was?" Celeste asked, finally managing to find her voice, meek and quiet. At least it didn't quiver in fear.

The sky had turned dark and the earlier breeze kicked up into a full-blown wind. A gust lifted up Celeste's ruined sundress, and a breeze whipped a lock of Neecie's blonde hair across her face. Neecie pushed it behind her ear with a pudgy hand, leaving a fresh streak of dirt across her cheek.

"Maybe we should put Sarge back in the pen and head up to the house," Celeste said, grasping her hands together to keep them from shaking. "I think it might rain."

"Nah," Charlie said with the certainty of a meteorologist. "Big Mama said it won't rain 'til after the game starts, and we're all inside."

"Maybe she's wrong." Celeste glanced at the horizon, worried Big Mama might not be as all-knowing as everyone thought. The sky glowed with an eerie-red cast, and menacing, black clouds rolled toward them. "I think we need to head back."

"Not 'til you meet Sarge," Neecie said. Insistent, she stomped her foot. "Shake his hand, pwease." She draped her arm across his neck and patted him. "He wants to be your fwiend and it makes him sad Lest's 'fraid of him."

"Okay," Celeste said, agreeing to anything in order to get the kids back to safety.

The darkness consumed the sky at an alarming rate, and she willed herself to take a tentative step forward. She would shake the dog's paw, make sure Charlie latched him into the kennel, and usher the kids back to the big house. Celeste took another few jerky steps until she stopped in front of Neecie and Sarge. She leaned down and held out her hand, which trembled only slightly.

"Shake, Sarge," Charlie said.

The dog lifted his paw into the air, and Celeste wrapped unsteady fingers around it and shook. At the exact moment they made contact, lightening split the sky and a rumble of thunder followed. Sarge jerked his paw away and his ears flattened back against his head, as he whimpered and moved closer to Neecie.

"He's scared," Neecie said. "Poor Sarge." She lifted her hand and rubbed it down his neck.

"Come on," Charlie said, pulling at Sarge.

As the first pelts of rain splashed down, Celeste straightened, and the hair on the nape of her neck prickled when she noticed that the sky had turned into a thundery darkness.

The storm was on them, and it was furious.

Another streak of lightening lit the sky, and a few seconds later thunder boomed, shaking the ground. Sarge lunged upright and bolted away from the barn, running blindly across the field toward a thicket of trees at the edge of the woods.

"Sarge." Neecie screamed and started after him. Celeste reached out and stopped her, but Neecie struggled against her grasp. "Sarge, come back. I gotta get Sarge." She tried to pull away, but Celeste held fast.

"No, Neecie. You need to get back to the house." Celeste knelt down and took Neecie by the shoulders.

"But what about Sarge," Charlie asked, a troubled frown creasing his young brow. "We can't leave him out here. He's afraid." He cast a worried look after the puppy who disappeared into the forest.

"Poor Sarge," Neecie said, and even with the rain sheeting down, Celeste could tell she was crying. "We gotta save him, Lest." Neecie gave her a pleading, pitiful pout.

Celeste, torn between the need to get out of the storm and usher the kids to safety, realized they wouldn't budge until they thought the dog was safe. She knew what she had to do.

"If I go after Sarge, will you two promise to go straight to the house?"

Neecie and Charlie both nodded, their earlier unblinking stares returning. Celeste's heart tugged at the sight of them standing there drenched, like orphans in the midst of a storm. They were cute kids. She couldn't imagine how their mother had deserted them. Or why? What kind of heartless creature would desert such charming no-neck monsters?

"Pinky promise," Celeste said and lifted her little finger in a crook.

Charlie hooked his little finger to hers. "I promise," Charlie said.

"Pwomise," Neecie said and imitated her brother's actions.

"Okay, now run. And fast." Celeste stood and shooed both kids toward the house, pushing a clump of drenched hair behind her ear. "Charlie, take care of Neecie and get to the house quick."

Charlie nodded and took Neecie's hand, pulling her behind him as he took off in a jog.

"Come on," he said, tugging harder as Neecie moved along with a reluctant step.

"Save Sarge," she said. "Pleaaazzze, Lest."

Celeste contemplated the kids, both of them soaked, the rain coming down in sheets of gusty wind.

"I promise," she said, her voice bouncing back in the whipping wind.

Seriously considering she'd lost her mind, Celeste turned to run toward the forest after Sarge.

Max was frantic when everyone returned to the big house, and he realized Neecie and Charlie weren't with them. He checked in the movie room where the adults had gathered to watch the Falcons take on their latest opposing team, and then in the play room where some of the younger kids had settled down to watch The Lion King again. Did they never tire of watching the same movie over and over? He expected to find Neecie and Charlie glued to the screen, but they weren't there. Where could they be?

Not wanting to alarm Big Mama, he darted out the back door and jogged down to the pavilion. Possibly they had stayed behind, intent on some game, but they were nowhere to be seen. Lightning flashed and thunder rumbled. Damn. The storm was hitting earlier than he'd thought. He stood under cover of the gazebo while sheets of rain fell. He panicked.

What kind of father was he? He should have kept a better eye on them, but he'd been too preoccupied trying to talk to Celeste, but she'd disappeared after the food was served anyway. He'd seen Charlie and Neecie wander off with their cousins after they'd eaten. He wracked his memory. When had he seen them last? He peered across the lake, then back across the field toward the barn. Where the hell were they?

The puppies. He should have thought of that earlier. Of course, Neecie would have talked Charlie into taking her to see Sarge. She was enthralled with the dog. He ducked his head and took off, the rain and wind driving him from behind. He'd almost made it to the barn when he saw Neecie and Charlie running toward him, their heads down, the downpour impeding their progress. He increased his pace and met them halfway.

"Where were you?" he said against the wind.

"We went to the kennel," Charlie said, refusing to look at Max. "We shouldn't have gone, but Neecie wanted—"

"You need to learn to tell her no," Max said. "Come on, let's get y'all to the house and dried off." He picked up Neecie and took Charlie by the hand. "This is a nasty storm and none of us have any business out in this mess."

The wind picked up and he jogged as fast as Charlie could keep up with him. They'd made it past the pavilion and halfway up the hill when Neecie began to cry, whimpering into his neck.

"Don't cry, you're safe. Daddy has you," Max reassured her.

"But what about Sarge?" Neecie sobbed. "And Lest."

Max stopped mid-stride, and Charlie bumped into his leg.

"What do you mean?" he asked, putting his finger under Neecie's chin and pulling her face upwards. "What do you mean, where is Lest?"

"She means the bridesmaid," Charlie said, hunkering close to Max's leg, trying to shield himself from the onslaught of rain.

"You mean Celeste?" he asked. A panic seized his heart when Neecie nodded yes. Max broke into a run. The back screen door screeched as he opened it, and he delivered them inside the back service entrance, the one closest to the pavilion walkway. He put Neecie down and squatted to their level. "Where's Celeste?" he asked.

"She promised to find Sarge," Charlie said.

"Where's Sarge?"

"He got scared and runned away," Neecie said.

"What does Celeste have to do with Sarge being afraid?" Max asked, dreading their response.

"He ran into the woods, and Celeste promised to find him if we'd come back to the house." Charlie squeaked the toe of his shoe against the ceramic tile. "Neecie wouldn't come back until Celeste promised to find Sarge."

"You're telling me Celeste is out in the storm looking for one of the puppies?" He couldn't believe what he was hearing.

Charlie and Neecie nodded in unison.

"Go to your rooms and get out of those wet clothes. I'm going back to search for her," Max said. He stood and glared down at his children. "Change your clothes. Go to the playroom and watch the movie with your cousins. Do not pass Go. Do not collect two hundred dollars and do not go back outside. Do you understand me?"

They both nodded.

"We'll talk about this later." He turned and darted back out into the storm.

"Damn," Celeste said as her dress caught on another twig. In the thicket of trees, the wind was less abrasive and the bite of the rain was muffled as it crashed through the leaves, a softer patter by the time it reached her. She pushed another willowy limb aside and made her way along an overgrown trail. She was drenched and cold, and her skin was starting to pucker.

"Here, Sarge," she said. Where was the damn dog? She'd been tromping around for at least ten minutes, and she hadn't seen or heard a sound from the escapee. And in a way she was glad, even though she had promised to find him.

A horrific thought zipped into her conscious. What would she do, if she didn't find him? What would she tell the kids? Or Big Mama? She imagined Neecie crying, void of her earlier playfulness. And it would be Celeste's fault if she didn't find Sarge.

But worse, what would she do when she found Sarge? She wasn't likely to throw her arms around him and carry him to safety. After all, he was a D O G. Her biggest childhood fear. Celeste tried to get a grip on her meandering thoughts. Who was she kidding? Dogs were her adult phobia too.

She stopped and took in her surroundings. Come to think of it, so was being alone in a forest in the middle of a storm. What had she been thinking when she agreed to go after the puppy in the middle of a downpour? Her stomach churned and her heart picked up an extra beat or two. Celeste decided she'd continue her search for five more minutes and then she'd head back, Sarge or no Sarge.

Celeste forged ahead and another rumble of thunder vibrated the ground when she heard a whimper.

"Sarge?"

A muffled yip replied.

"Sarge, where are you?" She stopped and listened. Another whimper answered her from the right, off the path in the brush. Celeste stepped across a bed of ferns and pine straw, the ground soft and pliable beneath her sandals, and she cringed. She was not a nature girl.

Reaching out, she pulled the limbs of a bush aside and found Sarge curled up at the base of a pine tree. He lifted his head and his ears perked up, his brown eyes sad and afraid. Another flash of lightening cut through the darkness, and Sarge whined, lowering his head again.

"Come on, Sarge," Celeste said. "Let's go. I'll walk you back and keep you safe."

He rolled his eyes upward. Celeste was pretty sure he wasn't convinced.

"Come on, boy. Work with me here." Celeste couldn't believe it; she was trying to reason with a puppy. "Don't make me try to pick you up. Walk back for me, okay?" There'd be no way she could carry a forty pound puppy through the woods.

The pleading tone of her voice must have gotten through, because Sarge sat up and cocked his head to the side. He appeared to trust her, and Celeste exhaled a sigh of relief. Progress. When she reached down to pick him up, she heard a horrendous crashing sound.

She straightened and jerked around, the first thought flashing into her mind: bear. Did they have bears in south Georgia? Big, black, vicious bears with sharp teeth that could chew up a thin woman and a German shepherd puppy with a few quick bites? Her second thought: coyote. Her heart skipped a beat, and she realized that she had no other choice but to grab the dog and run like hell. She had to save herself and Sarge.

Whether it was a bear or coyote, there was something large making its way through the thicket coming straight toward them.

CHAPTER SEVENTEEN

୬ଡ଼ୠ

In a sheer panic, Celeste reached for Sarge at the same time that he lunged to his feet. She jerked backwards. And her heart hiccupped into her throat. She waited for the attack. First by Sarge, and then by whatever crashed through the woods.

But instead of attacking, Sarge stepped in front of her, growling a low, menacing snarl. Amazement took over her fear. He lowered his head, the hair across his shoulders rising as his ears flattened against the side of his head, his eyes narrowed to slits, and his tail stood straight out. He'd taken a defensive pose, prepared to defend her.

"Ah, Sarge," she said out loud, thinking how honorable the little shepherd seemed, standing there ready to take on the creature who stalked them. Her throat tightened and hot tears burned, threatening to escape. They were about to die, but Sarge, noble warrior pup, stood ready to protect them to the end.

The sound of brush being trampled came closer and closer, and Sarge barked, spitting, nasty sounds, warning growls, his lips pulled back and his muzzle wrinkled in a snarl. He took off in an aggressive run, to take on whatever threatened them.

"No, Sarge," Celeste screamed. "No."

"Celeste? Sarge?" A deep, male voice called out their names as the underbrush parted, and a dark figure pushed through onto the overgrown path. Max lunged forward as Sarge charged him.

"Down, boy," he said. The dog had halted his run and hunkered down barking in warning when recognition dawned on him. "Down, boy. It's me," Max said, his voice soothing. Sarge relaxed and sat down on his haunches and lifted his paw. Max took the proffered paw and gave it a quick shake. "Good boy."

"Oh my," was all Celeste could manage to say as she stepped away from the tree. Relief flooded through her. Their attacker was only the tall, handsome, wonderful Max. Not a bear, not a coyote or a lion or a tiger. But a dripping wet, sexy hot Max. Her knees turned to jelly, and her body sagged like a limp noodle. She grabbed hold of a tree to steady herself. Max moved toward her with Sarge leading the way, woofing a few barks, like Lassie guiding the way back to Timmy in the well.

"Thank God I found you," Max said, relief sounding in every syllable. He reached for her, and she slid from the tree into his arms. "You okay?"

She nodded in the affirmative and snuggled against his chest. She was safe and instinctively knew that Max would protect her. He rubbed his hands up and down her arms.

"You're freezing. Let's get you back to the house and warmed up." He bent to slide his arm underneath her legs and hoist her up when she stopped him.

"No. There's no need to carry me. I can walk." The last thing she wanted was to be carried through the forest like Tarzan and

Jane. "Help me get Sarge back. I've got to get him back to his pen."

"He'll be fine, but are you sure you're okay?" With one eyebrow raised and his brow wrinkled in concern, he didn't seem to believe her.

"Yeah, I'm fine. Lead the way and help me with Sarge." She eased away from his chest and took a tentative step. Thankfully her legs cooperated. She lifted her face upward and the rain splashed down, pelting her face. "Let's get out of here."

"You got it." Max reached for Sarge and scooped him into his arms and started down the trail, looking back at her. "Everything all right back there?"

Close on his heels, she trudged along behind him and nodded. "Can we walk faster?" she asked, hoping the trip back would happen much quicker than her search had taken.

And miraculously it did. In only a few minutes, they were exiting the canopy of trees and making their way across the clearing. The relentless downpour still sprayed furious waves of rain their way, the wind a howling force to walk against. Their trek seemed to take twice the amount of time to cross the clearing as it had to navigate the woods, but they finally made their way to the barn. Max placed Sarge on the ground, before he opened the door. He reached for Celeste and guided her inside before he followed in behind her with Sarge on his heels.

Inside the barn, Sarge braced himself and shook off in a wild frenzy, spraying his own private deluge.

"Now if drying off could be that easy for us," Celeste said, looking down at her dripping wet sundress, clinging to her like she'd been vacuum-sealed.

"No kidding." Max laughed. "No sense drying off now, we still need to make it back to the house." He walked over to a stall gate and opened it. "Come on, Sarge. Let me get you settled, and I'll get your littermates out of the rain so Celeste and I can get dry too."

Celeste leaned over and examined the spacious stall. The floor was swept clean and seven cushy pet beds lined the wall with bowls of water placed nearby.

"Nice digs," she said.

Sarge obediently trotted into the stall and curled up on one of the beds, laying his head on his paws.

"Good boy," Max said. "Give me a few minutes to get the others inside before we start for the house."

"Don't they have cover in the kennel?" For all of her fear earlier, she thought she remembered seeing a state-of-the art facility.

"They do, but this is a nasty storm, I'd prefer to have them in here, and if we didn't have a house full of guests, you can be assured Big Mama would have them up at the house."

He walked to the door, and Celeste followed him.

"Hold the door open so the wind won't slam it shut," he said. He braced himself against the wind and flashed a wink her way before he ran outside.

Max unlatched the kennel gate and called for the dogs. All six followed him as he led their way to the dry safety of the barn. They shook off and dutifully jogged into the stall to join Sarge. Max latched the stall gate behind them.

"There, all safe and sound." He brushed his hands together. "All in a day's work." He moved toward her. "You ready to head—"

A flash of lightning lit the sky and a split second later a loud crack of thunder rattled the barn.

"Close the door," Max said. "That storm is right over us. We can't risk trying to make it back until the storm passes. Rain's one thing, but lightning is another. I won't jeopardize your safety simply to get you dry." He reached the door, helped Celeste close it against the fierce wind, and slid a bolt in place, then flicked a switch turning on a buzzing fluorescent light.

Realizing warmth wasn't in her immediate future, Celeste leaned against the wall and succumbed to a shuddering of cold chills. A wave of exhaustion drained through her, and she wanted to cry but willed her tears to stay put. She didn't want Max to see her break down, didn't want him to think he needed to console her. When, in fact, all she really wanted him to do was embrace her, so she could snuggle against his warmth and feel safe and protected.

"Big Mama's bound to have something out here we can use to get you dried off," Max said as he rummaged through a storage cupboard, desperate to find something for Celeste to cover herself with. Anything. There were dog treats, ear cleansing solution, and various other products used for the dogs as well as a stack of towels and a blanket. He'd hit the jackpot. "Aha. I knew it." He pulled out a towel and held it out to her. "Wrap this around you, once you're somewhat dry, you can use the blanket."

"There's a blanket in there?" she asked, taking the towel and looking at it before sniffing it.

"It's clean," Max said, hoping she'd hurry up and cover every exposed curve of her body. The once flowy dress was now stuck to her like a second, transparent skin. He could see her nipples, taut and peaked through her dress, and every ounce of his energy was being sucked dry trying to keep from taking in an eyeful of her lean curves.

"But what are they used for?" she asked.

"To dry off the dogs or whatever," he said, knowing he sounded impatient. He pulled the towel out of her hand and wrapped it around her. "Trust me they're as clean as the towels at the house, and at the moment, beggars can't be choosy."

He took one of the towels and buffed it across his hair, then pulled his shirt over his head and ran the towel across his chest and abs, before flipping it over his shoulder and drying off his back. He grabbed a chambray shirt hanging on a hook and shucked it on, buttoning two of the buttons. When he shifted his attention back to Celeste, she stood wrapped in the towel, staring at him.

"Nice," she said. Her lips curved in a slow tempting smile, or so it seemed to his libidinous thoughts: explicit, carnal images that raced through his mind. But he discarded the tempting possibilities. He needed to think about how cold he was, how wet and uncomfortable, because the last thing he needed in his drenched jeans was an erection. Or to seduce Celeste on a mound of hay during a raging storm.

"So, where are the horses?" she asked. She made her way toward him, her steps slow and languid. Enticing.

"We haven't housed the horses in this barn for years. Papa Joe built a larger stable for them on the other end of the property, south of the house."

"Oh," she said and stopped a few feet away from him. She reached up and played with a curl, flipped it over her shoulder. He reminded himself how cold he was, but a persistent memory recalled the springy softness of her hair, the gentle scent of her.

The towel did little to hide her curves, and, if possible, she was more enticing standing there with the straps of her sundress showing above the circle of white cotton, than she did in nothing but her drenched dress. He imagined her naked beneath; her smooth, creamy skin ready for his touch. Damn. So much for covering her up in one-hundred-percent white, opaque cotton—the image seemed to fuel his imagination and rampant libido.

"How's Sarge?" he asked, trying to distract her, to change the subject playing through his mind. He moved closer to the stall and checked on the dogs. They were all curled in their beds, heads down, waiting out the storm. He turned back to Celeste. "Tell me how you wound up in the woods chasing a wayward pup."

"I came down here to eat, away from everyone else, and found a picnic table by the larger barn," she said.

"That's where you disappeared to. You wanted to be by yourself?"

"Not necessarily alone...I needed to get away for a while."

"I see," he said, but he didn't. He didn't understand why she would be compelled to leave the pavilion and seek a spot where she could eat alone. Possibly he'd misread the gleam in her eye that he'd interpreted as interest, and the glint was only a reflection of the harsh fluorescents. "And you discovered the puppies and couldn't resist?"

"No. Oh no. I could have easily resisted. I'm afraid of dogs." She shuddered. "Scare the hell out of me."

"How did you wind up with Sarge loose and you on his trail?"

"The kids came out and Neecie enticed me to meet the kittens and Charlie suggested we visit the...puppies." She shivered again. "They failed to tell me the so-called puppies were half-grown shepherds, or I might have reconsidered their gracious offer for an introduction." Her teeth chattered.

"They're actually four months old, the last litter of Big Mama's favorite, Daisy."

"Last litter? Is Daisy okay?"

"She's fine, but she won't be bred anymore. Since Daisy's getting older, Big Mama wanted to breed her one last time and keep the pups for the family. She's promised Sarge to Neecie, Charlie gets his own, but he hasn't picked out his favorite yet. I'll get one, if I want, and the other three will go to whomever Big Mama decides deserves one of her beloved Daisy's offspring."

"I take it you're all fond of big dogs?"

"We've always had shepherds. It's a given, never thought about them being big."

"You can imagine my surprise when we rounded the corner and came face-to-face with seven huge dogs."

"They aren't huge. Trust me, they'll get bigger."

"And Neecie and Charlie said we were meeting puppies—" She stopped. "Those are not puppies." She pointed toward the stall.

"I'm sorry you were frightened, but they're puppies until they're a year old. I believe the definition for puppy is a young dog, younger than a year. And technically they fit the bill. They're puppies."

"Okay, puppies they are." She shot a nervous glance toward the corner of the barn.

"Seriously, Celeste," he said, concerned for her. "If the kids had known you were afraid of dogs, they'd have never brought you down here, and if I'd been here, I wouldn't have let any of this happen. I apologize that you were afraid."

"Don't worry," she said. "I managed to grow up with dogs in the house. It's not like I haven't been around them before. I prefer to stay away from anything larger than a Yorkshire terrier. Although Sarge might have changed my mind." She smiled. "Maybe a little."

The storm seemed to have stalled overhead, one lightning strike, followed by thunder, after another. He noticed that her lips had turned slightly blue, and she shivered again. He walked over to the cupboard and pulled out the blanket.

"Come here," he said and reached for her hand, pulling her along with him to a mound of hay in the corner. He tossed the blanket down. "Now sit," he said and she obeyed, settling down and drawing her knees up to her chest. Max pulled the blanket around her shoulders and tucked the other ends around her legs. "Do you want to take off your dress? You can wear this shirt." He pulled at the edge of the chambray.

"No, I'll be fine," she said. "This storm won't last much longer. Right?"

Without responding, Max sat down beside her. She had no idea how long one of the obstinate storms could linger.

"You didn't answer me," Celeste said, a panicky sound in her voice. "Can it?"

"What?" Max asked.

"Last much longer? Are we stuck here in the barn?"

Another rumble of thunder rattled the rafters and a few of the puppies whimpered.

"We'll head back as soon as the worst part of the storm passes," he said.

"Promise?"

"Should I take this personal?" he asked. "You don't like being stranded out here with me?"

"Actually, I might like it too much." Her voice had taken on a husky undertone, and she lifted her lashes as she said it, the shine in her eyes a definite come-on and had nothing to do with the overhead lights. She leaned dangerously close, and he felt the knot in his stomach pulse a surge of lust through his entire body, and his erection rose and throbbed against the confines of his soaked denim jeans.

"You're very tempting," he said.

"Then kiss me," she said, her breath a whisper, warm and wispy against his mouth and cheek. She shrugged the blanket from her shoulders.

"Do you really think we should?" he asked, knowing that the answer was yes and no. They should, but they shouldn't. And he knew in that instant that he wanted her more than he'd ever wanted any woman in his life.

She slid her hands around his neck and pulled him gently toward her, closing the miniscule distance between them, and when their lips met, she said, "Quit thinking and kiss me."

CHAPTER EIGHTEEN

೧೦⊶ல்

Celeste's mouth melted against his, softly at first, but when he deepened their kiss, an urgent promise of undeniable pleasure took over. She ran her hands up the back of his neck into his hair, holding him close, and his breath blew warm against her cheek, his entire length relaxing against her as he wrapped his arms around her. She reclined, the blanket a soft barrier between her and the bed of hay. She inhaled the sweet scent of the straw.

"I didn't mean for this to happen," she said against his lips, unnerved by the aching heat coiled deep inside her.

"Ummm, but I'm glad it is," he said against her neck, his lips tickling a row of tiny kisses until he stopped and nuzzled her collarbone, the sensation tantalizingly lush. Her heart hitched up a beat and her breath caught in her throat.

She didn't realize she had an erogenous zone there. Who knew?

Bracing himself on his elbow, Max peeled away the damp towel and tossed it aside, then slowly lifted the hem of her dress. Celeste pushed his hand away.

"Not fair. This time you should be the first to take your clothes off," she said, her voice sounding wispy, the idea of seeing him naked flaring lascivious thoughts.

"That's what you think?" he said, the corner of his mouth pulling up in a playful, naughty grin, his brow lifting in question. "So you don't want me to do this?" He pushed one of her straps off her shoulder, allowing the tips of his fingers to trail down her arm, leaving a track of goose bumps in their wake, and her nipples tightened at the thought of him touching her all over.

"No, I don't. I believe I should do this." She unhooked the buttons of his shirt, allowing it to swing open, and she pushed it free exposing his chest and abs. Celeste ran her fingers across the bulge of his pecs, his chest smooth, enjoying his skin prickle beneath her touch. When she lingered, rubbing her fingers across his hardened nipples, his lids fluttered closed, and he reached up and pulled her hand away, holding it tightly.

"You're driving me insane...you have no idea what you're doing to me." He opened his eyes. "Possibly I shouldn't confess this, but I've wanted you since the moment I first met you."

"Nice," she managed to say, her voice low, "but you're still undressing first." He moved his arms so she could shuck off his shirt and toss it aside. She relished the sight of him. "Nice body. All the hard work, I presume." She wanted to touch him again, but resisted the urge, the enjoyment of looking enough for the moment.

"And workouts five days a week." He leaned toward her and cupped her cheek with his palm and kissed her softly on the corner of her mouth. A tender, delicate kiss. More caring than what she was accustomed to. "You are absolutely, breathtakingly beautiful," he said on a whisper, still brushing his mouth against hers, his hand running along the length of her thigh. "The sight of you warms my heart."

Her heart sprinted, and her senses raged in turmoil. Max was the most charming, the sexiest, man she'd ever encountered in her life. She knew she should put a stop to their mutual seduction, but there was no way she could halt what they'd put into motion. And she didn't want to. She inhaled a ragged breath, her heart pounding, frightened by her sensual vulnerability.

"I'll admit there's more than my heart getting warm here," she said, trembling, eager for him to touch her all over, to experience his skin pressed against hers. She reached for the button on his jeans and clumsily worked it free, then grasped the pull on his zipper and inched it downward.

Abruptly, Max rolled away and stood, kicking his shoes free, then stripped his jeans from his hips and down his legs. He stood before her, the glory of his erection still covered by his boxer briefs.

"Shall I do the honor?" he asked, his voice hoarse and low, sultry, as he indicated his last piece of clothing, the cotton damp and clinging, exposing every inch of his enormous bulge. "Or do you want to?"

"Allow me." Enjoying the sight of him, Celeste stretched languorously against the blanket before she raised herself with deliberate slowness. She held his gaze, brushed her wet curls over her shoulder with a flick of her hand, her eyes never leaving his until she knelt before him. She shifted her attention to her mission, hooked her fingers in his waistband, and pulled. "Oh my," she said on a soft breath, his endowment another compelling factor to his charm.

"Now is it my turn to free you from that drenched mess of a dress?" Max asked, and she forced her mesmerized gaze to shift upward to his face. "Reach up," he said, and she raised her arms over her head so he could lift her dress free. He tossed it aside, and it landed with a plop next to the towel. He knelt beside her and then eased her back against the crisp cotton of the blanket. "I can't believe this," he said. "I'm a lucky man." He lifted her hand and kissed her fingertips.

She quivered, and it wasn't from the cold. Her body was on fire, and the pulsing between her thighs left her short of breathless. The only thing left between the two of them was her thong, and in a frenzy she reached to wrench it free. He stopped her.

"I'll take care of that," he said into her hair as he planted kisses along her temple. Then he leisurely trailed his mouth across her cheek, finally reclaiming her lips. She kissed him back, a deep kiss, all tongue, and the whole time she wished he was inside of her. He lifted away and trailed his kisses down the pulse of her throat, traveling lower, pressing his mouth against her chest, his lips warm and soft.

When he reached her breasts, he stopped and lifted his head.

"You wouldn't mind if I—" He lowered his head again and flicked his tongue, barely grazing her nipple, causing it to peak into a tightened, darkening nub. Her breasts felt full, heavy, and when he cupped his hands underneath them, a steady heat pulsed through her entire body.

"Could we please hurry," Celeste asked on a deep inhalation, arching her back and pressing her body closer to his. His erection pulsed between them. "I want you now."

"Some things shouldn't be rushed." Max smiled, watching her through half-lidded eyes. He took her hand and placed it on his chest, and she felt the tattoo of his heart beating in rhythm with her own. "I want you so much, my heart is about to explode."

His gaze held hers, provocative, sensual. She reached up and traced the arc of his brow, the hairs smooth beneath her touch.

"You're stunning," she said, overcome by his physique, the weight of his body braced above her. Gorgeous to the point he bordered on beautiful. Charming to the point he could tease her affections out of retirement. Her hand drifted across the stubble of his cheek, and then she traced her finger along his squared jaw, across his lips.

"You, my sweet Celeste, are exquisite," he said against her finger. "Now where were we?"

He dipped his head and found her lips again. And her mind and body continued their steamy journey toward sexual bliss, her last lucid thought zipping through her mind. Her resolution was doomed. She'd realized it the moment the storm had trapped them in the barn. Celeste might have sworn off men, but there was no way in hell she could swear off Max Riley. Not now, not ever.

Constraint. The thought buzzed through his overloaded brain, and Max focused his attentions on Celeste as he held her in his arms and kissed her. He'd dreamed of making love to her for the past two weeks and imagined their first time together as special, memorable, certainly not a seduction in a barn. But there was no way in hell he could stop what they'd put into motion, so regardless of their surroundings, Max planned on relishing every inch, every curve of her enticing body.

His heart drummed a surge of happiness. She was beautiful, but his feelings ran deeper than her physical allure. Half of his thoughts struggled with his common sense; he truly believed he could care about her, and the realization made him want her even more. Which was preposterous, because he had no business thinking of any long-term liaison with her. Max lifted his head and took in the sight of her, making a mental note that all the women he'd known before paled in comparison. He didn't believe Celeste could possibly look more phenomenal than she did lying beneath him on a bed of hay.

"Hey," she said, pursing her mouth, her lips pinked and slightly swollen. She grabbed the back of his head and pulled his face close to hers. "Come back."

"You like to give orders?" he asked, the idea of a woman taking control a titillating aphrodisiac.

"Sometimes," she said. "Kiss me."

"At your command." He leaned into her and their lips touched again.

He adored kissing her; it was the best excuse in the world to smell the scent of her, to touch her face, to play with her hair. And he especially loved her lips, soft and full. Overcome with the need to taste her, he sucked her bottom lip into his mouth, and she moaned, humming a delicious vibration through him. His erection surged, and he had to concentrate, using sheer willpower to keep from giving in to his desire to enter her.

He deepened the kiss, running his hands across her breasts, then down her waist, hips, and thighs. He cupped her buttocks and pulled her closer, and she gripped him tighter, her body moist with the heat between them.

"Now. Now," she said and sighed, a breathy, heated sound. She pressed her body closer to his and wrapped her arms around his neck. "I need you now."

Max couldn't believe his good fortune. She craved him as much as he desired her.

He drew back and studied her face. Her eyes fluttered half open, and she gazed at him.

"You have no idea how much I want you," Max said.

"I think I do," she said. She smiled and slid her hand between them, wrapping her fingers around the length of him, and he gasped at her touch. Her warm fingers gently squeezed and every ounce of blood left his brain and surged south, causing his balls to ache and his erection to swell rock hard. "Make that know," she said.

"Do you?" he asked.

She nodded with a sly smile, then wriggled her hips back and forth and managed to drive his desire higher. Max felt as eager and out of control as a teenage boy in the backseat of a car and realized he needed a distraction, so he decided her breasts required special attention. He cupped them both in his palms and rubbed his thumbs leisurely back and forth across her nipples.

"Do you like this?"

"Hmmm." He took her hum as a yes by the way her nipples tightened beneath his touch and she nipped her lower lip with her teeth.

"How about—" He leaned down and kissed her left breast, then swirled the tip of his tongue around the pert, hardened nub. "This?"

When she didn't respond, he discovered her head nodding in the affirmative while she squeezed her eyes shut and arched her hips.

"Open your eyes," he said. "I want you to watch me while I enjoy you like my favorite ice cream." Her lids fluttered open and once he could see the bright blue of her irises, he continued finding out exactly what she liked and what she loved.

"What flavor am I?" She sounded breathless.

"Pistachio." He grinned. "From now on, I think," he leaned down and licked a path from the creamy swell of her breast to her nipple, "I'll call you Pistachio." He grazed his teeth across her nipple and bit it softly, and she pushed her pelvis against his thigh. She felt warm and wet, and he focused on her breast as he sucked and his tongue rubbed against her puckered nipple.

He shifted and stroked hot fingers across her thong before grasping the elastic and gently tugging. She lifted her hips, and he whisked her underwear down her legs and tossed it aside.

"Be careful," she said, twisting her head and watching the flimsy silk land. "Don't throw it too far."

"Relax," he said, turning her face back to his. "I'll buy you a dozen more." Max slid his hand down her belly and across her pelvis, and in response she ground her hips upward, rotating herself against his hand. "We need to concentrate on what makes you feel good, so we can do it over and over again."

"Everything feels good," she said on a hum, as he rubbed his hand downward and parted her, his fingers gliding across her sleek, wet skin. Her hips picked up a faster rhythm. An acute throbbing began in his temple and matched her pace, pulsing its way into his erection. His brain and body were in chaos, and he knew he couldn't wait any longer. He wanted her too much. Rising to his knees, Max reached for his jeans and pulled out his wallet, grabbed a condom, then tossed his wallet aside.

"You're prepared. Good," she said, lifting herself on her elbow.

He tore open the package and quickly sheathed himself. He pushed down on his erection, and the tension inside his gut twisted and his balls tightened with anticipation.

"Always safe," he said.

"I like your motto, among other things." Her voice sounded low and thick, and Max thought it was undoubtedly the sexiest sound he'd ever heard.

He moved back in place beside her, and she wrapped her arms around his neck and clung to him.

"Do me now," she said, as his erection nudged her leg. He rolled on top of her, his thighs tensing. She pushed her pelvis upward, and he slid between her legs, her luscious warmth enveloping him. He held her hips and moved forward. She gasped, and he exhaled, the slippery friction shooting sheer delight through his nerve endings.

And then they found their tempo, and they rocked in a sensual dance, their rhythm quickening with frenzied thrusts, until her nails dug into his back. She muffled her scream against his shoulder as she climaxed, her sleek wetness pulsing around him, and unable to contain himself, he joined her with his own explosive orgasm, his body shuttering.

Max clutched her close and took a deep breath to calm his pounding heart. He was happier than he'd ever been in his life.

And as he pulled away, he already missed her.

CHAPTER NINETEEN

ॐ

Incredible. Celeste reclined against the hay, staring upward at the rafters overhead. Forcing herself to count to twenty-five before she said anything, she turned her head so she could see him. Fantastic. He lay beside her, a serene satisfied countenance on his face, a smile playing at his lips. Reaching over he took her hand and entwined his fingers with hers. Phenomenal.

She'd experienced the best sex of her life. The most intense orgasm. Ever. Extraordinary. She smiled and wanted to tap her toes, but forced herself to remain still. To relish the afterglow. Possibly the evening was over the top because of the fresh, country air, or the fact a storm raged outside, thunder rolling and rumbling, but moving farther away. Rain still pattered a soothing racket on the tin roof. She shivered, realizing she was cold, the heat of passion sizzling away, the chill of the barn forcing her back to reality.

Max rolled over onto his side and pulled the edge of the blanket around her.

"Better?" he asked.

"Yes, thanks." She snuggled closer to him, and he wrapped his arms around her, holding her, the same grin pulling at his mouth. "Why are you smiling?" she asked.

"Because I'm incredibly happy," he said. "And I haven't felt this content in a long time. Actually, I don't think I've ever felt as satisfied as I do right now. Thank you." Max lifted her hand to his lips and planted a kiss to her palm. She hadn't realized men could be so caring, so gentle. Sweet. But then, Max wasn't any man.

And the scary thing about it was that she felt the same way. Content. She told herself she shouldn't be comfortable, but her heart told her to go for it.

Max held her close a few moments longer, the silence between them soothing, the drumming of rain slowing down to a few tappity taps, the wind no longer howling, the thunder dissipating in the distance. The storm had passed, but what turbulence lay in store for her now that she'd slept with Max? And the fact she liked him. Probably too much. But she pushed the thoughts away, determined not to allow anything to dampen her blissful mood.

Max rolled to his feet and reached for his underwear.

"As much as I don't want to, we probably should get dressed and head back to the house," he said, pulling his boxer briefs onto his hips.

Celeste clutched the blanket around herself and sat up. "Do you think anyone has missed us yet?"

"With the game going on, probably not." He picked up her dress and wrung it out. She cringed as he twisted the delicate crepe, knowing the sundress was a total loss. "I think that's about as dry as I can get it." He handed the dress to her, and she slipped it over her head, then pulled the blanket back around her. Max picked up his jeans and fluffed them out, the drenched denim making a whacking sound. He tried to squeeze them, and Celeste laughed.

"Good luck with that."

"Here, help me." He handed her the legs of the jeans. "Hold on tight and I'll twist." She grabbed and held on as he wound the jeans around, wringing out as much water as he could, his biceps bulging with the effort. "There," he said, giving them one last wrench. "Thanks for your help. We make a good team." He winked and flashed his smile.

"Anytime," she said and felt her cheeks flush warm, liking the idea of being a team with him. She wasn't sure if he was smooth or sweet, but at the moment it didn't matter.

"Now let's see how easy they'll be to get into."

"This should prove interesting," Celeste said, watching as he pushed first one foot then the other into the legs of the jeans. He pulled them to his knees then started wiggling his ass as he tugged them upward, finally managing to get them to his hips. Celeste laughed and clapped her hands.

"You did it. Great job. And an even better show."

"My pleasure to entertain you." He bowed, smiling. "I don't think this will be as entertaining," he said as he pulled on the chambray shirt and started to button it. Celeste reached up and moved his hands away.

"Let me do that for you." She stood and took her time fastening each button until she reached the collar, then she stood on her tip-toes and kissed him.

"Thanks," he said, when she pulled away.

"I'll button your shirt any time."

"No. I mean thanks. For spending time with me. I guess we owe a huge thanks to Sarge for running away, or we wouldn't have been stuck here in the barn together."

"You're right, because my plan was to avoid you," Celeste said, reaching for her thong and pulling it on.

"Why would you want to do that?" he asked. He pulled a huge piece of straw from her hair. "I've enjoyed the time we've spent together. Haven't you?"

"Yes, I have. In fact, I've enjoyed it too much."

"There no such thing as too much, if you take pleasure in someone's company." He turned her around. "Let me get the hay out of your hair. We might have some 'splaining to do if we get caught coming in the back door with your hair looking like this."

Celeste giggled as he pulled and tugged a handful of hay from her wayward curls. Then he turned her around and kissed her again.

"When we get back to the house, I suggest you take a hot shower. I'll meet you downstairs in thirty minutes. We'll catch the end of the game with everyone." He smiled and tucked a curl behind her ear. "Sound like a plan?"

"You meant the two of us hang out in front of everyone?" she asked, a nervous flutter causing her heart to skip a beat. "In front of your mom and Becca?"

"Yes, in front of everyone. Becca's concerns about me are unfounded and my mother needs to stay out of my business." He rubbed his hands through his hair. "I know it might not seem like it, but Serena means well, she simply has a poor sense of priorities sometimes." He took Celeste's hand and looked her in the eye. "I like you and I want to see more of you. A lot more of you."

"How will we be able to do that? We live over two hundred miles apart," she said, pointing out the obvious. "I have my career, you have your farm. I can't live here and you can't live in Atlanta." She was attracted to Max, but at the same time, she was aggravated by the conversation, the discussion squelching her earlier euphoria. "I want to see you too, but let's admit the fact there's not much of a chance for us to see each other. We can enjoy each other's company while I'm here, and maybe a few weekends here and there, but I'd prefer to keep it on the down-low so as not to upset anyone. Your mother. Becca. The girls."

If Trudi and Patrice found out she'd slept with Max, she'd never hear the end of it, especially after their conversation earlier in the day. She'd rather wait and see how things turned out between her and Max before she confessed anything to her friends. After all, she might not ever have the need to tell them.

"But to be honest, I'm not certain the long-distance thing would work out," Celeste added.

"So what you're saying is that you want to see me on the sly while you're here and then possibly indulge in a clandestine fling? But only maybe because you aren't sure it would work out?"

Celeste winced. Saying it like that did make it sound harsh. Uncaring. And that wasn't how she felt. At all. But she knew that's all it could be.

"Yes. For the weekend. For now," she said, knowing it wouldn't be enough, but she had to try and be reasonable for the two of them. After all, not only was there the geographical undesirability of their predicament, there was also the ex-wife on the lam. And the kids. She forged on, refusing to make eye contact. "Then I'll go back home to my life and you'll stay here and settle back into yours. You won't even realize I'm gone."

"You really believe that?" He exhaled slowly, then lifted her chin with his fingers. "Tell me again that you seriously believe we'll be satisfied with a weekend fling and you'll be content with never seeing me again."

"I'll see you at the wedding," she said, ignoring his meaning.

"There's no chance we could see each other before?" he asked.

She moved her head in the negative, and he released her chin.

Max's heart squeezed at Celeste's response.

"It's daunting," she said.

He felt bruised. He'd finally met a woman he could potentially care about, and she had cold feet. Make that glacier feet with icicle toes.

"Work with me," he said and decided to lighten the mood. "You're stomping me like a barrel of grapes. Do you need to turn me into a fine wine? Someone worth having dinner with?" She laughed. He felt like there might be hope yet.

"You're already dinner worthy. More than dinner, actually." She chewed on her bottom lip. "There's so much against us to begin with. Is it fair to start something?"

"What's against us? The miles?"

"It's not only the GU factor."

"Then what is it?"

"Your ex. The kids. You have dogs. Your mother. Becca." She exhaled a deep sigh. "And I have my career. Do I need to name anymore?"

"My kids? What do they have to do with this?"

"Well. I'm not particularly a kid person, and you have them. There are children in your life."

"Yes, that tends to happen when one has offspring. They're my kids, and they're pretty spectacular, even if I say so myself. But my having kids shouldn't weigh against me regarding the fact I want to see you again," Max said. "I want to spend time with you. I'm not asking you to spend time with me and them." He would need to get to know her better before he considered introducing her as anything more than a friend. Merging their relationship with the kids was certainly something they could tackle in the future if things worked out between them, but they'd never know if they didn't try.

"And I certainly don't intend on bringing the dogs with me when I visit, and my ex shouldn't be an issue. I haven't heard a word from her since she left. During our divorce proceedings, we communicated through our attorneys, and when it was finalized, she didn't even show up."

"That might eventually be an issue," Celeste said. "Or one day she might show up. Your mother is convinced she'll return and reclaim her family." Celeste fidgeted with her fingers. "There's a lot to consider here. I knew I should have stuck with my conviction."

"What was that?" Max asked. He didn't recall her discussing any strong principles.

"I'd sworn off men," she said without much passion. "Not long before I met you, actually. It's been a battle to keep my word ever since." She glanced at him, her countenance accusing, but her lips smiling. "If I hadn't met you, I would have kept my word."

"Are you saying I'm too tempting to resist?" He wiggled his eyebrows, enjoying the way she eyed him.

"I'm not saying that at all," she said. He felt confident she was kidding from the expression on her face and the way she purred the last few words.

"Then why don't we name the good things we have going for us?" Max said.

"Okay. Shoot."

"You intrigue me."

"You scare the hell out of me."

"I don't think that can be classified as one of the good things. Try again," Max said. "Because I think you're unforgettable."

"I know you are," Celeste said. "I don't think I want to play this game."

"We aren't playing. This is serious. I'm trying to make sense of how I feel about you and why."

"What does that mean?" Celeste asked.

"I've known you for two weeks, and ever since I first met you—no, make that the moment I first saw you—I haven't been able to get you out of my mind, and I've wanted you in every possible way."

"In two weeks? I'm supposed to believe this?"

"It can happen. I'm living proof." He thumped his chest.

"You're too good to believe, and I don't." She stressed the negative.

"Believe me. I'm a fine Merlot, aged to perfection, and wanting to have dinner with you. Next weekend. In Atlanta. What do you say?" He stepped closer and stretched out his hand to her, but she side-danced and ducked out of his reach.

"What if I don't want to go to dinner?" She countered, and circled away when he moved toward her.

"Name it, whatever you want." He stopped in front of her, calculating how he could scoop her into his arms, knowing if he kissed her, she'd be his.

"What if I want to go to see a sappy chick flick and eat too much popcorn." She waltzed backward, slow and sexy, towards the barn door.

"I say, tell me what movie and where, and I'll purchase the tickets in advance on Fandango." He followed her as if she were the Pied Piper playing a magical tune.

"Or I'd rather paint my apartment. From top to bottom." She lifted her brow in challenge and stopped her retreat, her back against the barn door.

"I'll bring my blue tape and finest Purdy brushes." He put one arm on either side of her, trapping her against the door.

"You would do that for me?" She batted her lashes, and he smiled. God, she was beautiful.

"I would do anything for you."

"What if there's a huge sale at Neiman's I don't want to miss?" She ran her tongue across her top lip, and he thought he would come out of his skin.

"I'll wear running shoes so I can keep up." He bent his head narrowing the distance between them, and Celeste laughed.

"A man willing to shop? I must really have you then," she said.

"Oh, you have me all right. So what do you say? You won't keep me a secret. And dinner in Atlanta next weekend?"

"Yes, anything you want," Celeste said, lifting her mouth to meet his. "How could I ever say no?"

CHAPTER TWENTY

❧❧

"I should have told him no."

Celeste paced a path from the front door to her couch and back, while she clasped her hands and tried to stop their trembling. She'd daydreamed through every waking hour over the past week thinking about seeing him again. And now that he was on his way, she found herself dreading their encounter, but at the same time craving his touch. To absorb his warmth. Smell the distinct male scent of him.

She glanced at the clock. Two o'clock. He'd left Tyler almost four hours earlier.

Hot desire curled between her thighs, making her jeans feel too tight. She rushed into the bedroom and stood in front of the full-length mirror: skinny jeans, camisole and boyfriend cardigan made a perfect ensemble, especially combined with her new ankle boots.

But was it right? She turned her wrist in order to see her watch. Did she have time to change? Of course she didn't. She made her way back to the living room.

What had she been thinking? Her and Max?

He had kids. But he kissed like a dream, and he was sweet and kind and thoughtful.

And he lived four hours away. But Max made love as if the only reason for his existence was to ensure her happiness. And he knew exactly where and when to touch her.

Reality check: he had an ex and…kids. Two cute, irresistible kids. And she had her career, and there was no room in her life for a divorced man with children.

And no way in hell did a long distance relationship fit into her plans.

But she liked him. Possibly too much.

And he would arrive any minute.

The doorbell chimed, and Celeste jumped. Her pulse galloped a race of its own, and she wiped her palms across her upper thighs. She could always hide in the bedroom and act as if she weren't home.

Another ring followed and then a third in quick succession.

"I should have said no." She reached for the doorknob.

Celeste smiled her megawatt smile, and Max felt as if he'd been sucker punched: a perfect upward blow to his diaphragm. He'd anticipated seeing her again with a teenaged angst, which he found both exciting and confusing. The drive up to Atlanta had seemed to take forever, and finally after days of anticipation, she stood in front of him.

"Hey there," she said and took a step back so he could enter.

She was as beautiful as he remembered, maybe more so, and he had to remind himself to breathe.

"For you," he said and held out a bouquet of roses. He stepped inside, and she closed the door behind him.

"Beautiful," she said, taking the flowers from him. "What a stunning color. They're—"

"Lavender," he said. "Sterling Silver is the name." She moved through the living room toward the kitchen, and he followed, stopping at the edge of the bar that separated the two rooms.

"You know roses?" she asked and flashed him another one of her gorgeous smiles. One of her real ones, not the one she used on television. She opened the under-the-sink cabinet and pulled out a vase and began filling it with water. "Which wouldn't surprise me."

"Nah, the girl at the shop told me," he said. He hiked his butt onto the bar stool and glanced around. The living room had a comfortable someone-really-lives here ambiance to it. Bright blue and green throw pillows graced the couch and books lined a huge bookshelf. "Nice place. But I can tell you don't entertain children very often."

"Pardon?" she asked with a quizzical scrunch to her brow

"White?" He pointed to her couch and an overstuffed chair.

"Oh, yeah," she said. "No kids here. I see my nieces and nephews at my parents' house." She arranged the flowers in the vase and set them on the bar. "In fact, I rarely have company. I almost always meet the girls out. We used to hang at Becca's place sometimes. Before she met Marcus."

"Speaking of," Max said. "I didn't call Marcus. He doesn't know I'm here."

"I'd wondered if you were going to mention your visit to him." she said with a kitten-in-headlights expression on her face. "Becca doesn't know either."

"You didn't mention our dream date?" he asked.

"No," she said. "I didn't tell any of the girls you were coming." She joined him at the bar. "And what's this about a dream date?" She smiled. A real smile that made him want to slide his hands around her smooth, pretty neck and pull her to him, so he could kiss her throat. She was close enough for him to smell her perfume, and he remembered how the scent of her ramped his libido into overdrive.

"Dream. Date," he said, sounding like a fool. "Yes, our dream date." He forced himself to focus on the plans he'd made. There'd be time for kissing later. "First, a movie." He pulled two tickets from his back pocket. "How does Breaking the Rules sound for starters?"

"Really?" she laughed. A funny, sort of girl giggle that made a warm, fuzziness settle over his chest. And from the delighted expression on her face, he assumed he'd chosen correctly.

"As I understand, it's the number one romantic comedy. You approve?" he asked.

"Oh, yes." She grinned. "Perfect."

"Good." He looked at his watch. "We have exactly thirty-eight minutes to get there before show time." He stood. "Are you ready?"

"As ready as I'll ever be." She slid off the stool. "Let me grab my purse."

How could she ever be ready for a man like Max Riley? He helped her into the car and positioned her seatbelt, his hand brushing against her arm. A tiny tingle of lust zinged through her, all the way down to her feet where it sizzled, leaving her toes curled. Celeste smiled a thank you when he closed the passenger door. He walked to the driver's side.

"What? No Porsche?" she asked when he slid behind the wheel.

"Not for a road trip. I thought the hybrid was a better choice. Better for the environment. And mileage."

She liked the fact he thought green. Actually, she liked everything about him. She'd forgotten how good looking he was until she'd opened the door, and her heart palpitated into a stroke-worthy frenzy. The flowers were gorgeous and unexpected. And she'd been especially thankful for something to do with her hands, because her first instinct had been to grab him and tear his clothes off. She'd been fighting the urge to kiss him ever since he first arrived.

Celeste watched him from the corner of her eye as he guided the car through the parking lot of the apartment complex and onto Virginia Avenue, his hands strong and certain on the wheel; everything about him exuded confidence.

"So, a movie first?" she asked. When he'd mentioned dream date, she couldn't help but wonder what else he had in store. "Then what?"

"I remember what you said in the barn," Max said. He raised his brows and wiggled them. "As I recall, you mentioned shopping. A huge sale at Neiman's to be exact."

"Shopping?" She couldn't believe he would take her shopping.

"Yes. I googled it and there's a huge sale this weekend at Lenox. And after we load up on too much buttery popcorn, we're hitting the sales."

"Are you sure?"

"Absolutely. I believe I owe you a thong or two."

"Only one," she said. He remembered everything. Most men she knew would have forgotten her lost thong the minute they discovered its fate of flying overboard.

"And dinner afterwards," Max said. "I made reservations at Chops."

"Chops. Great choice," she said. He had no need to pull out all his tricks: flowers, a great romantic comedy, shopping, and dinner at Chops. Seriously? She was already a sure thing. She craved him more than she'd ever wanted any man, and it took every ounce of willpower she possessed to keep from jumping his bones in the middle of Saturday afternoon traffic. A friends-with-benefits fling with Max might prove more enticing than she'd originally thought.

Celeste repressed the urge to hum as she unlocked her apartment door. Her feet ached after their sprint through Lenox Mall, and she still couldn't believe that Max knew how to shop. He hadn't complained at all regardless of how many times she stopped to check out a deal. And the dinner at Chops was sheer perfection. No other way to describe it. Max certainly knew how to impress.

"Thanks for a great time," he said. He followed her into the apartment and dropped her shopping bags, one of them from Victoria's Secret held her replacement thong, onto the dining room table.

"No. Thank you." She plopped her purse down next to the bags and turned to face him. "I hope you don't mind, but these boots are coming off." She pulled off her boots.

"I think I'll join you." Max eased out of his shoes and socks, then wiggled his toes in the carpet. "The mall trip was reminiscent of walking the lower forty acres at the farm." He laughed, and the sound filled her heart with a surge of happiness.

"You certainly delivered everything you promised, and almost all that I bargained for in the barn," she said.

"Almost?" he asked. "What did I miss?"

"Painting my apartment from top to bottom."

"Well, we can catch that next weekend. I'll come equipped with the drop cloths, tape and brushes. Tell me the color, and I'll have the paint too." He moved closer, and she breathed in the crisp, sexy scent of him.

"No need to paint. The apartment's good as is." She laughed and held up her hand, placing it on his chest. And the strength of him, steel hard, beneath her hand rocked her with a surge of want.

Next weekend? She needed to make it through the night. She hadn't intended to allow him to weasel his way into her life, but he'd managed to talk her into what had turned out to be the perfect date. A faint memory of her swearing off men flittered in the back of her mind, but the left side of her brain where all of her common sense resided apparently went on holiday because she couldn't remember why she'd sworn off men in the first place. Max had totally blown her vow to give up the opposite sex.

He glanced down at her hand and lifted a brow.

"Too close?" he asked.

"Is there such a thing," she said and laughed again, a forced noise that made her sound as nervous as she felt. She dropped her hand and stepped around him. "How about a glass of wine? Or a beer?" They hadn't discussed sleeping arrangements when they'd made their plans, but she knew as well as he did where a drink could lead.

"What no tequila?" he asked and feigned disappointment. "Have I taught you nothing?"

"Sorry." Celeste winced. She should have thought to purchase a bottle. "I didn't think—"

"I'm teasing. A beer would be great." He followed her into the kitchen and moved behind her when she opened the refrigerator door. "Let me help you with that." He grabbed a beer and the bottle of wine, his thighs brushing against hers as he leaned forward. A spark flickered between them. She stepped back and leaned against the counter. He'd felt it too; she could tell by his demeanor, and the way he stepped back as if he'd been shocked.

"Wine glass?" he asked.

"Behind you." She pointed to the cupboard.

He busied himself with pouring her wine and opening his beer. He handed her the glass and tilted his bottle. "A toast?"

Max moved closer, warmth radiating from his body, igniting a flush that warmed her from head to toe, and she lost the ability to talk. She loved the scent of him, and his nearness made her head swim and an unusual giddiness filled her with an obscene delight. She hoped she wasn't smiling like the Cheshire cat, but he didn't seem to notice.

"To Celeste, may every day be happier than today," he said. He clinked his beer to her glass and then took a swig.

"Nice," she said. "I like. And here's to you, Max Riley. Thank you for today." She took a sip of wine, and he stepped beside her.

He slipped the glass from her unresisting fingers and put it on the counter next to the fridge along with his beer.

"Now, let me do what I've waited all day to do." He cupped her cheeks with his hands and tilted her face upward. He was so close that his breath fluttered past her ear and tickled her neck.

"And what would that be?" she dared to ask.

Max wrapped his hands around her waist and lifted her onto the counter. The air around them seemed to crackle and pop.

"This." He rested his hips between her thighs, and his mouth touched hers in a tentative kiss, a sweet caress. He lifted his head, releasing her from the kiss, and they both seemed to hold their breath.

"Wow." Celeste exhaled. "All day, huh?" She curled her arms around his neck.

"What I imagined doesn't compare to actually kissing you." He hummed against her lips, and the vibration sizzled its way from her nipples straight to her crotch.

"There's no reason for you imagine any longer." She pressed her mouth to his and kissed him, escalating the sweet kiss to a ravenous one, all mouth and tongue. She wanted him, and she wanted to make sure he knew it. He tightened his embrace and returned her kiss, his mouth warm and moist against hers, their tongues dancing a sensuous promise of sex.

His body heat radiated against her, his biceps and abs hard, and all she could think about was him inside her. He pulled her to him, and she leaned against his chest, as he dipped his head and claimed her mouth again. His erection swelled and rubbed against her jeans, the delectable pressure causing her to wiggle herself closer. She ran her fingers through his short, cropped hair, across his neck, and down his back, enjoying his solid muscles beneath her hands.

His hands slid underneath her camisole and cupped her breasts, and when he flicked his thumbs across the lace of her bra, her nipples peaked taunt and strained, and all she could think about was his mouth and the wonderful happy trail it was capable of creating. She moaned.

With deft proficiency, Max relieved her of the boyfriend sweater, and left her upper body clad in her silk camisole and lace bra, the cool air in the kitchen doing little to chill her hot, toe-curling need to do him.

He slipped the delicate straps of the camisole from her shoulder and the pads of his fingers left a trail of tingly bliss in their wake. His touch made her hot, and she loved it.

Celeste wrapped her hands around his neck and hitched her hips forward, his hardness pressed against her. As he planted kisses on the plane of her shoulder, she allowed her hands to run down his back, until she could reach the bottom of his shirt. With one quick movement, she pulled it up and over his head. No way would she allow him to strip her first.

"Yum," she said. The sight of him made her sizzle like melted butter on a high heat. His skin glistened in the diffused track-lighting of the kitchen, and his nipples peaked tight. She leaned down and licked a path from one to the other, and his muscles tensed beneath her touch.

"Let me make this an equal playing field. Lift your arms." He pulled the camisole over her head and dropped it on the counter with one hand, while he unhooked her bra with the other. The delicate lace fell away, and he tossed it aside.

"Beautiful," he said. All of his attention focused on her breasts, as he cupped them with his palms. "You are perfection." He bent his head and sucked a nipple into his mouth, nipping it with his teeth, softly, causing her nipples to tingle and throb. A shiver worked its way through her abdomen, and she groaned a guttural pleasure deep in her throat.

"You like?" he asked.

"Very much."

"Good, because I have a few more things I'd like to lick and bite on you."

Celeste slid her hands to the top of his waistband, where his erection surged, hard and enormous.

"Ditto," she said. She unhooked his belt buckle and pushed it aside, working on the button of his jeans until it wiggled free. Although feeling impatient, she inched down the stretched-tight zipper, running her tongue across her upper lip in anticipation. She hooked her thumbs into the waistband of his jeans and tugged until they were past his hips so they could drop to the floor. He kicked them aside and stood before her clad in his boxer briefs.

"Appears someone's glad to see me?" she teased.

"You keep getting ahead of me," he said. Max lifted her from the counter, and with uncanny speed, her jeans were discarded and before she realized what was happening he'd slid her back onto the counter. "Now we're even."

The granite was cold beneath her bare buttocks, the lacey silk of a thong doing little to cover her. Max brushed his hands up the side of her thighs, while he nuzzled kisses into the bend of her neck.

"You're perfection," he said, moving his palms inward in order to meet at the intersection of her legs. He pressed his thumbs against her crotch, and she let out a soft moan, his touch inundating every nerve in her body with the need for release. Thoughts of her king-sized bed fifteen feet away began to surface, but he slipped his finger under the edge of the lace and pulled it aside, teasing her, and the idea of her bed fizzled into the background of her mind.

"Oh, please," she said, but couldn't find the words to express what she wanted, so she arched her back and pushed her hips forward instead. She yearned for him to touch her, his fingers to caress her, and when his finger found its way home, a sliver of light shimmered in the back of her brain. He stroked her with a circular motion before slipping inside.

"You're wet."

Wet didn't come close to describing her body's reaction, and the only relevant thought she could muster was the need to have him inside of her. Deep inside her.

"I want you now," she said, the idea of her comfortable bed dissipating along with every thrust of his pleasure-giving fingers. She ground her pelvis against his hand. "Now." Her voice was breathy, heated.

She pushed at his boxers, and he reached down to help her shuck them down his legs. He grabbed his jeans and pulled out a condom.

"I've thought about making love to you every waking minute this past week," he said.

"I think I've been dreaming about this my entire life," she said. She'd never desired any man the way she wanted Max. He ignited a passion she'd never experienced before.

He slipped her panties off and left her naked and exposed. His for the taking.

"Wrap your legs around me," he said, and she followed his instructions, circling her arms around his, his erection nudging the wet sleekness between her thighs. "Are you ready for me?" he asked, his voice jagged, husky. Low.

"Yes, oh yes. Yes. Yes." She thrust her pelvis forward, and he slid an inch inside her. She gasped. "More." She wanted him inside her. She wanted him to fill her up.

She ground her hips in circles, and he pushed in a few more inches. She grabbed the back of his head and pulled him to her.

"I want all of you. Now."

And he obliged, driving forward until his thighs met hers, and she let out a small scream. Her body shuddered, as tiny ripples of pleasure spread throughout her body, vibrating until her ears rang.

He waited and when her trembling subsided, he began to move, and she met him thrust for thrust. They moved in unison, with complete abandon, and she dug her nails into his lower back, pulling his hips closer. Desire burned until she reached a frenzy of pent up friction, and her body's need for release took over, and wave after wave of her orgasm slammed through her. When all the tiny slivers of her nerve endings consummated their seizure of pleasure, Celeste realized that Max had stopped moving and was holding her, still perched on his erection.

She'd never be able to drink another glass of wine at the bar again without thinking of Max.

"My turn?" he asked.

Max lifted Celeste from the bar, her legs still wrapped tightly around his waist, and walked toward the bedroom. She nestled her face on his shoulder and hummed a contented sound that made him feel powerful. Wanted. Good.

He enjoyed the way she made him feel about himself.

When he reached her bed, he withdrew and eased her down against the pillows and braced himself above her. He couldn't believe he'd managed to hold back, but he didn't want to come too soon. He planned to pleasure her the entire night. He wanted to rock her world and leave her wanting more.

He cupped each of her breasts with one of his hands and traced his thumbs across her nipples, hardening them into tiny peaks of darkened pink. He leaned down and grazed first one and then the other with his mouth, sucking and nibbling until she writhed beneath.

She reached for his erection, which surged upward against his belly.

"I want you again," she said.

He gasped when her fingers wrapped around him and slid down his shaft. He grabbed her hand and pulled it away.

"No," he said. "It's my turn to pleasure you. Lie still and let me show you what I have in store for you."

He parted her with his fingers and dipped his head between her thighs. He flicked his tongue across her and took his time raking his tongue round and round. Flick, lick, flick. She squirmed and arched her back, pushing herself closer to his face. He pressed a finger inside and danced a double duty, until he closed his mouth on her and sucked until she came again, pounding her fists against the sheets.

"Are you trying to drive me insane?" she asked. An expression of sublime bliss settled on her face. "Because I want you again. Inside me."

On his knees above her, he lifted her legs onto his shoulders, and he eased himself between her legs and pushed into her. She gasped. He sighed.

She felt warm and wet—her tightness encasing him the most delicious sensation he'd ever experienced. Better than the first time.

Max began to rock, gently at first, before he built up speed, pushing into her, and she mirrored his thrusts, time and again. Until she rotated her pelvis and the unrestrained buzz pulsated straight through him. He throbbed with the need for release but forced himself to think about nothing, to make his mind go numb, until the need to come subsided, and he picked up his pace again.

She muttered breathy moans, grabbing wads of sheets until she reached out and ran her hands up and down the muscles of his arms. And he pumped deeper, holding his breath against the rare, intense feeling, until he had no other choice but to exhale in a rush of air. He bit her ankle and pumped his hips with a ferocity that she met until he couldn't hold back any longer, and he climaxed. He held onto her legs, still propped on his shoulders, a wave of goose flesh erupting over his entire body. He held himself in place until the over-sensitive phenomenon of post-orgasm subsided. He settled beside her, sweaty and spent.

"Wowza," she said. "That was incredible." She turned her head on the pillow so she could watch him.

"Glad you enjoyed it," he said. The way he felt about Celeste wasn't only about the sex. The sex was the cherry on top. Celeste made him comfortable as if he'd found home; she made everything more pleasurable. And he planned on making her return the same sentiment about him.

"You didn't plan on sleeping tonight, did you?" she asked.

"No," he said. "Not at all."

Because he knew the minute he'd pulled away that he hadn't had enough.

Sunday afternoon, Celeste stood in the apartment parking lot in the warm September sun as Max drove away. He waved when he turned and disappeared from sight, and she stood there waving for a few moments after he was gone. Looking like an idiot and feeling like one too.

She hated to admit it, but the weekend, although a whirlwind, fell under the category of perfect. And she teetered on the precipice of liking him too much. She should have never allowed him to visit.

When Max'd wooed her into seeing him again, she should have said no. No with capital N capital O. That should have been her answer. And here she'd gone ahead and let him talk her into seeing him again next weekend.

For some unfathomable reason, she seemed to have a hard time turning him down. What had happened to her conviction to stay away from the dating world and focus on her career? Or remembering her rules?

If Trudi knew Celeste was seeing Max, Celeste could imagine Trudi ordering Celeste to "focus." But focus seemed to be the last thing she could do when Max Riley was around.

Now she'd have to worry about what she'd do if Becca and the girls found out. Or when her career put a screeching halt to the fling she knew they should have never begun.

CHAPTER TWENTY-ONE

৵৽৽

Celeste strode down the hallway on her way to meet with the program director. When she received the summons to report to Mr. Chandler's office, she instinctively realized her career was on warp-speed forward, and she'd have little time to offer Max. She ran her hand down her straightened locks and willed her heart to remain calm.

The past month had been a blissful whirlwind, and she'd enjoyed the past few weekends she'd spent with Max, every second of their nightly phone calls, and all the cute texts they'd shared. There was no doubt he was near perfect in every sense of the word, but her time had come, and if she wasn't mistaken, she was about to receive her coveted spot as the weekend AM anchor. The next rung on the ladder to her success. Finally.

She stopped in the hallway and gave her short-waist jacket a quick tug and made sure her pencil skirt was straight on her hips before she rapped a quick knock on the door.

"Come in."

Celeste took hold of the doorknob with a steady hand and opened the door.

"Ah, Celeste," Mr. Chandler said as she entered. He glanced at his watch. "Prompt as always. One of the many qualities I admire about you." He stood and indicated she should join him at his small conference table. "Please sit."

"Thank you, sir." She settled in a chair and waited while he joined her.

"You've done some great reporting lately, and I've followed your progress closely. Frankly, I'm delighted with what I've seen, and this coming Saturday I'm putting you on as weekend anchor." Mr. Chandler smiled and reached across the conference table ready to shake. "I'm excited to be the one to let you know."

Celeste grasped his extended hand and pumped it in acceptance.

"You won't regret this decision." Celeste managed to stop her smile before it widened into an idiotic grin. The warmth of pride spread across her chest, and she resisted the urge to place her hand across her heart to try to still it. She'd never felt this proud in her life.

AM weekend anchor today. Atlanta's premiere Primetime anchor tomorrow. Soon she'd be on her way to New York. Move over, Diane. Get ready to retire like Barbara.

Returning to the cubicle in the newsroom, she slumped into a chair and rested her head against the high back. She closed her eyes. Finally all of her hard work, and the major effort to never stumble over her words, had paid off. Could life be more perfect? The fast track for her career had arrived, and she wanted to stand up and yell woo hoo.

She jerked forward, and her eyes popped open.

Shit.

Max and their weekend plans.

Memories of the time she'd shared with him in Atlanta flooded her mind, including a sharp reminder that the upcoming weekend would be the last chance for Max to visit Atlanta before preparation for the peanut harvest would consume his days. Although they'd already discussed Celeste traveling to Magnolia Oaks during his busy season over the next few weeks, she'd had mixed emotions. After all, she'd see his kids again: the quiet and reserved Charlie and the irresistible Neecie.

The whole situation scared the hell out of her. And although Max seemed to idolize her, and she, in return, adored him, possibly her new position would be the perfect excuse to put an end to their fling. After all, a long-distance relationship with a divorced man with children was against her rules.

The trill sound of her cell phone interrupted her thoughts. No need to view the caller ID, the ring tone was dedicated to her mother.

She sighed before she answered.

"Hi, Mom."

"Hey, Precious. How's my baby girl?" Her mother, always in a good mood, sounded exceptionally chipper. "Do you have something to tell me?"

Celeste groaned. Of course her daddy already knew her good news. He and Dave Chandler were best friends; both of them had been at the station for years.

"You've already heard?"

"Yes, your father called me. We're both so proud of you."

"Thanks." Celeste could hear the happiness in her mother's voice and her own heart swelled with pride. She'd made it. Finally, she was on the way to the career her mother had given up.

"We want to take you out to dinner to celebrate. Are you free Saturday night?"

A dozen thoughts crashed and whirled inside Celeste's mind. She put the receiver down and rested her face in her hands. She'd need to call Max and cancel their weekend plans. Her heart hurt at the thought of missing their Sunday morning ritual of lying in bed watching the news, but there'd be no more watching the weekend morning report for her; she was now the anchor.

"Celeste?" Her mother's voice droned through the phone. "Did you hear me?"

Dinner to celebrate. She couldn't tell her parents no, but they didn't know anything about Max, and Celeste wasn't ready to tell them either. Actually, she didn't have a clue if she ever would. There was the remote possibility that her relationship with Max could lead to something someday, in a few years, but not now. Not so soon. She wanted to have fun, enjoy him and keep it simple. And there was the problem of the kids. And his ex.

"Celeste?" Her mother sounded on the verge of hysteria. "Are you there?"

Celeste picked up the phone. "Yes, Mom. I'm here."

"Thank goodness, you had me worried. What were you moaning about? I thought something had happened."

"You heard me?" She hadn't realized she'd actually made any sounds aloud.

"What's wrong? Something's not right, I can hear it in your voice. You should be ecstatic and instead you sound more like someone with a bellyache."

"I'm not feeling well." She couldn't explain to her mother that her career had collided with her love—make that—personal life. "About Saturday night, can I get back to you?" Celeste asked. "I have some things I might need to rearrange and I'm not sure if I'll be available."

"Of course, honey. Let us know."

"I will. Bye, Mom." Celeste ended the call and drummed her fingers on the desk. If she didn't see Max Saturday, they probably wouldn't see each other until the end of October at the wedding. And that was a month away.

What to do about Max and the weekend?

Celeste hit speed dial number two on her cell.

"Trudi," she said when her friend answered. "I need to call an emergency girlfriend meeting."

❀ ❀ ❀

"Emergency girlfriend meeting, my ass," Trudi said. She jerked open the door to Buckhead's elite Diva Day Spa and Salon and glared at Celeste when she ducked inside, escaping the afternoon glare. "How could you have forgotten our appointment with Becca?"

Celeste cringed as Trudi continued to berate her for a total lack of consideration for Becca's upcoming nuptials, the hum of her voice drowning out the light tinkling of piano music playing throughout the spa. Celeste wasn't saying much in return. She hadn't mentioned her promotion because Trudi was right. What kind of a friend was she?

Becca and Marcus were getting married in a month and deadlines were approaching much too fast, and the last thing Becca needed was one of her bridesmaids, one of her best friends, not keeping her end of the bargain.

And Celeste had forgotten all about the appointment with the bridal image consultant.

How could she fail to remember that today was their day for sample hairdos and makeup? Becca would have a conniption fit if she realized Celeste had not remembered, and the last thing Celeste needed was to instigate a bad case of bridezilla with attitude. Especially since Becca had been on edge ever since the Stock the Bar party and seemed to grow antsier with each passing day.

"You're not going to tell her our appointment slipped my mind, are you?" Celeste asked, eyeing Trudi with a sideways glance.

Trudi stopped inside the lobby of the plush salon and slung her hair over her shoulder with a lift of her chin and jerk of her head. She was pissed. Celeste waited, anticipating another reprimand.

"Of course I'm not," Trudi fired back. "Why in the world would I want to live through that drama? She'll never know." Trudi pointed her finger at Celeste. "And you owe me one."

Trudi turned on her heel and stomped through the lobby filled with plush velvet couches, satin pillows, strategically placed lights showcasing bushy palms, and trifold Chinese partitions.

"Actually, for good measure, make it that you owe me two." Trudi sailed past the antique mahogany reception desk and marched down the hall.

"Excuse me, may I help you—"

"We have an appointment with Delilah," Trudi said over her shoulder.

Grateful that Trudi didn't plan on ratting her out, Celeste followed behind and took in a deep breath allowing the scents of the salon, sweet lavender mixed with vanilla and musk, and the background music to calm her beat-up nerves. She didn't want the drama either. The last thing she needed was Becca and company upset with her when every complication possible seemed to be raining down like men at a Weather Girls concert. Taking another step toward her goal in life now seemed cluttered with too many hurdles, teetering on too-high heels. Life could be such a tightrope.

They made their way to the bridal suite, and Celeste followed Trudi through the pink satin curtains. They went from elegant posh to what she would classify as over-the-top princess girl. Every possible shade of pink assaulted her senses, and she wondered if someone had accidentally exploded a bottle of Pepto Bismol in the room. She'd never seen so much pink satin, velvet and netting in her life. A vase of stargazer lilies exploded on a sidebar, their strong aroma hanging sweet and heavy in the room. If she were ten, she'd love it, and a little thought niggled in the back of her head: wonder what Neecie would think? Her stomach roiled at the frou-frou décor, but what did she expect from a consultant who called herself the Diva Designer of the Brides? Becca sat in the stylist chair, pumped high, a white cloth draped around her, looking every bit like a bride-to-be on speed. An expression of relief washed across her face.

"Good, there y'all are," Becca said much too fast, her voice high-pitched and uncharacteristically edgy. She glanced at Patrice who sat in a chair beside her writing notes in her ever-present journal. "It's already five after two, and I'd said to Patrice that I was worried the two of you'd forgotten since I didn't call and remind y'all, and you know Delilah said we needed to be prompt, since there are four of us to work with. And I've been worried sick the past few days with all of the final arrangements coming up, and I need y'all more now than I ever have. And I thought y'all had forgotten." Becca finally took a breath.

"We'd never forget you," Trudi said. She regarded Celeste and lifted an eyebrow. "Would we, Celeste?"

"Never," Celeste said. Except on the day she'd received word that the weekend anchor position for Morning AM was now hers. The same day she realized she would need to tell Max she couldn't see him for a while. Possibly never again. The same day she needed her best friends for a consultation on what to do? What not to do? All colliding on the same day she'd already committed to be there for Becca. And friends always came first regardless of the problems raining down. Men or no men.

Delilah sauntered into the room, tall and erect, her beauty-queen looks defined by faultless makeup.

"Ah. Good, you'zall here," she said, her accent some odd combination of southern drawl, a Yankee clip blended with something that sounded oddly like fake French, but Celeste couldn't quite place it. Possibly it was Russian.

"We can ztart." She checked her watch. "Almost onz time." She leaned against the counter, backed by a wall of mirror, and indicated they should take the seats pulled up next to Becca. Celeste and Trudi obeyed and gave the Diva Designer their complete attention.

"Let me ezplain what we will be doing today. Here's my portfolio and book of themez…ideas, if you will." Delilah took a leather-bound volume off the counter and placed it in Becca's lap.

"I've already gone over some of zis with Becca, and az the bride she understands. We'll pick her theme, and I'll work with each of you and instruct my assistantz on the best makeup for your own faces and styles, while ensuring we complement Becca and make her shine on her special day. We'll also try out several hair-stylez…updos, down-dos, but I also want to enzure you three understand your duties as well." She gave each one of them a perusing stare. "Which of you iz the maid of honor?"

"She hasn't deci—"

"Yes, I have," Becca said, cutting off Patrice.

Patrice turned to Becca, Bambi-eyed and mouth opened in a little O. Trudi leaned forward, and Celeste sat ramrod still, wondering who Becca had chosen.

"I have one out-of-towner coming in. My cousin from Texas," Becca said.

"What cousin?" Celeste chorused with Trudi and Patrice.

"Actually she's a second cousin from Daddy's side of the family. Y'all know I have family in Texas."

"Yes. Family you haven't seen in your entire life." Trudi's face had turned red, and unfortunately, the shade clashed with her hair.

"That's not true," Becca said. "We drove to Texas for a vacation when I was eleven, and if you remember, they came to visit us when I graduated from high school. She's five years younger than me, but Mom and Dad thought it would be a nice family gesture for me to ask Molly to be my maid of honor. I gave it a lot of consideration and decided it would prevent any hard feelings amongst the three of you, so I called her and asked. She said yes, she'd love to." Becca pulled a folder out of her voluminous purse and plopped it on top of Delilah's portfolio. "I have a picture of her, and we can do her practice makeup when she arrives the week of the wedding."

"As if you'll need to be worrying about last minute things like your cousin's makeup," Trudi said, not trying to hide her annoyance.

"Be nice, Trudi. I chose Molly so I wouldn't hurt your feelings."

"Not being chosen as your maid of honor does not hurt my feelings," Trudi said.

"It does mine," Patrice said.

"I find it annoying and totally impractical that you chose a second cousin you've seen a whopping two times in your entire life," Trudi said. "That's all."

Celeste could tell Trudi wasn't going to let Becca's selection for maid of honor go easily, but she kept quiet. She had other things to worry about.

"Yeah," Patrice said. "You chose a cousin over us? We've been your best friends for almost twenty years. What's up with that?" Patrice shut the journal, slumped back in the chair, and stuck out her lower lip. Patrice did pouty-face quite well, Celeste noted.

"Ladiez, ladiez. This iz not the time to quarrel, you should discuss this amongst yourselves later. Possibly it is a good time for some tea—"

"I suggest it's a good time for a glass of wine," Trudi said.

"I'd prefer a mimosa. This room makes me think I should indulge in a lady's drink." Patrice pointed at Celeste. "What about you?" Celeste stared back at her, amazed that Patrice could still talk over her puffed-out lower lip.

"Frankly, I could use a smooth sipping tequila. Chilled and straight-up."

"That makes me want my favorite," Becca said. "A tequila sunrise. That's my and Marcus's drink."

"Sorry, ladiez. I can help you with the wine and champagne, but I have no tequila." Delilah picked up a phone and requested a round of mimosas before turning back around. "Now, can we getz to work?" She cocked an eyebrow defiantly. "Let's zee the picture of this cousin."

Becca pulled out a photo and Delilah perused it. "I see no problemz with this. There is no worry for you, Delilah will take care of the...maid of honor when she arrives." The diva creator turned and smiled at the girls, and Celeste had the distinct impression she'd stressed maid of honor, as if she were pouring a little salt in a wound or two. Or three. And enjoying it. "I prefer to do the sample hair first, so once we decide, we can then do the makeup and get an idea of the finished product."

Becca started flipping through the tabbed section for updos.

"I love this." She jabbed a finger at an elaborate swirl of loose curls, pulled into a semi-formal, whimsical style. Not very Becca-ish, but Celeste kept her mouth shut.

"Ah. Youz want to try to wear your hair up?" Delilah seemed delighted at the challenge. "You have so much hair, so lovely, so soft. A beautiful shade of blonde. I'm surprised you don't want to wear it down."

"I think she should wear it down." Apparently, Trudi still felt cantankerous.

"Her hair would be lovely if she wearz it up." Delilah lifted a brow and challenged Trudi with her stare.

"But what about my hair?" Patrice asked, pulling at her spikey cut. "How will we style my hair to complement Becca's?"

"There iz always the option of extensions."

"Great idea." Becca clapped her hands. "If I decide to wear my hair down, you can have long hair for the day."

Celeste couldn't believe she'd heard correctly. Becoming a bride had turned Becca into someone else. The old Becca, the real Becca, would have never thought hair extensions were a good idea. Where had her sweet friend gone?

"Extensions?" Patrice stuck out both her lips.

"You know our motto, Tous pour un, un pour tous," Celeste said. "It's Becca's day and if she wants us all to have long hair, we will."

"What does that mean again?" Patrice asked.

"All for one, one for all," Becca said. She repositioned herself in the chair, so she could see all of them, but Delilah jerked her head back around. "Sit forward, pleaze."

"That's right, I remember now." Patrice grinned, melting the pout from her face. "And Becca is the wandering one. Dark-tan-man."

"It's d'Artagnan, and I'm sick of this Musketeer crap," Trudi said. "I never agreed that Becca is our d'Artagnan. I firmly stand with the belief that I am, and she is a Musketeer."

"The other day you said Becca was d'Artagnan. Why do things always have to be your way, Trudi?" Patrice asked, her earlier sulk returning.

"Because," Trudi said with a flourish, "I'm always correct."

No one spoke, and a stunned silence sucked the air from the room, while Delilah layered chunks of Becca's hair in huge ringlets. When Becca tried to turn her head to see Celeste, Delilah tossed the curling iron aside.

"I cannot work with diz energy in the room." She braced her hands on her hips and glared in the mirror, eyeing each one of them through their reflection.

Celeste lifted her hand to her mouth to hide her smile, but it was too late. Becca caught her reflection in the mirror, and they both started to giggle. A few seconds passed before Patrice chortled along, and then Trudi laughed with them.

"All for one, one for all." Celeste hiccupped between fits of laughter.

"I will give you ladiez a moment to collect yourselvez so I can continue my work," Delilah said. She stormed from the room.

"Who, may I ask, is the bridezilla here?" Trudi said, pulling a tissue from her purse and dabbing at her eyes. "That felt good. I haven't had a good laugh in a long time."

"Me either," Becca said, sitting up straighter in the chair. "I needed that."

"Ditto." Celeste still felt the endorphins running through her, the belly laugh the medicine she'd needed. No matter the problems in life, she could always depend on the girls to help make things right. "I have something to tell you guys."

"Tell us quickly, before Von Hilda returns," Trudi said.

"Von Hilda?" Becca started to laugh again. "That's a good one—"

"I'm taking over as weekend anchor for AM Atlanta." There she'd said it. Fast and quick, interrupting Becca to ensure she made her announcement before Delilah returned, and Celeste chickened out. After all, it was Becca's day, but she did want to share her news.

"OMG." Patrice grinned from ear-to-ear, her pixie features morphing into upturned curves and dimpled cheeks.

Becca squealed, jumped out of the chair, and leaned down to engulf Celeste in a hug, covering her in a cloud of curls and white cape. When Becca pulled away, Trudi stood there staring at Celeste.

"You've known this since we talked this morning?"

"Yes." Celeste stood and faced her.

"And you haven't said anything to me?"

"I didn't want to distract—"

"From my day?" Becca blinked, and Celeste would swear she saw tears.

"OMG. How sweet." Patrice hopped up and threw her arms around Celeste. "I'm so proud. I know how much this means to you."

"You're on your way," Trudi said solemnly, still staring at Celeste. "But you didn't tell me." Celeste felt a tug of guilt. She and Trudi knew why the subject hadn't been brought up.

"I know, when I called this morning I was thinking about—"

Trudi stopped her with a bear hug, motioning for Becca and Patrice to follow suit. They all stood with their arms wrapped around one another, in the middle of the nauseously pink, lily-scented room.

"Congratulations, my friend," Trudi said. "All for one, and one for all." She pulled away from the group hug. "Now what about that emergency girlfriend meeting you needed?"

CHAPTER TWENTY-TWO

❧

Celeste breathed a sigh of relief.

"Well, I don't know what I should do," Celeste said, beginning to explain as they all settled back into their respective seats, but before she could finish an attendant arrived with a pitcher of mimosas and four glasses. She placed the tray on the counter and grinned.

"Here you go, ladies," she said. "Delilah said I should bring a pitcher. She thought you might need it." She gave them all a quick once over. "Deciding on the right makeup and hairstyle can be so stressful. Enjoy." She exited as quickly as she'd entered.

"I think I might have a certain respect for Von Hilda after all," Trudi said as she stood and served the drinks. She lifted her glass. "Let's make a toast to good friends and to being here for one another."

Celeste lifted hers too, and they all clinked their glasses together. "To good friends," she said.

"So what's your problem?" Trudi asked, back to her normal self, straight-to-the-point and no sugar coating. Anything.

"A man—"

"Man?" Trudi said, annoyed. "I thought we were talking career here. Your new position, taking the spot as weekend anchor? I thought you had a real problem." She huffed and sat back in her chair, taking a long draw off her drink. "Not an issue with a man." Disgust dripped from every syllable. "Who is he?"

"Max—"

"Max?" Becca, Trudi and Patrice chorused.

Celeste nodded.

"Have you seen him more than you've told me? I only know about the one weekend." Trudi scrunched her eyes. "Are there a few details you've failed to mention?"

"I can't believe you," Becca said. "After I asked you not to."

"Wow. Lucky you," Patrice said.

"I knew about the one date, but y'all certainly kept the rest to yourselves," Trudi said. "I'd say that was a little deceptive on your part. You should have told one of us."

"I told you not to get involved with him," Becca said. "If you'd listened to me, we wouldn't be having this conversation." She sipped at her champagne cocktail and glowered at Celeste over the rim of her glass, which made images of Serena dance through Celeste's head. She cringed. She'd prefer sugar plums any day, and she didn't know what they were.

"Don't look at me that way," Celeste said. "The evil glimmer in your eye is oddly reminiscent of the glares Serena shot my way during the weekend at Magnolia Oaks."

"The old witch gave new meaning to 'if looks could kill,' didn't she?" Trudi chuckled. "Your affair with Max might be better than a series on TruTV after all."

"I'm not having an affair," Celeste said.

"Right," Trudi said and took another swig. "Go on," she urged.

Celeste didn't care for the skeptical gleam in Trudi's eyes, but she continued with her current dilemma.

"I was ecstatic when Dave Chandler told me he was moving me to weekend anchor." Celeste sighed. Where should she begin to explain her happiness when she'd heard the news? "I've wanted this for a long time, and it felt like I was walking on a cloud all the way back to my cubicle. Then I remembered." She took a fortifying drink waited for her friends to react.

"Remembered?" Patrice asked. "Remembered what? The looks Serena gave you?" Patrice blinked. "I don't get it?"

"No," Trudi said with a snap. "That is not what she remembered." Trudi turned on Celeste. "Can we get this moving? If you were a witness on the stand right now, I would chew you up and spit you out, and we aren't working with much time here. Von Hilda could return any minute."

"Max," she said again. "I remembered Max, and I felt horrible because I was so happy about my career finally moving in the right direction, I didn't immediately realize I wouldn't be able to see him."

"Exactly how much have you seen him?" Trudi scrunched her brow and eyed Celeste with a suspicious glare. "I thought this thing between you two was only a hookup that night on the lake and the one weekend he drove up."

"I told you to stay away from him," Becca said again. "But you wouldn't listen."

"I've seen him every weekend since Labor Day."

"Every weekend?" Becca said, sputtering a mouthful of mimosa on her white cape.

"Uh oh," Trudi said and pointed out the spill. "Von Hilda's gonna be pissed at you."

"I don't care." Becca turned on Celeste. "You've seen him every weekend since Magnolia Oaks?"

"Well…yes." Celeste winced. The idea for an emergency meeting to discuss a situation she hadn't exactly been the most forthcoming about might not have been a good one. Now she'd need to confess everything. "He's driven up every weekend for the past month."

"You didn't tell us." The accusing pout on Patrice's face almost triggered guilt. But not quite. Celeste had enjoyed herself. Every minute of every weekend, and she'd do it all over again.

"Aha. You've seen him more than the one weekend?" Trudi accused and didn't wait for a response. "There's more than what you described as the most 'perfect date' you've ever had?"

"You had a date?" Patrice asked, stung. "I didn't hear about it."

"What about this perfect date?" Becca sat forward, spilling more of her drink to join the orange stain from earlier, and gave her a Serena-glare. "What have y'all been doing?"

"Didn't she tell you about him arriving with prepaid tickets for the mushy comedy he took her to see and tackling the crowds while shopping at Lenox, hitting the sales at Neiman and Nordstroms?" Trudi smiled, enjoying herself. "With Max."

"A man who shops," Patrice said. "How utterly delightful. A dream come true."

"And a man who takes a woman for a late night supper at Chops," Trudi said and winked at Celeste. "You shouldn't try to keep secrets from the sisterhood. I didn't realize you hadn't confessed the entire experience to all of us."

"Chops?" Becca was flabbergasted.

"I love Chops," Patrice said.

"When did you ever go to Chops?" Celeste asked, beginning to think she didn't know her friends as well as she thought she did, but guilt hit her for keeping her own secrets.

"Well, I bet I would love it if I ever had the chance to go." Patrice pouted for a beat, but immediately brightened. "How was it? What'd you eat?"

"I had the scampi-styled lobster." Celeste hummed, remembering the succulent lobster melting on her tongue and the loaded baked potato she and Max had shared. The evening had been bliss. The entire day—priceless.

"Are you sure it's a good idea to indulge in midnight lobster dinners?" Becca asked, the Serena-look plastered on her face intensifying. She tapped her hands on her belly and hips.

"What is that supposed to mean?" Celeste asked, appalled by the idea that sweet Becca would dare imply she'd gain weight.

"We've already had our last fitting, the dresses will be ready in two weeks," Becca said. "This whole wedding has me paranoid. That's all. I'm not sure I can handle any more last minute changes. Adding my cousin as maid of honor last minute is enough."

"Don't make her go bridezilla on you," Trudi said. "Becca bitchy would probably be an over-the-top experience. You know how mellow people can be when you push them over the edge."

"Crazy," Patrice said. "I've seen it happen before."

"With Becca?" Celeste asked. Becca never went off the deep end. When her ex-fiancé, Harold Houdini, cancelled their wedding after the rehearsal dinner two years before, Becca had remained calm. Or so it had seemed at the time.

"No, of course it wasn't Becca," Patrice said, waving the idea away with her hand.

"Please tolerate me," Becca said. "I don't want to get fanatical over anything. I'm worried about the wedding. Marcus and me. All the plans. You don't know what it's like...the final stages of planning a big wedding. I really wish we'd run away to Vegas to get married." Becca finished the few sips left of her drink and held the empty glass out to Trudi. "Pour me another one."

"But no one would know you're married. Because what happens in Vegas, stays in Vegas," Patrice said.

"You don't really believe that?" Celeste asked. Patrice could be so gullible, and it worried Celeste at times. "You do realize that's only a tourism ad?"

Trudi laughed and handed Becca a refreshed mimosa, and Becca turned to Celeste. "I can't believe you kept Max's visits from me." Becca slumped back in the chair and rubbed her hand across her forehead. "I'm confused. I want Celeste to be happy...but I don't want Max getting involved in a relationship when he's not ready...I don't know." She focused on Celeste. "Have you slept with him?"

"Have you?" Patrice sat forward, her interest heightened.

"Of course they're bumping nasties." Trudi grinned. "So how's it been going?"

"Fabulous."

"That's the problem with going into a relationship with zero expectations," Trudi said. "You remain relaxed and act like yourself." She made a face and cringed. "How scary is that? Actually going on a date and being the real you? I mean, who does that?"

"The next thing you know," Patrice said, "a booty call has turned into an attraction between two people who might possibly really like each other. Late night hookups, or in your case weekend hookups, segue into a relationship." Patrice smiled. "Bada boom, bada bing."

Everyone stared at her.

"What did you say?" Celeste asked, flabbergasted that Patrice could be so insightful.

"And you know this why?" Trudi's voice took on its defense attorney threat, along with the way she narrowed her eyes, scrunched her brow, and pursed her lips.

"I read it. Somewhere. Seventeen percent of couples start their long-term relationships as no strings attached." She pointed at Celeste. "Proved point."

"I'm not in a relationship," Celeste said, wishing they'd allow her get to the point. "We're having fun together."

"So, this thing with Max is supposedly only a physical fling?" Trudi asked, the expression on her face screamed she wasn't convinced. "Sex only. No emotional involvement?"

Celeste nodded, beginning to doubt she knew the real answer herself, and all she really wanted to do at the moment was discuss her quandary about the weekend.

"Then why are you so worried about your promotion interfering?" Trudi asked. Trudi was good, real good. Celeste would never want to be in the witness chair and be grilled by her. Ever.

"Well, I'm not. It's not the promotion, it's the fact our plans won't work out now. The timing is off. He has kids. He's divorced. And I like him. But he lives so far away. But none of it matters because what we have is only a physical thing, but I'm having fun, and I'll miss our time together. That's all," Celeste said, as confused as she sounded.

"You do know that the initial raging attraction doesn't last," Trudi said, all-knowing.

"It doesn't?" Patrice asked, sounding disappointed.

"Well, I can dispute you on that one." Becca grinned and slurped at her drink.

Celeste and Patrice gasped. Becca going up against Trudi?

Trudi turned to Becca with a smug grin. "The statistics—"

"Can we focus here?" Celeste interrupted, not wanting the discussion to turn into a debate on love versus sex. They'd engaged in enough heated conversations to know that Patrice and Becca were eternal romantics and Trudi the interminable pessimist. Celeste rode the fence. "I need y'all to concentrate on my current problem for now."

Trudi swiveled back to Celeste.

"Go on."

"We were enjoying some time together on the weekends. And that's my problem. Max is supposed to come this weekend, but I think I should cancel."

"Explain," Trudi said.

"He normally arrives Saturday morning and since I worked the weekday shift, I've been free to spend all day Saturday and Sunday with him. But this Saturday, I'll be at the station until the afternoon."

"So, he comes a little later and you see him Saturday night," Patrice said.

Celeste stared at her. Patrice made complete sense.

"But I'll be exhausted."

"I told you not to get involved," Becca said, moving her head slowly back and forth, the pained expression on her face predicting doom.

"Why don't y'all go out for dinner and make it an early night?" Trudi said. "I don't see a problem here."

"I'll have to get up at three in the morning in order to get to the station on time. I'll have to be in bed by eight. At the latest."

"And going to bed early is a problem because?" Trudi wiggled her brows.

"I'll need my rest…and I don't get a lot of sleep when Max is around."

"Oh, God, and I have to listen to this why?" Becca put her hands over her ears. "Hear no evil."

"Suck it up, Becca," Trudi said. "You're going to have to admit that your best man is sleeping with your best friend."

"He's Marcus's cousin. He's fragile." Becca shot an accusing glare at Celeste. "And you're going to hurt him like Marcus and I were worried that you would. Max is a country boy."

"Max," Celeste said, "is so NOT a country boy." She knew exactly how worldly he was. And as far as she was concerned, country boys were hot.

"Y'all sleeping together will still ruin my wedding." Becca's voice quavered.

"How in the world do you think we'll ruin your wedding?" Celeste asked. "You're being totally irrational. It's not like we'll have sex at the reception."

"Why not?" Trudi asked. "Sounds like fun." She wiggled her eyebrows, and Celeste waved her off, trying not to laugh. She turned back to Becca.

"I don't know," Becca said, worry lines wrinkling the space between her brows. "But something will probably go wrong. Serena will have a hissy fit."

"Serena doesn't know," Celeste said, knowing good and well she was kidding herself.

"She'll know," Trudi said. "Trust me."

"I asked you to leave him alone," Becca said. "He's no match for someone like you."

"She's not going to hurt him," Patrice said, reassuringly. She turned to Celeste. "Are you?"

"I don't plan to." Celeste took a drink. Had she possibly started something that would end in disaster? In someone getting hurt? The way her stomach churned and her heart ached, she wondered if it might not be her, instead of Max, who would walk away scathed. She forced herself to refocus her thoughts. No one would get hurt. They were only having a good time together.

No big deal.

"So cancel this weekend and see him some other time," Trudi said, her voice abrupt like the thud of a gavel hitting wood. "We don't have anything to discuss here."

"But that's my dilemma. See him when?"

"Next week," Patrice suggested with her wide-eyed innocent moue.

"He'll be too busy with harvest next week," Celeste said. "I was supposed to go down to Magnolia Oaks for a weekend or two before the wedding."

"So go during the week." Trudi sounded exasperated.

"Did you not hear me? He'll be busy with the peanut harvest." Celeste clenched her teeth and sounded as exasperated as Trudi. Didn't she understand? There was no time for the two of them to get together. Her coveted career move and Max's peanuts had put a screeching halt to her seeing him for the next month.

"I bet picking peanuts is tedious," Patrice said, nodding her head.

"They don't 'pick' peanuts." Trudi looked at Patrice as if she'd grown a horn in the middle of her forehead.

"How do they get them off the trees?"

"Really?" Celeste chorused with Trudi and Becca, and Patrice shrugged her shoulders and held out her palms.

Trudi dismissed her with a wave of her hand. "If y'all have the hots for one another, the flame will burn brighter if you can't see each other for a month. And when you see each other again, the attraction will be stronger. If he wants you now, he'll still want you the weekend of Becca's wedding. Just think, free fireworks." She winked at Becca who flinched.

"I didn't plan on any fireworks," Becca said.

Trudi leaned forward and took Celeste's hand. "Look me in the eye, and Becca, you and Patrice listen to me too. I want to know if y'all agree with what I'm about to say." Trudi turned toward Becca, who nodded. She turned back to Celeste. "You have what? A month invested in this guy?"

Celeste nodded.

"You had how much time invested in Josh? Over a year?"

Celeste nodded again.

"Hey, I saw Josh the other night, did I tell y'all?" Patrice asked. "He was with a girl that was the complete opposite of Celeste."

"Really?" Becca asked, interested. "What did she look like?"

"Who cares?" Trudi asked.

"No makeup, jeans and T-shirt with a hoodie. I'd guess she knows how to toss a football. A real guy's kind of girl—"

"We don't care," Trudi said, teeth clinched, her patience dissipating.

"Why do you think he'd date someone like that?" Becca asked.

"Because Celeste's beauty and brains scared the beejeebus out of him," Trudi said. "He wasn't confident enough to handle her career. He wants someone to be his equal, and Celeste was better than Josh."

"She looked like a nice girl," Patrice said.

"I'm sure she is, and she can play toss with him in the park on the weekend while our girl here is reporting the news, so can we all please FOCUS?" Trudi turned back to Celeste. "Let's face it, this thing with Max started as a fling—"

"It is not a thing," Celeste said. She really wished they'd stop trying to turn her meetings with Max into a relationship.

"Whatever," Trudi said, and continued on, "It's only been a month, and he has kids, and if you remember your rules, you personally don't want any 'no-neck monsters.' And neither do I. So taking a break for a month might be the thing you need to do. Focus on your career, which you might recall is your primary goal. Take out your cell phone and call him. Or be a coward and text him first. Inform him that you have to cancel this weekend and be sure to let him know about your new position. If he understands, he might be a keeper."

Celeste nodded her head and a surge of relief washed over her. Trudi was right. As always. Trudi must have noticed something in Celeste's expression because she clutched her hand and squeezed it.

"Focus. I said he might be a keeper, but we need to get you through this weekend and behind that anchor desk, well-rested and confident. You don't need a distraction right now." Trudi turned to Becca and Patrice for confirmation. "Do we all agree?"

"Agreed," they said.

Celeste pulled out her phone and took the less confrontational way out. As she composed her text to Max, the tug on her heart made her wonder how something so right for her career could make her feel so sad?

CHAPTER TWENTY-THREE

৵৽

Max cell phone vibrated on his way back to the main house. Whatever the message, it could wait until he arrived. He looked at his watch. Three o'clock. Charlie would be home from school already, working on his lessons with Big Mama's guidance, allowing Max the freedom to handle paperwork before it was time to join the kids for dinner.

He shrugged his shoulders, loosening the tightened muscles in his neck. He'd spent the past three days hiring the seasonal workers to help with the harvest, and he was tired. He and his dad, and their four full-time hands, all had their work cut out for them over the next month. Big Mama had orchestrated the opening of the dorm where the seasonal workers would be housed, and Brick was there now overseeing the airing out of the facility ensuring all beds were outfitted with linens.

Luckily, Mother Nature had been kind, and she'd sent enough rain throughout the growing season that there had been no need to rely on the backup irrigation systems. Max smiled, realizing their good luck. The ideal season. After the past two drought-ridden years, he had a feeling that this would be a perfect harvest, and there hadn't been one in a long time. Looking back, every year seemed to have its critical issues, but the family always managed to pull through. Some seasons better than others, but this year, he had a feeling Celeste was a lucky charm. His heart warmed at the thought of her, and he couldn't wait to see her again. Two days to go, and he'd be on his way to Atlanta.

The upcoming trip would be his last one until the wedding, since timing was always crucial during harvest. He'd suggested Celeste visit him at Magnolia Oaks for a few days throughout October. Although he'd be slammed working alongside all the workers, there was no way he'd miss out on spending a few hours with Celeste if she visited. He knew it was selfish, but he planned to make the time to spend with her. He'd already forewarned Brick that he'd be otherwise occupied for a few of the days.

He'd toyed with the idea that it was time to introduce Celeste as more than one of the bridesmaids to Charlie and Neecie, but he hadn't discussed it with her yet. And although they'd only known each other for a little over a month, the idea made him happier than he probably should be. The whole thing with Celeste felt right. Like a favorite sweatshirt, worn-out and comfortable.

But was an introduction to the children too soon to consider? Did he dare expose the children to Celeste, especially since she had an aversion to kids? Maybe what the two of them shared could never evolve into anything more than friends with benefits. A weekend fling. A long-distanced weekend fling at that. And subjecting Charlie and Neecie to another loss was the last thing he'd want to do.

Max drove his truck under the porte cochere and jammed the gearshift into park. He ambled out of the cab, pulling his cell from his pocket as he moved up the stairs. The notification of a text from Celeste glared on the screen, and he tapped the touchscreen as he walked into his office off the main foyer.

Great news! I received the position as weekend anchor. Bad news. I start this weekend and need to cancel our plans. ☐ Call me. Xoxo Celeste.

Max collapsed into his chair with a rush of air. Cancel their plans? He was more than disappointed. Yet, she'd received the anchor position, and he knew how much it meant to her. He smiled, proud for her. Good for Celeste. She deserved it.

He decided to call her, thinking there had to be a way to convince her they could still see each other. The line rang with no answer, and at the precise moment that he was mentally creating the message he'd leave, she answered.

"Hey," she said, and he smiled at the sound of her voice.

"Wow, I didn't think you were going to answer. Congratulations," he said. "I'm so excited for you. It's always a good thing when exceptional people reach their goals."

"Thanks."

"How does it feel?" he asked.

"Like a dream come true. Well, the beginning of it anyway." She laughed, sounding nervous. "You got my text?" she asked. "Well, that was dumb. Of course you did." She laughed again.

"Yeah, yeah, I got it," Max said, the sound of her voice coursing warmth through him. Contentment.

"So about this weekend—"

"I was looking forward to seeing you, and I'd love to celebrate with you."

"I'm sorry, Max. That's not a good idea," she said. "I can't."

He would bet money he heard regret in her voice, so he tried again. "Are you sure? I can drive up and take you to dinner? No big day. A simple night?" he said and waited, hoping.

"I can't see you on the weekends anymore. Maybe I can once I'm accustomed to my new schedule and the early hours, but not for a while."

"What about you coming down? Any chance you could get away for a day or two during the week?" he asked. "I could make the time. Get away and entertain you. We could hang at the cabin. Take out the pontoon."

"I'll still be working shifts during the week as an on-the-scene reporter. I'm not sure, how it's all going to work out," she stumbled over her words, and Max thought he heard her clear her throat. "I'm sorry, but it might be the wedding before I see you again," she said and sniffed.

"Are you sure?" he asked, disheartened. The wedding was still weeks away, and he didn't want to wait another three weeks before seeing her again.

"No," she said. "I'm not sure of anything right now." She cleared her throat. "Except for the fact I took a big step toward my ultimate goal. Thanks for the congratulations. It means a lot to me."

"Sure. Of course," he said and stopped, gathering his thoughts. "I can't wait until the day I turn on Friday's 20/20 and you're there hosting the show." He forced a strangled chuckle. "Watch out, World News Tonight."

She laughed, but it sounded oddly like a sob. "I'll be in touch."

"Yeah, me too," he said. "We can still talk every day, if that's okay with you."

"I'd like that," she said and her voice sounded lighter.

"Maybe a little sexting?" He chuckled.

"I'd love that," she said and laughed along with him.

"I promise I'll pick up your telecast on cable. I'll be watching."

"Thanks. Bye." She ended the connection, and the screen of his phone flashed. The call was over. He was alone. His weekend plans no longer an expectation. He had nothing to anticipate, but three weeks of hard work, and a wedding that seemed a century away.

Max sat in his office for over an hour staring out the window, thinking about life and its successes, happiness and disappointments, struggling with feeling proud for Celeste while crushed by the fact he wouldn't see her anytime soon. He'd decided it was time to focus on paperwork when someone knocked on the door.

"Come in," he said, and twirled his chair around to face whoever entered.

Serena pushed open the door and stood in the threshold, waiting, and when she didn't say anything, he said, "Yes?" To act busy, he moved some papers around on his desk.

"Do you have some time to talk?" she asked.

Max lifted his eyes. She had on a dress more suited for afternoon tea at the club than a day at home, with a sweater hanging loosely from her shoulders. Her blonde hair was pulled up in what she called her Breakfast at Tiffany's-do. She looked more like a movie star who'd missed out on her dreams than she did a mother.

"About?" he asked, sounding more perturbed than he intended. The phone call with Celeste had left him frustrated, and his nerves were as ragged as if they skated on the edge of a circular saw.

"Sissy," she said, pausing in her annoying way. Waiting. For what, Max never knew.

"I don't have anything to say about Sissy." He'd managed to push thoughts of his ex from his mind. After two years, he was on the road to the next phase of his life, and he didn't want to think about Sissy or discuss her with his mother.

"Humor me," Serena said, standing before him with her hands clutched in front of her, waiting as if there was something she wanted to say, but not quite sure what it was.

"I really don't want to discuss her with you or anyone else." At the moment, he didn't want to think about Sissy. He was ready to move on with Celeste, to find out where their relationship might lead. He stood up and moved toward his mother. "Is there anything else you want to discuss? Such as Charlie and how well he's doing in school, or Neecie's dance recital coming up in a few weeks?"

Surprising the hell out of him, Serena took his hand and led him away from his desk to a small sitting area in front of the fireplace.

"Talk with me, Max." She settled into a chair.

"About? I'm not interested in discussing Sissy."

"Please." She lifted her hand and indicated the chair across from her. "Sit. We need to talk."

He lifted his brow, skeptical that such a conversation could lead to any good, but he sat anyway. Maybe she would finally say what had been on her mind for his entire life. Fill in the mystery of all of her pregnant pauses. All of the waiting moments she'd peppered throughout his life.

"What do we need to talk about?" He swallowed her bait. Line and sinker.

"Family."

Max tilted back his head and laughed. An aborted noise, void of any humor. A sound full of disappointments and misunderstandings. "You want to talk about family?"

"Yes. Family. Particularly yours." Serena folded her hands in her lap and smiled one of her fake smiles, and Max returned the gesture with an equivalent lack of warmth. "About Charlie and Neecie. You and Sissy."

"Sissy?" Max said, horrified that she would mention Sissy's name in the same sentence with the word family. "Sissy isn't our family, Serena."

"But she is." Serena reached over and took Max's hand into hers, she stared downward as she ran her thumb over his knuckles. He wanted to pull away, take his hand from her grasp, but in some ironic twist he enjoyed her touch. He'd so seldom ever experienced it.

"What's this about?"

"Sissy called me," Serena said.

He jerked his hand away. "Why the hell would you talk to her?" he asked. His fury boiled in his gut and his pulse vibrated in his ears, a whooshing noise that ebbed and flowed with each beat of his heart.

"She wants to come home."

"No way in hell," Max said.

"She made a mistake, and you have no other choice but to give her another opportunity to prove herself." Serena paused. "For the well-being of the children." She searched his face, and he sat immobilized, torn between wanting to walk out the door before he said something he shouldn't or bashing his fist through the drywall. "Sometimes you have to swallow your pride, and you need to put your children first, Max. You need to give Sissy a second chance."

He didn't need this. He didn't care for Serena's tactic of using guilt in order to force him to allow Sissy to come home. To take back the very person who'd betrayed him. And for the sake of his children? The sake of family? He didn't think so.

"Would you have taken Dad back?" Max asked, staring his mother in the eyes. "If he'd done this to you? Betrayed you?"

"He did," she said. Her face crumpled, as if she would cry, but the moment passed, and she straightened her shoulders. She took a deep breath. "And I did take him back."

"No," Max said, shaking his head in denial. "Dad adores you. The two of you have shadowed each other my entire life. I'm sorry, but I don't believe you."

"Trust me," she said, her blue eyes telegraphing her despair, her face poised and unaffected as alabaster. "You were much too young to remember. Still a baby. You were a baby when a young couple joined our congregation, the wife was a gifted musician and became the church organist, and we became friendly with them. He was the manager of PPP."

"Whitaker's? The peanut processing plant?"

"Yes, exactly. It was called PPP, Inc. back then, but it's the same company." Serena paused. "There was an accident, a fire, and he was killed. Died going back into the plant to save some of his employees. He managed to save them, but he didn't make it. The entire incident was devastating."

"I know the story. He's considered a hero. But what does his wife have to do with it?"

"His death left Marlena a widow. Young. Healthy. Beautiful. And sad. Your daddy was always telling her his repertoire of jokes, all of the ones I'd heard a hundred times before. All the jokes I didn't laugh at anymore. But she hung on every word and laughed at every punch line. Giddy like. Just as I did when I'd fallen in love with Brick, back when we were first out of college and so in love nothing in the world could tear us apart. Nothing until Marlena laughed at everything he said and made him feel special again." Serena produced a handkerchief from God knew where and pressed it to her nose.

Max wanted to ask what happened, but when he saw the glimmer of tears, he didn't want to know, the shock of his father's infidelity not yet burning a firm root in his mind.

"Silly me," she said. "At first, I was relieved that he was giving her attention, after all the poor thing had lost her husband. Seemed to me, she deserved some happiness, a few laughs. And every Sunday morning, she'd work her magic on the church organ, while little did I know she was also working her same magic on my husband."

"Dad had an affair?" He couldn't believe the actual thought had escaped his lips. He knew the minute you breathed something aloud, verbally into the universe, the words had the potential for truth.

"Yes, your daddy had an affair. Broke my heart, he did. He crushed my spirit, but I survived. Didn't have any choice really. My mama came to me and told me exactly what I would do."

Max waited, not wanting to know, but realizing he had to.

"She reminded me I'd married well, and the Riley family's image could, and would, withstand the scandal. Family came first, she said. Mama told me that Brick and I would heal, and we would move on, and I should act as if nothing had ever happened." She paused and took a calculated breath. "Somehow the whole affair never leaked, no one gossiped. Thank God. Marlena quietly disappeared. Brick swore he didn't cheat, claimed nothing happened between the two of them, so I chose to forgive him and never mentioned it again, and he's been by my side ever since. And I'm not ashamed to say that I've loved him back. My mama was right. If I had left, I would have missed out on the greatest love of my life." Her last few words were a whisper. "I took him back and held my head high for the Rileys, and I've never regretted it. Family—means everything, and you will do your duty. After you forgive her, you'll find a way to love her again. If Sissy comes home and asks for forgiveness, you will take her back and make your family whole again."

"But you didn't."

"Didn't what?" Serena tilted her head to the side.

"Make our family whole again," Max said. "If it weren't for Big Mama, I wouldn't have felt loved."

Serena gasped and fluttered her handkerchief as if to dismiss his words. "You don't understand. We love you…it was never our intention to make you think we didn't." She moved her head back and forth as if to clear her thoughts. "Big Mama was always there for you, and you were always such a happy child. We were a family. And that's my point." She studied his face for a moment. "A family. That's what your children deserve, and you must remember that Sissy is their mama."

Max stood, a wave of sorrow consuming his spirit. She didn't get it.

"Giving birth doesn't make someone a mother," he said. He walked out the door and left Serena sitting alone.

CHAPTER TWENTY-FOUR

"Did you watch my newscast this morning?" Celeste asked her mother. She took a tight sip of chardonnay. After surviving her first weekend as anchor for Atlanta AM like a pro, her second Saturday proved much more challenging.

Mom drank her tea and looked over the rim at the overstated restaurant Dad had chosen for their belated celebratory dinner. She placed her glass on the table and picked up her fork.

"Yes, darling, of course I did." Mom busily pushed a chunk of potato around on her plate. "I wouldn't have missed it for anything." She lifted her fork and took a bite. Mom wouldn't look Celeste in the eye, and she busied herself by dabbing at the corner of her mouth with her napkin

"There has never been a more charming news anchor," Dad said, strategically stabbing his fork into a serving of prime rib. He sliced through it with his knife and winked at Celeste. "Except possibly your mother." He took a bite and chewed.

"You old charmer," Mom said, dimpling like a school girl at his compliment, still in love after almost forty years. She reached over and patted his arm. "That's why I keep you around."

"What did you think?" Celeste dared to solicit the opinion she dreaded to hear.

"You've been doing fabulously, dear. Really you have."

"Go ahead and say it, Mom," Celeste said. "Until this morning."

"All reporters have their moments, Precious. You'll toughen up with time. God created all kinds of people to handle different professions. Like nurses, for instance. It takes a certain fortitude to be in healthcare. God knows I could never do it. I'd cry all the time." Her mother smiled. "But God made some people who can remain strong for others during a time of need." Mom reached across and patted Celeste's hand. "Soon you'll be breezing through the most heartbreaking of stories without a blink of an eye. Trust me. You can do it and you will."

"Listen to your mother," Dad said. "She knows what she's talking about. Never stuttered a word on the air, waltzed through every story. You'll be like her before you know it." He sat back, and Celeste noticed an extra roll around his middle. Her father had gained weight without her realizing it, and a web of crow's feet crinkled the corner of his eyes. He was aging. And she hadn't paid attention. She dared a peek at her mother and saw the same fine lines etching her face. Celeste put her wineglass down and reached for her mother's hand.

"Your daddy's right, you know," Mom said, her typical encouraging self, as she grasped Celeste's fingers. "The stories about children are always the hardest."

Celeste leaned forward, hoping to make the connection between them stronger, yearning to absorb some of her mother's strength.

"Oh, Mama, it was horrible." Celeste wouldn't break down again. Her crying jag at the station earlier, after the Noon Update wrapped, should have been enough. Celeste forced back the lump in her throat, but to her horror she felt the prick of tears. She blinked them back.

"I know, I know." Mom patted her hand furiously. "It's one thing to report the week's recaps, the overnight breaking news. Those stories you're prepared before, but the on-the-scene breaking news stories can sometimes pull the rug out from under you. You need to hop back up and keep on going."

"Like an energizer bunny," Dad said, laughing, trying to lighten the mood.

"I don't think I handled it very well," Celeste said, remembering the horror of the moment the report had come in. The panic that'd seized her, the cold slivers of fear when the on-the-scene reporter announced, 'Breaking news...now on the scene...where the body of a four-year-old girl has been found...drowned in a nearby lake...' And then the images of a little girl, looking frighteningly like Neecie, and the pain that'd gripped her heart. Nausea had roiled in her belly and she'd stumbled over the next report, her focus destroyed with the sorrow she'd felt for an unknown family who'd lost their baby.

"You did fine dear," her mother said. "Next time you'll do better and soon none of the reports will affect you."

"They've never affected me before," Celeste said. "I've reported murders, accidental deaths."

"But have you ever reported the death of a child?" Mom asked. "Bad news about children, now that's different."

"I'm a professional. No news should shake me. Especially children. Face it, Mom, I have a major case of kidphobia."

"Kid what?" Mom asked.

"Phobia," Dad said. He took another bite of prime rib, and Celeste made a mental note to discuss his eating habits with him later.

"Mom, I have a serious no-neck-monster phobia."

"I think you read too much classic literature while you were at Georgia, if you want to know what I think," Mom said. She picked up her tea, but sat it down without drinking. "What do you mean by a kidphobia?"

"Children are sweet, but I don't ever want any children of my own."

"Of course you do, sugar, everybody wants children," Dad said.

"Not everyone. Trudi and I don't plan on having any kids."

"Trudi." Her mother humphed. "Let's not compare you to Trudi. Now that one is a piece of work."

"Feisty, she is," Dad said.

"I didn't exactly describe her as feisty. I said piece of work." Mom turned to Celeste. "I don't know how I missed this."

"Possibly it's because you've always doted on Ryan and Adam."

"Celeste," Mom said. She splayed her hand across her chest and sucked in a sharp breath. "You're jealous of your brothers?"

"No, not really. Daddy made up for it." Celeste smiled at her father. "I enjoyed being Daddy's girl. It didn't really bother me that you preferred the boys over me. By the time I might have cared, I'd met Trudi and Becca. Patrice. And since you were preoccupied getting Ryan and Adam through high school and sending them off to college, it gave me the freedom I wanted to hang with my friends." Her mother's forehead crinkled in concern. "I didn't suffer for it."

"I had no idea you felt that way. How did I miss it?" The corners of Mom's mouth pulled downward.

"No harm done, please don't worry. I love you." Her mother didn't tend to agonize over too much; she always remained upbeat, ever the optimist, and Celeste didn't want to be the one to cause her to worry. "And I've always known you love me."

"You think I preferred your brothers over you?" Mom shook her head. "No, I didn't. They needed me more. The boys were never good at entertaining themselves, and they were always fighting with one another. They were five and seven when you were born and into everything. I always prayed and thanked God every night that he'd sent me such a good baby girl. You were never demanding. And always seemed to prefer your daddy over me."

"You're a good mama," Celeste said.

"Am I?"

"Yes. Of course you are."

"All I ever wanted was to have a family. Bring up healthy, happy children."

"And you did, Mom. I love you. You did a great job with me."

"But you don't want children?" By the confusion on her face, Celeste could tell her mother was still trying to fathom her revelation.

"My upbringing has nothing to do with why I don't want to have offspring." Why had she brought the subject up? She wasn't really in the emotional state to expose her very essence. The day had been rough enough already.

"But you used to play with baby dolls," Mom said, refusing to believe her daughter's confession.

"Most girls play with dolls."

"But don't you love your nieces and nephews? Your own flesh and blood?"

"Actually, Mom, I love them. I do. But I don't care to be around them. Haven't you ever noticed I tend to be scarce when they're around?"

"I always assumed you were busy. With your career, your friends." Her mother chewed on her bottom lip and thought for a moment. "But you always send such nice gifts. Expensive gifts."

"Payoff, Mom," Celeste said. "Because I always try to stay away, except for Thanksgiving and Christmas, and when I do come around, I keep my visits short and sweet. So imagine my surprise when I was affected by this morning's story. That poor little girl." Celeste willed the image of Neecie's face to dissipate before any tears could return. "I can't imagine what her parents are experiencing. Her mother...and father." Celeste stumbled on the last word imagining the grief Max would experience if something ever happened to Charlie or Neecie.

"Obviously, you do have a soft spot for children, and you're now realizing it." Her mother smiled, looking as if she'd found a chip in Celeste's armor.

"No, no," Celeste said, turning her head back and forth, her hair swinging against her cheeks. "No, I don't. I have a friend with children, and I was imagining his grief if something happened to one of them."

"A friend?" The comment had piqued her mother's interest. "Lot's of people have children. Why are you so concerned about this particular friend and his children?"

"Well, I've actually met them—"

"Are you dating someone who's divorced?"

"No," Celeste said, convincing herself she wasn't telling an untruth. Even though Max was legally divorced, they weren't technically dating. They'd hooked up; they weren't seeing each other. "He's Marcus's cousin, the best man for Becca's wedding. His son and daughter will be in the ceremony."

"I see," Mom said, and the expression on her face made Celeste think her mother did, in fact, think she understood way too much.

"I met the kids Labor Day weekend," Celeste said and inwardly cringed. She hadn't planned on discussing Max with her parents. Parents didn't need to know about their daughter's flings.

"I'm sure it was a lovely time." The implication in her mother's voice matched her face.

"It didn't mean anything," Celeste said. Her mother's perception could be so damn annoying. Were mothers born with a sixth sense when it came to their offspring? "I went down to meet Marcus's family, to support Becca. Of course, Max was there, and it was inevitable that I'd meet his children. I met everyone. Cousins, nieces, nephews. Brothers. Aunts. Uncles. Everyone. Meeting Max's children did not mean anything special."

"Of course not, Precious."

Celeste humphed. She found the all-knowing smile on her mother's face incredibly annoying.

"His name is Max?" Mom asked.

Celeste nodded, refusing to look her mother's way, and focused on her dad instead.

"I'm sure you'll tell your daddy and me the entire story all in good time." Mom reached over and took hold of Dad's hand. "Don't you think so, Daddy?"

"Sure she will." He winked. "When she's ready."

"I don't have anything to tell," Celeste said with emphasis.

"Of course you don't, dear."

Celeste focused on the napkin in her lap, so she didn't have to watch the understanding gloat plastered on her mother's face. Mom might think she knew something, but she didn't. Max was only a fling. His kids meant nothing to her.

But for some perplexing reason, she couldn't get the thought of him and his children out of her mind.

CHAPTER TWENTY-FIVE

రిల్లా

Max, restless after a long day in the fields, listened to the soft breathing of Neecie and Charlie in their adjoining rooms. He envied their ability to slumber regardless of whatever was going on around them. Damn. To be young and innocent again. What wouldn't he give?

According to his watch it was nine thirty. He'd talked with Celeste earlier, but she'd cut him short. She had dinner plans with her parents and promised she'd talk with him later. She'd seemed preoccupied, out of sorts, and the sound of her voice made him believe she'd been upset. But she hadn't mentioned anything in particular. Maybe he could get it out of her when they talked later.

Max rolled to his feet, stood and stretched out the kink in his back. He needed a nightcap, something to help him relax, chase away the relentless thoughts of Celeste he couldn't seem to get out of his mind. He'd really missed seeing her over the past weekend.

He strolled over to the mini-fridge he kept in his suite at the big house and pulled out a beer, but decided he'd go for tequila instead. He grabbed the bottle and a glass and walked onto the gallery. The late September night held an unusual chill, and a shiver slithered through him when his bare feet hit the floor. He sat down and poured three fingers, settling back and gently rocking the chair with a push of his toes. The old rocker offered a sense of security; it was the same one Big Mama had used to rock him when he was a toddler. He'd heard many a story during sunsets while being rocked. He'd repeated many of the same stories himself after Charlie and Neecie were born.

Family. Roots. Heritage.

Everything Sissy had given up when she'd left. And now she might want to come back? He didn't think so.

Regardless of what Serena said, Max wouldn't take Sissy back for the sake of the Riley family reputation. Unlike his father's suspected clandestine affair with the organist, everyone knew about Sissy and Pastor Dick.

He hadn't brought up Serena's accusations with his father yet. He still wasn't sure how he felt about Brick being unfaithful. He'd had a lot to think about over the past week and half, and he thanked the Lord he'd been preoccupied with the harvest and his evening talks with Celeste. Or the whole situation would drive him crazy.

From the corner of his eye, Max caught a flicker of someone approaching along the verandah, and he rocked forward and lifted himself from the chair.

"Big Mama, what are you doing out here?" he asked and reached for her elbow to guide her inside. "It's too cold for you to be running around outside in your robe."

"And much to chill for you to be without your shoes," she said, allowing him to escort her through the doorway.

"We need to talk," she said, her voice low so the children couldn't hear. "I think there are some things I need to clear up for you about your daddy and Serena."

"Such as?" He answered in a whisper, not eager to have a conversation, still unsure how he felt about Serena's revelations.

"Let's go downstairs so we won't wake the children. No sense having them groggy during Sunday School." She started for the door. "Get your slippers and meet me in the kitchen."

"Your mother tells me she had a discussion with you the other day," Big Mama began, straight to the point. She sat in her favorite Queen Anne chair in front of the kitchen fireplace, a small fire burned in the grate.

"Yes. We talked." Max watched Big Mama's face for an indication of what she was thinking, while he purposefully kept his own expression guarded.

Big Mama pressed her lips together. "Maybe I should have told you years ago, but I didn't see any need. It all happened such a long time ago, and I didn't foresee Serena ever mentioning anything to you. What did she say?"

"That Dad had cheated on her and Grandma insisted she take him back." Max didn't want to elaborate. Short and sweet. Succinct worked for him.

"Did she tell you that Brick swore on the Bible he never slept with Marlena?"

"No, she didn't mention the Bible." Serena had been so certain, he tended to believe it. "Did he?"

"He swears he didn't, and I believe him. You know your daddy used to sing in the choir, and Marlena'd stay after Wednesday night Bible study and play the organ while he practiced his solos. After a while, Serena convinced herself that the two of them were having an affair." Big Mama shook her head with a pained expression on her face, as if she couldn't believe what she was actually saying. "Your parents and Marlena and Chuck had been very close. It didn't seem unusual to any of us that Brick was protective of Marlena after Chuck died. At first, Serena didn't seem to mind, but once she got it in her head that the two of them had become a little chummier than they should have, all she could think of was the fact Marlena was a lonely widow and your daddy was a married man." Big Mama paused. "I don't need to tell you that your mother can be a little odd. A downright icy bitch at times, and when I first met her, I didn't understand what your daddy saw in her. Gave me a new understanding that love is blind when he brought her home from the university hell-bent and determined to marry her, but he seemed to adore her. And I've always preferred my children happy. After you came along, she turned all of her attention to you, and I think she was almost relieved when Brick started paying attention to Marlena, since she no longer had to split her time between the two of you. But after a while, she got suspicious. Once she felt her world was threatened, it all became another story. When she accused him of sleeping with Marlena, Brick swore on a Bible he was innocent. And Marlena denied it as well, but Serena wouldn't listen to them. Hindsight, she probably had a case of postpartum depression, but in those days we didn't know about any such a thing."

"What happened to the other woman?"

"You mean Marlena? No need to be disrespectful. She had a name, and she was not the other woman. There was no possibility Brick's friendship with Marlena might have grown into an affair. When your mother confronted them, Marlena was devastated. Papa

Joe and I had the unfortunate experience of watching the drama unfold right here at the house. Brick and Marlena both swore up and down that they were only friends."

"I bet."

"None of that, now. Talk to your daddy yourself."

"Why would I want to do that?"

"To get his side of the story." Big Mama said. "Marlena packed up and moved the very next week. She'd lost her husband, lost her two best friends. She didn't have anything to stay in Tyler for."

"Where'd she go?"

"Moved back to Tennessee. With her people, where she belonged," Big Mama said. "You have to know your daddy dotes on your mother. He would have never cheated on her, and I believe he's proved his love for her every day of his life. Serena has her faults, I won't argue that one. But she loves your daddy. After everything settled down, she refocused all of her energy on Brick. She knew she would be a fool to give up her position with our family, and I've no doubt her mama drilled the importance of respect and family into her head."

"She implied as much. Said I needed to take Sissy back for the same reason."

"Now there, my boy, is where the two of us disagree. We're talking apples and oranges here." Big Mama's brow wrinkled and her cheeks flared a bright pink. "Sissy is nothing but a two-bit harlot. She ran off and left you with those two babies. And there is no way in hell I'd ever condone you taking her back. That harlot needs to fry in hell as far as I'm concerned."

"Tell me how you really feel." Max tried to smile. There was one thing about Big Mama, she always spoke her mind.

Big Mama reached over and grasped his hand with hers, her grip still strong. "Max, I love you as if you were my own son. I raised you, and I have to admit I'd do harm to anyone who ever hurt you. And Sissy is riding high on that list."

"I know, Big Mama."

"But, son, if you take her back, you won't be doing your family a favor. You'll be setting them up for another heartbreak." She patted his hand. "Go talk to your daddy. Listen to what he has to tell you."

Max padded down the back hallway debating whether he would talk to Brick or not. He loved his father, but frankly, he didn't care whether his father had an affair or not, and he didn't want to hear Brick's advice about keeping a family whole. He'd trust Papa Joe's advice on family more than his father's.

When Sissy deserted them, he'd been lost. Left alone with two small kids, he could barely take care of himself much less a two-year-old baby still in diapers and a four-year-old who kept asking when his mommy would be home. And Max didn't have any answers for him. Not the first few days any way.

He'd been worried, thinking the worst, but hoping for the best, when it came to light that Pastor Dick was missing as well. Adding the facts together didn't take a rocket scientist to know what had occurred. So within a few days after her disappearance, the worry that his wife might have been kidnapped, possibly murdered, morphed into anger with the speculation that she'd run off with the youth minister. Pastor Dick had left a wife but, thankfully, no children. The fact the law held Max under suspicion for a month added insult to his injury.

Scandal ensued. The kind of scandal a small town thrives on like a frenzied maggot infestation feeding on a three-day-old carcass. Max managed to ignore the looks and whispers he encountered in public. When he finally heard from Sissy, he'd allowed his anger to rage, and after two months, he finally moved back to Magnolia Oaks. He told himself it was for the children, but if he were honest, he needed Big Mama and Papa Joe as well.

Max realized he no longer rambled through the house, but had stopped in the main foyer, the same foyer he'd entered two years ago holding Neecie in his arms and clutching Charlie's hand. He'd returned home defeated and lost, his heart deflated, full of bitterness. He'd busied himself with work, staying away for long hours, sometimes twelve to fifteen hours a day, and he'd refused to return to the small ranch house on the east side of town that he'd shared with Sissy. The thought of walking into the home they'd shared as a family made his heart wrench.

Big Mama took over for him with the children, and when he decided to sell his house, she'd hired a crew to help pack up all of their belongings, and she'd supervised the process. Max had no idea what happened to any of Sissy's things. He'd never asked. And he didn't care. He hoped Big Mama had sent it all to the dump.

Hindsight, Max had loved Sissy when they first married. That blind kind of love that sees no flaws, but he'd been nothing but a kid. Twenty-three was too young to know whether he truly loved her or not, and she'd only been twenty when they'd married. She'd run off the week of her twenty-fifth birthday. If she'd stuck around, he'd been willing to make things work. But she made that decision for him. Sissy wasn't the woman he thought she was. He hadn't known her at all, because he couldn't fathom how a woman could run off and leave her children.

After moving back to Magnolia Oaks, nothing had helped with the insult of her desertion except nonstop work, excessive workouts at the gym, and an occasional date with a tequila bottle. Six months into wallowing in self-pity over his predicament and the house in town sold, Big Mama gave him a come-to-Jesus talk. She'd basically told him to put on his big boy pants and hitch up his suspenders. His children needed him. So he sucked up his pride and resentment and became the man she'd taught him to be, the father he needed to be, focusing on the care of Neecie and Charlie.

But after two years, the time had come for him to take care of himself. To concentrate on his own needs and desires, and he finally felt prepared to share his life with a companion. Someone to talk to and someone with whom he could exchange thoughts and dreams. Someone to hold. Someone to love.

He wasn't surprised that Celeste managed to get through to him. He was ready to move on when he'd first met her in August. And his attraction to her was tangible. She intrigued the hell out of him, and he liked the comfortable feeling of home he experienced when he was with her. She made him feel happy and relaxed. He wished he understood her jumpiness whenever he was around. She was more skittish than a cat on a hot tin roof. He smiled at the memories.

"Son."

Max turned at the sound of Brick descending the stairs. His father approached belting his robe around his waist.

"Big Mama said you wanted to talk to me. What can I do for you?" Brick stopped at the foot of the stairs.

Meddling old coot. Big Mama probably knew Max would ignore her suggestion and had intervened making sure that he and Brick talked.

"No, I'm good." Max turned to move past his father and started up the stairs, but Brick reached out and stopped him.

"I think I have an idea what this is all about," Brick said. "And I could use a night cap. What about the two of us tipping back a Wild Turkey and allowing me to explain a few things?"

Max permitted his father to turn him around, and he followed Brick to the bar at the far end of the main room. Brick placed two highball glasses on the counter and started to pour when Max reached out and took the bottle of bourbon from his father.

"Let me turn you onto something new." Max grabbed a bottle of añejo tequila.

Brick held up his hands and waved them as if to ward off an evil spirit. "Whoa, there." He laughed. "Your old man doesn't have any business slamming any shots of tequila."

"This isn't your average shooting gold," Max said. He took two brandy snifters from beneath the bar and proceeded to pour. He handed one to Brick and took the other for himself. He lifted his glass. "See the dark color. This is an extra añejo and has been aged for over three years. This is a fine spirit and demands respect. This tequila should be sipped neat." He swirled the liquor and inhaled the rich, earthy aroma, and Brick followed his lead.

"Pleasant bouquet," Brick said. "I'd swear there's an oaky scent to it."

"Not surprising, since it's aged in oak barrels." Max took a tiny sip and savored the woody piquant liquor. "Nice," he said. "Although I'll admit I prefer a nice reposado served straight-up."

"Here's to hoping we can figure out what makes our women folk tick and manage to find a life of happiness once we know," Brick toasted. He smiled before taking a drink.

Max hiked himself onto a bar stool and cupped the snifter between his palms.

"Is that a possibility?" he asked.

Brick laughed. "Probably not. I haven't figured it out yet, and I'm not sure Daddy has either."

"If Papa Joe hasn't, I'm sure we won't," Max said and paused for a moment. "We don't really need to talk," he continued. "Big Mama was mistaken."

"Shoot, boy. You know that's not true. Big Mama is never wrong." Brick laughed again and leaned forward on his elbows. "Your mama confessed she'd bent your ear and brought up that mess with Marlena. I don't know what in the world compelled her to tell you about that fiasco. I thought she'd gotten over the imagined affair a long time ago. I guess you never know what's going on inside a woman's head."

"No, sir. You're right. I don't think we have a clue." Max chuckled to fill the silence, but the sound didn't hold any humor.

"Big Mama seems to think I need to make sure you understand that there was no affair."

"She already convinced me." No sense confessing that he actually didn't care one way or the other.

"Do you have any other questions for me?"

"No, sir. I'm good." He finished his tequila. "Is that all?"

"There is something else I believe we should discuss," Brick said.

"What would that be, sir?"

"Your mama seems to think that Sissy should come home. That she should come back and y'all patch up things between you. And on the other side of the ring, Big Mama is hell bent and determined that Sissy coming back will happen when hell freezes over."

"And what do you think?"

"Do you love Sissy? Miss her?" Brick asked.

"Not in the least, sir. The thought of her actually repulses me. Her running off with another man destroyed any feelings I had for her and put the final nail in the coffin as far as our relationship goes. But what disturbs and frustrates me the most is the fact I don't understand how she could leave her children. What kind of person deserts their own offspring?"

Brick shrugged his shoulders, his pained expression evidence of his agreement with Max. "Son, I have no idea." Brick rubbed his temples with his fingers as if he tried to erase the memory of Sissy's actions by soothing his thoughts with the circular massage.

"I know it's hard for you to understand," Brick said. "But I love your mother. She certainly has her peculiar ways. Downright odd at times, but I believe, and I always have, that I was put on this Earth to love her. Protect her. And that's what I've done. I don't begrudge a single minute of it. I adore her and in some strange way she completes me. Who am I to second guess love?" Brick paused. "But if you don't love Sissy, I highly recommend that you stick to your conviction, because one single day is too long to be saddled to a woman you don't love."

Max mulled over his father's words. His old man made perfect sense. Twenty-four hours with someone you didn't love could seem like an eternity.

"You know, Dad, I believe that the foundation of a relationship is being faithful and honoring commitments." Max looked Brick square in the eye. "I might eventually forgive her, and possibly I already have, because I'm tired of being angry about the whole damn situation. But I don't love her." Max stopped as he realized something. "And I question if I ever really did."

CHAPTER TWENTY-SIX

৵৵

Monday night after work, Celeste huddled with the girls around the bar at the loft Becca shared with Marcus. They'd met at Becca's insistence to go over some outstanding wedding plans, but Celeste suspected the meeting was a disguised girlfriend meeting to calm Becca's premarriage jitters. A spread of appetizers was artfully arranged on a silver platter and displayed on the marble bar. They'd all waited patiently while Becca mixed each one of them their own tequila sunrise while she explained it was her signature drink of choice. And, without taking a breath, she chattered on asking how the bartenders could possibly serve one hundred guests their own individual drink of the beautiful concoction that was an art in of itself?

"Possibly you need to consider another signature drink," Trudi suggested, "or you'll need to have the venue mix a batch of premixed sunrises, and they'll be pink instead of the gradation colors of a sunrise?"

Becca gasped like someone had twisted her Lei D designer panties in a knot. "A tequila sunrise can't be pink."

"In that case, you might not be able to serve them," Trudi said. "Choose another signature drink—"

"I think I might go to Magnolia Oaks to see Max," Celeste announced out of nowhere. She paused and waited for her friends' reactions. She couldn't believe how much she'd missed spending the last two weekends with him or, more amazing, the intensity of the gnawing desire to see him again.

"I'm seriously considering visiting him," she said.

She meant it. For real. She was going.

Or maybe not.

"I think I'll drive down," she reiterated.

"Are you now?" Trudi asked in the disbelieving way only Trudi could achieve: by rolling the R and stretching out the U. She blinked in rapid succession three times then flared her upper lids so the whites of her eyes showed. She stared at Celeste. The Trudi dare stare.

"I'm not sure you should." Patrice added her opinion.

Celeste shot her a glare, but stopped herself before she said Who asked you?

"Don't go," Becca said. A worried frown puckered her forehead.

Maybe Celeste should suggest the bride indulge in a shot of Botox before the wedding? She smiled at her snarky thought. She probably needed a paralyzing dose herself, an entire face-full actually, considering all the moping she'd done since taking over as weekend anchor. At last she had what she wanted—her career on the fast track—but instead of feeling ecstatic and relishing every moment of her new position, for some unfathomable reason, she now wanted to spend time with Max. Celeste took a deep breath and sighed. If only she could figure out what she wanted.

The whole situation was like having an itch, and no matter how much she scratched, it wouldn't go away. And since she'd met Max, her new position didn't seem like enough.

"I know. The idea is crazy, isn't it?" Celeste's desire to see Max deflated somewhat at her friends' lack of enthusiasm. "Do you think traveling four hours south for a fling is insane?"

"Yes, it is," Trudi said. She nodded her head as if to indicate how zealously she concurred. "You'd be an absolute lunatic to go." She jabbed the straw in her drink, churning the ice and blending the drink to murky pink. "What's wrong with the men in Atlanta?"

"I thought you swore off men," Becca conveniently reminded her. "So please explain why you are considering this?" Becca grinned, but only her mouth curled, there was no humor in her expression, and if Celeste didn't know better, she'd swear Becca was being insensitive.

"I did swear off men."

"It didn't last very long," Trudi said in her deadpan tone. "What was it? Two weeks and then you slept with Max."

Celeste wasn't surprised by Trudi's response. She expected Trudi to be blunt and to the point. She exhaled a huff of air as if she'd been punched in the stomach. Sticks and stones could break her bones, and words could hurt like hell.

Trudi was right.

Again.

"Cut me some slack. After I stopped seeing Josh, I didn't go out on a date for months before I met Max. Months," Celeste said. She chewed her bottom lip. In the scheme of things and in her defense, six months didn't seem that long, and since her friends appeared less than supportive, Celeste wished she hadn't mentioned visiting Max. She wasn't sure why she had. Had she subconsciously wanted them to talk her out of it? "And besides," she added. "I didn't mean to sleep with him. It was an accident."

Trudi and Patrice burst out laughing.

"Do you hear yourself, girlfriend?" Trudi asked. She took a swig of her drink. "I hope you realize how you sound."

"I think the idea of going to see Max is incredibly romantic," Patrice said. The expression on her face glazed over with an angelic glow. Patrice still believed in love and princes on white horses, but to Celeste's amazement, the shimmer diminished, and Patrice tilted her head in concern. "But we've already discussed this and you need to focus on your career and yourself. You can wait until the wedding to see Max again."

"Wow," Trudi said.

"Are you for real?" Celeste asked. She couldn't believe that Patrice made perfect sense. A contemplative silence fell between them. Celeste imagined what her friends were thinking: Becca was obsessing about the wedding; Trudi was contemplating her next rendezvous with the bartender of the week; and Patrice was daydreaming about a prince and a horse.

"My wedding is less than two weeks away, and there's still so much to do." Becca confirmed Celeste's suspicion. She'd been worrying about the wedding. "I need y'all. Please tell me I can depend on y'all. Lei D wants to film the first commercial next month. Fabien and Marcus are furiously working on the story boards now. But, bottom line…I'll need to work, and we still need to—"

"Focus," Trudi demanded. She gave Becca the glare. "You have your gown, we all have our dresses and the final fitting was a success, the venue is scheduled, the menu and flowers chosen. What are you concerned about?" Trudi asked.

"The cake," Becca said. "I forgot to order the cake." She turned to Patrice. "And you didn't remind me." Her chin quivered. "None of you did."

Celeste wanted to remind Becca that the maid of honor could have reminded her. Oh wait, she was a distant cousin, a thousand miles away, but Celeste bit her tongue and sucked up her nasty thought.

"Don't freak," Patrice said.

"We already know that you'll use McEntyre's. As if your mother and grammy would allow you to use any other bakery," Trudi added.

"You simply need to do a taste testing and decide—"

"The flavor, the icing. Choose a cake topper," Celeste finished.

"We can help you. Do you want me to set up an appointment to do a tasting?" Patrice asked.

"Would you?" Becca puffed a deflated breath. "Don't tell my mother that I forgot to contact McEntyre's. The idea that I'd use them was so engrained in my mind that I mentally checked it off my to-do list, and I've been so busy helping Marcus and Fabien with the campaign for Lei D's new clothing line…listen to me, now I'm stressing." She took a staggered breath. "Where did all the time go?"

"You know time goes by faster when you get older, and since you're thirty now, it'll fly by faster and faster every year," Patrice said.

"And you shouldn't be trying to do so much." Trudi pointed out. "Helping Marcus with the advertising and fulfilling your obligations as the Lei D girl is a lot to handle while you're planning a wedding. But you know we're here for you. We always will be."

Becca moaned and covered her eyes with her hands. The sound reminded Celeste of worn-out brakes scrubbing against rotors.

"We'll take care of the cake," Celeste said. "You don't need to worry about it. You want the traditional yellow with the cake square icing and glaze, and pink rose buds...don't you?"

"Yes," Becca said, brightening. "I am so lucky to have the three of you."

"You know we've got your back," Trudi said.

"Always," Patrice confirmed.

"Forever," Celeste said.

They spent the remainder of the evening discussing the wedding, and no one mentioned Celeste's threat to travel south to visit Max again. But Celeste didn't forget it. She leaned back in her chair and tried to shake off the tension tightening her spine. She felt desperate, as if a noose hung around her neck while her toes teetered on the edge of a tilting chair. She was thirty years old, unmarried, with her career taking off, and her heart pining for a man with children. Things weren't going as she'd planned.

And the idea of seeing Max again, even coming face-to-face with Charlie and Neecie, seemed appealing. She needed to talk to Max.

The next morning after a quick phone call, Celeste threw her overnight bag into the back seat, slid behind the wheel, fastened her seatbelt, and headed south.

She smiled to herself as she guided the Acura onto the freeway.

Talk hell. She needed to see him.

The country and kids and dogs, oh my. And insatiable, hot kisses. Oh, yes, yes, yes.

CHAPTER TWENTY-SEVEN

❧⊰

Celeste sat cross-legged on the floor at the coffee table along with Max, Charlie and Neecie beside the fireplace in the front room of the big house.

"One more time, one more time…pwease, Lest?" Neecie asked. She smiled a sweet, beguiling grin, and if Celeste didn't know better, she'd swear Neecie batted her lashes. How could anyone say anything but yes to such a captivating little no-neck?

They'd played games before dinner and, after dinner, they continued their marathon with a third game of Candy Land, and a few rounds of Hi Ho Cherry-O and Chutes and Ladders. Celeste secretly prayed that they didn't own a junior version of Monopoly. Losing at Candy Land or Hi Ho Cherry-O was no big deal, but losing at Monopoly was another issue all together. She royally sucked at being a land developer and landlord and no matter how she calculated her strategy at buying properties she never seemed to invest correctly. She never passed go or collected her two hundred dollars. She always seemed to go to jail. Straight to jail. And she never ever had the Get Out Of Jail Free card.

"I weally, weally want to play again." Neecie reached over and cupped Celeste's cheeks with her warm, pudgy hands. "Can we?"

"I don't know," Celeste said, amazed by the fact that Neecie's slightly sticky hands hadn't totally turned her stomach upside down. In fact, there was a soft, sweet smell to the snuggly little girl, and Celeste found herself fighting the urge to scoop her up and give her a hug. "It's up to your dad."

Max lifted his lashes; the soft glow from the crackling fire reflected in the darkness of his eyes. A funny sensation stirred in her womb, and she'd swear her ovaries palpitated. What was wrong with her? She didn't particularly like no-necks, but she'd actually enjoyed every minute she'd spent with Max and his enchanting neckless monsters.

"Nice stall tactic, Neecie, but you know it's a school night. It's time for you and Charlie to get ready for bed." Max forced his expression into a stern scowl, and Celeste imagined how much effort it took for him not to give in and agree to another game. "Both of you tell Celeste good night. We'll go find Big Mama so she can help y'all."

"I don't want to." Neecie stuck out her bottom lip in an exaggerated pout. "I was having fun."

"So was I," Charlie said. "But Dad's right. We need to go upstairs. I have a test tomorrow and Big Mama is gonna quiz me one more time." He sounded far too grown up for his six years, but the little boy exposed himself when he looked at Max with adoration. "I promise I'm gonna make an A."

"I know you will, champ." Max ruffled Charlie's hair and stood up, reaching out his hands toward his children. Charlie jumped up and grabbed one outstretched palm, while Neecie took her time and reluctantly grabbed the other. She scruffed her foot into the carpet, one last diligent effort to prove she wasn't ready to admit defeat.

"I wanted to play another game with Lest," she said, and her bottom lip trembled.

"Come on," Max said and gave her hand a tug. "You'll get to see Celeste again in less than two weeks."

"I will." Neecie turned to Celeste and brightened, a dimple showing in her cheek. "Are you coming back to see us again?"

"You'll see her at the wedding, silly goose," Max said. "Remember. Celeste is a bridesmaid and you're the flower girl?"

Neecie's mouth rounded in wonderment. "It's aweady time for the wedding?"

"Sure is," Max said. "And you need to get up stairs and work on some beauty rest. Let's go." He moved toward the foyer with the kids. "Hold tight," he said to Celeste over his shoulder. "I'll be back down in a few."

Halfway across the immense room, Neecie broke away from her father's grasp and made a beeline back to Celeste.

"I need to tell Lest something," she bellowed. She ran to Celeste and collapsed into her lap. "I had fun pwaying games with you, and Sarge wanted me to tell you he's sowwy he didn't get to see you."

Celeste laughed, secretly glad Big Mama opted to keep the puppies at the kennel for the night. "Tell him I said 'hi.'"

"And somethin' else," Neecie said. "I need to tell you a seekweet." She cupped Celeste's cheeks again and nestled her face into Celeste's hair. "I wish you were my mommy," she whispered, her soft breath tickling across Celeste's neck. She hopped up and dashed across the room, passing Max and Charlie. When she reached the foyer she turned. "Night, Lest. Sweet dweams."

She disappeared around the corner with Max and Charlie on her heels.

Celeste struggled from her cross-legged position on the floor to sit on the hearth. She hugged her bent legs to her chest and rested her chin on her knees. She rocked herself gently and stared at the flames, watching the flicker of light burn yellow, orange and red. Smoke curled and dissipated up the chute, and heat radiated from the hearth, warming her. Or was she flushed from Neecie's secret wish? She brushed her fingers across her face touching where Neecie's sticky hands had clutched her earlier.

Her mommy?

Neecie wanted Celeste to be her mommy? Where had the sentiment come from? She couldn't imagine what had propelled the little girl to whisper such a wish.

Celeste tried to make sense of it, but she couldn't. They'd been around each other twice. The day of the fiasco with Sarge, and the time they'd just spent together. Could Neecie be so starved for the attention from a mother that even Celeste would do? Surely not.

Face it. Celeste wasn't exactly the motherly type. And she didn't want children. Ever.

Surely Neecie could perceive Celeste's aversion to kids. Did no-necks not have a sixth sense?

Celeste's resolve wavered at the memory of Neecie running toward her, long blonde curls swinging, a happy grin dimpling her cheeks, and the gummy-sweet aroma of little girl engulfing her when Neecie had collapsed into her lap.

And her ovaries ached again. She attempted to shake off her illogical reaction. What was up with her woman parts getting involved in her inner battle?

Celeste rubbed her temples, trying to calm the thoughts that weaved around inside her mind, in and out, up and down, like a little kid creating an image with an Etch A Sketch. She groaned at the contented hum purring through her body. What had she gotten herself into? The fling with Max had manifested and taken on a life of its own. Not what she'd intended at all.

She'd never imagined a divorced man with children being part of her life. In fact, the very idea made her cringe in the past. But she'd spent the entire evening playing board games and, without the slightest hesitation, had enjoyed herself.

The girls would never believe her when she told them. And she could almost hear Trudi say, Celeste, what is wrong with you? Don't you remember your own rules?

Celeste shrugged. She remembered them, but she was beginning to wonder if rules were that important after all.

Max tucked the blanket around Neecie. "Snug as a bug in a rug," he said and kissed her on the forehead.

"Can Lest come tuck me in?" Neecie asked, her lids fluttering heavy with sleep.

"No," he said. "I think you'll be asleep before I can get back down stairs. Sleep tight."

Neecie rolled over on her side and slipped her thumb into her mouth, a habit Max and Big Mama were reluctant to end considering what she'd been through. Allowing her to suck her thumb while she drifted off to sleep couldn't hurt anything orthodontia couldn't correct later.

He moved to the door and flicked off the light, leaving the room illuminated by the soft glow of Hello Kitty night light. Outside in the hallway he stalled for a moment and tried to get a handle on his tumultuous thoughts before returning down stairs.

That morning, he'd been ecstatic when Celeste had called and asked to come down for the night. After all, the past two weekends had been torture. Although he'd struggled with how to handle the afternoon after the kids came home from school, the issue solved itself when everyone arrived at the big house at the same time.

Celeste had pulled in behind him when he returned to the house from the fields, and neither one had time to exit their vehicles before Big Mama arrived with Charlie and Neecie. The kids had tumbled from the car in excitement, with Big Mama on their heels, grinning like a Cheshire cat. Which only made Max wonder if the timing of their arrival had been coincidence at all.

When Big Mama winked, Max knew he'd been played. He should have never mentioned that Celeste was coming down for the night. Sly old fox. Apparently it was in Big Mama's plans to expose Celeste to the kids.

He understood Big Mama's intentions. After all, he wanted Celeste to get to know the kids as well, but he wasn't sure it was the right time. Although he'd intended to talk to Celeste about hanging with the kids, he'd never broached the subject. And he had a gut feeling it might be too soon.

But there they'd been; Neecie jumping up and down, blonde hair swinging, a silly grin of happiness causing her face to glow, and Charlie seemed to bounce a little on his heels, his enthusiasm contained behind his reserve. But Max recognized his delight. Max was amazed at their reaction; he presumed that they'd bonded to Celeste over the Sarge incident the day of the picnic.

When they'd begged to play games and Celeste had assented, he'd had no choice but to agree. After all, he was a package deal, and if he and Celeste potentially had a future together the kids would be part of their life.

He sent up a quick prayer that her spending an afternoon with the kids wasn't too soon, because he supposed that two children could be overwhelming for a career-focused city girl. Although he was a firm believer that all things happened for a reason, he hoped that the afternoon had played out as it had for a good one.

After all, Celeste had enjoyed herself. Or so it seemed.

Max pushed his worrisome thoughts from his mind and picked up his pace. He hurried down the hall eager to see her alone.

Laughter and sweet kisses would be the perfect climax to a fabulous day.

Max smiled to himself, convinced happiness was in his future after all.

CHAPTER TWENTY-EIGHT

త∞ల

Max crouched before the hearth at his cabin and opened the damper. He grabbed twigs from the tender box and busied himself building a base for a fire.

"I can't believe how chilly it is." Celeste shivered and made a brrrr sound.

Max stopped what he was doing and turned around. Celeste busied herself with unhooking the straps on her high-heeled, platform sandals. She took them off and pushed them aside, then reclined on the couch and curled her legs underneath her. Max grabbed a throw off the back of the chair and covered her.

"This should keep you warm until I get this fire going."

He turned back to the fireplace and lit a match to check the draft. Satisfied that the flow was wafting upward, he extinguished the flame and layered more sticks, before he stacked kindling crisscrossed and perpendicular so it created a foundation.

"Building a fire is an art, isn't it?" Celeste asked.

Max turned to her and laughed. "I guess you could categorize it as a specialized skill." He stacked two mid-sized logs on top and lit another match, touching it to the twigs. He sat on the hearth and watched the yellow flames flicker and curl. Finally satisfied with the crackling noise the starter twigs made as the fire caught, he shifted his attention to Celeste.

"Impressive," she said. "There's something incredibly sexy about a man who can build a fire with such finesse."

"Thank you," he said. He supervised the fire for a moment longer before he settled on the couch next to Celeste. "Well," he began. "What did you think?"

"I already told you, you are obviously a master fire starter."

"No, I mean this evening."

"You mean dinner?" she asked. "The food was fabulous. Does Big Mama always cook gourmet meals?"

"I think she was showing off for you. She doesn't normally go all out. Chicken marsala isn't a typical menu, especially on a Tuesday night."

"I have to admit it was better than any I've ever tasted, and the potatoes and almondine green beans," she paused and licked her lips. "A culinary delight." She made a smacking noise. "Yummy."

"I'm glad you enjoyed it," Max said. "And did you see the way she grinned from ear to ear when you told her how good it was. No doubt about it, you made her day."

"Good. I'm glad." Celeste smiled her megawatt smile, the one he'd come to know as her real smile. "Make sure she knows I only give compliments where they are due."

"I'll do that." He shifted his attention to the fireplace to ensure the kindling had caught. "But actually, what I was really asking...what did you think about this afternoon? Spending time with Neecie and Charlie."

"I'll confess, the afternoon wasn't what I'd expected," she said, and when she paused, he turned his head so he could see her. Her expression was guarded, but she smiled, and he breathed a sigh of relief. "I should have realized," she continued. "But I was so amazed that I'd decided to drive down, I guess I didn't fully think it through. I didn't take into consideration that Tuesday was a normal work day and school day. And you're a family. Life goes on. Right?"

Max nodded. She seemed to connect the dots. Life with him would mean every day family things. Work. Kids. School. Homework. Baseball practice. Games. Dance class. Recitals. Not much glamour in his life. But there was a lot of love. And satisfaction. But did she see it that way? He waited for her to go on.

Celeste lowered her eyes and focused on the velour throw. She didn't want to see his face full of expectation. Had she made a mistake by coming to visit Max? There was no question that she enjoyed spending time with him. She liked him. Probably too much. And she did want to know where her feelings might lead and learn if he felt the same way about her.

But the kids. She couldn't get emotionally close to the children. What if she decided the family unit didn't work for her? She'd been a fool to come. Follow your heart. Where had that sentimental bad advice come from? She entwined her fingers in the silky fringe of the throw and combed the soft strands. A hush stretched between them. Not a calm, comfortable silence, but a strained awkward quiet.

An ill-at-ease situation she'd created with her impetuous trip. She didn't particularly care to admit she was ever wrong, but she should have listened to the girls and waited until the wedding to see Max again. In a controlled environment without any expectations. A good time celebrating Becca and Marcus's love. But here she was alone with Max in his cabin after spending the afternoon with his family, and she wasn't sure what she wanted.

She inwardly cringed at the thought that she could potentially hurt others with her indecisive behavior. Although she wasn't prepared to make any decisions about their future, she had the distinct impression from Max's silence that he might expect her to. She decided to suck it up and make the best of the night.

"The entire afternoon…dinner, this evening was nice," she said. She smiled and her lips quivered, but she tightened her cheek muscles and the smile stayed put. "I enjoyed myself. I had no idea that Candy Land could be such fun."

Max laughed. He draped his arm across her shoulder, and she felt him relax.

"Good. I was hoping you'd say that," he said. "Are you ready for your next sample of tequila?"

"Sure," she said. "What's the next flavor?"

Max stood and walked to the kitchen. "They aren't flavors. They are classifications. And I think it's time for you to taste an extra añejo."

"So I've graduated to the big girl tequilas, have I?" She drew a deep breath and exhaled, relieved he'd changed the subject. If they kept talking about the afternoon with the children, she was fearful her allergies to no-necks might kick in and she'd break out in the hives. Big itchy whelps. Which could put a damper on the remainder of their evening.

Max returned with a bottle of tequila and two crystal glasses. The tumblers were round and sported a diamond and wedge cut.

"Nice glasses," Celeste said. She picked one up and rested it in the palm of her hand. "I love the shape. Are they Waterford?"

Max settled next to her again and busied himself with opening the bottle.

"I have absolutely no idea." He laughed. "Serena bought them. So probably." He took the glass from her and began to pour. "The class of tequila is defined by its color and the length of time it's aged. This tequila is a premium class. The finest of the fine." He lifted the glass and whiffed, before handing it to her.

"No ice?" she asked. The idea of sipping the tangy liquor room temperature made her stomach lurch and her mouth water.

"Yep," he said. "This one should be sipped neat." He took a drink. "Go ahead," he urged. "Try it."

Not quite believing the flavor would be as refined as he promised, she took a dainty sip, and surprisingly found it palatable. "Nice." She took another drink. "I like it."

"What a perfect way to end a great day," he said. He eased his shoes off and propped his sock-covered feet on the coffee table. "Our peanuts passed the USDA inspection, and we should have everything sold by the end of the week. A great day at the office so to speak. I came home and enjoyed an afternoon with my kids. A great dinner with my family, and now I'm enjoying a drink in front of a roaring fire with a very special woman." He lifted his glass in toast. "Here's to a beautiful woman, who I am lucky enough to spend time with...I would toast to the losers who have lost you, but what's to say other than I'm glad they did. So here's a simple toast to a fabulous evening."

Celeste lifted her glass and touched the edge to his, her cheeks burning hot, and she wasn't sure if it was the fire, the tequila, or the expression on Max's face that made her flush. She took another drink and decided to relax and enjoy the tequila. She pushed her earlier doubts about the day from her mind and decided she agreed with him. The night was perfect and from the reflection of firelight in his eyes, she had an idea it was about to get a lot hotter.

When Celeste drained her tumbler, Max reached over and took it from her. His fingers brushed hers and she saw him scrutinize her from below his thick, dark lashes. A cruel trick of nature to give a man such luscious lashes.

He bent his head and touched his lips to hers and inhaled, taking her breath away. She hummed at the light contact. A soft, barely there kiss that would have crumpled her knees if she'd been standing. He stroked her neck and shoulders with feather-light touches that prickled her skin with desire.

"You're so beautiful," he said against her mouth, before he intensified the pressure of their kiss. He teased her with his tongue, the flavor of the tequila fueling the heat between them. His hand brushed her breast, then settled against her ribs. The heat from his fingers seared through her blouse, and her nipples tightened at his provocative touch.

She wanted his skin against hers, and she convulsively reached for his shirt and managed to unhook the top buttons, enough so she could slide her hands inside his shirt. The skin on his rock-hard chest was hot and soft as silk. She ran her fingers along his etched abs, along his ribs, around his waist toward his back. He stiffened and pulled the shirt over his head and shucked it aside.

Celeste gazed up and relished the sight of him. His tanned chest smooth, his muscles lean, his abs ripped. He reminded her of a romance cover model. The fact he still wore his jeans was somewhat troubling since they hindered her entire view of his gorgeous, too perfect body. She unbuckled his belt and unhooked the button of his jeans, reached for his zipper and inched it downward. He sucked in a deep breath, his muscles rippling. She tried to pull the pants from his hips.

"Let me help with that," he said. He stood and husked his jeans aside. "Looks like you need to catch up." And before she knew what was happening he'd whisked her jeans and top aside and exposed her to the rapidly warming air, leaving only her bra and thong between her and the elements. He exhaled, and his expression provided evidence that the investment in the red silk lingerie was worth every penny.

"The sight of you drives me crazy," he said. His voice was low, husky. He touched the side of her face and trailed a finger down her neck, across the crest of her breasts. Her nipples ached for his touch, and she arched her back thrusting her chest forward, but his finger kept its course southward teasing the delicate skin of her belly and hips, until he reached the vee of her thong where he stopped his descent. He pressed against her groin and stoked the throbbing ache between her thighs. He rubbed a circular motion with his thumb. "You like?" he asked.

"Very much," she gasped, and when he slipped his finger under the edge of her thong, she almost cooed her excitement, a lightning rush of adrenaline fueling an insatiable desire, a yearning to have him inside her. She ground her pelvis against his hand, amazed that his touch alone could leave her on the edge of climax. "I want you now, please," she managed to say. She tugged on his boxers. "These need to go."

"Not yet," he said. He cupped her breasts with his hot hands and dipped his head, stroking one breast with his tongue and then the other. Through the lace of her bra, he flicked his tongue across her peaked nipples, and she moaned with the need for him to pull the bra aside.

"Off, off," she said and swatted at her bra with her hand.

Max obliged by reaching behind her and unleashing her breasts from the dainty lace. Celeste reached up and grabbed her breasts, the relentless throbbing driving her wild for his touch. "You...touch...here."

But instead of doing as he was told, Max pulled her hands away and took his time to lick his way from one breast to the other, skimming and swirling his tongue against her hypersensitive skin, every touch pushing her closer and closer to the edge of orgasm. The man was a maestro.

"Pistachio. So very, very good," he said, humming the words against her flesh.

And all the while he tasted her, his hands caressed her, hungrily, greedily, up and down her torso, to her thighs and back, as if he tried to consume her with his touch. When his finger slid under the lace of her thong again, her legs instinctively parted, and he touched her in the best spot of all. Quivering desire swelled within her, and a whimper escaped her lips.

Max pulled her thong and slid it down her legs and when he started to toss it aside, Celeste grabbed his arm.

"Careful," she said and her gaze darted toward the fire. He laughed and dropped them on the table.

"Better?"

"Yes."

"Are you ready for me?" he asked.

She couldn't find the words to express how much she wanted him, so she simply nodded.

Max stood and made a slow show of sliding his underwear past his hips, watching her watching him. He smiled when his erection bounced free and she reached out to claim him.

He eased her back on the couch and stretched himself down beside her.

Max wrapped his arms around her and gloried in the fervor they shared. He'd never met a woman who could make him feel so complete. He loved the smell of her, the touch of her skin, like a fine creamy silk. She arched beneath him, inviting him in.

"I'm ready for you," she reminded him. She raked her nails down his back and crushed him closer.

When she locked her legs around his hips, he had no other choice but to find his way home. And he did.

They moved in synchronized harmony, rocking each other's worlds until they were both exhausted and sated.

Later lying in bed, Max watched Celeste while she slept, knowing she was the one. Believing that all things happen for a reason.

And praying she knew it too.

CHAPTER TWENTY-NINE

వ≈

At eight-thirty in the morning Celeste and Max left the cabin. Unusually timid with one another for two people who'd spent such an intimate evening, they said their good-byes surrounded by a chill, fog-shielded sunrise.

"Call me when you get home," Max said. "So I'll know you arrived safely."

"Why don't I text instead?" Celeste asked. "You'll be working, and I've already interrupted your week as it is."

"No, not at all. You weren't an interruption. I enjoyed every minute you were here."

He slid his hands around her face and cupped her cheeks, placing a light kiss on her lips. Memories of the night before stirred within her, but she knew she needed to shake off the reaction to his touch.

"It was a good time," she agreed. "But I was a distraction for you and your family. That wasn't fair of me. I was being purely selfish coming down here on the spur of the moment."

"I like spontaneous decisions, especially when they culminate with me having the chance to see you." He grinned his boyish smile, and he almost tripped her up.

"What I'm trying to say is," she paused, knowing what she needed to say, but not sure how to go about it.

"What is it?" Max tilted his head to the side and waited. "Is something wrong?"

"No. Not wrong. I think it might be best to give each other some space between now and the wedding," she said. "Time to think."

"About?"

"Things," she said. "Us."

"Did I do—"

"This isn't about you," she said. She struggled with the sensation that she was five years old again and in the midst of an inner battle, on the verge of a tantrum, trying to understand herself and what she really wanted. "I don't know what I'm thinking right now," she said with a light, fake laugh.

Max stared at her for a moment. He didn't smile in return.

"I have my career," she said. "And I'm not sure how I fit in with all of this." She lifted her hands indicating the whole of Magnolia Oaks, the cabin, the lake, the children. "I enjoyed myself immensely. Probably too much. But I think I made a mistake coming down yesterday."

Max started to say something, but she lifted her hand in protest.

"I need time to think." A hot, stinging prickled behind her lids. "Forgive me."

Celeste jerked open the door of the Acura, tossed her overnight bag into the back seat, and slid behind the wheel. She started the car and rolled down the window. "Tell Neecie and Charlie I had a nice time, and I said good-bye."

She pulled away and made the mistake of glancing in her rearview mirror. And like Lot's wife, punished for her secret longing, she felt like she'd turned into a pillar of salt.

The Acura bumped along the drive, the crunch of the rock and gravel beneath the wheels echoing in the still morning air. A sad, empty final sound followed her exit, while a miserable silence consumed the car.

And all she could think was chicken shit. Chicken shit.

Fifty miles south of Atlanta, Celeste abandoned her inner argument and decided to call her mom. After all, battling with herself for the last three hours during her drive northward had gotten her nowhere.

"Hello, Precious." Mom answered on the second ring. Although she could always depend on her mom to be available when she needed her, Celeste still breathed a sigh of relief.

"I want to get your thoughts on some things," Celeste started the conversation.

"Sure, what's on your mind?"

"Do you recall about a month ago, when we went to dinner with Dad to celebrate?"

"Yes, of course. It was a lovely time. Dad had the prime rib—

"I don't want to discuss what we ate, Mom," Celeste said. She had to reel in her mother or she'd take off on a tangent and waste fifteen minutes of conversation time discussing the entire evening. Celeste didn't have the time for chit-chat; she wanted to get to the point. "We discussed kids."

"Yes," Mom said, dragging out the word as if she was already mentally deducing what their conversation might truly mean.

"I'm curious to know about your decision," Celeste said. "How you decided to be a stay-at-home mom and give up your career."

"Once I met your father and we married, it was an easy decision for me. I wanted a perfect family. To be a wonderful mother," Mom said. "I always knew I wanted children. I loved playing with baby dolls, and when I was nine or ten years old, I made the proclamation that I wanted eight children. Four boys. Four girls. Your grandma laughed at me and said, 'That's what you think now.' And of course Mother was right, because when I found out about the birds and bees and realized what I had to do to have children, what giving birth involved, I changed my mind." Mom laughed and Celeste giggled along with her, remembering her own disillusionment when she'd discovered what sex entailed. The idea of boys putting their private stuff in her private places seemed so unbearably gross. But luckily she'd outgrown her juvenile perception.

She grinned to herself, thinking of last night with Max, but she forced her thoughts back to the conversation at hand and straightened her toes, her foot pressing the accelerator. She sped ahead.

"So you changed your mind from eight to three?"

"Not consciously. Things played out that way," Mom said. "Two boys two years apart and they were a handful. That's why it took me five years to finally have my girl. But having you made our family complete."

"You never missed your career?"

"Not really. I've always been a family-centric girl, not necessarily a career-focused one. Let's face it, I'm not a feminist. I'm a mother. A wife. A homemaker. And a grandmother. I love my life." Mom paused. "What are we really discussing here?"

"I've always been career-centric," Celeste said. "It's almost as if I'm the complete opposite of you." She'd never thought about their differences that way before. She'd focused totally on her career. Her mother had forfeited hers for a family. Celeste didn't want children. Children had always been her mother's dream.

"You know, Precious, it doesn't have to be black or white. There is a gray," Mom said. "Your life can come together in a way that will allow you to have a career and a personal life that includes a family. If that's what you want. You can have both, after all this is the twenty-first century. We're well into women's liberation. Come on, we've had the right to vote for almost a hundred years." Mom laughed.

"You're correct," Celeste concurred. "And parenthood is no longer viewed as an obligation, but as an option, and some women choose to not only postpone motherhood, but choose to bypass it altogether. Trudi and I have discussed this numerous times, and she and I both agree that offspring are not in our future."

"I hope you don't take this wrong," Mom said. "But I don't think foregoing motherhood would be such a bad decision for Trudi. In fact, a motherless Trudi might be good. But you on the other hand—"

"Mom, seriously, I can't believe you. Trudi is one of my best friends, and I love her. How could you say such a thing?"

"Listen to you," Mom said. "Defending Trudi's right to motherhood. You just explained that she didn't want children."

"Right. Her decision. Not your opinion whether she should have them or not." Celeste hated that her voice had taken on the defensive tone she'd used in her teens. She digressed, and the conversation wasn't going as she'd planned. "I don't want to discuss Trudi. Whether she wants children has nothing to do with what I want to discuss." She tightened her grip on the steering wheel and focused on the heavier traffic she'd encountered closer to metro Atlanta.

"Which is?" Mom asked.

"How you knew? When you decided to give up your career for Dad and the boys?"

"I wanted to be home, and I knew it. I'm afraid I can't give you an explanation of a life shattering moment. I made the decision because it was the right one for me." She paused. "Is there a decision that you need to make?"

"No, no, not at all. I'd been thinking about my career. About yours. And I was curious what your determining factor might have been."

"It's a life choice," Mom said. "When the time comes for you to make such a decision—"

"But I don't want—"

"I know. You don't want children. You want your career. I understand. But I'm saying, should there ever come a time that you want to make a decision, you're smart enough to figure it out. You'll find the right place for your heart and your mind, and you'll follow it. And it'll be the right decision for you. Trust me."

Celeste smiled. She did trust her mom. Kind-hearted and always optimistic, she could depend on her. Always.

"Thanks, Mom. I appreciate you."

"I love you, Precious."

"I love you too."

"I'm here to talk whenever you need me."

"I know." And she did know; she could always rely on her parents. They'd always supported her. She assumed that was part of the family package as well. Always knowing you had someone you could depend on. "Bye, Mom."

"Bye, Precious."

Her Bluetooth disconnected and the iPod continued a blaring tune. Not certain that her mother's revelation or words of wisdom had guided her to an understanding of her own inner turmoil, Celeste focused on the expressway ahead.

She felt as if she'd been lost for a long time. Would she ever figure out the road home?

CHAPTER THIRTY

✀

Max pulled into the drive to Magnolia Oaks. With the peanut harvest behind him, he'd have time to focus on the curriculum for the class he'd finally agreed to teach at the community college winter semester. Teaching would give him a purpose. And the planning would occupy his thoughts. And time.

He'd need something since Celeste had pretty much blown him off. Although, he hoped by the wedding she'd reconsider. He believed there was a special connection between the two of them, and he still held hope that she would realize it too. Quite possibly that was what had spooked her.

A low layer of clouds cast a gray hue to the late afternoon, and he unconsciously followed the drive, almost allowing the truck to drive itself past the row of oaks and gangly, tall pines. Over the past four days, he'd beat himself up, counting off everything he'd done wrong.

First, he should have told Celeste to drive to the cabin. But he hadn't wanted to hide her, as if he was ashamed of her. Nothing could be further from the truth.

Second, he shouldn't have allowed Celeste to run into the children. She wasn't ready, and he'd known it.

Third, when they all had accidentally arrived at the house at the same time, he should have insisted the kids go with Big Mama and not have allowed them to spend time with Celeste. That mistake was probably the one he regretted the most. Neecie had asked about Lest at least ten times every day since Wednesday. When would Lest be back? Where was Lest now? Wasn't it time for the wedding because she wanted to see Lest.

Celeste hadn't been ready and now he'd given his children some false sense of...of what? That their dad might have a girlfriend? That they might have a mother again?

Max tried to shake off the impression of impending doom because he held firm to the idea that everything happened for a reason. And everything would turn out fine. Yesterday was history, and he still had tomorrow. And next week. And the wedding. And seeing Celeste again.

Max walked toward his office, but before he could reach for the knob, Serena opened the door and held it wide, smiling.

"Look who's home," she said. She stepped aside and behind her stood Sissy. She looked the same, maybe a little fluffier. Still cute.

Pert.

But evil.

"Hey, Max," she said, flipping her long hair over her shoulder.

With a heartfelt pang, he thought of Neecie with the same blonde locks. He moved into the room, his mind numb. What the hell was Sissy doing in his office?

"I'll leave so y'all can talk," Serena said and stepped out, closing the door with a click, leaving the two of them alone.

Max stared at Sissy. A dull, deadened ache spilled through his gut. The mother of his children, and he couldn't feel anything more than a distrustful loathing.

"I assume you want to see Charlie and Neecie." Of course that was why she'd come, trying to make amends with the children. To see them. If what his mother had told him was true, she'd possibly come back to try to patch up things between them. But there'd be no way he would ever take her back. Now that he knew what true happiness could entail.

"Hmmm. I wanted to see you first." She'd stopped about three feet away and glanced up at him from beneath lowered lashes, a playful smile pulling at her lips. He knew the expression well; it was the same flirty expression she'd wooed him with when they'd first met. She took the few steps to clear the distance between them and splayed her hands against his chest, the same adulterous hands that had recently touched Pastor Dick.

Max forced himself not to cringe at her touch.

"I thought you and I should get reacquainted before I see Charlie and Neecie again," she said.

She reached up and ran a finger down the length of his jaw, stood on her tip-toes and pressed a moist kiss against the corner of his mouth. Like she used to. But her lips were oddly cold, and Max jerked back and wiped his mouth with the back of his sleeve.

"What do you want, Sissy?" He had no use for any of her kisses, for her seduction. She could save all of her wiles to use on other men. He put his hand up and held her away from him. Sissy sucked in a deep breath, as if he'd struck her.

"Aren't you glad to see me?" She tried using her innocent look: eyes opened wide, a few bats of her lids, her mouth a silly, little O shape. That one didn't seem to work anymore either.

He gritted his teeth. "I'll ask again, and why don't you try to find it in your lying, cheatin' heart to come up with an answer this time. And try a truthful one. What do you want?"

"Let's sit down and catch up on life." She settled in a nearby recliner and waited.

"I'll stand, thank you."

"Suit yourself," Sissy said and for a brief moment he thought he saw something flicker in her eyes, a warmth reminiscent of their first few years together, when he'd thought they'd been in love. But he knew better now, and his heart ached at the thought of their bogus love and all the wasted years, but most of all he hurt for Charlie and Neecie.

"So what do you want to know?" Max asked, angry with himself that he wouldn't—couldn't—simply tell her to go. "Are you moving back to Tyler?" He flinched when he asked, not really wanting to know her answer, worried about the direction their conversation would take.

"Well," she said, smiling, all dimples and duplicity, "that depends on whether you'll have me back."

Max felt as if he'd been sucker punched. He should have seen that one coming. Serena had been correct after all. Sissy wanted to come home.

"I don't think that's going to happen, Sissy."

"You wouldn't give me another chance?"

"Not until hell freezes over."

Sissy stood and advanced toward him again, each step deliberately slow, each step appearing stealthier than the last. She stopped directly in front of him.

"I made a mistake. Can't you find it in your heart to forgive me? Allow me to come home where I belong. To be a family with you," she paused, "and the kids. I bet Neecie's all grown up, not a baby anymore. Come on, Max, give me another chance." She leaned in to kiss him again, but he stepped aside. She teetered off balance.

"I don't think this is a good idea," Max said. "I've moved on. I don't have feelings for you anymore." In the back of his mind, Serena's words haunted him. Family first. Sometimes you have to swallow your pride. Bullshit. "You need to stay away from me, and tell me what you came here for."

"I came because I missed my family, the people I love the most. I want to make amends."

"You don't run out on the people you love. You don't desert your own family." Max didn't see an ounce of truth shining through her eyes. If she'd wanted her family back, wouldn't she have asked to see the children? Demanded it, instead of trying to seduce him? He didn't believe a word she was saying. He knew what it was like to look into someone's eye and see the truth. And at the moment he was looking into deep pools of blue, a muddled mess of deceit and lies.

"What is it that you really want, Sissy?" Max asked. He pinched the bridge of his nose and concentrated on forcing his lips closed and holding back the expletives that wanted to spew from his unforgiving lips. Why the hell had she returned? He pushed his hands through his hair in exasperation. He'd spent two years learning to overcome her deception and focus on the future. On the kids. And now that he'd met Celeste, he had hopes for a new relationship. Why would Sissy raise her Medusa head and complicate his life all over again? Mess with his brain. He lifted his head, stretching his neck and rolling his shoulders in order to release the tension griping his spine. He gritted his teeth and stared her in the eye. "Why are you here?"

"I love you," Sissy said. Her lips lifted into a persuasive smile, winsome, almost believable, but Max wasn't convinced. "I realize what I did was wrong. I should have never left the way I did." She paused and lifted her hand as if she implored his forgiveness. "I regret everything. Would you not consider giving me a second chance?"

He moved back a step. Thought better of it and took another protective step away from her.

"Please explain to me how I can trust anything that comes out of your mouth? And while you're at it, why don't you also explain how you think I can find the strength to forgive you?" He clamped his jaw and forced his words through clenched teeth. "Excuse you? Or consider giving you another chance?"

"We had something special once, and I know you can find it within yourself to forgive me. You're a good man, Max Riley."

"Bullshit." The words exploded through his lips. "You threw everything away when you disappeared. If there was a chance for us, it disappeared the day you left. I do not have a smidgen of emotion left for you Sissy."

She didn't seem to understand what he'd said. Sissy sidled up close and pressed against him.

"Make love to me like you hate my guts—rip out all of the disgust you have for me. Purge your soul, so you can care for me again" She tickled her tongue along his jaw, her tongue warm, her breath hot.

Max pushed her away and she stumbled backwards, an expression of disbelief on her face.

"Max, I don't understand?"

"Understand what, Sissy? That I despise you? Because that would seem clear to me. I'm not sure what's clouding your vision," Max snarled. "Maybe it's all the sin and deceit in your world that's veiled your sight. Maybe you can't see the truth anymore."

"I see the truth." Sissy smiled. "You're angry right now, but once you have a few days to cool down," she almost hummed the words, "you'll take me back. I'll make you take me back."

Max glanced at the clock above the fireplace. One o'clock. Big Mama and the kids would be home from church soon. He needed to get Sissy away from Magnolia Oaks before Charlie and Neecie arrived home.

"There's no car outside," Max said. "How'd you get here?"

"The bus. Serena picked me up in town."

"How kind of her," Max said, and vowed to have a few choice words with Serena. How dare she bring Sissy to their home without his knowledge? Big Mama would blow a gasket when she found out. "Where do you plan on staying?"

"Here?" Sissy tried another one of her coquettish expressions.

Max's stomach roiled. "No way in hell are you staying here." He reached out and grabbed her arm. "Get your things. I'm taking you to town."

After registering Sissy in a cabin and paying for five nights, Max moved away from the registration desk of the Quality Lake

Resort fifteen miles northwest of town near Lake Seminole. Twenty miles from the Oaks. Hopefully enough distance between his children and a woman with no car.

Sissy waited across the lobby, one lone bag on the floor. Leave it to her to show up in Tyler penniless and looking like a waif. All of her earlier self-assuredness was gone, and she appeared lost. Max enjoyed a jab of self-satisfaction before he heard Serena's voice inside his head. Family. The children need their mother. Family comes first. You and Sissy belong together. Max massaged his temples trying to ward off the unwelcomed thoughts. Serena's guilt trip sermon was the last thing he needed bouncing around inside his head. He needed a clear mind to deal with Sissy. And he prayed the five days he'd paid for the cabin would be long enough for the two of them to work out their differences and send her on her way. She needed to be long gone before they left for Atlanta.

Max inhaled a deep fortifying breath. This was not how he'd anticipated spending the week before the wedding.

An hour later, Max unloaded the last bag of groceries into the cupboards of the tiny lake cabin.

"This should get you through a few days," he said.

Sissy had busied herself with unpacking, placing items in the dresser and hanging a few pieces of clothing on hangers. She stood in front of the small sink in the bathroom placing her toothbrush and paste, a brush, and a small cosmetic bag on the back of the vanity.

"There," she said. "Like home sweet home." She flashed a bright smile and moved the few steps from the bathroom to the kitchenette. "I can't thank you enough for taking me in, Max. I don't know what I would've done if I hadn't had you to depend on."

She gestured as if she intended to reach for him, but Max backed away.

"I'm not taking you in, and you can get it out of your head that you can depend on me because you can't. And I'm not sure why you came back to Tyler," Max said, but he motioned between the two of them. "But the two of us. It's not happening. You can get any idea of a reconciliation out of your head."

"I know this is hard for you," Sissy said. "But Serena told me that she talked to you about the importance of family, and I believe in my heart that you'll do the right thing."

Max waited, and an expectant pause grew between them. He waited for her to add the full ammo to her artillery. The moment she played the guilt card about Charlie and Neecie needing their mother.

"If you'll spend some time with me the next few days, I know I can make you understand that I've changed," Sissy said. "I'm truly sorry for hurting you. And if you give me a chance, I'll make it up to you. You'll see. You'll want me back."

"I'll give you minimal time in order to determine where you're going and how fast." Max moved to the door and pulled it open. "And I will not want you back."

He slammed the door on his way out.

"What the hell were you thinking," Brick asked, his voice raised.

Max quirked an eyebrow at Big Mama. Brick never raised his voice to Serena. Max, along with Big Mama, Papa Joe, Brick and Serena sat huddled in his office. The strained silence the five of them that had endured through dinner could have choked a giraffe. But now that the children were in bed, everyone had donned their boxing gloves.

"There's no need to shout, Brick. I have perfectly good hearing." Serena lifted her chin and gazed at each of them. "Sissy called me. She wanted to come home. How could I deny her?"

"Easy," Big Mama said. "You could have said no. Real simple and to the point. That piece of white trash has no business here." Big Mama gritted her teeth. "I can't believe you were so dumb."

Serena gasped. "There's no need to get nasty." She turned to Brick. "Are you going to allow your mother to talk to me that way?"

"This time, Serena, Mama's right. You should have never encouraged Sissy to come back to Tyler, and you certainly shouldn't have brought her to Magnolia Oaks." Brick held out his hand imploringly. "Don't you understand? That was wrong. You were wrong."

"And unannounced at that," Big Mama pointed out. "Blindsiding Max that way. You should be ashamed of yourself."

"It was not my intent to 'blindside' anyone." Serena sat up straight and squared her shoulders, as if she sat for a formal portrait. "I think you all know I believe in family first."

"Well, you have a strange way of showing that you believe in family first," Papa Joe said. "Because I don't think bringing Max's ex to the house was a family thing to do. It just wasn't right."

Max almost fell out of his chair. Papa Joe rarely voiced his opinion, especially about family matters. He'd always relied on Big Mama to handle them.

"You all can gang up on me if you want, but I stand by my decision, and I think I did the right thing." Serena dabbed at her eyes with a kerchief, but Max would swear he didn't see the first glint of a teardrop. "Sissy should be home. Back with her children. It'll make up for the scandal, and over time people will forget about her and the youth minister."

"People will never forget about Sissy running off. You're delusional if you believe they will," Big Mama said.

"Are you telling me they never forgot about Marlena?" Serena said, her voice lowered. She turned to Brick. "They remember?"

"Oh, good Lord, Serena," Brick said. "There isn't anything for anyone to remember. Nothing happened between Marlena and me. You imagined it. Big Mama thinks you had postpartum depression, and I'm inclined to agree with her."

"Give it up, Serena. You were never wronged. Only by your own imagination. All that drama was in your head," Big Mama said. "However, the drama you've caused for Max is real." She paused and turned to Max. "Now what are we, as a family, going to do about this fine mess?"

"I'll handle it," Max said. "She asked for a few days. That'll give me time to talk with my attorney and determine where I stand legally if she insists on seeing Charlie and Neecie." Max closed his eyes and rubbed his temples. Sissy opening old wounds for him was one thing, but hurting the children was another. And it was the last thing in the world he wanted to come from her visit.

His children came first. He'd protect them at all costs.
He'd figure out the right thing to do.

CHAPTER THIRTY-ONE

Tuesday evening Becca called an emergency girlfriend meeting at five o'clock, and the four of them met at her loft. Their meeting would be the first time Celeste had seen them since she'd returned from Tyler.

"I can't believe it. This is a catastrophe," Becca said. She reclined against the black leather couch, and Miss Kitty snuggled into a ball of fur in her lap.

"I knew it was a bad idea to have a distant cousin as your maid of honor," Trudi said. "The idea reeked of an impending disaster."

"Don't be so harsh," Celeste said. "No one could possibly have known she'd be struck with appendicitis three days before the rehearsal dinner."

"I didn't know people could still get appendicitis," Patrice said. "I thought there was a vaccination for it."

Celeste studied her face, waiting for the grin. Or a laugh. But Patrice blinked instead.

"You're kidding right?" Trudi asked.

"Patrice, there are vaccinations for the flu, the measles, mumps, rubella, among other things, but there isn't a vaccination for appendicitis," Becca said with a shake of her head.

"Too bad there isn't a vaccination for denseness," Trudi said.

Celeste smacked Trudi's arm. "Trudi."

"Pardon?" Patrice said.

"Never mind," Trudi said. "Let's focus on the issue at hand." She turned to Becca. "Our bride has no maid of honor."

Becca groaned. "To be honest, between the four of us…I can't wait for the whole affair to be behind me." She leaned her head against the back of the couch. "Don't misunderstand me, I'm excited to marry Marcus, but sometimes I wish we weren't having such a large wedding."

"You don't mean that," Patrice said. "You'll be beautiful. Marcus will be handsome. The day will be perfect and you'll have fabulous memories of the day you married your prince."

"You, my friend, are a hopeless romantic," Celeste said. Since her return from Tyler, she hadn't felt as optimistic about the rosy possibilities love could offer.

"Sentimental dreamer," Trudi added.

"Call me what you want," Patrice said. "But I know that all of us will find our special someone, not because I'm a hopeless romantic or sentimental dreamer, but because we deserve it. Becca's found hers already." She turned to Celeste. "What about you, Celeste? Have you found your special man in Max?"

Celeste felt heat burn across her face, and she prayed the tell-all sign of flaming cheeks didn't give her away.

"Actually, I don't think so," Celeste said. She hadn't confessed her impetuous trip to see Max.

Trudi gave her the stare. "What are you not telling us?"

Celeste lowered her lids so she couldn't see the whites of Trudi's eyes and expelled a breath.

"Whatever do you mean," she stalled.

"You went to see him, didn't you?" Trudi accused.

"Did you?" Patrice asked.

"Celeste?" Becca sat upward with a start and startled Miss Kitty. The cat jumped off her lap with a loud meow and scampered under the coffee table.

"Was the sex not good?"

"Tell us everything."

"Why did you go?"

Their questions jumbled together in their rush to know what she'd done.

"I drove down last Tuesday and came back the next day. And in hindsight I shouldn't have gone. I actually told him I thought we should give each other space."

Becca gasped and clutched her hand to her chest. "Please tell me you didn't hurt him? The last thing I need at my wedding is a best man who's in tears."

"Don't be melodramatic," Trudi said. "Max is too much man to blubber at a wedding." She zipped her glare to Celeste. "No matter what our own femme fatale has possibly done to him. Dish. What went down."

"I didn't think before I drove down…I was in such a rush to see Max…I didn't think about the children."

"Oh. The no-neck monsters," Trudi said. "They were there?"

"Of course they were," Becca snapped. "They are his children. They live with him. Where else would they be?"

The three of them stared at her and waited. Celeste searched for the words to convey her confusion, explain her jumbled thoughts and emotions, but she didn't know where to start.

"We played games."

"I bet you did," Trudi said, the tone of her voice suggesting that she knew exactly what kind of games they'd played.

"With Max?" Patrice asked.

"No. You've got it wrong. Real games. Game, games. We played board games with the children."

"The children?" Trudi asked. "You mean the no-necks, don't you?"

"Actually, they're quite charming. I don't really think of them as little no-neck monsters—"

"Please, please, please tell me you haven't crossed over to the other side?" Trudi's eyes widened, and she held up her hand as if it was a wand and she could banish Celeste's words with a flick of her wrist.

"You spent time with his kids?" Becca asked. She groaned and shook her head from side-to-side. "This can't be good. What did you do to them?"

"I didn't do anything to them," Celeste said. She crossed her arms. "What kind of ogre do you think I am?"

"What's an ogre?" Patrice asked.

"It's a terrible person who hurts children," Becca said.

"I didn't hurt the children," Celeste said. "I had a wonderful time. We played Candy Land and Hi Ho Cherry-O—"

"Quick." Trudi stood and moved toward the bar. "I need a drink. I cannot believe what I'm hearing."

"We played games in the front room for the afternoon, before we had dinner. Big Mama cooked chicken marsala to die for—"

"You ate dinner with the family?" Trudi asked. "I thought you said this was a fling. A pleasurable thing between two consenting adults. A fun sexual romp with no strings attached." Trudi made a hideous sound that screeched from somewhere within her. "And a fling, by the way, does not include playing games with no-necks and eating dinner with the entire family." She slapped her hands, palm down, on the counter. "Did I teach you nothing?"

"Who won at Candy Land?" Patrice asked. "That was always my favorite game."

"You did let the children win, didn't you," Becca said. "You know you're not supposed to win. Correct?"

"We all won a few, no one monopolized the winning. We played fair." Celeste reached under the coffee table to scratch Miss Kitty under the chin. Did she dare share Neecie's wish with her friends? She ventured a glance at Becca, who watched her through narrowed eyes, and thought better of the confession. "Later, when we were at the cabin, I started thinking."

"Aha," Trudi said from the bar where she poured herself a glass of wine. "So that's when you started thinking. After playing games and eating dinner?" She took a sip of wine. "Can I pour one for anyone else?"

"I need one," Becca said.

"Me too," Patrice said. "And I think y'all need to stop giving Celeste such a hard time." She reached out and patted Celeste's arm. "I think it sounds like a perfectly lovely time. As if you were part of the family."

Trudi returned, balancing four glasses of wine between her hands and passed them around.

"And that's where my problem lies," Celeste said. "I didn't mean for my fling to turn into something more than a good time with a man hotter than asphalt in August." A throaty sigh escaped at the memory of his rock-hard body. "The man is gorgeous. No doubt about it. But dammit. He's so sweet and kind. And he makes me feel like a goddess." She scooped up Miss Kitty and snuggled her close, but the cat protested with a hiss and jumped down.

Trudi laughed. "That cat never has liked you very much."

"That's because she knows Celeste doesn't like animals," Patrice said.

"But that's not true anymore," Celeste said. "I like animals and…"

"And kids." Becca finished for her.

"Yes," Celeste confessed. "I enjoyed spending time with them, and they like me. I mean really like me. I have no idea where this thing with Max might have led, but I couldn't get close to the children. What if the relationship didn't work out? Because let's be honest, I live four hours away and I'm not giving up my career for anyone…I couldn't hurt the children. And I should have considered them when I let things move so fast."

"Yes, you should have," Becca said. "But you didn't, so how did you leave things with Max?"

"I told him I needed time to think and we should give each other space. That we shouldn't talk before the wedding."

"Wow," Patrice said. "What did he say?"

"I didn't give him the chance to say anything. I left."

"You left him hanging?" Trudi asked with a sly smile. "Now that's my girl. Never allow the man the upper hand. Keep them guessing. That's what I do. Simple and unattached." She tapped the rim of her wine glass to Celeste's in salute.

"One of these days," Patrice said. "The right man will walk into your life, and the love bug will take over. And you, Miss

Know It All, will fall in love. Mark my words. Your day will come."

"We'll see," Trudi said. "But that time is a long way off. And in the here and now we have Celeste's problem." Trudi turned her attention to Celeste. "He hasn't tried to call you?"

Celeste shook her head.

"Have you tried to call him? Text him."

"No."

"You've had a week to think," Becca pointed out. "What have you decided?"

Before she could answer, Marcus walked through the front door, balancing two bags of take-out, and from the aroma wafting in with him, Celeste guessed it was Chinese.

"Delivery guy is here," he announced as he deposited the bags on the counter.

Becca jumped up and rushed to the kitchen where Marcus pulled her into an embrace and kissed her.

"Awwww, y'all are such a perfect couple," Patrice cooed.

"Get a room," Trudi said and made a retching sound.

"We have one," Marcus said and wiggled his eyebrows.

Celeste and the girls laughed, and Marcus busied himself with pulling out cartons and placing them on the counter.

"What's the girlfriend meeting about?" Marcus turned to Becca.

"Molly's in the hospital for an emergency appendectomy," Becca said. "And I have no maid of honor."

"I'm not interrupting a discussion of who you'll choose to take her place, am I? Because I can leave."

"No. That's not why I called everyone over," Becca said. "I really wanted to drink wine with my friends and lament yet another decision I need to make."

"Which one of us will you choose?" Patrice asked.

Celeste inwardly cringed at the expression of hopeful anticipation that clouded Patrice's face because her heart skipped a beat with similar expectation. After the ceremony, the maid of honor walked up the aisle with the best man. And that would be Max.

"I've given the situation a great deal of thought. And I've decided that all three of you will be my maids of honor. I need to choose an additional attendant or not have one at all."

"All three of us as maids of honor?" Patrice asked. The hopeful anticipation crumpled into a mask of confusion. "How can we?"

"Let's face it," Becca said. "Being the maid of honor is an honorary title, and it can be a lot of fun, but it also entails a lot of work. And who has been by my side the entire time?" She moved from behind the bar to the couch where she embraced Trudi and Patrice and motioned for Celeste to join them. Celeste scooted over and joined the group hug. "The three of you. The dress fittings, the trips to the Diva Day Spa, which I might add…one trip was torture, but y'all endured two… and Patrice handled the cake. I could go on and on with all y'all have done." Becca pulled away and walked back over to Marcus and wrapped her arm around his waist. "But the fact is, each of you deserve the honor. So, although whoever the gods are who bestow the rules for weddings suggest having no more than two, I'm breaking the rules and having three."

Celeste swallowed a funny lump in her throat and batted her lids to keep from forming tears, Patrice beamed like she'd been handed a kitten, and Trudi glowed with a proud blush on her cheeks. The mood in the room vibrated with happiness.

"But Marcus has a best man and three groomsmen," Patrice pointed out. "Won't that present a problem?"

"She's right," Trudi said. "Your wedding party will be lop-sided."

"I actually have an idea how to rectify the missing bridesmaid," Becca said.

"And what would that be?" Celeste asked. The sparkle in Becca's eyes piqued Celeste's curiosity.

"You'll see," Becca said. "Come on, let's eat before everything gets cold." She opened the cupboard and pulled out a stack of plates.

"Indeed, ladies," Marcus said. "Help yourselves. Anyone interested in sesame chicken? Some fried rice and crab rangoon?"

"Sounds awesome," Trudi said.

Celeste followed Trudi and Patrice to the kitchen, and they took turns loading their plates. Trudi and Celeste erupted in a fit of giggles when Patrice tried to scoop lo mein with a spoon.

"I almost forgot," Marcus said. "I talked to Mom today and you'll never believe what she told me." With expert precision he clamped the strings of lo mein with chopsticks and lifted a portion to his mouth.

"What did she have to say?" Becca asked.

"Big Mama's hopping mad. Mom's exact words were 'mad as a hornet.'"

"What's upset BM?" Trudi asked.

"Trudi." Celeste chorused along with Becca and Patrice.

"How many times must I tell you? Do. Not. Call. Big Mama. BM." Becca made a tsk-tsk noise and then pinched her lips together.

"Okay." Trudi laughed. "Sorry. Sorry. No more BM."

"Why is Big Mama mad?" Celeste asked.

"You'll never believe it. I tried to call Max to confirm, but his phone's ringing straight to voicemail." Marcus took another bite of noodles and chewed.

Celeste put down her chopsticks, a wave of nerves killing her appetite. And Marcus still chewed; the moment it took for him to chew seemed like time stood still.

Celeste wanted to shake him and ask, what is it?

He finally swallowed.

"Sissy's back. And Big Mama's having a hissy fit."

"Sissy?" the girls chorused.

"The ex?" Trudi asked, zipping her dagger glare straight toward Celeste.

Celeste managed to nod in the affirmative while her emotions rode a tsunami of disappointment. A wave train, rising like the tide, squashed every hope and dream she had for her and Max.

"Well, girlfriend, I presume there's no decision for you to make," Trudi said in her matter-of-fact way. "Seems as if it's been made for you."

Celeste deflated. She'd been on the precipice of figuring out what she truly wanted in life, and now it didn't matter.

If only she'd remembered the rules at the beginning and stuck to them. If she had, she wouldn't be fighting back the tears that burned behind her lids.

And trying to figure out how she'd face Max again.

CHAPTER THIRTY-TWO

෨ఄఄఄఄ෨

"Now tell me again why you didn't go to your mother's?" Max asked. He'd met with Sissy three times over the past four days; checking in to determine if she was still in town, and hoping every time when he entered the cabin that she'd be gone. But no such luck.

She apparently had the patience of a black widow with a nicely spun web.

Since he didn't trust Serena any farther than he could toss an elephant, he'd left strict orders at Charlie's elementary school and Neecie's pre-school that only he or Big Mama could see the children or pick them up. In case Serena or Sissy had plans for a sneak attack.

But Sissy had obeyed Max's wishes. During the day, she'd stayed at the cabin and hadn't ventured to Magnolia Oaks or tried to see the kids at their schools. She was waiting patiently.

He'd met with his attorney and determined that Sissy could take him to court and regain visitation rights. Although, according to her, she didn't have a dime to her name, so he wasn't concerned she'd trump him with the legal card. Yet.

However, her persistence with seducing him hadn't waned, and he'd fought her off at every visit, so he sat across the room on a kitchen chair leaving the expanse of the room between them—his defense against another attempt to seduce him. She seemed determined to win him back with sex, which he actually found amusing.

"The last I heard, Mama remarried and moved to Pittsburgh," Sissy said. "I haven't heard from her since I left. I don't know her address."

Max wasn't surprised. Sissy's people had never been family-oriented. They were a selfish bunch who preferred to feed their own vices. Her daddy had run off with another woman when Sissy was eight years old, and her mother loved liquor. And men. Lots of them. Max wasn't surprised that Sissy had latched on when she'd met him. His family and stability had been a life-line for a girl growing up without nurturing parents. And given her upbringing and family history, he shouldn't have been surprised when she left. Max wasn't fond of clichés, but the apple dropping from a tree fit Sissy and her family perfectly.

He hadn't asked about what had happened between her and Pastor Dick, and she hadn't offered any insight. Frankly, he didn't care, and he still found it difficult to mention the man's name without a gurgle of bile burning his gut.

"I've been thinking," Sissy said. "I realize I've gone about this all wrong." She ducked her head and lowered her lashes. "Calling your mother. Coming home without permission. And trying to seduce you every time I see you. I know I was wrong trying to force myself on you. I guess deep down I hoped you still felt something for me. Desired me. I apologize.

"I realize I need to prove myself. Start all over. I don't know what I was thinking or that I actually believed I could waltz in here and you'd take me back. Love me as if nothing had happened between us. So, can I please ask for a little more time. Now that I don't have you...or Charlie and Neecie anymore, I realize how important family is and I want y'all back. If there's a way. I'm willing to wait for you to reconsider. To give me a chance. To prove myself to you and the kids. I'm their mother and I want to come home." She finally looked him in the eye.

Maybe she was smart enough, after all, to realize that sex wasn't the ammunition that could win the battle. It was the kids, and her counterattack caught him off guard.

Max sought out Big Mama as soon as he arrived home. He found her in the kitchen mixing up a batch of homemade buttermilk biscuits. Charlie and Neecie sat at the table, their heads bent over their homework.

"Dad."

"Daddy."

Both kids clambered from their chairs and threw their arms around his waist and legs.

"Hey guys." He ruffled Charlie's hair with his knuckles and smoothed a hand down Neecie's cheek. His children. His family. His life. "Why don't y'all go out and play with the puppies for a little while." There was still two hours of daylight, and the afternoon was reasonably warm for October.

"But I haven't finished my homework," Charlie protested.

"See my pwetty picture." Neecie held up a crayon drawing for his perusal.

"You can finish your homework later," Max said to Charlie. He took the drawing from Neecie and placed it on the refrigerator, securing it with a magnet. "You are my little artist."

He ushered them to the door. "Thirty minutes to romp with the puppies and then back to your school work. Sound like a deal?"

"Yes, sir," Charlie said and bolted out the door, Neecie hot on his heels.

"What was that all about?" Big Mama asked.

"I need to talk," he said and settled on a stool next to the counter where Big Mama took shortening and dipped it into a mixing bowl of flour and milk and worked magic with her hands.

"I'm waiting," she said.

"It's about Sissy."

"Pshaw," Big Mama snapped. "I don't have nothing to say about that little tart."

"I need closure. I admit I'm confused, but I'm leaving for Atlanta Friday morning, and I need closure on the situation here."

"It's an easy decision if you're asking me," Big Mama said.

"I'm beginning to think she might be serious."

"Serious? Serious about what?" Big Mama asked. She lifted her hands from the dough and wiped them off on a towel. She shoved the towel aside and put her hands on her hips. "Don't you tell me you're going soft for her."

"No. I'm not. But what if she's sincere? What if she does want to come back and be a family. Be a mother to the kids. Do I send her away or support her staying in Tyler?"

"You're too nice, Max Riley, for your own good. Would you seriously consider opening your heart to that woman and giving her another chance after what she did?"

"But if Charlie and Neecie could have their mother again, shouldn't I at least consider forgiving her. Allowing her the opportunity to prove herself?"

"Boy, I know you're smarter than you're sounding right now. She gave birth to them, but I haven't seen her act like much of a mother."

"You're right. I know. Giving birth doesn't make someone a mother."

"You've got that right. Look at Serena. I tend to think of her as your daddy's wife more than as your mother, and she gave birth to you."

"That's true. Serena hasn't been the most loving mother figure, but at least she stuck around. And now that's Sissy back—"

"If you were looking for someone to give you an opinion based on both sides of the perspective, you've come to the wrong person because I wouldn't give that trailer trash another chance. I'd send her packing and to be honest, I don't know why you haven't." Big Mama huffed and her face flushed a splotchy red. "She cheated on you. She ran off with another man who, might I point out, was married to someone else, and she deserted you. Allowed you to divorce her."

Max flinched, he took each word like a blow to his abdomen, his ribs, his chest, like the final round of a Muhammad Ali fight. He braced himself for the knockout.

"And she relinquished any rights to her children. What kind of woman does that?" Big Mama finished with a final punch. "She hurt you, Max. And when she did, she hurt me, and anyone who hurts Big Mama's family has made an enemy for life. But I raised you to forgive. To be a good man. A simple man. To follow your heart and always do the right thing." Big Mama paused and tears glistened in her eyes. "I'm not going to tell you what to do. You need to find the answer yourself. What's best for you. For your family." She turned back to her biscuit making and dumped the dough onto the floured board. "But whatever you decide, I'll support you. Because that's what family does."

"Thanks," he said.

"But I do have one question for you," Big Mama said. "That girl from Atlanta. I thought you had a hankering for her? What're you gonna do about her?"

"To be honest, I think I have more than a simple hankering for her, but with Sissy here, things are complicated. I have a lot to consider." Max stood. "I appreciate you talking to me."

"Did I help?"

Max shrugged. "I don't know."

Outside the kitchen window, the children raced by with Sarge and his litter mates. The children ran with abandon, their faces flushed with delight. Max headed out the back entrance, and with a screech and a wham, the screen door slammed behind him.

"Hey guys," he called out.

The children turned and ran toward him, and the puppies followed. Sarge led the pack, tongue lolling to the side, his ears perked; he galloped toward Max.

"Sit," Max commanded, and all seven puppies obeyed. "Looks as if Big Mama has taught them well."

"Vewy well," Neecie said and threw her arms around Sarge's neck. "I love you," she said in the dog's ear.

Charlie stood behind her, his hand resting on the neck of his favorite of the litter, a male he'd named Buddy.

"Come on, Neecie," Charlie said. "Let's get the puppies back to their family."

"Family?" Max asked. "I thought we were their family."

"We are," Charlie said. "But Daisy and Duke are their real parents, and they're down at the barn."

"Yeah," Neecie agreed. "Sometimes the puppies miss their mommy and daddy." She jumped up and started off at a trot. "Come on, Sarge. Let's go find your mommy."

Max watched Sarge, Charlie, and Lady take off after Neecie with the remaining five puppies fast behind.

Mommy.

Neecie said, let's go find your mommy.

Not daddy.

Mommy and daddy. A family. A unit. A whole. A support system.

Max steeled his shoulders. He finally knew what he had to do.

CHAPTER THIRTY-THREE

೭⊶⊰೨

Celeste couldn't believe how quickly the night of the rehearsal dinner had arrived. For the past three days, like waiting for a root canal appointment, she'd dreaded the moment she'd have to face Max again.

She parked her car and glanced in the rearview mirror. The sapphire hue of her designer, stretch-satin sheath proved a perfect complement to her eyes, and she knew, if she said so herself, she looked damn fine.

The dress fit her to perfection. Figure-flattering didn't come close to describing the way the ruched bodice hugged her like a second skin. The sheer mesh detail at the top and back finished off the seamless combination of sexy elegance. She was rocking it. Luckily, her true emotions didn't reflect in her baby blues.

Her heart ached. But she couldn't be sure whether it was a bad case of heartburn or possibly because her heart had crumbled into a million broken pieces. Or the fact she wore a body-shaping, mid-thigh Spanx under her dress. She prayed she wouldn't need to pee all night because it would take a complete undressing to get the damn body-hugging underwear pulled down. Celeste sighed. Sometimes she didn't think things all the way through.

If she had to suffer to be a femme fatale, at least she was rock hard and sexy. And that's all that mattered.

Now if she could act as strong and confident as she appeared.

She studied herself in the mirror one last time, dabbed a tad more burgundy-tinted lip gloss to her lips and smacked. She puckered her lips and posed.

Someone tapped on her driver window and she jumped. Trudi's face appeared through the smoke-tinted glass.

"What the hell are you doing?" Trudi asked, her voice muffled. "Get out of the car."

Celeste grabbed her clutch purse and shawl from the passenger seat and joined Trudi, who grabbed her by the elbow and ushered her toward the front door of the venue.

"Now remember," Trudi said. "You are beautiful. You are strong and confident. You are a career woman. Ignore the fact that the man you love has chosen his cheating, lying ex over you. Never ever forget who you are and that you are better than the both of them combined."

"Gee, thanks for the pep talk." Trudi's words accentuated that every step she took burned as if she walked over a path of burning coals with abscessed feet. And it had nothing to do with her four-inch Madgley Mischkas. They were divine. But her walk of shame wasn't.

"Is Becca here," she asked.

"Yes, I think everyone's here. But us," Trudi said. "I was waiting for you in the parking lot. I didn't want you to make your grand entrance alone." She stopped short of the front steps.

"Sometimes a girl needs her best friend to lean on. And I'm here for you. Let's go knock 'em dead, sweetie."

Celeste's insides churned to the beat of an imaginary cha-cha when she took the steps to the landing and intensified to a crescendo of pure panic when she advanced toward the door. Would her biggest fears find fruition when she saw Max? Could she hold herself in check when she saw him with his ex?

She'd never seen a picture of Sissy, but Celeste imagined her as blonde and petite. Cute. Like a porcelain doll. Not tall and lanky like Celeste.

One thing she knew for certain. She'd always remember the rules in the future. Never again would she put herself through such turmoil of emotional anguish. Ever.

An attendant opened the door, and Trudi took her arm again.

"Are you ready?" she asked.

"As much as I'll ever be."

Celeste stepped inside the entryway.

Celeste mentally ticked off time the second she entered Villa Gardens. One hour. They had one hour in the garden to rehearse the wedding, before retiring to the dining room for dinner. Two hours for dinner. A total of three hours. Three miserable, sad hours, before she could go home and drown her sorrows. Alone and desolate with her thoughts and regrets.

She glanced around the foyer; they were alone.

"Where is everyone?" she whispered, lamenting the moment she would face Max, but also wanting the meeting to be done and in the past.

"Please join the wedding party in the gardens, ladies," the attendant instructed.

He led them across the vestibule, past the bar and dining area, and onto a terrace that spanned the length of the building and opened onto a stoned walkway threading through the grounds. Celeste sucked in a lungful of evening air. The venue was as magnificent as she remembered: a magical combination of waterfalls and gardens leading to the stacked stone pavilion where the wedding party gathered. The remainder of the family congregated on the terrace enjoying cocktails and hors d'oeuvres.

"There y'all are." Becca called from across the lawn. She and Patrice rushed toward them, a man in their wake, but Celeste refused to focus on anyone but Becca. She dreaded facing Max; the mere sight of him could cause her heart to disintegrate into smaller shards.

"Hello, Fabien," Trudi said and thrust out her hand in greeting.

At Trudi's welcome, Celeste shifted her attention to the man who accompanied Becca, and breathed a sigh of relief. It was Fabien. Safe and trust-worthy. Tall and debonair, Becca's friend and coworker always radiated a sophisticated grace.

Becca threw her arms around Celeste.

"Great news," Becca squealed. She apparently had already had several glasses of champagne from her flushed cheeks and the fact she'd squealed. Becca never squealed.

"The weather forecast for tomorrow is in our favor. The skies will be clear and the temperatures in the low seventies. Ideal for an outdoor wedding."

No one ever knew what to expect from Atlanta weather in October, but it appeared Mother Nature was on Becca's side. The evening was warm and Saturday promised to be glorious. Blue skies. White clouds. Sunshine. And warm.

"Fabulous news, indeed," Fabien said. "Good to see you both again." Fabien gave Celeste a quick hug.

Becca clapped her hands. "Now that you're all here, my three maids of honor, I want to announce that the lone bridesmaid will be…" she held out her hand toward Fabien.

"Fabien?" Trudi asked.

"Yes," Becca said, eyes aglow with excitement or the influence of alcohol, Celeste wasn't sure which.

"I love it." Trudi laughed. "Who better to be your bridesmaid other than your fourth best girlfriend?"

"I'm glad you approve," Becca said. "I thought you'd agree with my choice."

Becca looked over Celeste's shoulder toward the entrance and gave a little hop. "Big Mama and everyone from Tyler have arrived. Now that everyone's here, we can begin." She rushed away and left Celeste with Trudi, Patrice and Fabien.

Celeste grabbed her mid-section. "I think I'm going to throw up."

"No, you're not," Trudi said. "You look like a million bucks, so act like it. Now suck it up and turn around. You might as well go ahead and get this over with."

When Celeste turned around, Big Mama strode down the walkway with Charlie and Neecie at her side. When the children spied Celeste, Neecie broke away and ran straight toward her.

"Lest! Lest!"

Celeste knelt down in time to catch Neecie in her arms.

"Lest, you wook vewy booteeful." She clasped Celeste's face and pressed a wet kiss to her cheek. "I bwought you a present, but I can't tell you what it is." She leaned her head closer. "Itza seekweet," she whispered.

"Another secret?" Celeste asked.

"Stand up and give me a hug," Big Mama demanded.

Celeste glanced up to find Big Mama standing above her, and knowing Big Mama, she did as she was told. Pulling away from older woman's embrace, Celeste noticed Charlie standing to the side, reserved as usual.

"Hello, Charlie, you look mighty handsome tonight." The little boy beamed at her compliment.

Celeste dared a glance to see who else had entered. Papa Joe remained on the terrace, Serena and Brick by his side, and walking across the side lawn was Max.

Alone.

He walked straight to her and pulled her into his arms.

"I apologize," he said to everyone standing around them. "But I've needed to do this for nine days. Nine long, miserable days." He pressed his lips to hers.

"Daddy likes Lest, Daddy likes Lest," Neecie sing-songed while jumping up and down.

"I'll take the children and go inside," Big Mama said. She turned to everyone else. "I think these two have a few things to discuss. Let's give them some space."

Trudi flashed a thumbs up. "Come on, y'all," she said. She hooked arms with Fabien and Patrice and pulled them away. "Let's get a drink and find out who's bartending this fete."

Big Mama turned to Max. "Make it snappy. We've got a wedding to rehearse." She herded the children back to the terrace, leaving Max alone with Celeste.

Max took her hand and led her down a side walkway. "Let's go this way. I already scoped out a cozy spot, right around the corner over here."

"You did, did you?" Celeste asked. A bundle of tingling nerves and struggling with a crazy, stomach flipping wave of happiness, she followed him, not sure what was happening. Where was Sissy?

Max stopped in front of a waterfall and took both of her hands in his.

"I understand that there should be a certain degree of guessing to make a new relationship intriguing. But head games have never been my thing, and since you're already inside my head. Inside my heart, I—"

She placed a finger over his lips, shushing him. "You're correct. Head games are bad. Very bad."

"Let me finish," he said. "I've rehearsed this and if you interrupt me I might forget the important parts—"

"I think you've already said them." Inside my head, inside my heart reverberated through her mind, and she knew she was smiling a huge idiotic grin, but she didn't care.

"I'm too old to play cat and mouse love games. And the fact is…you're under my skin, in a good way. You have me. I would sacrifice anything to have you in my life. So now, I need to figure out how to make that happen. Do you want to give it a try? To figure out how we can make us work?" He paused.

"You would sacrifice anything for me?"

"Yes, you. Ever since I first met you, you made me feel at home. Complete. Like I'd found the missing puzzle piece to my life." Max caressed the side of her face, his touch like a whisper. "I know it sounds crazy, but you're the one. The only one for me."

"Forgive me, but I'm confused," Celeste said. "I heard Sissy was back. In fact, I expected to see her with you. Tonight."

"She did come back, but she had ulterior motives," Max said. "Apparently, she and Pastor Dick are expecting their first child, and they concocted a plan to bilk me for some money. Sissy seemed to think she could seduce me and then in a month or so convince me the baby was mine, and I'd pay her support money. I have no idea why she thought I'd entertain the idea of touching her, but I knew she was up to something when she didn't ask to see Neecie and Charlie."

"You can't be serious? She didn't see the children?" Celeste couldn't imagine what made that woman tick. The more she learned about Sissy, the less she could fathom what type of human she was, and she probably didn't want to waste any time trying.

"No. She barely mentioned them. When I drove out to tell her I thought it was time for her to leave town, I stumbled upon her and Dick..." he paused, "how should I say...in a compromising position. Walking in on them like I did, I foiled their plan, and Sissy came clean."

Celeste couldn't think of anything to say and simply shook her head in disbelief.

"Enough about Sissy," Max said. "She and Dick are gone, and after our last encounter, I don't anticipate seeing them again."

"Did seeing her again stir up any old—"

"Absolutely not. In fact, I struggled with how much contempt I held for her. I'll admit the entire week was difficult, and compounded with the fact I didn't have you to talk to, it was more unbearable." He wrapped his arms around her. "Now back to the speech I practiced. If I remember correctly, I was at the part where I say, you're the only one for me."

"But why am I the one for you?" she asked.

"It has nothing to do with your fabulous baby blues or your kissable lips. I enjoy your company. When I'm with you, I'm comfortable. Relaxed. I love your drive, how you've always known what you wanted and how you pursued your career. Your loyalty to your friends. The way you've supported Becca. There's something about you that makes me happy. So what do you say? Can we give us a chance?"

"We do have a lot to consider," Celeste said. There was her career. His farm. She lived in Atlanta.

But the memory of the desolation she'd endured over the last week, first not talking to Max and unsure of their future, and then thinking she'd lost him altogether, reminded her that some things might not be so important after all.

"But I'm willing to compromise," she said.

"And you realize I come as a package deal," he said.

"I know. You. Charlie. Neecie." The warm fuzzy sensation she'd experienced with Neecie's hug and whispered secret spread through her.

Max hooked his finger under her chin and lifted her face to his.

"I love you, Celeste. You captured my heart when I first kissed you." And, as if to remind her, he pressed his mouth to hers, a light, sweet kiss, and Celeste swooned under the intensity of his gentle caress. He lifted his lips from hers and gazed into her eyes. "We'll take it one day at a time. We'll figure it all out. Between the two of us."

"You mean the four of us, don't you?" she asked.

Max laughed his warm belly chuckle that always enticed her to join him. "So…are you game?"

"Game on," she said.

CHAPTER THIRTY-FOUR

❧

The next evening, the wedding ticked through Celeste's mind like the reel of an antiquated 8 mm film: frame by frame.

The happy couple: Becca smiling at Marcus beneath the arch of the stone pavilion, while they recited their vows; the guests watching from the lawn seated on an eclectic combination of antique pews and chairs.

The proverbial question: "Does anyone know why this woman and this man should not be joined together in holy matrimony?" And even though she didn't expect a response, Celeste's heart hitched and missed a beat, relieved when no one shouted, "Run, run."

The officiate: "I have the pleasure of introducing you to Becca and Marcus Blake."

The guests: standing, erupting in applause.

The recessional: Max and Celeste following Becca and Marcus up the aisle, the happy couple waving to the guests.

The afternoon sun: sliding into dusk, painting the sky a palette of reds and oranges against a backdrop of blue.

Becca and Marcus were married.

※ ※ ※

After posing for countless photographs and a smile-breaking stint in the receiving line, Celeste entered the reception tent. The entire space was adorned in pink-pastel, canopy fabric draped at varying heights, and crystal chandelier fixtures hung from the ceiling offering a warm, buttery glow, a contrast to the rosy hue of the soft, romantic up-lighting.

White lilies, pink roses and gold-encrusted branches, dripping with crystals, sprouted from vases centered on table rounds swathed in white satin. Gold chiavari chairs circled every table, each set with white bone china and sparkling glassware. The entire room glittered.

Becca and Marcus made their way toward a sweetheart table elevated on a dais front and center. The table, adorned in satin and tulle, was draped with a flower garland entwined with roses, lilies and greenery. But Becca didn't appear to notice the décor. The happy couple couldn't take their eyes off one another. Becca glowed with adoration; Marcus beamed a giddy, goofy grin: the two of them the embodiment of true love.

On a mission to locate their assigned seating, Celeste trailed behind the girls and their dates. They found the table reserved for the maids of honor where Fabien and his date Corey were seated to Celeste's right, and a place card with Max's name was to her left. Celeste smiled. Becca had changed the seating assignments at the last minute. A true friend forever.

Her gaze shifted to the adjacent table where the groomsmen, along with their wives, searched for their delegated seats. Max raised an eyebrow, lifted his palms upward and mouthed where am I?

Celeste hooked a finger, made a come hither motion, and indicated here.

He stepped away from the groomsmen and joined her.

Max's heart beat in a contented rhythm at the sight of Celeste. The connection between the two of them drew him to her like a moth to light, and since she'd confessed her feelings for him, he was determined to ensure their relationship held a chance. Come hell or high water. He'd make sure of it.

Max settled on the chair next to Celeste and took her hand. He pressed a light kiss to her palm.

"I've scored the best seat in the place," he said. "I'm a lucky man."

Celeste blushed and the tinge of pink made her appear sixteen. The night couldn't be more perfect, and he intended to ensure she had a fantastic time.

"What can I get you to drink?" he asked.

Max and the other men at the table excused themselves to go to the bar leaving Celeste with Trudi and Patrice.

"Remind me again. How you met your date?" Trudi asked Patrice. "I don't recall meeting him before."

"He's someone new."

Trudi smiled. "Don't lie to me. He's from 1-800-Boy-Toys isn't he?" Her tone was playful, but suggestive.

Patrice gasped. "I. Would. Never. Pay. For. A. Date." She huffed, crossed her arms, and tapped a beat with the toe of her shoe.

"Right," Trudi said. "And neither would the heroine in your favorite movie. What's the name of it again?"

"The Wedding Date," Patrice said, immediately forgetting her indignation, her voice a dreamy coo. "I LOVE that movie."

"Didn't she pay for her date?" Trudi asked.

Patrice nodded her head. "Yes."

"Well, everything turned out well for her, didn't it? So fess up. Who is he and how did you meet him?"

"He's the new guy at work. I thought I told you about him."

"Not that I recall—"

"You mentioned him to me," Celeste said. "And I know you didn't call the 1-800 service for him." She wrapped a protective arm around Patrice's shoulder. "Trudi's being spiteful, because all the men she dates have to work on Saturday night, and she had to pay for her date."

Trudi's mouth gaped open. She snapped it shut. "I. Did. Not."

Celeste and Patrice laughed.

"Touché," Trudi said and joined their laughter. "Point taken. I was only teasing."

"So was I," Celeste said. "Remember, all for one, one for all."

"Forever," Trudi said. Her gazed drifted to the table of honor. "Can y'all believe Becca's married?"

"The first one of us to waltz into the sunset of marital bliss," Celeste said, and for once the observation didn't leave her with the shudders. Instead, she experienced a fuzzy warmth oddly reminiscent of romantic bliss.

"Becca's absolutely radiant," Patrice said. She exhaled a deep sigh. "I'm happy for her, and I can't wait to find my true love." She turned to Celeste. "How do you know?"

"How do I know what?" Celeste asked.

"When he's the one?"

"Who's he?"

"Don't play dumb," Trudi said. "It isn't becoming on you. Patrice can get away with the dense persona. You, not so much."

"Hey," Patrice said. "I resent that."

"No, you don't," Trudi said to Patrice and shifted her attention to Celeste. "Answer her question. How did you know that Max was your knight in shining armor?"

"I haven't said he's the one."

"Yeah. Right," Trudi said. "We all know that you know that he's the one. So confess."

"Max is your true love," Patrice said, her voice lowered to a whisper. "He's your one." Her eyes rounded in excitement. "He's the one for you," she reiterated.

"I don't know if I can admit that," Celeste said. "But he's special and I think—"

"You don't think…you know," Trudi said. "I can see it in the way you look at him and the mushy expression on his face when he stares at you." She lifted her chin and waved at someone across the room. "Like right now." She smiled and nodded. "See him. Standing in line for your drink and watching you."

Celeste caught Max's gaze. He smiled and her heart did a little skip and then galloped. And her stomach fluttered a happy dance. The girls were right.

"He's the one," she said on an exhaled breath. "My prince."

An hour later, Becca and Marcus danced their first dance as man and wife, followed by Becca's dance with her dad, which they combined with Marcus's dance with his mother. When the song came to an end, the DJ called the group to order.

"Could I have everyone's attention, please?" he asked, speaking into the mic. "And Becca will you join me?"

On cue, Becca took her place next to the emcee, her bouquet in hand, the background song a chanting number about putting a ring on it.

"All the single ladies please join me," he said in a suggestive baritone. He walked onto the dance floor and encouraged the women to join him. "Come on, now. Don't be shy. I believe you ladies know what's coming next," he said.

Celeste watched in amazement as not only the young women, but the mature as well, in addition to Fabien, swarmed the floor and jostled themselves into position. Patrice claimed a spot on the frontline and planted her tiny high-heeled feet in a competitive stance. Fabien stood near the rear of the throng, easily towering over his competitors.

Trudi remained seated, and Celeste leaned around Max and glanced at her. Trudi shook her head.

"There's no way I'm getting trampled over a bouquet of flowers I have no intention of catching," Trudi said and crossed her arms. Celeste could feel the back and forth swooshing of the tablecloth as Trudi swung her leg in defiance.

"Come on," Max said. "Get out there." He reached for Celeste's arm at the same moment Becca leaned into the mic.

"I spy two ladies who have ignored your invitation to join the fun," she said, and pointed their way.

Everyone turned, and the DJ made a beeline for their table.

"Ladies, ladies on the floor now." He'd reached their table and made an effort to pull Trudi's chair aside so she could stand. "A beautiful woman such as you should vie to catch the bouquet," he said. "Instead of sitting here like a wallflower."

Celeste could see the glint in his eye and knew immediately the DJ planned to be a contender for Trudi's attention. Poor guy. He had no clue. Trudi would eat him up and spit him out.

"If I'm going, she's going," Trudi said between clenched teeth. She glared at Celeste.

"Go on," Max said. "It's part of the fun."

At his urging, Celeste and Trudi both stood, and the crowd applauded. Celeste followed Trudi onto the dance floor and the two of them joined Fabien on the periphery of the crowd. She felt foolish; she'd never been a "catch the bouquet" kind of girl.

The DJ rejoined Becca and hiked the music up a notch.

"Now listen to the song and put your hands up, shake them all around, and get down with your bad selves."

The women lifted their hands and pulsed up and down, some moving side to side. Celeste wasn't sure if they followed his instructions or whether the song amped up their anticipation to a frenzy. Regardless. He was good. Real good.

"Be forewarned," Becca said. "I've been practicing, and I'm not making this easy for y'all."

"All my single ladies get ready." He turned to Becca. "Okay, let it rip and let Cupid work the magic," he said. "On the count of three." He paused. "One."

Fabien leaned down. "Come on. Get with the fun. Just lift your hands." He lifted his own two feet above everyone else and waved them around.

"Two."

"Right," Trudi said, turning to speak to Fabien while half-heartedly lifting her arms. "Like I'm trying to catch that thing."

"Three."

A chaotic surge of women pushed forward, and Celeste watched in dismay while the bouquet sailed up, up, up and over the crowd, spinning out of control and straight toward Fabien's outstretched fingers, and at the exact moment she was certain he'd caught it, the flowers grazed his fingertips and twirled straight toward...

Trudi.

The flowers landed with a soft whoosh in Trudi's outstretched arms, and she instinctively crushed them to her chest. For a mere second, a look of pure panic plastered across her raging pink face before she lifted her eyes.

"This isn't mine," she said. "It's yours." She flipped her wrist and with a ricochet toss, the bouquet landed in Celeste's hands.

Celeste gawked at the battered bundle of blooms. Had she legally caught them? A nervous niggling of nausea weakened her knees.. Whether she had or not, they were in her hands.

"And the next lucky lady to be married will be..."

The crowd parted and Becca rushed forward.

"Celeste," she cried and wrapped her arms around her neck. "I'm so glad you caught it," she said. "This is perfect."

"But I didn't—"

"Of course you did," Trudi said, and took Celeste's arm. She tugged her away from Becca. "You lucky girl, you. And you weren't even trying to catch it." She leaned into Celeste's hair and whispered in her ear. "Never, ever tell anyone that thing touched me. And remember, possession is nine-tenths of the law."

Trudi broke away from Celeste and reached a hand out to her date. "Come on, handsome. Let's get a drink."

In the background, the DJ took over once again and commanded everyone's attention. "And now for the garter toss."

Within thirty minutes, the reception was in full swing. The dance floor was packed, and even Neecie and Charlie danced and hopped to the music.

Celeste had retired to the table to take a breather. She sipped champagne and observed the celebration, considering whether she should slip off her sandals and massage her feet. Everyone was having a blast. A good time. No doubt.

"Our next song is a special request," the DJ said in the background.

"Excuse me," Max said, breaking her reprieve. Celeste turned toward his voice.

"Hey," she said. "Where've you been?"

"Making a special request, and the next song is our dance."

"Our dance?" she asked. "I didn't know we had a dance."

"We sure do." He reached for her hand and she followed him, as a marimba rhythm started to play.

He swung her onto the dance floor, and the melodic blend of horns and cha-cha rhythms, reminded her of their first dance at the country club two months before.

The song—it was the same song—and he'd remembered. You had to love a man who paid attention to the little details.

His strong arms supported her, and she swayed along with him, their bodies in tune. She rested her head against his shoulder, and his breath fluttered across her neck, a wave of desire shivering down her spine. She loved the pressure of his palm against her waist as he guided her through their dance, and when he pulled her tighter, she noticed the crowd.

"I think we're causing another scene on the dance floor," she said.

"To hell with them," he said. "They're jealous."

"You're ruining my reputation with your family."

"Do you suggest I make an honest woman out of you?" he asked.

"Hhmm, we might need to consider a way for me to save face." She giggled.

"I know exactly what I need to do to save your reputation," he said.

"You do?"

"Definitely," he said. "Marry me."

"Marry?" She knew she wore her surprise on her face, but he didn't seem to notice.

"I know it's soon, but I've never been more certain of anything in my life."

"But—"

He placed a finger over her lips. "No buts," he said. "Promise me you'll give me the chance to court you and convince you that the only choice you have is to say yes." He smiled and her heart melted.

"Okay," she said. "I promise."

And they sealed the deal with a kiss.

EPILOGUE

𝕒𝕠𝕠𝕤

Four months later

"Without a doubt," Max said. "Your landing the anchor position at WGSW calls for a celebration" He padded in socked feet into the kitchen. "Champagne or tequila?"

"Tequila, please," Celeste said. "A reposado. Chilled. Straight-up."

"That's my girl." Max beamed.

Celeste rested on the couch, with Sarge at her feet and Lady sleeping in her lap. The cat purred up a storm, content with her place in life. And Celeste knew how she felt. After Neecie revealed her big secret the weekend of Becca's wedding, presenting Celeste with Pumpkin's offspring, the kitten had found a place in Celeste's heart. And Sarge came later, although no longer small, her little protector would always have her heart, no matter how big he grew.

A small fire warmed the cabin, and Celeste basked in the cocoon of cozy happiness surrounding her. She gazed at the engagement ring glittering on her finger, and twisted it so the firelight would reflect the diamond's brilliance. She sighed.

Max returned with their drinks and settled beside her.

"Here's to the best weekend anchor southwestern Georgia will ever have." He lifted his glass to hers. "I'm proud of you."

Celeste smiled and chinked her glass to his. "And here's to the most handsome man in the world." She sipped her tequila and snuggled into the crook of his arm.

"I have the blueprints for the addition," Max said.

"Great, let me see." She and Max had decided to build onto the cabin by adding a formal dining area, expanding the family room, and adding four more bedrooms. A bedroom for Charlie and one for Neecie, and two for any potential future Tylers. Celeste's womb did a funny pulse at the thought and her ovaries tingled along with it. She placed a hand on her stomach; stupid girl parts betraying her again.

"I'll show you later." Max waggled his brows and Celeste laughed. "We have some celebrating to do."

"I'm so happy." Celeste reached down and rubbed behind Sarge's ear, and he thumped his tail against the rug.

"The house should be completed in May—"

"The wedding in July."

"We're firm on the day, correct?"

Celeste nodded.

"Big Mama knows?"

"She knows. She's already planning—"

"You realize that you made her the happiest woman in the world when you told her you wanted to get married at Magnolia Oaks."

"I believe her exact words were 'plum tickled pink.' Whatever that means."

"It's probably akin to 'happier than pigs in poop,'" Max said.

"Like me." She pulled his face to hers and kissed him. "I love you, Max Riley. You complete me."

"We're family." Max reached down and petted Sarge. "Right, guy?"

Sarge moaned his agreement, and Celeste laughed.

"Family," she agreed. "Building a home and planning a wedding."

"You're not going to worry yourself silly over who will be maid of honor are you?" Max asked.

"Oh no," she said. "That's decided."

Month: July

Place: Magnolia Oaks

Matron of Honor: Becca

Maids of Honor: Trudi and Patrice

All four girlfriends living happily ever after…

Well now, that's another story. Or two.

TEQUILA 101

Admit it. We've all done it at least once, and I'm not talking about dancing on tables. We've all held our breath and dubiously eyed a shot glass filled with golden liquid. The process begins with salt on the back of your hand (or the rim of a shot glass); lick the salt; tip back your head and swallow the tequila; immediately bite into a lime.

But tequila isn't just for shooting, and tequila connoisseurs will tell you to savor the taste and aroma of the liquor instead of gulping it.

A little bit about Tequila: Mexican law requires tequila be produced, bottled and inspected in Mexico, specifically in the state of Jalisco or Gujanajuato, Michoacan, Nayarit, and Tamulipas. Tequila is made from the juice of the blue agave plant, which is distilled and fermented. Although Mexican law mandates tequila must be at least 51% agave, the best tequilas are 100%. Any tequila that is not 100% agave is considered a mixto tequila. Mixto tequilas can be produced outside of Mexico.

Types of tequilas:

Blanco (silver/white):

Bottled soon after distillation, silver tequila is not aged over sixty days and can be either pure agave or mixto. Blanco tequila is used in fruity drinks, such as margaritas.

Oro (gold):

Gold tequila is actually silver tequilas that contain caramel and or oak extracts for coloring and flavoring. The gold is a sweeter tasting tequila, and considered smoother, and is the preferred tequila for shots. Golds are also used in mixed cocktails.

Reposado ("rested"):
Reposado tequila is aged in wood barrels or casks for two to twelve months. Considered a sipping tequila, reposado has a robust flavor and can be either 100% agave or a mixto. In addition to sipping, reposado is excellent for shots or in cocktails.

Añejo ("old"):
Añejo tequila is dark and smooth due to the aging process of at least twelve months in oak barrels. The barrels can be either white or French oak, and sometimes used bourbon barrels are utilized. Considered a vintage tequila, añejo should be sipped neat.

Extra Añejo (ultra-premium):
Considered a newer class tequila, extra añejo is aged for twelve months to three years or more, but no more than four years. Sip neat in a snifter to enjoy the excellent aroma of the new ultra-premium class of tequila.

Note: Mezcal is produced from the maguey agave and other varieties of the agave plant. Tequila is only produced from the blue agave plant..

Sip and enjoy!
And while you're at it, experience romance, discover love, and *Believe*!

Sneak peek...

TEQUILA SHOTS ~ MAKING THE RULES
A Novella

CHAPTER ONE

"All for one, one for all," Trudi said. She held up her neon colored shot glass. *"Tous pour un, un pour tous."*

She looked magnificent standing on the beach in her purple string bikini, the top so small the cloth barely contained her abundant cleavage, the ocean and sky painting a backdrop, her red hair flaming.

Celeste and Patrice lifted their shots in unison, but Becca held back. She wasn't sure she was ready for a full week of partying. Spring break in Panama City Beach so wasn't her. The excursions her best friends could talk her into. And they always managed to find trouble.

Every time.

And here she was again.

Sucker.

"Isn't it a little early to be drinking?" she asked. She scrutinized the pink fluorescent shot glass she held in one hand, a lime in the other.

"What?" Trudi pushed her sunglasses on top of her hair and glared at Becca: her stare like a Hawk ready to swoop down on unsuspecting prey. Becca cringed at the look. If looks could kill, Trudi qualified as a serial killer.

"It's five o'clock somewhere," Celeste said. She paused and waited for Becca to join the revelry and toast, but Becca didn't budge. She wasn't ready to slug down any liquor at eleven thirty in the morning, much less tequila.

Becca watched as Trudi changed tactics and tried another angle. She smiled.

"We all agreed that PCB was the place to be." Trudi swept out her arm indicating the entire beach to the west of them. "The Redneck Riviera. Paradise on the Gulf Coast. Just look at all the sinful debauchery."

Becca zipped her gaze and took in the sight of the beach swarming with half-naked college kids. School flags waved in the breeze above pop-up canopies outfitted in the colors of the kids' alma maters. A countless number of other beach goers—drinking, throwing Frisbees, and partying in general—dotted the coastline. The whole scene pulsed with a frenzied rhythm.

Since Trudi insisted they stay near all the MTV action, the four best friends had rented a condo next door to LaVela—the largest nightclub in America—and Spinnaker Beach Club. Near the camaraderie? No. They were in the middle of the craziness.

A posse of guys sauntered past: tanned and lean, their swim trunks hung low on their hips, hats turned backwards, dark shades covering their eyes. One of them sported a T-shirt emblazoned with Party Naked. When they spotted Trudi, they all stopped.

"Hey gorgeous," the tallest one called out.

Trudi turned and gave them her gotta-love-me smile.

"Hey," she said.

"Why don't you invite us over for a drink?" one of the guys asked.

Trudi held up her finger. "Hold on a sec. I'll be right there." She turned back to Becca. "Don't you see?" she asked. "This is where the boys are, and this is where we want to be. So come on…loosen up."

Trudi dropped to her knees, sloshing tequila in the process. She knelt before Becca who perched on the rented wooden lounge chair.

"Come on, Bec," Trudi said and then licked the spilled liquor from the side of her glass. "We're here for our final hoorah. It's our last college Spring break." She looked at Celeste and Patrice for reinforcement. "Right, girls?"

"Yes," Patrice said. "We all agreed that coming to PCB would be our opportunity to," she paused, thinking for a moment, "well, it's our last opportunity to raise hell."

"You know you want to," Celeste urged. "When we graduate in May, our life as independent adults begins." She raised her shot again. "Here's to the four of us. Best friends forever." She grinned her megawatt smile and pushed a chunky brown curl away from her face.

"I'll drink to that," Trudi said. "To the four of us through thick and thin. Through the good times and the bad. We have each others' backs. Forever." She licked the salt, downed her shot, and bit a wedge of lime. Celeste and Patrice followed her lead, and then they all turned to Becca in anticipation.

Becca stalled a moment longer. She really should have stayed in Athens and worked on her marketing research paper. She eyed the golden, pungent liquor and winced. She really shouldn't be drinking. Her belly rumbled in disgust.

"Bottoms up, girlfriend." Trudi pumped up her hand in encouragement. "Get with the program."

Her mouth watered at the thought, but Becca finally lifted the shot to her lips, squeezed her eyes, held her breath, and then gulped down the fiery liquid. Her nose burned and a numb sensation slid down her throat. There. She'd done it.

They were official. Their Spring break had begun.

Trudi sauntered over to the five guys waiting at the edge of the surf. Patrice and Celeste followed.

Becca stayed under the safety of the umbrella.

"Hey," Trudi called out. "Where're y'all from?" She didn't care. They were cute, and her plan for the entire week included flirting and drinking, dancing and drinking, and flirting some more. Anything to help her forget Sean; they'd broken up before Christmas, and she needed to let go. She needed a distraction.

And spring break in PCB was the diversion she needed. If Becca wasn't interested in having fun, that was her problem, and Trudi had no intention of allowing Debbie Downer to ruin her good time. She loved Becca, but sometimes she was so infuriatingly tight-assed.

"I'm from Florida," answered the one wearing the Party Naked shirt.

"Well, duh," Patrice said "We're all from Florida right now, 'cause that's where we are. She means where are y'all really from?" The guys stared down at Patrice.

Trudi shook her head. Patrice was cute as a pixie, but most of the time she was an airhead.

"Yes, she's serious," she explained with a shrug of her shoulders. "Humor her."

"We're Tigers," he said.

"Waaaaaar Eagle!" they all chorused in unison.

"Hell no," Trudi said. "Y'all are from Auburn?"

"Yeah," Party Naked said. "Is that a problem?"

"What do you say girls?" She winked at her best friends. "You think these wimpy Tiger boys can hold their own up against us Dawgs?"

"Shit," the Naked shirt guy said. "You girls from UGA?"

"Yes, we are," Trudi said. Celeste and Patrice backed her up with hand pumps and woof, woof, woofs.

"So …" She inched closer, near enough to smell the scent of his lotion: pineapple and coconut, mixed with surf and sweat. He smelled divine. "You think you can handle some real women?"

"Hell, yeah. I can," he said low enough for only Trudi to hear. "My name's Blake."

"Hi ya', Blake. A pleasure to meet you. I'm Trudi," she said. "You interested in having a good time? And I mean, a real good time."

"I sure am," Blake answered.

"This is Patrice." Trudi indicated her petite friend: all five feet of her perfect body in a teensy bikini. "And this is Celeste."

"Hi." Celeste wiggled her fingers at the guys and flashed her favorite grin: the one she planned to use in front of the camera when she nailed her first new reporter assignment. Trudi knew the smile well. Whenever Celeste practiced her camera-ready smile, she made the girls grade her on a scale of one to ten. She usually made a perfect score.

"We're on our way to LaVela," Blake said. "Wanna come?"

"Coming's exactly what I want to do," Trudi replied, making certain insinuation dripped from every syllable. Blake grinned.

"LaVela. That does sound fun," Celeste added. "We're so there. Right, Patrice?"

"Sure, but let's do another shot before we go," Patrice said. She lifted her brow and flipped her dark hair behind her ear. "You guys wanna join us?"

"Hell, yeah," all five of them chorused.

They weren't men of many words, but Trudi eyed Blake with his shaggy, blonde hair and crystal blue eyes edged with thick lashes, a scruff of beard along his jawline, and decided she wasn't looking for a philosophical conversation anyway.

Blake and his friends followed them over to the spot the girls had claimed as their "homebase." Staking their claim, Becca relaxed on the loungers that the foursome had paid a hundred and fifty bucks to rent for the week. Trudi opened the cooler they'd packed with beers, ice, more beers, and nestled on top, like a golden treasure in a chest, a fifth of Cuervo.

Trudi pulled out a package of neon-colored, disposable shot glasses and passed them around.

"Bad ass," Blake said.

"I'm an expert at packing for the beach," Trudi answered. "The correct glassware adds a touch of finesse."

"You're so full of shit." Celeste laughed and grabbed the tequila. She poured a round for everyone, except Becca who didn't hold out her glass for a refill.

"She bought them because she likes the colors," Patrice explained as the guys simultaneously tilted back their heads and downed the liquor. She stuck out her bottom lip in a perfect Patrice pout. "Y'all didn't wait to make a toast?"

Trudi laughed. "We'll toast on the next go 'round."

"Are they old enough to drink?" Becca asked. "What if you're serving alcohol to minors? Which is against the law and potentially dangerous."

"Y'all underage?" Trudi asked and gave him another once over.

"No," Blake said. "We're plenty legal, but we might be dangerous," he added, his face a cocky smirk.

"I'll bet you are." Salacious thoughts danced through her mind.

And she planned to find out just how dangerous.

※ ※ ※

Celeste trailed behind Trudi and Blake, while Patrice and one of Blake's friends tailed her. They'd wandered through the entire complex, losing first one of the guys and then another as they succumbed to the lure of the different themed party rooms. They finally stopped at the pool deck. The blare of techno music vibrated and thousands of spring breakers pulsed in time with the music. After two shots of tequila, the frenzied motion of everyone around her, in addition to the relentless noise, left Celeste dizzy and confused. She worried that the incessant pressure might rupture her ear drums.

A guy to her left poured beer down the chest of a girl and lapped it up with his tongue. Celeste couldn't believe the girl's reaction; she threw back her head and laughed allowing him full range to lick and suck. The girl didn't seem to have an inkling that she'd wind up a sticky mess, not to mention her lack of dignity. Celete was beginning to think that spring break wasn't such a good idea after all. Who were all these insane kids? Did none of them understand the meaning of scruples?

An emcee yammered into a mic and a parade of bikini-clad ingénues pranced across the stage. The crowd roared its approval, as if they were third century participants at the Colosseum celebrating the victorious kill by a popular gladiator. Celeste didn't understand the show of admiration and praise. It wasn't as if any of the girls had yielded a sword and fought a bear to its death. They were scantily clad women jiggling like a tray of half-congealed jello shots.

A wave of party goers surged like a tsunami toward the stage, and Celeste was swept along with the flow. She found herself in a sea of strangers and neither Trudi nor Patrice were anywhere in sight. A hot panic coursed through her. Patrice was so small, a crowd of this size could crush her. And Trudi? Well, Trudi could take care of herself, no doubt, but what about her own safety? A sweaty, hairy chest pressed against one shoulder and the buxom wonder of some skanky girl doused in enough perfume to kill the scent of a skunk pressed against her back. Her face was exactly an inch away from the tattooed back of a skinny dude who apparently held a fascination with dragons, because she was staring into the fiery breath of one.

A hulk of a dude pumped his fist in the air and chanted to no one in particular, "Show your tits, show your tits!"

Celeste didn't have any intention of showing her breasts or anything else. She pushed herself through the crowd, battling the surge of bodies like fighting a riptide. For every two steps forward, she stumbled back one. Her heartbeat thudded in her ears, and the sensation of smothering pressed against her chest. She couldn't breathe.

She forged ahead determined to make her way to an exit, because if she didn't escape the madness, she'd go bat-shit crazy.

What was she doing in party central? In the largest night club in the world?

Terry Poca

Terry writes sassy, smart, sensuous romance and believes true love stories never end. Join her characters on their journeys as they experience romance and discover love.

Terry graduated from Kennesaw State University with a degree in Education, Secondary English. When not writing and brainstorming the remainder of The Tequila Series, she reads her favorite authors, watches movies and her favorite television series, and hangs out enjoying life with her one true hero a.k.a. her husband.

She lives in metro Atlanta with her husband, two spoiled Plott hounds, and one bossy, alpha Pomeranian.

Terry is currently contemplating cross-bow lessons in preparation for the zombie apocalypse.

Terry loves to hear from readers so please contact her at

terry@terrypoca.com or visit her website at www.terrypoca.com.

You can find her on Facebook at

http://www.facebook.com/TerryPocaAuthor

CPSIA information can be obtained at www.ICGtesting.com
Printed in the USA
LVOW11s2259100814

398503LV00001B/196/P